The
Reluctant Hero

**Book One
of the
The Zradian Chronicles**

**The Reluctant Hero
The Professor And His Son
The Doomsday Bomb**

James Apps

Published in the United Kingdom
TAUP UK
Sheerness
Kent

The Zradian Chronicles is dedicated to my cat, Sophie, whom I treat as a companion knowing fully well that I am her unpaid servant. It is my delusion that I speak for her in saying that we both like Procul Harum's *Whiter Shade of Pale*.

I am also under the delusion that I understand what the song is about; mainly because when it was first played it seemed to make an awful lot of sense.

James Apps

Author's note: I have made a few small changes in the text and corrected some errors on all three volumes. James Apps 2020.

Contents:

Do not be Afraid of the Rodents!

Prologue

Star Station One:
Zradian Standard Time: 11:07:03:04

The space time continuum squeaked rather than ripped and made way for the huge Star Station. The massive ship wobbled, found its centre and settled into orbit. For two complete orbits nothing happened. And then as the Star Station came alive nothing continued to happen. Inside everything seemed to happen. Lights worked. Screens worked. Zradian Pairs took their places. Stood on guard. Glared angrily at each other according to his station. Discovered that whatever they did nothing could get in and nothing could get out. No messages, no stores, no weapons, no food. Especially no food. Grat and Trag the civilian Leader Pair ordered the operators to try again. Nothing. None of the matter transfer ports worked. One enterprising Pair took a look out the conveniently placed viewport and just to make sure took another, longer, look. Unable to contain their distress they told Grat and Trag that the mighty all fighting Star Station was in the wrong place.

Oops!

Earth: January 7

Arthur Renfrew stared at the pictures. There should only be two moons at this time and in this sector not three. Not only that one of them was moving in the wrong direction. It was smaller too and that was another problem. The new moon was only visible by radio-telescope. He sat for a long time thinking about it. What was it? Debris? One of the nine moons gone rogue? If that had happened then the whole world would have known about it. If it was an extra moon then where did it come from? A moon shifted from another axis? Or, and the or worried him. Artificial? If it was artificial whose was it? He reached across the view table and slid one of the prints under the magnifying lens, and with a few quick finger movements on keys he had a blow up on the screen. He split the image and called up a spectrometer read out.

The read out told him most of what he needed to know. Too many metal compounds and some plastics. It had to be artificial. Whose? Which nation had put it there. Again he tapped keys searching this time for recent launchings. Nothing. The screen read an emphatic zero. The new moon circulating contra-wise to the others was artificial, agreed, but if nobody on Earth had put it there then that question, Professor Arthur Renfrew thought, was one he personally couldn't answer.

Julian finds a home

Constable Bates and his partner Constable Fish were bored.

"Fishy, how long we got to sit here in this bloody car..."

"...waiting for something to happen before we go bloody loopy?" finished Fish, as Bates paused in his sentence.

"Depends on what the sergeant has got in store for us," Bates said and toyed with the radio microphone. It was Fish's turn to drive and as usual the afternoon shift was turning into another boring wait for something to happen. They had eaten their burgers, dutifully put the rubbish in the bin, and waited. During the last hour calls had come but nobody asked them to respond.

"It's like we been invited to a party and nobody..." began Fish

"...wants to bloody talk to us. What are we, working coppers or ..." said Bates

"...some sort of ornamental garden gnomes decorating the bloody street?" said Fish.

"Yeah, that's what I say," replied Bates and grabbed the microphone when it crackled into life. "Batesy here, sorry, Tango Delta three, what do you want?"

"Okay Tango Delta three, attend a disturbance on the Bywater Road junction with Peel Street, two youths seen running from a fire..." Fish started the vehicle and Bates listened to the description and what had happened. He put the microphone in its rest and related the message to Fish who grinned as they headed at high speed toward the Bywater Road. Close to their destination they saw two youths fitting the description hurrying along the road in the opposite direction to theirs and with total disregard to any other traffic, and great skill, Fish did a U-turn and raced after them. The skinny one saw them and started running heading into an alleyway followed more slowly by his mate.

Fish skidded the car to a stop. Bates jumped out and ran after the two youths catching the slower one by his collar in the traditional fashion and held him. Fish raced past but the skinny boy was gone.

"Missed the bugger," said Fish, breathlessly when he returned.

Bates held his captive against a wall and glowered at him. "Right, arsehole, why did you run?" he said.

"You frightened me," he said.

"Name?"

"What?"

"What's yer bloody name?" demanded Bates.

"And who was the other skinny gutted..." Fish

"...bugger, and what were you doing?" Bates.

"I don't have ter say nothin'"

"Oh you will, you will, especially when we take...Fish

"...you back to the scene of the crime what we was asked to attend," Bates

"So, shut yer gob and you come along with us," said Fish.

There were two Fire Units blocking the road when Bates and Fish arrived with their prisoner and, as usual Fish parked where he felt like doing so and the two officers piled out dragging their captive with them.

The fire was out and the owner was talking to one of the fire crew. The other crew stood beside their unit which Bates and Fish noticed was commanded by that useless bugger Weddell. Perversely they smiled at Weddell and greeted him cheerfully.

"Got here in time to put the fire out did you Sidney?" asked Bates giving his prisoner a rough push forward when he hesitated.

Fireman Sidney Weddell glowered at Bates.

"Guess not..." Fish

"...you don't normally so why start now?" Bates said as the two officers walked past and rudely interrupted the conversation between the shop owner and the fire officer.

"This the grot bag?" asked Bates.

The owner looked startled. "Yes, yes, that was one of them."

"Do you know him?"

"No, but I know the other one," he said.

"Well? Who is he?" asked Fish.

"He is a boy named Julian Renfrew; a well known firebug," said the owner.

"Right, then we may as well take this one in..." Bates

"...to chokey, and then waltz out in the motor and get this bloody Renfrew kid," Fish.

"I'll stash this bugger in the car and my mate will take a statement," said Bates.

The owner watched them, puzzled as they both walked back to the car with the prisoner arguing about whose set of cuffs they were going to use on him, and as they passed Fireman Weddell the other boy said it was Julian who set the fire.

"It was him what did it!" the boy said.

The owner was even more puzzled when they drove off without taking a statement from him.

Julian hid in his room.

He felt helpless. There was nothing he could do, nowhere he could go and with the conviction that Grot would let him down and dob him in he could think of no way to put the blame on somebody else.

Footsteps outside the door and a knock frightened him, but he was reassured when the handle rattled and his mother called out. "Julian! Are you in there? Do you want something to eat, oh dear, you've been so quiet, my darling boy, what's wrong, let me in, there's a love." She said.

"You on your own?" he demanded.

"Yes, yes, of course. I'm worried about you," she said.

He moved out from the corner between his bed and the wardrobe and went to the door and unlatching it he stood back waiting for an invasion but it was only his mother. He put up with her smothering hugs and when she had finished he followed her downstairs listening to her chattering but not taking much notice of what she said. A meal was whisked out of the kitchen and placed on the table in front of him. Steak and kidney pudding, with potatoes, good vegetables and gravy, his favourite, and as usual it was delicious.

"Your father will be home soon, so tell me, why did you come rushing in so quick and disappear up to your room. Have you done something wrong?" she said looking at him intently.

"Grot, I mean Gary got into trouble," he said, blushing.

"That stupid little shit," said his mother.

"Yeah, he tried to..." but whatever he was going to say was cut off when there was a loud knocking on the door. His mother got up to answer it and whilst she was doing that he gobbled up the remains of the pie, wiped his mouth with the table cloth and stood up to listen to what was happening at the door. He caught a glimpse of police uniforms and that was enough. He raced into the kitchen, flung open the back door and ran out into the back yard and stopped.

What stopped him was the strong arms of Constables Bates and Fish.

"Now sonny Jim, you wouldn't be..." Bates

"...wanting to do a runner, now would you?" Fish.

"Oh fuck," Julian said.

Julian Renfrew stood obediently to attention. His face remained expressionless although somebody watching him carefully would have seen the slight twitch in the corner of his mouth, and may have noticed the fingers moving almost imperceptibly. What they wouldn't have noted was the contempt he felt for the older man who sat in his comfortable chair drinking coffee from a huge mug marked '50 - but still lovable', who now and then fondled a large raspberry iced bun with obvious pleasure. Julian had eyes only for the piece of official looking paper resting on the blotter pad.

"You are to be discharged today Julian," the older man said.

"Yes sir," said Julian.

"You are fortunate that somebody has come to collect you -" pause and a penetrating gaze of beady eyes staring out from the fat face. "Sent, evidently by your father and accompanied by a member of your local church so I believe."

"Yes sir, I am fortunate sir." Julian spoke precisely with a minimum of expression. Experience had taught him to answer the Governor politely. Sarcasm or saying nothing was likely to make the old fart angry.

"It is more than you deserve and I am sure that with your record you are bound to let them down," the old man said.

"Yes sir, I expect I will let them down, but I will do my best to be a better citizen as you have attempted to teach me here sir," Julian replied hoping that he was putting it on enough but not too much.

"A penitent?" said the Governor, and the two screws either side of Julian sniggered.

Arseholes, Julian thought, they are both arseholes.

The door opened suddenly and a head poked in and a voice called out cheerfully. "Party to collect young Renfrew," it said, and a hand opened the door wider.

Richard Byrde walked in followed by a young woman. Julian groaned when he saw her. She was beautiful, busty with long flaxen pigtails and an ample figure that was firm and full of health. And although he might have expected her to be involved she was the last person he wanted to see. Didn't she know it was embarrassing enough with bloody Richard Byrde coming to claim him without her being in on it too?

"Hello Julian," said Byrde. "Good morning mister Lavery, this is Angela Breen from the Christian Mission, she is here on behalf of the Church. She is here to oversee the arrangements we make for Julian's rehabilitation. She has powers to veto any adverse arrangements, but she assures me that so far everything is fine."

In a daze that centred mainly on Angela Breen's bosom, Julian signed papers, shook hands, collected his civilian clothes, showered and changed, and finally followed Byrde and Angela out of the Institution to freedom.

"Friends are we Angela?"

"I have taken on the task of looking after you."

"Right, okay, but we can do things together, right?"

"Such as?"

"Well, you know, we can sort of..." he began and quailed under her gaze.

"I hope you are not suggesting we do anything naughty?"

"Er, well, no, not anything naughty, you know me," he said.

"Only too well," she said.

He gave up all attempts to chat her up and spoke only when she spoke to him. She gave him a key when they got to the house and led him up to his bedroom.

"My room is across the passage, and Michael's is at the end. Paul has the room down below, and there is a common lounge and dining room. Bathroom along the hall; a toilet, and another downstairs. Sort your stuff out and read through the papers on your bed. Your Probation Officer will deal with you after this and you will have to report at the proper time or it is back inside and I am sure you don't want that do you?"

"No but I can't help thinking I have swapped my cell for a more comfortable one out here," he said.

"Oh I am sure you have," she said, and giggled.

Bloody self effacing bitch, he thought, and looked around the room. The only thing that was good about it was he was at least free to go out whenever he wanted, providing he did as he was told. He shuddered. The sudden thought hit him right in the centre of his conscience. Angela might want him to go to church. He groaned aloud this time.

"What's the matter?" she asked giving him one of her disapproving looks.

"I suppose you're going to pray over me now are you?"

"I always pray for you Julian," she said rather too smugly.

He groaned again.

"Don't worry, I won't force you to go to church but I think you ought to go and thank the people there for the help they have given you," she said, and from the hard glint in her eye he reasoned that he had better not refuse.

"I suppose you are right," he said. "I should thank them, after all their kindness, I should."

"Of course you must," she said, and left him to settle in the room smiling as she closed the door behind her. And as he sat gazing at the closed door he remembered how he was rescued by the holy rollers from a cold night under Kew bridge. Christ! He was drunk that night and they took him in. "I ought to be grateful," he said to the closed door that still seemed to have Angela's pious imprint on it.

Julian sat in his room that first night aware that he had a long way to go. His first impression of his flatmates was that they were a pack of self righteous bastards. Michael, who was in charge made him feel uncomfortable. He looked at him the way the beak had in court and Julian disliked him and at the same time was scared of him. He remembered the court and all that happened; his mother getting tiddly, his father looking at him and shaking his head, writing him off as a no hoper.

From the moment he entered the court room Julian knew that things would go against him. Grot didn't stand a chance under questioning; the shop owner recognised them both; the fire service report said the fire was deliberately set; the damage done to goods and equipment cost a lot; other witnesses had seen them, and Grot had nicked booze, which was why he got caught. Julian's father refused to speak up for him; his mother was obviously drunk and maudlin and had to be taken away, and when the beak looked at his record he decided to 'make an example of him'.

"I shall send you to the young offenders unit where you will, perhaps learn something useful. Let me see, we have a guarantor with mister Byrde who has been kind enough to offer you a job when you are released. Under those circumstances we will sentence you to two years. We would prefer you serve the full sentence," the Beak said, and Julian felt a deep pit open in his belly.

The same beak put Grot on probation.

Two years passed and he stood facing the Governor waiting for mister Byrde to come and claim him. His father refused to have him back in the house, and his mother, feeling even more lonely, took to drinking, effectively creating an even greater rift between her and Arthur. Julia Renfrew, never the most sweet talking woman when drunk became foul mouthed and angry as her marriage fell apart, and her dearly beloved son Julian languished in prison.

Julia Renfrew was surprised when Angela Breen, a young woman from the local church called on her to talk about Julian's release.

"My Julian belonging to the church!" She said when Angela explained that her mission had decided to put her in charge of Julian's rehabilitation. "Fuck me! Julian a bloody holy roller? Nah," she said.

Angela smiled. "Well yes Mrs Renfrew, you sent him to the Sunday School, he is a member of the youth club. I think your husband insisted," she said. "And as a fallen person he comes under our care. The probation service is glad to hand him over to us." She didn't tell Julia of the time the mission found him lying in his own vomit on the steps of Kew Bridge, and the Pastor, recognising him as one of his flock had given him some help. She assumed Julia knew about that.

"Shit, so what happens when he comes out then?"

"We find him a place to stay and help him to get started again." Angela explained and screwed up her face when Julia offered her a drink from her gin bottle. "No thanks, not when I am working."

Julia watched Angela go and taking a sip from her bottle wiped her lips with the back of her hand and said. "Stuck up tart!" She stood in the passage with the bottle clutched in her hand as Angela turned out of the gate and walked off along the street. She kicked the door shut and staggered back to the living room where she poured some gin into a tumbler adding tonic. She was feeling the effects of the gin she had drunk earlier but nevertheless her aim with the liquid was unerring. She took a long drink, coughed, spluttered a little, put the tumbler down on the coffee table and wiped her mouth with the back of her hand.

"Arseholes! What a bastard! I nearly choked on that!"

She sank down into her settee and took the glass in her hand putting it to her lips and swallowed the contents steadily. This time it went down smoothly and with a lopsided grin she poured another and held the glass up to the ceiling.

"Fucking arseholes, my little Julian out of fucking chokey," she said, and took a drink thinking of what her husband would say. "I know what the stuffy old bastard would say," she said pursing her lips, "Oh no, as long as he darkens not my door." She giggled at her mimicry and finished the drink.

"Bloody stupid old prat!" She said and fell backwards onto the arm letting the empty glass roll on the carpet, she dropped off into a drunken sleep.

Arthur Renfrew, fully aware that his son was soon to be released found her late that night and with a sigh carefully carried up to her room and put her to bed.

"Goodnight Julia," he said and shuddered.

He watched her for a while shaking his head slowly wondering what had happened to her since they were married. She had given up work for a few years to look after Julian and when the boy started school she had taken a part time job but when Julian got into trouble she gave that up and tried to sort him out. The problem was that Julia was too soft on him and Julian didn't help. He had 'learning difficulties' so they said but it was not that; Julian was a liar, a cheat, a petty thief and a fire raiser. Arthur had bailed the boy out of trouble too many times to be sympathetic to him and when he left school and became involved in a string of petty crimes in the company of the boy known as Grot, Arthur had overruled Julia and insisted Julian find somewhere else to live. The tragedy was that Julia's foul mouth and her self centred attitude had not helped Julian at all.

He looked at the once desirable woman he had married and realised she was now an alcoholic, who hated him and had an abhorrent dislike of sex; the opposite of her son who in his mean way tried to do it all the time.

He went downstairs, locked up for the night, made a cup of tea and went to bed, read for a while glad that they had separate rooms as well as separate beds. The thought of sleeping with Julia was not a pleasant one.

Beginnings

On the planet Zrad, in the Sirius β star system, the Usurper who became Consul of Sector Green Four instinctively knew that as much as sex, shelter and food was a basic need there was one more essential requirement. And that was space in which to live. Lebensraum. And the trouble with Lebensraum was that in most cases the people who already lived in it most often objected to being pushed out. Faced with an overwhelming force of arms the people of Sector Yellow One through to Five reluctantly moved out, a warning to be ready for the same to Sectors Red and Blue. Resistance was futile. But, fed up with fighting a bloody hand to hand war the Usurper solved the problem with a short, but effective Nuclear strike, and established himself as President of the Second Republic.

The new President set about consolidating his victory with harsh measures against all opposition. He pushed the northern people out of their pleasant land banishing them by conquest to the rough lands of the west of what later was to become Sector Blue. They took with them their skill of husbandry and farming as well as the old religion that was long forgotten in the southern states. The worship, or at least the knowledge of the teachings of a former national hero Glord the Glorious went with them. The new regime oppressed the worshippers and it became a capital offence to belong to any group that worshipped Glord the Glorious who, as Zradian history recognised, was the founder of the First Republic and the most effective leader Zradia had ever had. It seemed that although he was a national hero the new republic baulked at admitting him to the land of the gods. Quite simply they did not believe in them. Dissenters to the new rule, some Glordists amongst them, escaped to the hills and hid; others fought back and died, and some, more foolish than brave, took up political opposition. These Pairs[1] became more and more isolated in the Senate, and frustrated by their inability to be heard, they decided on a more telling protest. On the day that the new President finally declared the revolution over these few members met secretly and planned their protest.

"We will show the people that there is a proper opposition to this Usurper," said their leader.

And so it was decided to plummet en-masse from the tenth level windows and smash to death on the roof of the Presidential hover

---

[1] *Zradians are born as Pairs. One is passive and one is assertive. They sometimes refer to each other as Twins but they are in fact two halves of one person.*

wagon as it arrived at the door of the temporary government centre and by doing so take the usurper with them. They stood in a row holding hands and when the arrival of the wagon was immanent they launched themselves from their perch. Their timing was perfect and with a yell of defiance mixed with much fear they dived out the windows at the exact moment when the hover wagon halted at the door. Unfortunately they chose the wrong side of the building. Their broken bodies were found by an urchin Pair from Sector Blue who picked their messy pockets before reporting their magnificent political gesture.

Oops.

But according to Zradian scientists there was a bigger problem. The radiation levels rose quickly, and the lowlands beneath the mountains became a wasteland fit only for outcasts and the throwbacks from Sector Blue. The land area in the northern sector was not large enough to support everybody; the Lebensraum was shrinking. The Twin Consuls were ordered to find more land, and so with all the resources they could scrounge from the Military funds, and with the aid of the fanatical Polisocs, the Zradian Political and Social Police, they searched the skies for an unsuspecting planet. They found the small blue and green planet Earth and decided it would make a perfect colony for their burgeoning millions. The problem was that any probe would take a long time to return any results, and what was more frustrating was that by the time the probe returned the situation on Zrad would be much worse. What they needed was a means of getting an invasion force to Earth quickly and to follow up just as fast.

"What we need is a matter transfer system that will work over enormous distances," said the Scientists, and were disappointed and rather put out when their masters instructed them to get on with it. The concept was easy as far as the scientists were concerned, over short distances; it had long been known as the means of delivering weapons but the long distances eluded them until the invention of the super-conductor. Helium gas superconductors were used in space to encase small, sensitive objects and responded to matter transfer systems so well it was discovered that objects could be sent to points in space at 0.5 light year intervals apart. The simple matter of seeding a chain of beacons was obvious once they had discovered what the heck had happened to the first ones. The result was a method of sending large, dangerous objects such as Star Stations long distances in space to desirable planets. Of course the method was horrendously expensive and needed a lot of resources to keep going. Any invasion had to be, as the accounts department said, cost effective.

"Do you realise that this little planet is virtually unoccupied?" said the High Leader Pair (Population)

"And from the data the planet has plenty of water and enough land mass to support at least twenty billion Pairs," added the High Leader Pair (Territory)

"And not only that but the minerals and other raw materials are more abundant than on any other planet we have probed. It also has a slightly higher oxygen count than Zrad," enthused the High Leader Pair (Physics)

"But they are not all that developed industrially which means there will be no standing armies to put up a really good fight," said the High Leader Pair (Military) rather despondently.

"Oh, yes, we hadn't thought of that," said Population, Territory and Physics together quietly with a modicum of fearful respect.

"Still, we could send a mission?" said Territory, excitedly.

The High Leader Pairs looked at each other and nodded their heads. They could send a mission.

On the four hundredth anniversary of the founding of the Second Republic, Zradian Scientists sent a mission comprising of one Mother ship equipped with four probe ships Paired by a team of mixed discipline Pairs trained to gather data and observe. The team included two mathematician Pairs, and two Astro- Physicist Pairs to calculate accurately the distance between Zrad and Earth. The Mother ship arrived in the Solar System to take up orbit around the small third planet and drop Paired probes to the surface.

Whether it was the fault of the technician Pairs or the poor design of the Mother ship's major systems, or if it was merely a fickle accident of fate the records will never show, but a few Mother ship orbits after the probes were released something went dreadfully wrong. Two of the four probe vehicles, each with a pair on board crashed in one of the mighty oceans and sank to the bottom.

"Gravity is low and re-entry speed is too high; the shields burnt up and I am afraid our Pairs were cooked," said the Leader Pair. "Increase the shielding on the next two probes."

One landed safely in the desert land of what would be known later by Europeans as the Sahara, and the other crashed on the top of Mount Ararat killing its occupants and creating a problem for Theological historians, and a convenient myth for the opponents of Darwin's delightful Origin of Species.

The occupants of the successful landing probe, although delighted to be safely down on Terra Firma, were disappointed when they discovered that communications with the Mother ship itself was defunct. Their on board computer screen relayed one continuous message whenever they tried to tune into their mission control.

Source Disk Malfunction

And that, they surmised, meant nothing doing. They were stuck on a planet with nothing but their own meagre resources and the hope that the local inhabitants would be kind to them.

In fact it worked out that the local inhabitants worshipped them.

The Pair, whose name was Dogo and Doog, introduced themselves through a series of clever signs and sand drawings and pointed out to the locals the place in their cosmos where they came from. Dogo, the more exact Astrophysicist, used a portion of their probe ship's furniture as a permanent plan. He marked the exact spot in the African sky where the planet Zrad was to be found. He explained that Zrad circulated a small pale Star which was part of a binary system but, unable to translate their own name into the local language, shrugged his shoulders and spread his hands wide and said.

"This is the star we come from."

The Shaman stood before them covered in skins and a fair daubing of wet Camel dung, and bright spots of red and white paint and repeated the information in his own language.

"Dog's star, place you Dog people come from, little star up there!"

He pointed with his holy stick and stomped his foot three times and cocked his leg higher for a short period.

"Little Dog's Star?"

"Dogo nodded, annoyed that however much they corrected him the Shaman never seemed to get their names right. He was on the verge of correcting the man once again but he was too late; the whole tribe was dancing around them in a vast circle chanting while the Shaman called out the cadence.

"Why do they call us both Dog?" Dogo asked his twin.

"Bulgers[2] if I know," said his twin.

The Pair remained with the tribe for nearly five Earth years constantly torn between staying with the probe and wanting to explore. With a need to keep occupied they did what they were most capable of, and that was to teach the people many things. They learned the lore of the tribe and was a bit disturbed when they learned the tribe called themselves the Dogon people. Doog was sure that this piece of information was likely to cause someone at sometime some problems. He hoped it wasn't them. Shortly before the end of the fifth year the computer signalled that the Mother Ship was expecting them. In fact they had to dive back into the probe

---

[2] *A small smelly Zradian mammal.*

smartly before the automatic system closed the hatches and the whole thing lifted off. They had no time to apologise to their hosts or to make arrangements for their children to be handed over to surrogate fathers. They had to leg it for the ship before it took off. The probe docked into its slot, and within a few periods they were aboard a deserted Mother ship staring at the screens. Apart from themselves and a pair of curious rodents from the planet Earth there were no live Pairs on board.

Dogo looked at Doog and shrugged.

"I suppose there's no chance we could go back to Earth?" he said, a statement and not a question, which according to the data scrolling down the screens and the obvious signs the ship was about to head back home, was quite true.

"None at all," his twin replied. "The ship has suddenly been reactivated under the Emergency Code and there's nothing we can do about it. I'm sorry my twin but we will not survive the journey either."

"Why not?"

"The computer says because of reduced power the trip will take approximately one thousand orbits and we have no female Pairs."

"Can we not deep freeze ourselves?"

"We could try."

They walked to the cryogenics bays and stared glumly at the boxes. The monitor above the boxes told the story.

Power Outage - Area not scheduled for re-allocation of energy resources

Despondently they walked back to the central control room and sat in the comfortable seats to watch the progress of the ship as it was charted on the Nav-Graph.

"What do we do now?" asked Doog.

"We eat, sleep, shit, entertain ourselves and when we have finished doing that we start over until we experience terminal trauma," replied Dogo.

"What is terminal trauma?"

"Death, the ultimate alternative lifestyle. There's a lot of it about," said Dogo.

He wasn't smiling.

They sat silent and brooding for many periods, and Doog, the more optimistic of the Pair pressed the entertainment codes and waited for the large screen to activate. Disappointingly it displayed only one message.

Power Outage - Area not scheduled for re-allocation of energy resources

"Bulgers, we may as well give up now," Doog said, and slumped in his seat.

The journey lasted nearly three hundred four hundreds and as the space weary Mother Ship eased into the grip of its home system it signalled its arrival with a stream of data and suggested it send a probe to collect a delegation of Pairs. It's request was refused and instead the President of Zrad dispatched a battleship of Polisoc Stormtroopers with the intention of arresting the occupants. The Polisoc battleship locked itself in orbit around the Mother Ship and electronically ordered its ports to open. Fighting craft filled the platforms and as soon as the airlocks were closed Stormtroopers poured out and ran hup hupping along the platforms to the inner portals, and poured into the labyrinth of dimly lit corridors. One Troop ran to the control centre and the rest explored the living and working quarters. They found the remains of Dogo and Doog lying on the floor beneath their comfortable seats and for a few short periods the Leader Pair and his troop stood and wondered.

"Just bones, white bones looking like they been gnawed by animals," he said, and turned toward a sudden pattering rustling sound that poured from every hole, orifice or aperture in the central control room.

"Bulgers!" he said, and like the rest of his troop he tried to shoot his way back to the fighting craft but there was no escaping the mass of ravenous rodents that saw them as a welcome feast.

That some Stormtroopers survived the onslaught of the surprised but happy animals was a miracle. That two fighting craft loads managed to get back to the battleship was another; that several breeding pairs of rodents managed to stowaway on board the craft and hence the battleship was to be expected. That nobody noticed their arrival on the planet Zrad was a matter for the maintenance crews to worry about. Constantly looking for ways to supplement their inadequate salaries the maintenance crews discovered a lucrative source of income by selling the Rodents as laboratory animals.

Thus, the arrival of the long lost probe during the latter part of the Second Republic was a welcome addition to the Zradian President's acquisitions and from that he saw a whole new world of conquest and honour. The old arguments in favour of invading the Earth were revived. The President ordered an immediate invasion.

"We want it, get working and let our people colonise the place. We need it." The President's word was law and with the enthusiasm of the truly frightened, the fanatic and those keen on making lots of money, the people and the military got on with it.

It should be noted that one of the most enthusiastic customers of these illicit Rodent traders was C&D Developments who were currently employed as consultant contractors engaged in reviving the old Star Station system.

They needed Rodents, they said, because live Polisoc prisoners were becoming increasingly scarce.

On Earth about ninety-five years before the Mother Ship's arrival at its home planet, a group of anthropologists working in North Africa discovered the Dogon tribe and wrote screeds of notes explaining how the simple people knew about the star they, the anthropologists knew as Siriusβ. The anthropologists dutifully recorded the details, including in their notes a description of the so-called Gods from the Dog Star who, the tribal shaman said, came to visit their ancestors in a metal ship. To show them what he meant the shaman produced a precious icon of beaten metal inscribed with a crude star map and a pictograph of two beings standing in front of a flying saucer.

The group of anthropologists just as dutifully allowed their findings to go public and wondered why they became the butt of stage comedian's little green men jokes. On the whole the experience for the anthropologists was disappointing. The experience for the Dogons was hardly enlightening either, but then they were too busy dying out to be too much concerned with the anthropologists' embarrassment.

One hundred years later and some four hundred and twenty years after Dogo and Doog's enforced stay Professor Arthur Renfrew, an Anthropologist whose hobbies included amateur Astronomy and Aikido discovered a strange new satellite in Jupiter's orbit. He was invited to speak about his findings at the highly prestigious Science and Philosophical Forum held in the West London University Humanities Hall. He spoke about the new satellite, explaining the unusual spectrum; the odd orbit; and postulated the theory that this so-called moon might be artificial. It was the part about who might have made it and sent it there that got their full attention. Professor Renfrew explained, quite clearly, how he thought that the new moon was placed there by an alien intelligence. What spoiled the effect was the question flung at him from the floor by a tipsy student.

"What, you mean like aliens, little green men?"

"If you like, if there are little green men," Arthur replied.

The audience erupted in laughter, but the next day on the media the story made headlines and Arthur became the butt of comedian's jokes. He expected the comics and satirists to make jokes about him but what annoyed him most was that the media called him the 'Nutty Professor'. Arthur Renfrew had never considered himself as potty.

In the lounge bar of the Drunken Clown pub, sipping foaming ales Professor Renfrew remarked to his close friend Richard Byrde that he was somewhat disappointed by the reception of his comments. Byrde, knowing his friend was not disposed to a sense of humour, declined to make any comical observations and dutifully made sympathetic noises.

"It seems to me that the public has been fed so much disinformation about what to expect from a meeting with Aliens that they are unwilling to listen to the truth when it is staring them in the face. I mean, why did they have to run that little green man story when all I really said was that the satellite could possibly be artificial."

"Well you were sceptical about our own ability to build one and get it into orbit around Jupiter," said Byrde.

"But all I wanted to say was that it was too big for any known space project to launch. It had to be built off world by us or Aliens. I never mentioned little green men or flying saucers."

"I know that, you know that, and so do the powers that be know it but what didn't help was the revival of the Dogon Siriusβ story on the telly." Byrde said, trying to sound neutral.

"But why little green men?"

Byrde wanted to say 'why not' but he knew that Arthur would take such a facetious remark the wrong way and short of grovelling apologies and much backtracking on what he had already said he would not be placated. Instead Byrde shrugged his shoulders and sipped his beer.

"These journalists are all the same," he said.

"Yes, twist your words around every which way and never write what you actually said."

Byrde was glad when Arthur suggested they play darts, and with a sigh of relief he even bought the next round of drinks when it was not his turn.

He also took care to let Arthur win a few games.

Byrde and Arthur walked to the corner together and stood for a moment or two before going their separate ways.

"Oh well, I suppose it is back to Julia for me," Arthur said, and Byrde felt sorry for his friend's reluctance. Julia was hard to handle at times which is why they met at the Drunken Clown. Arthur sometimes made a brave attempt to take her out to dinner or to a show but Julia always drank too much Dutch Courage before she left the house, and always had to be taken home early 'feeling poorly'.

"Yes and I must get back to Emily," Byrde said.

"Ah yes, dear, delightful Emily. I envy you Richard. Emily is a lovely woman and a good friend as well. In my own way I love her and as I often say, I am so glad you both enjoy each other."

"Thank you Arthur and goodnight, thanks for the evening," said Byrde.

"My pleasure mostly, and thanks for the chat. A little bit of relaxed sanity helps you know," he said, and with his hands stuck in his trouser pockets he strolled off. Byrde watched him go and then with a light step he turned and walked across the street. "Shoot!" he said, jumping the last pace onto the kerb as a hover car hurtled along the road towards him headlights blazing and engine revving. Quickly he flattened himself against a doorway watching in horror as the car skidded onto the pavement, lurched sideways and hurtled past him to crash against a lamp post.

The vehicle settled slowly on its canopy; two men staggered out and limped off supporting each other to disappear around a corner. Byrde stayed where he was for a few moments and before the neighbourhood reacted he hurried away feeling guilty, but thinking that the vehicle was aimed at him. Arthur's making you paranoid, he thought rationalising the thought by dismissing the men as drunken joy riders but he realised that the car had started up only when he had crossed the street and unless the driver was a complete moron he was sure that the vehicle was deliberately aimed at him. At home he told Emily of the incident and although he was tempted he did not ring Arthur. "I'll tell him next time I see him," he said.

The President

The trouble with being President, thought the President, was that Pairs expected you to be a President. What he really wanted to be was to be left alone to get on with his life and enjoy a little murder and mayhem, intrigue and blatant perversity. He liked a little blatant perversity. Especially when it meant Pairs screaming and dying on the floor of the Great Hall. He loved to watch the Dog Squad drag the bodies away; he liked the way the victims heads bumped up and down on the flagstones. It was fun to yell and holler at the Pairs and watch them grovel but when it came to actual administration he hated it. What he would really like to do is play fourball, the dangerous national sport, or get drunk; he could get drunk easily, too drunk to play fourball.

In fact he was holding a drink in his hand which, he was pleased to describe, was the finest Gin and Tonic to be found this side of the Galaxy. As far as he knew anyway. He liked Gin and Tonics and always liked to capitalise the name as well. The royal We.

"We are fond of Our Gin and Tonics," he said, and watched the courtiers and the servants grovel. "Bring me another!"

As if by magic a Gin and Tonic appeared on a tray borne by a grovelling Pair who trotted in balancing the tray between them trying to hurry and trying not to spill any. Scum. Almost not quick enough. Pig fodder!

The Pair grovelled back behind the screen and with a flourish he lifted the drink to his lips and sipped it. Nectar. He focussed on the robed Pairs kneeling before him and was satisfied. Apart from the illusion that there seemed to too many of them they looked as if they were following protocol; waiting patiently and nervously for him to speak. Power. That's what he liked, power but without the stupid responsibility. He sipped again and then with a foppish flourish he put the glass gently on the small tray built into the arm of his throne. What he really wanted to be was an Emperor.

"We wish to hear your report," he said, watching the Twin High Consuls twitch, uncertain whether to rise or to remain face down and read from there.

"You may rise and address Us," he said.

The two Pairs rose from their prostrate position nervously eyeing the guards who touched their swords ready to draw. The Dog Squad soldiers looking smart in their red and black uniforms, polished boots and distinctive badges showing the Lupe logo that belonged only to the President watched impassively. The President looked at them fondly, happy that they would kill anybody he asked them to with no compunction. Loyal to a fault they were also well paid and exempt from investigation by the Polisocs, the dreaded Social and Political Police. His Pairs.

The Twin Consuls were speaking and from the moment they started he realised he hadn't understood a word.

"What?"

The Twin Consuls stopped talking and huddled.

"Your Honour?"

"Begin again," he said.

They shuffled uncomfortably and began their report speaking nervously but directly to him more or less balancing out between eye contact and a proper use of protocol. He had to follow their movements carefully as whenever he looked directly at them they shifted their gaze to avoid him. Most frustrating.

"You shall speak directly to Us," he interrupted, and smirked when they huddled again. He waved the guards back and was pleased to hear all the swords sliding back into their scabbards as one. Nice discipline.

He contented himself with staring at the Twin Consuls and watching their faces reddening with a mixture of fear and embarrassment. They finished their report without further incident and immediately dropped prostrate on the floor.

"We have questions. Please rise and answer them."

The Twin Consuls stood and again they huddled, waiting.

"These Rebel scumbags you talk of; are they not merely a rabble to be eliminated by Our Glorious Armed Forces or can the Polisocs not destroy them and throw them to the pigs or, better still, have them ripped to death in the squares for Us to watch?"

"It seems, forgive us your Honour, that these low scum are gathering in an organised force in the Outlands beyond the Wastelands. They..."

"We have not asked a second question!"

The Twin Consuls cringed.

"Your Honour!"

He glared at them.

"They are easy to kill your Honour but not so easy to catch. They slide off into the contaminated Wastelands where it is unsafe to travel. They do not care for the radiation any more than we do but they seem to be immune from it. It is said they follow the teachings of Glord the Glorious our Proud Ancestor..."

The President stood quickly and spilled some of his drink, and agitated, he bore down on them with his terrible gaze. "You will not mention that name in my Honourable Presence!" he roared, and stayed the guards with a wave of his hand.

"This is the truth your Honour!"

"So be it; bring another Gin and Tonic!"

The drink appeared, and anticipating his need the Drinks Pair had another ready on the tray. The terrified Pair hovered nervously behind the throne.

He sipped the fresh drink and stared out across the Great Hall feeling the weight of decision upon him and something else too. Fear? Fear of what these upstarts in the Wastelands could do? He wasn't so drunk as to miss the main thrust of the report, confused and a little befuddled yes, but too drunk, no. We will not be frightened. We will not give in to doubts. We will overcome.

"Arrange to seek them out and destroy them. Send troops. Send Stormtroopers if you have to and bring me their Leader Pairs strapped to the back of a war wagon. Kill them!"

The twin Consuls cringed deeper and squeaked.

"Yes Your Honour."

Capital letters, he liked that. He sat in his throne watching the Twin Consuls grovel backwards out of the chamber noting with amusement that they were almost line perfect, but then, they were well practised at it.

So the Rebels were getting stronger? He had to admit his own private sources had told him as much. He tried to remember what sector the rebels operated from. South and Yellow, he thought, had to be yellow because that was where the scum came from. Or ran to. He remembered that was the sector the new Zradians had conquered the Northern Lands from where his ancestors had fought the last great battle before the nuclear wastelands cut them off from the rest of the world. The battle destroyed the Northern Lands and drove the inhabitants south and into oblivion. Got rid of the Bulgers; a memory, yeah. Now that was a war, he thought, that was one Bulger of a war. He licked his lips and thought about the films he saw when he was a young Half Pair growing up with his Twin in the family rooms. He recalled the thrill of learning about their history and the part his own family had taken in it. When he became President he remembered the satisfying feeling as he strangled his Twin and threw the body to the Polisoc pigs.

He grabbed the remaining Gin and Tonic and thought about the piddly little planet they were going to take over in place of their own battered remnant. Too many Pairs and not enough room, that was the trouble. One large inland sea, named the Sea of Zradia in that boring fashion Zradians have of naming things, was a natural barrier between east and west but because of the contamination in his time had never been exploited. And there was the the vast stretches of shallow water to the south forever locked away by the contaminated hills where the battles had been fought and where, so he was told, the statue and shrine of the dead leader of the first Republic of Zradia was worshipped daily by its devotees. Well, he had banned all that. Nobody was allowed to worship, mention, write or refer to the name of Glord the Glorious. The book containing all that was known about their nation's founder was hidden in a secret vault somewhere in First City along with the Pairs who had placed it and other valuable artefacts there. Let them eat their own knowledge. Scum.

None of the land was worth a Bulger's fart, and invading Earth seemed to be the only solution.

"Bring Us the report on the invasion of Earth!"

A Pair scuttled from the rows of petitioners and prostrated themselves on the flagstones.

"Your Gracious Loving Honour, we humbly salute you!"

"Bulger shit, you've stuffed up again haven't you?"

"Your Honour, it was not our fault, we only delivered the report."

"Read it!"

The Pair read the report from the prostrate position and sobbed pathetically when they delivered the final words and held the flimsy sheets out for the scribe to take. They released the flimsies and moved quick but not quick enough. The guards cut them to pieces with their wicked double blade swords before they reached the aisle. The sweepers with their wheeled buckets and pumping hoses hurried in from the wings and washed away the mess.

The President grunted. Sometimes, he thought, the guards could be a bit too hasty, he had wanted to ask them some questions. Oh well, not to worry, there were plenty more Pairs where they came from. Low level Greens didn't really count for much anyway.

He took the sheets from the scribes and re-read them. Earth, a planet one and a half the size of their own existing habitable land mass with a piddly population of some four billion Half Pairs, and as a whole was barely one third the size of Zrad. The population was a primitive people who had yet to make more than a tentative step off world. Why, it was only recently they had discovered nuclear weapons. All that was needed to control the stupid creatures was a Star Station and a Doomsday Bomb. The invasion would be a troop exercise as well as a massive blood letting of course. Tell the Bulgers about the Doomsday Bomb and invade anyway. The earthlings could figure it out if they were bright enough. Slavery or oblivion, it was up to them. Resist and win and the Planet would disappear in a puff of matter; lose and the planet would be ours. The new colony of the second republic of Zrad. And why not.

The problem was putting the Star Station in place. It seemed that the problem was with seeding the way stations and keeping track of their locations. There had been a cock up. Now they had to start again and this time it had to be right. The turns were rolling around to his birthday and he wanted, so desperately wanted, to announce the new colony on this four hundred's birthday or at the latest the next.

Bulgers! How can they be so incompetent.

"Scribes!"[3]

Two panting Pairs came scurrying and stood before him their screens ready and their anxious faces gazing expectantly up at him.

"We request expediency with the placement of Star Station Two. There will be a gift to the Pair that finds Star Station One. We wish Star Station Three to be commissioned immediately."

The scribes rattled the keys with quick incisive fingers and within two small periods handed him a sheaf of flimsies. He perused each in turn and chose one, dumping the rest in a waste bin. The material would be recycled for him to use later. He smirked knowing that his message would be on its way to all his senior staff and immediately acted on. He had added 'on pain of death', the scribes had added the phrase, he corrected, and that would get them moving.

"Who shall we give the contract to?" asked the senior scribe Pair and grovelled nicely with the grace of much practice.

"Clard and Dracl of course," he said, and thought about the Pair and decided that after the contract was completed he would find a way of honouring them. Oh yes, that uppity Pair were going to get a shock.

He gazed across the Great Hall at the anxious Pairs waiting to speak to him or waiting on his pleasure, guards ready to kill, courtiers ready to do his bidding and prisoners waiting for sentence. He would condemn a few prisoners to death, yes he would, guilty or not they would die.

"We wish to interview the prisoners," he said and glared at the cowering Pairs waiting at the lower door. "Bring them to Us."

Guards marched prisoner Pairs to the central circle and threw the first Pairs to the floor. The others waited in line held up by their guards and forced to witness what was about to happen.

"The charges, tell Us the charges."

The nearest guards barked the charge out and looked at him waiting for orders.

---

[3] *In general other than the President most Zradians assumed that the Twin High Consuls, Consuls and the Vice Consuls were the most powerful and effective civil servants in the republic. In fact it is the Scribes who attend the President in his personal department who have the most power. It is they who interpret his garbled orders - those they don't like are cleverly altered to suit. Troublemakers within the civil service are weeded out by the Scribes at most levels of administration according to their own code of conduct.*

"And what else have they done to offend Our Person?"

"Er, they called you names your Honour, they might have drunk illegal Outlands brew your Honour?" A question, not a solid charge, but as far as he was concerned the idea was good enough.

"And what did they call Us?"

"We cannot repeat the words in your Honour's presence," said the guards deferentially and he noted, with a certain amount of embarrassment.

"Never mind, kill them now," he said.

"You bastard!" screamed the condemned Pair. "We never said anythi....arrgh!

The guards' swords swished in tandem and heads rolled on the flags. He watched the cleaners drag the bodies away and ordered the next set of offenders forward. Twenty two Pairs later he was bored with executions and sent the next six Pairs to the Polisoc labour camps.

"We are tired," he said, and stood up ready to leave the throne. The court Pairs grovelled on the floor and he noted with amusement that two prisoner Pairs took the opportunity to escape. He walked unsteadily to his chamber and lay down on his futon watching the world behind his closed eyelids spin around in time to the world underneath his bed. Bulgers, I'm pissed again, he thought, and batted away imaginary blue Bulgers that seemed to want to join his fantasy world. Whilst the President slept, the servants washed the Great Hall floor down, the drinks Pair replenished his dwindling stocks and the scribes wrote the latest missive so that it made sense. Lights dimmed; and the heating automatically readjusted. Out in the Great Hall and throughout the Palace life continued. Prisoners were fed and beaten, guards marched or relaxed off duty and staff went back to their interrupted tasks. The Dog Squad elite guard went to their barracks to train and relax and look at the posting list to see who was on assassination duty for the next few turns. Kitchen staff cooked the sausage for the troops and fashioned the food portions for the Consuls, and the Representatives, and stole rations for themselves and their families. In the environs of First City the Pairs went about their business. The Pairs in Sector Red continued to despise those in Sectors Green and Yellow and tried to ignore the Pairs in Sector Blue. Those in Sector Green looked disdainfully on the Pairs in Sector Yellow and resented the superiority of those in Sector Red and grew increasingly more scared of the Pairs in Sector Blue. The Pairs in Sector Yellow dealt with those of Sector Blue at a modest profit on illicit goods and offered connections to those in Sector's Red and Green to the menials of Sector Blue. This group offered illicit goods at an exorbitant cost to the greedies of Sector Green and refused to deal with those of Sector Red.

The Pairs in Sector Blue tolerated the Pairs of Sector Yellow and disliked the rest. Sector Blue Pairs were scared of each other.

But all Pairs were equally scared of the Polisocs. They were not alone in this; everybody except the President, the Dog Squad and the Zradian People's Rebel Army. The Rebel Army were the only people on Zrad who openly shot at the Polisocs with the intention of killing as many of them as possible. All other Pairs who shot at the Polisocs usually did so in self defence. Especially the Pairs from Sector Blue.

The Labour Camps continued to operate their brutal shift system and the poor, unfortunate Pairs who were sent there cursed everybody, especially their glorious President.

In the Wastelands over the hills south of Sector Blue the Rebel Army patrols gathered refugees from the Second Republic, vetted them and those found some to be unsuitable were sent back. The rest were recruited, trained and added to the ranks. To give credence to the President's perception that the rebels operated from Sector Yellow many of the rebel's niggling raids took place on its borders with Sector Blue. The reason was quite simple: the lands south of Sector Yellow were virtually uninhabited, and it was through there the rebels could smuggle their most excellent Outlands Brew, the beer of choice for most Zradian citizens.

And that fact was another annoyance the President had to endure.

No Smoke...

Julian Renfrew stared out the window watching a black and white dog piddling against a lamp post. He concentrated his mind and tried to will it to piddle on the cable cover and electrocute itself. It didn't, and with a quick scuff of its feet it ran off sniffing the pavement. Frustrated at his impotence Julian turned back to his breakfast and picked up the slice of burnt toast and wished he had enough butter to spread on it.

He hated burnt toast.

He hated most things; his father, the flat, the morning and having to get up to go to work. He hated work. No he hated having to work. He hated his flat mates, especially that smart arse Michael who had banned him from the kitchen, and stopped his mates coming round. And now he was asking awkward questions about the rent money and his share of the bills.

"I got the money in the bank, ain't I?" Julian explained.

"Yes, well, we need the cash now to pay the bills, your share plus what you owe from last month, and then there is the extra you owed for the net," Michael said, and added, "Get it for us tomorrow because the rest of us are getting fed up with paying your debts. When Angela was here it was different, you paid up on time. You don't do your share of the housework, and we had to chuck you out of the kitchen because you wouldn't do your share of the cooking, and now we have to keep badgering you for the bills. Where's the money Julian?"

"I got commitments," Julian said.

"Yes, to Donald Best, a bloody loan shark. That's where the money is going. You had better sort it out matey or..." Michael said leaving the rest unsaid.

"Well I have. I've got all sorts of commitments what you have no idea, and okay, I'll get the money tomorrow. You know I got nothing better to do than to waste me bloody lunch break getting cash out for you to give away to other people, when all you had to do was let me use me debit card and pay into the accounts like what I suggested," Julian said, pouting and glaring at Michael.

"Oh shut up Julian you know damn well you have to pay them on time like everybody else, now why don't you go to your room and stop making the house untidy."

That was typical of Michael. Bloody rude.

He threw the toast on the floor unable to eat it and grabbed his jacket. May as well go to bloody work, he thought, at least bloody

Richard Byrde supplied tea and coffee and with a bit of luck he might be able to bludge some food from the canteen.

He hated being broke too.

It was all bloody Donald Best's fault; the man who loaned money to you but wanted it back at huge amounts of interest. He had tried pay-day loans once but ended up with nothing in his bank account even when his salary was paid in. That had cost him a session with the Church and Richard Byrde who was still deducting the amount owing from his pay. He hated that too. He hated Donald Best but most of all he hated Denny Block the man who collected Donald Best's debts. Denny Block was hard to resist. Impervious to argument however well reasoned, Denny had a knack of extracting money from reluctant clients. His method was simple. Pay up or end up in hospital.

He hated the thought of that.

In fact Julian Renfrew hated the world and everything in it. Except perhaps his doting but drunken mother. His mother, whose home was for ever open to him but denied because his father wouldn't let him live there. One day he would Kung Fu the old fart and kick him out of the house. As Julian walked down the slope to the main road he thought about his father. The stuffy old Professor teaching Anthropology or whatever it was to arty farty students at West London Uni. Him and his stupid star gazing. Professor Renfrew was a jerk. Instead of helping him out the old man sided with Bates and Fish, and let the court put him inside. Okay, so the old man had asked mister Byrde to give him a job when he came out, and that was bloody good of him, but he wouldn't let him go back home. And now he was bloody broke. He borrowed money from Donald best to pay the bills, spent the money on a night out with his mates and ended up borrowing more. The trouble was he didn't have the money in his account to pay Michael and that meant borrowing more from bloody Best.

"What a bastard, everyone's against me. It's not fair!" he wailed.

He walked across the street and crossed the park. Birds sang in the trees and flitted around eating things. He scowled at them and with a smooth movement he picked up a handful of gravel from the pathway and flung it into the nearest tree.

"Serves the little bastards right," he said as a flock flew noisily into the air and wheeled around behind him. That they continued singing after he passed annoyed him but at least he had had his short moment of revenge and shifted them from their rotten little perches.

"Noisy little shits," he growled and turned into the main road from the park. Byrde's plastics factory loomed at the end of the road like a prison which he was tied to like a slave to earn his pittance making poxy plastic tokens. Millions of the things all the same colour; the same shape and the same number everyday. It was a bloody boring, pointless task with no future to it unless you could call being in charge of the whole section of machines a future.

The trees that lined the street were full of blossom and pink petals fell like soft rain on the pavement to be crushed underfoot. He hated pink; it was the colour the stupid jerks in the institution used to help calm angry boys down. They said that pink was good for you and even after being out now for three and a half years he still hated it. Pink was gay.

He walked steadily to the gate and turned in ignoring the gate man's cheery greeting and went directly to his machine station. His fags were in his locker and he wanted one desperately. He was early and he had time for one smoke at least. Rules about not smoking at work and all the pubs and that had changed to allow those that wanted to smoke to have a place to do so. Byrde's company allowed smoking on the pad outside where there was a good shelter but it was a way off from the rest of the factory. Cripes, he thought, even in some of the pubs they had built separate rooms, and besides, the smokes were mild now with all sorts of things in them and hardly any tobacco. Grot smoked weed most of the time which he gave to Julian now and then. At least it was legal and you could buy it in the shops. Julian didn't like it much, it made him feel sick.

He hung his coat up inside his locker and donned his overalls. From the top shelf he grabbed his smokes and lighter and dashed off outside. Sod the bloody smokers pad, he thought, and instead he sneaked behind the waste bins where the plastic trimmings were dumped. The light breeze fluttered spilled flakes around his feet, and idly he picked one up and lit it letting the flame grow before touching it to the end of his cigarette. Like lighting fags with money, he thought, like in the old movies. He thought he heard a noise of somebody moving nearby and turned to look still holding the flake close to his cigarette. As he moved, the small flame, caught by the draught, flared up and burnt his face.

"Ouch," he hissed and dropped the burning flake his eyes streaming moisture and for a few moments he was blinded. Something hurt his foot and he looked down and gasped. The flake, well alight now, was one of several burning at his feet. He jumped sideways and slipped on more flakes kicking them across the pad. He hopped on one foot trying to dislodge melting plastic from his shoe but the flames were fanned by his movement and he had to bend down and shift it with his hand.

Black smoke wafted past his face and when he looked up he paled.

"Oh shit," he yelled.

The concrete pad between the bins was a mass of flame.

Instinctively he ran, racing through the wicket gate back into the factory coughing and spluttering and barged into one of the women workers. She staggered nearly falling but held him stopping his headlong dash.

"Wot is it Julian?" she said.

He fumbled at her trying to grab parts of her body but she pushed his hands away and glared at him.

"There's a fire," he said, and pointed to the door.

She let him go and looked out the door.

"Oh gawd, you're right," she said. "Come on! We gotta do summink!"

"What...?

"Shuddup an' git on the other end of an' 'ose," she said, and dragged him through the door..

"But Beryl..."

"Can it and grab the 'ose!"

Beryl hit the fire alarm and turned the water on. Julian staggered, working hard against the power of the water jet unable to let go the hose or direct it. Beryl calmly grabbed another hose and braced herself turning it on and coolly aiming the jet. She grinned at him and yelled.

"Brace yer legs Julian and work the 'ose down, s'easy once yer git the 'ang of it!"

He did as she said and between them they played water on the flames. She grinned at him and he thought, cor! I'll try her out later.

Richard Byrde enjoyed walking to work and on this fine spring Wednesday morning he took great delight strolling under the blooming cherry trees. The spring air was balmy with the perfume of blossom and noisy with the happy chirruping of birds and he felt good. This was one of his early days so he strode steadily timing his pace to arrive at the factory after seven thirty to give the workers a chance to get started. His father had said: "Give the staff the chance to settle in and they will work better. Giving them the first ten minutes is worth a mistake free shift." He smiled at the memory of those and other wise words when he decided to join the company. Fresh from his University degree he wanted to find his own way but stopped long enough to listen to his father.

"Plastics, Richard, is my life and if you want it then it can be yours too. All I ask is that you have patience and learn the art from the bottom up. If you don't want it then you are free to do something else. Does that sit well with you?"

"I'll do my best Dad."

His father nodded.

When both his parents died within a few months of each other Byrde was left with the business. In his will his father requested he keep the name Byrde and Ceedy and named Richard his successor. Ceedy, he remembered, was the man he always called Uncle Oscar. Long dead but he was once a regular visitor to the Byrde home. Oscar Ceedy's share of the business reverted to Byrde senior when he died which enabled Richard to expand. There were two requests his father made in his will that Richard Byrde found puzzling. The first clause was reasonably straight forward and quite easy to understand. His father requested that he keep the old Chinese cleaner, Tzu Wu, on the staff until he left or chose to retire. Byrde remembered his father's liking for the old man and when he asked what the relationship was between them his father smiled and explained.

"I owe him," he said and said no more.

The second clause puzzled him completely and when he asked the company solicitor to explain the man looked at him patiently and sighed.

"I'm sorry but the social club and the canteen is a contract in perpetuity and there is nothing you can do about it."

"Can I have a look at it."

"If you want but I am afraid there is no way out."

Byrde examined the contract and promised himself that at some time he would investigate the matter and make some changes.

As he walked he thought of old Tzu whose family name, Hu appeared on the supply invoices. He mused on that. An old obligation perhaps? His father owed Tzu what? He often puzzled this point on the way to work. He never found an answer. Then there was the plastic tokens. His company made millions of them and as far as he knew Tzu's family were involved with their distribution. The Woo contract his workers called it.

He was close to the factory now and it was with some satisfaction he saw the low buildings with the company name on the roof. Under the name was the environmental code and that was something to be proud of. His products helped keep the air in London clean and he breathed deeply enjoying the fresh scented air. His nose wrinkled and with a shock he realised he could smell, almost taste, something acrid in his nostrils. Smoke and burning. The factory! He ran.

He ran through the gate and yelled back over his shoulder.

"Call the fire brigade and get the supervisor."

Byrde dashed inside the building as the alarm started to jangle and workers streamed past him to the assembly points. He grabbed one of the men by his arm and stopped him to ask where was the fire.

"In the rubbish bins," the man explained.

"Damp the walls down," said Byrde.

The fire was out by the time the fire tender arrived, and all but one of the crew slammed their gear down in anger and grouped together muttering to each other in a dejected group. They brightened up a little when Byrde offered them a little something in compensation for their trouble. The one man that refused gave his name as Senior Fireman Sidney Weddell and he cheerfully explained that he would take nothing for himself if mister Byrde didn't mind.

"I have my duty to do sir and if you don't mind me saying so we get paid well for our work," he said, and looked disapprovingly at the others.

Byrde noticed with interest that the others pointedly ignored him.

Senior Fireman Weddell dutifully examined the burnt out waste bins. He fossicked around in the wet ruins concentrating on his task while the rest of the crew waited despondently in a group beside the tender. He examined the site and went from person to person talking to them asking questions in a clipped tight lipped manner, and taking notes until he was satisfied. Byrde stayed talking to the others trying to make them feel at ease.

"Sorry we were late," said one. "We got stuck in the mud, or we took the wrong turn or it was the wrong time of the month. You take your pick."

Byrde looked at the man's desperate face and smiled.

"Senior Fireman Sidney Weddell?" he asked, knowingly.

"Yeah, the bloke's a prat," the fireman replied.

"We haven't reached a fire in time since that berk has been in charge," said another.

"No," said a third, "and what's more on one trip he took us up a one way street and we got blocked in by a furniture van. The driver made us wait until he finished loading before we could move."

"We hate him," said a fourth, viciously.

Senior Fireman Sidney Weddell stood respectfully in front of Byrde and in his clipped tones delivered a brief report.

"We found a lighter and a packet of cigarettes on the pad. We are of the opinion that one of the workers started the fire. Outside the designated smoking area. Not on sir. Not on. We will note that in our report."

"Very good," said Byrde. "Carry on."

Fireman Weddell stared at Byrde with a peculiar indecisive look on his face as if waiting for Byrde to speak and wanting to say more.

"Could be arson," he said unable to resist.

"Could be an accident," replied Byrde giving the benefit of the doubt.

"That's as maybe, sir."

Byrde smiled and watched as Fireman Weddell turned sharply and marched to the wagon taking his position in the driver's seat. Byrde winced as the wagon jerked forward and rolled over the concrete entrance divider crushing the keep left sign leaving it twisted and battered. He shook his head. His sympathies lay with the crew. For now he had to organise a clean up and speak to Julian and Beryl. He had his suspicions, but unlike Senior Fireman Sidney Weddell he didn't take the incident personally even if it was his factory. He also had other, more pressing things to worry about, like the incident of a few nights before. He thought that and the fire might have been connected but when he realised it was probably Julian being stupidly lazy he relented and in a way felt thankful.

The maniac driver of the hover car outside the Drunken Clown was a bigger worry. He thought he was being paranoid about the incident but he had talked it over with Emily and although he had made light of his suspicions she had not.

"Don't forget there are people around who would do anything for a few Euros in their sweaty hands," she said.

But he didn't really believe that. Nevertheless he had promised to take more care and that made him a little nervous. Just thinking about somebody trying to murder him was enough to scare him. The fire was a relief in a way; it confirmed his optimistic view that accidents do happen even to the best and worst of people.

Tzu Wu

Most of the time, thought Tzu, he was happy. Sometimes he felt as if the world had stopped and was politely waiting for him to catch up. Sometimes it was the other way around, and when that happened he would breathe deeply and let the Chi flow. Today he was letting Chi flow gently and contentedly like a cat purring in the sun. His people were busy in the workshop cleaning the floor, in the canteen cooking, and outside stacking and loading boxes. He plodded on sweeping and shovelling making certain that nothing was missed. Now and then he would give some machinist a toothy grin and nod his head laughing when they laughed and smiling when they growled at him. When they asked him questions he answered in a pidgin English responding to the name Fu Manchu. He didn't mind the banal comments they made, or their assumption that he was just a Chinese labourer with very little between the ears. "Hey Fu Manchu!" They would yell. "You a silly bugger!" And they would nudge each other and wink when he answered back.

"Oh yes, sirry buggah orlight. Me Fu Manchu, sirry buggah!"

On Thursday's when he went out to the loading bay to talk to the delivery driver they took great delight in calling out to each other and laughing at him.

"There he goes again, Fu Manchu off to talk Chinky with the rice chewers!"

He wondered at their ignorance, but then what could he expect, most of them were little removed from poor peasants anyway. He looked up from his work and saw Julian working at his machine looking as if he was expecting something rotten to happen. That young man, he thought, was heading for a pile of trouble. Julian's father was right to approach the Kung Fu school and ask Tzu to take him on. Julian seemed to take to it well although he had seen too many Kung Fu movies and fancied himself as a star. Tzu offered to teach him.

"What's the catch?" asked Julian.

"No catch. You work for me part time and I teach you very good Kung Fu."

"Will I win fights?"

"Maybe."

"You teach me how to bop people and bop them good?"

"Maybe."

"Show me."

Tzu hit him and knocked him down. Julian got up yelling angrily and struck out with his fist. Tzu calmly knocked him back down again. Julian sat on the floor with his legs out in front of him tears streaming down his face. Tzu helped him up and explained that the day he could punch him and get his own back then he had learned enough. Julian was a good student and learned the basic moves easily and in return he worked for Tzu on his days off shifting and loading boxes as part of a gang of people in a warehouse attached to the building block where he did his training. The boxes were all marked in script that looked remarkably like Chinese that was incomprehensible to Julian. When he asked some of the others what they were loading they merely shrugged and said they did not know, all they had to do was load up and keep working. Julian didn't mind; because the work was light and sometimes as well as teaching him Kung Fu old Tzu paid him some money. Tzu discovered that if he was treated right Julian was almost likeable. That thought amused him and when he made his first report to Arthur Renfrew he said so and was puzzled by his friend's disbelief.

"Likeable? The kid's a rat bag."

"Maybe he is but with the right training and the proper incentive there are hidden depths in the boy," said Tzu calmly.

"They are hidden so deep nobody yet has been able to find them," replied Arthur with a shake of his head.

"Not so deep that he cannot find them given the right impetuous; the right influence and some encouragement," Tzu said, and wondered why he felt defensive.

Tzu swept steadily glad that the work was light, giving Julian a friendly smile as he passed his machine, glad when the young man smiled back. When he smiled Julian looked quite pleasant; handsome even, for a European that is. He mused on the irony, that soon Julian will be working full time on the plastic tokens and he, Tzu was about to bow to his family request and retire. He continued sweeping and laughed gently ignoring the amused looks of the workers as they shook their heads at him. The contract was already on Byrde's desk but he still had to give him samples for the second and third runs and of course he had to let the manager know he was about to quit. He planned to quit on Thursday morning after he collected his car, Byrde's old Mercedes, and leave the place in style.

He finished sweeping and leaned on the broom watching the other workers clearing up the piles of waste and wheeling the barrows to the bins. Byrde should install some washing bays to recycle the scrap himself rather than contract it out. The savings would be considerable. Tzu made a mental note to discuss the possibility with Byrde when he had an opportunity. His eyes twinkled a little as he thought about what Byrde's reaction would be.

These Englishmen didn't take Chinese people seriously enough. They seemed to accept Japanese expertise and he knew that mostly they had a sneaking suspicion that Chinese people were good at business. Tzu had made a lot of money playing on that attitude. Despite the years Europeans had bought goods from large companies that made their goods in China, his mother nation was still considered a backward peasant country of po-faced morons. He could sympathise with the Chinese government although he could never want to live there. The Chinese were an environmental disaster, he thought, an ecological time bomb that could either wreck the planet completely or find the means to help fix it. Tzu cynically plumped for the former. He had no faith in his own people. His fellow workers didn't seem to realise how many British businesses were owned by Chinese and Indian companies, or that it was Asia's turn at being number one.

He sighed and muttered. "They will never learn," and smiled; he was amused at their poor language skills. The factory workers treated him as if he was an idiot laughing at his mangled English yet most of them spoke their own language badly. Tzu thought about Queen's English, and smiled softly; he liked the Royal Family and Tzu could also be proud to be born British and therefore one of the Monarch's subjects, most loyal subject, he added.

The other cleaners completed their tasks and started putting their gear away so with a casual but steady plod he shouldered his broom and walked to the cleaner's cubby hole. He watched as the young men and women stacked their gear neatly and approved when one took the broom from him and placed it in its slot.

Another successful day at the office, he mused.

Tzu walked from the factory to the bus stop with the rest of the crew and as he went he began to slot his mind into the new market. The extra tokens would be manufactured mostly at Byrde and Ceedy but there would be a back up located in a factory in New Zealand. Tzu was proud of that. He had managed to locate the right place through a subsidiary in Sydney Australia and when the Australians had suggested they could get a better deal in Auckland's Albany Basin he accepted it. Ironic really but the subsidiary was originally part of the company whose bonus system worked on the tokens in exchange for goods idea his own company had taken over. It was simple really; a worker or gang of workers were committed to a safe working environment with on time delivery and no mistakes. Tokens were handed out to the lucky workers who then redeemed them for goods, supplied by Tzu's company, with a social club and canteen package if requested. He recalled the day, years before, when the two strange men had arrived in his office unannounced and had made him an offer he could hardly refuse. They had sold him the system which had cost his savings, his children's piggy bank money and the funds from the Kung Fu club. He had paid all of it back many times over and his family business was getting so big he had accountants to work out his inland revenue returns, and accountants to deal solely with his customs and excise. Since that time a package of tokens as samples had arrived with specifications and new contracts at intervals. This last one had called for some colour changes and a large increase in the order.

It was something to think about.

Right now he needed to produce his bus ticket. The operator looked pained as he fumbled myopically in his pockets for the pockmarked card and he was amused when the man almost sneered as it hiccupped in the swipe slot. The fare took a while to register but eventually it did and he climbed into a seat. The other workers followed him and took seats around him making a block of mostly Chinese at the front of the bus.

The operator looked resigned to his fate and Tzu smiled secretly to himself, and with one eye on the operator he spoke to his companions in Cantonese and soon they were laughing and joking and occasionally glancing at the operator and glancing away again. By the time Tzu reached his bus stop the operator was fuming.

Funny how a few well timed looks and a lot of laughter can upset a person, Tzu thought, as he alighted and gave the operator a rueful smile.

Duty is a fine thing.

The sword blade sang as it arced through the air. The twin blades splashed reflected light briefly, and as quickly dulled again. Kord breathed in and with a slow expiration of air he made a cut. There was a sudden sloppy gasping sound of flesh dropping in slices to a wooden floor and a grunt of satisfaction. Twice more the sounds were repeated and then with a faint metallic scrape the sword was sheathed.

Kord faced his twin and smiled. At his feet lay the mangled bodies of three Polisoc prisoner Half Pairs each dead from one of the eight classic cuts.

"Well done my twin," Krod said. "You have cut well."

Kord visibly swelled with pride. He was a good sword fighter but his twin was much better and this was praise indeed.

"Good enough to beat our target?"

"Maybe, maybe not, all we need is more practice. These scum," he kicked the dead bodies and sneered. "Are nothing; no competition really. Just targets to play with. We need some real fighting to keep us in trim but I suppose these creatures will have to do."

"At least they are soldiers and not City Pairs the Polisocs are giving us," said Kord.

His twin laughed.

At that point the Training Leader Pair entered the room.

"Neat cutting Pair, neat cutting; I hope you had them fight you?"

"We did your Honour. They fought well. One Half Pair actually walked out alive," said Kord. "But he quarrelled with the Polisoc Leader Pair. I am afraid his freedom was short and hardly sweet."

"Can't be helped, they're only prisoner scum anyway so they don't matter. I have some news for you. Your enemy target is on his way so now is your chance to get some real work in."

"Do we terminate?"

"Yes, our Glorious President has given orders that the subject Drogl and all who associate with him are to be wiped out. Show no mercy. Your orders are cut already, and when you reach the Transfer Ports data updates will be ready for you. Good hunting."

Kord and Krod bowed low.

"It is an honour to be chosen to thus serve our Glorious President," they said together with just the right amount of joy in their voices.

The Leader Pair bowed back with solemn faces. The trouble with Kord and Krod was that they meant it when they said they were honoured to serve and that, thought the Leader Pair, was what made them valuable operatives. The only drawback with such blind loyalty was they took their orders so seriously they would carry them out to the letter, and once launched on the mission were impossible to stop. The Leader Pair shuddered. The thought of being Kord and Krod's target was a nightmare only worse than being the target of Blard the Barmy and his psychopathic twin Bradl.

Now that was a trouser wetting thought to have in a Pair's mind.

Drogl, or D.G as he liked to be known was unaware of Kord and Krod's orders but even if he had he would not have worried too much. He was confident in his own ability to handle whatever came his way as far as actual fighting was concerned; also he was an arrogant Bulger who led a charmed existence that seemed to balance between life and death with equanimity.

If D.G was asked about his thoughts on being the target of a Dog Squad hit Pair he would have replied that he liked the challenge. He had a challenge already which taxed his ability to the limit; and that was how on Zrad he was going to get the hang of all the gismos they had given him. He laid them out on the bench and tried to recall what the technician Pair had said about them. There was an Atlas, and that was straight forward; he could use one of those all right, and with that was the Transfer Station Activator. Those two items he could cope with. What fazed him was the communications modules and the remote control units. These were fine to a point but they were controlled by a different monitor system which was linked to his electronic door and lock protectors. He was unsure of them and that sort of thing bothered him. He sighed and shoved them into his bag. All he could remember was the last remark the technician Pair had made to him before he left the workshop.

"These things are idiot proof; even the dimmest operative can use them."

He hadn't liked their grin as he put them in his bag too proud to admit that he hadn't a clue how to use any of them except the Atlas and the activator. He left the weapons to last and hefted the gas gun in his hand first and put it in the pouch. He counted the bombs and was happy they had given him twenty; the same number as the replacement gas capsules. They had also given him some cash and a credit card made out on the Bank of Hong Kong. He had asked for American Express but the reply was short and to the point.

"You get what we give you. We have an account with them."

He didn't ask why or through whom but just accepted the explanation at face value and asked for more American dollars and a few more Euro-dollars in place of his English pounds.

"It's a pity I cannot exchange Tokens, I understand the current exchange rate is quite favourable," he said, and grinned, pleased when the High Leader Pair walked smartly out of the room red-faced and angry.

He packed his kit which included spare underwear, his nail scissors, his blade sharpening tools and his favourite short knife. They wouldn't let him take a plasma gun or a sword. He was allowed to take his Glord the Glorious Token with him. That was his lucky charm and he always took it on missions. The problem lay, he thought, within his and Glord's twinship. The bond was strong and full of empathy but they had a unique streak in their nature. They could work alone and separately without going into trauma. When he and Glord worked together they were awesome but they were good as Half Pairs too. That was because of their Fourball training. You don't get to be stars at Fourball without developing a keen sense of other, he thought, with some satisfaction. Other Pairs didn't like it.

Other, the way of being an individual or, according to the Concise Oxford English Dictionary the word otherness is defined as 'the state of being different' and although D.G didn't feel different he knew what the separation meant.

"I am not different," he said. "Not different at all. I am the same as my twin. My twin is the same as me."

But deep down he knew he wasn't and that disturbed him deeply.

He finished his packing and marched out of the portal with his bag slung over his shoulder nonchalantly as if he didn't care and to his surprise he realised he didn't. That disturbed him too.

Glord saw him off and shook his hand as the technicians checked the Transfer Port coordinates. They looked more nervous than he did. The technicians gave him the thumbs up and with a final touch of his twin's outstretched hand he stepped into the port. The sudden sick feeling of transfer disappeared quickly, and with a sense of detachment he counted the number of changes. One in a remote block south; another to a port in Second City and one more to the Transfer Station above the planet Zrad and then the quick flicker of the cargo port in Star Station Two. The last, a supposedly risk free transfer to a point in the northern hemisphere of Earth, was almost a disaster. He dropped a metre to a concrete pavement in the middle of shoppers in a busy downtown centre on the western coast of the United States of America.

He dropped lightly and turned immediately to look up and adopted the ruse of pointing to the roof of a nearby male boutique.

"Did you see that?" he said, but was disappointed when he realised that nobody had noticed his sudden arrival. He looked around and shrugged. He looked at his dress and looked again at what other people were wearing. "Yeah but look at me in these threads, man I am a sartorial mess."

For the first time he appreciated what otherness was and with his credit card handy and no idea of what was cool he stepped into the boutique.

"Dress me baby," he said to whatever it was that came forward to serve him.

Kord and Krod suffered Transfer stoically. They hated it but as transfer was necessary in the line of duty they endured it. In fact there was a large number of things they endured in the line of duty. They were always polite to the Leader Pairs; tolerated the worst excesses of the Polisocs and did everything by the book except when it suited them. They saluted the Leader Pair of Star Station Two who, having no time for Dog Squad murderers, allocated them the worst cabin they could find, apologising that as they were only going to be there for a couple of turns then they didn't need luxury.

Kord and Krod were content, at least is was better than their last quarters, the loft above the pig pens in First City's Polisoc Headquarters. The food was better too, and it was with much enthusiasm and praise they asked for, and got, second helpings of the bland dinner time sausage.

"Yummy," said Krod, and smacked his lips with his tongue.

The servery Pair looked at each other and shrugged.

"Very good sir," he said observing the protocol and speaking as one.

Privately and later in the canteen mess room they told the story of the Dog Squad Pair who ate and enjoyed the bland sausage that everybody, to the lowest Half Pair, laced with the highly tasty spices the catering crew sold on the black market. In a way Kord and Krod's refusal to use such tasty condiments whether in ignorance or through a sense of duty helped the President's war effort. For the few days they were on board Kord and Krod's non expenditure on illegal substances denied a minute amount of funds to the enemy.

Everybody knew, but would never admit, that the origin of the spices was deep in the wastelands where the Zradian Rebel Army had their farms and breweries and from where they launched their attacks.

Kord and Krod, of course, would never use such illegal substances.

But then, as the canteen staff and all who came in contact with them agreed; Kord and Krod were a Pair of Bulger's arseholes. They were also about to be transported down to Earth on an important mission as soon as they were briefed. The briefing began that very evening and it was with enthusiasm and some excitement they entered the training room. The Pair Dral and Darl stood beside the HoloScope and pointedly looked at the clock.

"Sorry we're late," said Kord. "We sort of lost our way."

They didn't explain that the Pairs they asked to direct them had given them completely wrong directions, nor did they explain that after spending most of one period wandering in the dark somewhere in sector yellow they had almost but not quite transferred back to Zrad. It was the sudden spoken message from the Cargo Transfer Port speaker that alerted them to their imminent unwanted journey. They backed out of the port quickly and sighed with relief when the lights turned back to a steady green-red-green.

They sat in the chair at Darl's bidding while Dral hopped behind the control console and activated the holograph.

"First we will show you the latest update from our Earth archives and after that we have a little test for you," said Darl. "The content of which may be disturbing. Mental supervision may be necessary."

The pair looked at him with a puzzled expression and then turned to watch the image as the briefing began. They sat through to the end concentrating on whatever was before them, and when the images disappeared they waited ready for the test.

"Your reactions to this will determine your assessment," said Dral, and smirked.

"We will be staunch," said Kord and his twin nodded.

At first they did nothing when the new image appeared but with a shudder of fear and anger they left their seat and as the creature played and flitted around in circles first this way and then that they yelled with a primal howl and dived at it as one being. Their hands grasped nothing but light and with curses they tumbled over each other scrabbling for a grip ready to kill. The light vanished and the image disappeared and with embarrassed looks at each other and at Dral and Darl they asked. "What is it?"

"It's a kitten. It's a young Cat; smaller but similar in type to our Carnibeast. Your reaction is typical and now the rest of this briefing will be taken up with de-toxification exercises."

"What?"

"We teach you how not to react," said Darl, smirking even more facetiously than he had before. "It seems that we have an inherent tendency to chase them. Some of our Pairs have already died in the field trying to kill them."

"But why? Why the Bulger do we chase them?" asked Krod.

"It has something to do with the origin of our species," said Dral. "Too complicated to go into here; we have enough on our hands with this task. Tomorrow you will be here and let us get on with the briefing. It may take some time."

"Dismiss," said Darl.

Kord and Krod bowed slightly, saluted and with precisely paced and coordinated steps they left the room.

"Prats," said Darl as the portal opaqued behind them.

"True but we'll be rid of them tomorrow if we push it," said Dral.

As it turned out Dral and Darl passed Kord and Krod for active service within half a turn. By the time the mid meal break arrived they were utterly fed up with them and passed them anyway. If Kord and Krod chased cats and got killed for their efforts then let them get on with it; the Bulgers were insufferable, and as far as Dral and Darl were concerned they would hardly be missed.

"They're on our little list," murmured Dral and wondered where the phrase came from. To make certain that they had actually got rid of Kord and Krod they went to the Transfer Port and watched them flicker out of sight; transported, so the technician Pair said, to somewhere in darkest England.

It was in darkest England, or as dark as it could get with street lights burning and the lights of the buildings casting a glow on the city. Two Pairs who were given the task of watching the Earthmen their masters were interested in followed the old Chinaman along the street as expertly as they could given the circumstances. Zradian nights were not as dark as those on Earth and although they had good night spectacles it was still difficult to see what they were doing.

Tzu and his companion turned a corner into a street of glass fronted shops and in the opposite widows he caught sight of the Pairs. "I think we are being followed," he said to Arnold, his companion, a Kung Fu instructor from West London University with whom Tzu intended to arrange a seminar. Tzu repeated the warning and laughed softly. "I think our followers are good but not as good as they think. We will test them."

Tzu led the way into an alleyway and walked quickly along it to a dog leg turn around a couple of back yards where the pair stood quietly in a dark recess to watch. There was a junction of two alleyways at the far point of the dog-leg and Tzu gave their followers full marks for spreading out in pairs; approving of their swift but cautious progress as they explored all the ways before moving on.

"Be ready," Tzu whispered.

Suddenly there was a scuffle on the wall above them followed by a cat's yowl which was answered by another. Tzu froze and so did their pursuers. Beside him Arnold tensed up ready to move but it was unnecessary, two felines suddenly burst into full scream and tumbled down the wall to land spitting and swearing at each other ready to fight tooth and claw for territory.

What happened next surprised the cats and amused Tzu and Arnold. Their pursuers stopped, stared at the two animals and as one attacked the creatures who turned, struck out viciously, fur fluffed, tails erect and claws out to defend against the new threat. After a brief skirmish the two cats turned tail and ran. The four men chased after them howling and shouting, their voices both angry and frightened as they ran past Tzu and Arnold taking no notice of them.

"Come, let us see what happens," Tzu said, and the two men hurried after their would be trackers emerging to see that the cats, miraculously escaping death crossing the busy road were sitting on a low wall busily washing themselves.

"Oh dear," said Tzu. The four men were not so lucky; one was underneath a hoverwagon, one draped over a centre wall, a third lay still on the road and the fourth was still rolling head over heels from contact with a truck.

"How odd, I could swear they were actually chasing the cats," said Arnold, and as the traffic stopped the two men walked to the nearest body and knelt down to see what their followers looked like. He was surprised at what he saw.

"Arnold, look at this man's face, the eyes! See the eyes, they are odd," Tzu said. "We should have a look at the others quickly before the services arrive."

The two men hurried to where the second man was now slowly drooping backwards onto the roadway. Tzu eased him down to the paving and again noted the eyes, aware also that the man was still alive. "This one not dead." Together they eased him to a position where he could breathe properly and waited until the services arrived. The medical people pushed them aside without even a thank you.

"Come on you two, move along, there's nothing more to see. Let the professionals do their job," a constable said glaring at them menacingly.

"Ah so, Thank you verra much," Tzu replied.

Arnold giggled.

And the pair cheerfully walked away.

Angela.

Angela Breen knelt down beside the limp form on the pavement and spoke softly.

"How are you brother?"

The man groaned and spittle bubbled from his pale lips. She helped him sit up and examined the whiskery face and red rimmed eyes. There was a cake of dried matter tacked to his cheek that ran from one eye to his chin like a line of crystals on granite. Where the dirty collarless shirt covered his chest there was a rime of greasy dirt. She was sure he smelled of meths and unwashed body parts but she had her duty to do and so with a smile she spoke again.

"We can help you brother; we will give you succour and heal your hurts," she said and turned her head to see where the group was.

The man stirred and with a sudden movement reached out with a claw like hand and gripped her wrist. He drew her close to his face and mouthed words at her and with his other hand fumbled at her clothing.

"Come on darlin' give us a fuck."

Red faced with anger and righteous embarrassment she slapped his hand away from where it was reaching for her breast and when he tried to touch her again she smacked him hard on the jaw with her fist.

"Dirty old man," she said and stood up smoothing her dress.

She let the men pick him up and watched as they carried him to the van biting her lip and trying hard not to think of what the man was thinking about. Sinful thoughts; a sinful act outside marriage; disgusting; animalistic; rutting stags or pigs and dogs. At least the animals were innocent in their actions but this, this creature, this fallen creature should know better. She hated him.

"Oh Lord," she said. "Please help me to love such a one as this as you love us, and purge these sinful thoughts and feelings from my mind and body. She wondered why whenever she tried to pray for forgiveness she felt confused and her words seemed to tangle themselves up, like Alice.

"Twinkle twinkle little bat, how I wonder what you're at," she recited and stood staring across the river at the twinkling car lights. She wondered what she was at. Each night of the week and every Saturday evening the team came to the Embankment and searched the dark places for the down and outs to give them shelter and food for the night and in the morning teach them the Gospel. Every Saturday night without fail they met abusive men who called them names and made lewd suggestions to the girls and sometimes to the boys. Disgusting sex things and like as not they would throw up or do other things when they got to the refuge. Sometimes they caught one of the men masturbating and when that happened the boys would surround him and make him stop and pray for him.

It was usually men they took back to the refuge and sometimes they found dead ones and that was sad. She remembered one woman she found by the river in the winter frozen to death on the steps. The police had to break her body free and scrape flesh and clothing from the stonework with trowels. That was sad too because when the Church traced her family nobody wanted to know about her unless they could collect on her insurance. One relative even wanted to know if he was likely to benefit from her will and how much it was likely to be. Angela recalled that she had decked him too when he made an inappropriate suggestion.

"I'm not that sort of girl," she said, and felled him with a kick to the groin and a right cross to the jaw.

She packed her torch in her bag and glanced at Big Ben. Time to go home. Nine thirty, time for all good Christian Girls to go seek their beds. She had at least three quarters of an hour on the train and a ten minute walk at the other end and her sister liked to lock up at eleven. Cocoa at ten thirty.

She walked purposefully toward the tube station glaring at a policeman who looked at her lustfully. Was that all men thought about? Perhaps she should dress more soberly and not let her figure distract them. She knew her long flaxen hair and her shapely beach bunny figure was pleasant for men to look at but that was not what she wanted out of life; to be a sex object. She wanted to be treated properly like a good Christian girl should be treated.

The journey home was fraught with suggestive glances and she worried if it were her imagination that the men lusted after her or that she was lusting after the men. The second thought worried her and she hastily said a prayer to cover it, a tumbling, babble of words with no real purpose. In her room she read her Bible and thought about how her Lord had sacrificed Himself for her, and with her head bowed she prayed again. She prayed too that she might be spared doing drunk duty this Wednesday, she didn't mind Saturday but tonight and tomorrow night was a bit too much, and for some reason she couldn't pin down she began to pray for Julian Renfrew.

"Lord, protect him and bring him true understanding. Give him the strength to realise his weakness and give him the chance to see your truth before ...before, oh I don't know what before. Give him your Love and protect him from all harm. Amen." She finished off and with one last touch of her Bible she lay back in her bed and switched out the bedside lamp.

She woke the next morning to the sound of her alarm disturbed by the semi-waking dream she had had in which Julian featured, to her shame, as her lover. Naked and penitent she knelt beside her bed and prayed for forgiveness. To her surprise when she said Julian's name she felt her nipples harden and a warm lumpy feeling tighten in her belly. She prayed instantly to quell that feeling too.

Sinful, sinful girl!

On the Wednesday morning Julian walked into Byrde's office feeling nervous.

"Take a seat Julian," said Byrde, smiling.

Julian sat in the chair opposite and waited trying to appear patient but wishing the interview was over.

Byrde sighed leaning forward and placing his elbows on the desk touching his fingers together making a spire.

"Well, Julian, you had better tell me what happened out in the yard," he said and locked his gaze onto Julian's.

Julian dropped his gaze and took a deep breath.

"I was on my way to the smoking area for my usual morning smoke," he began. "I like to have one before I take over on the machine, and I saw a wisp of smoke cummin' from the bins. I went over to them and looked inside and saw some plastic burning so I sort of tried to pull it out didn't I? It burnt me 'and didn't it? I dropped the bit I got hold of and tried to kick it out the way but it was too late 'cos by then the air got to it and that was it. Flames shot up out the bin and bloody near burnt me 'air right off. I ran to get help but I got caught in the smoke and then me and Beryl got on the hoses."

Byrde shook his head a little and Julian's heart raced. I hope the bugger believes me, he thought, frightened.

"I'm sorry Julian, I misjudged you, because it seems that what Beryl told me was the truth. She said she thought you were going out for your morning smoke. The report from Fireman Weddell suggests that somebody had stopped there for a smoke because he found a pack of cigarettes on the floor and a lighter. Were they yours?" said Byrde.

"Yeah, they was. I was carrying my fags and my lighter ready to take one out when I got there because I hadn't got much time. I let go of 'em when I saw the smoke. I suppose I've lost 'em now?" Julian replied, contrite but with an eye on Byrde's reaction.

"Yes and maybe it's time to give up the habit?" said Byrde knowingly.

Julian grinned, and spread his hands, relaxed a bit now that the immediate threat was past. "After this lot I reckon that's a good idea, mister Byrde, I had no idea how a plastic fire can spread. Just imagine if someone deliberately lit the stuff in the right places. There would be no stopping it," exclaimed Julian. "I'm glad I was there on the spot to help put it out."

Byrde nodded and with a sigh he handed Julian a sheet of paper.

"That sheet is my written recognition of your quick work this morning, Julian, and you will find the increased rate in your pay next week. I have decided to give you a little extra bonus for helping to save the factory." Byrde stood up and reached out his right hand to shake Julian's and smiled warmly at him."Thank you Julian. Now, I suggest you get back to your work."

Julian took the hint and stood up ready to go. He shook Byrde's hand and turned to go out the door opening it on the second attempt and almost stumbling through.

"Oh, and Julian," said Byrde. "Next time be a bit more careful."

Julian turned back and gave Byrde a fleeting, frightened smile. What does the old fart know, he thought, and turned quickly out the door.

At the bottom of the stairs Julian stopped to read the sheet and got a pleasant surprise. A rise of six percent and a bonus of two weeks wages plus a notice of promotion.

"Please report on Monday at 8 am to the Chargehand's office to undergo stage one of the Charge Hand's program. Congratulations, we look forward to you working with us...

He put it in his pocket and walked boldly back to his machine with his chest out stroking his long hair back over his head feeling superior, and letting his grey eyes sweep over the figures of the women working on the machines. As he turned into his alley he saw Beryl and went to talk to her.

"You helped me out there a bit with mister Byrde," he said, grinning. "How about I buy you a drink after the shift and maybe we could go out after for a little bit of the old slap and tickle. What do yer reckon?"

For a moment she looked pleased and then her look changed to one of disgust and anger when she understood what he had said.

"Wot, wiv you?" she said. "If I go 'ome an' tell my ole man wot you jest said 'e won't 'arf give you an 'iding; you dirty bugger. I seen yer aht in the yard lookin' through 'oles in the bog wall. You ain't nuthin' but a pervert, you. You jest bugger orf before I call the super!"

"All I wanted to do was say thanks. Crikey, some people don't 'arf take on so," complained Julian, backing away from her as she leaned toward him with her hands on her hips glowering at him angrily.

"Go on, get lorst," she shouted.

Julian backed out into the alley and hastened to his own machine red faced and angry. "Fuckin' slut," he muttered.

From the balcony outside his office Byrde watched Julian walk across the factory floor stop briefly to talk to Beryl and afterwards hurry away to his machine. He saw Tzu look up and smile as he worked, like the other cleaners, steadily pushing the waste toward the bins. He thought about the connection between Tzu and the plastic token contract, and smiled as he remembered calling on Sherman Holmes to investigate when, Morrison, his solicitor explained that there was a water tight contract that tied in the manufacture of the tokens with the social club.

"Your father set it up with Oscar Ceedy when he was alive, I am afraid the conditions are binding, and, er, you wouldn't want to lose a valuable part of your operations would you?" said Morrison.

Byrde agreed but had set Holmes loose on it anyway. Predictably Holmes discovered that the contract was watertight and all he did was to waste his money and give Holmes a chance to get drunk at his expense.

That evening at home Byrde took a quick look into his empty garage. He was sad to see the Mercedes go but he agreed with Emily that they really didn't need a large car.

"You walk to work a lot and when you go to see anyone you go by bus or taxi so I want a car for me this time. I'm going to get a smaller one that fits in the garage and costs less to run. Besides, the new cars are as powerful as the old ones and they use less fuel and make less noise. And, don't forget, the bigger vehicles are not allowed to use the inner city roads anymore," she said.

She was right, twice he had gone into the city and had to park outside the inner ring and go by train. The trips by car, he agreed, were a waste of time, he may as well have taken the hover train in the first place. They got a good price for it and Emily took it into the dealer for the new buyer to collect on Thursday. Byrde turned and went into the house moving slowly into the kitchen and waited for a moment when Emily was not actually carrying anything. He put his arms around her and kissed her cheek letting his lips meet hers as she twisted around to face him.

"You saw the old car off all right then?"

She grinned and glanced up at him with a merry twinkle in her eyes.

"You are dying to know what I have chosen aren't you?" she said.

"Of course but you want it to be a surprise," he said.

"Naturally, so instead tell me about your day especially the fire," she said, and giggled. He kissed her again and sat in one of the dining room chairs so he could talk to her as she worked. And told her what happened including his interview with Julian.

"Do you think that Julian lit the fire, Richard?"

"I have my suspicions. He worked hard to put it out so I could hardly let it go without doing something. The problem is that he is a good worker and worth promotion but the other workers don't like him. I gave him a charge hand's job today. I hope I am doing the right thing."

"I'm sure you are Richard. My cousin called today wanting to know if you have any work for her drunken pet the delectable mister Sherman Holmes."

"Your cousin is a bossy bag and no I haven't got any work for Holmes," said Byrde. "I recall that the last time he was employed he caused a near riot in a church fete of all places!"

She giggled and said, with her eyes sparkling. "It livened the event up. He was so drunk that afterwards we had to get someone to carry him away. Julian was there with Angela and I remember how he panicked when she demanded he tell Holmes off for his rude remarks."

In spite of his dislike for Holmes and Emily's cousin, Byrde was amused at their relationship and the sometimes fiery results. The pair were a bit like Julia and Arthur Renfrew really.

"I should call Arthur," he said and left the table.

"Dinner will be ready in about ten minutes so don't be too long Richard," she called after him as he strode off to the room he used as an office.

Julia Renfrew answered and from her slurred speech and belligerent manner he knew she was already drunk. He was glad he hadn't used the screen, the sight of Julia in a drunken state didn't appeal to him.

"What do you want?" she demanded.

"May I speak to Arthur, please Julia?"

"Yeah sure you can..."

He heard the receiver rattle a little at the other end and then Julia's voice yelling.

"Arthur! It's one of your dumb friends on the blower..."

She thumped the receiver down and a few seconds later Arthur answered.

"Oh hello Richard, sorry about Julia I'm afraid she is having one of those evenings again. What can I do for you?"

Byrde told him about Julian and waited for Arthur's reaction.

"Watch him carefully Richard he is a crafty lad and likely to do some mischief. I suggest you don't let him get away with much more. In fact I think you should tell him that I might call on him if he doesn't shape up."

Byrde chuckled, he knew that Julian was terrified of his father.

"Richard, er, can we meet this evening later, er, in the Clown over a beer or two. I have to get out of the house, Julia's moaning is driving me crazy." Arthur said sounding anxious.

"Well I do have the dishes to do and some work to catch up on but if it is important then, yes, I suppose we can," Byrde said. "What is it about?"

"I'll explain when I see you. About eight thirty?"

"Sure," said Byrde. "See you."

He dropped the receiver into its cradle and let his fingers rest on it for a moment.

"Arthur, you sound mysterious," he said quietly.

Emily had served up the meal so they sat and ate sharing the small chores needed at table until at last they were sipping at coffee.

"I'll do the dishes now and then I will go out for a while to the Drunken Clown," he said. "Arthur wants a chat. I won't be long. Will you be all right here on your own?"

She looked up at him and nodded.

"I'll yearn for you tragically," she said and made cow eyes at him.

"Woman, you are irresistible," he said and would have plumped for staying at home. "I love you Emily."

She dropped her gaze and then looked up at him. There were diamonds in her eyes and warmth of joy in her look that gripped his heart like a loving hand holding a trembling sparrow.

There was no mockery in her voice when she replied and he kissed his name from her lips.

"I'll have my mobile with me," he said, releasing her.

Angela sat watching the television with her sister. They had put the children to bed and all that remained was to enjoy the evening and wait for Roger to come home from work. Leanne liked to watch the police dramas and the hospital ones and although Angela would have preferred to watch something more enlightening she watched too and was content. Since she had moved in with her sister she was happier. Living in the same house as Julian was a drain on her patience and she had to admit, a drain on her faith too. Julian and his mates were always ready to mock her Christianity, and to make matters worse she ended up cleaning his mess up behind him. Michael and the others refused to do it and she couldn't stand mess. Then there was the two couples in the other rooms. She disapproved of unmarried people sleeping in the same bed and hated the idea of living in the same house as fornicators.

She had wanted to spend Wednesday with Leanne and the children rather than out on the Embankment with the drunks. Leanne got lonely sometimes and besides, when push came to shove, she was prepared to take some time out for herself. After all, she worked hard at the mission. It was not every qualified social worker who was prepared to work for the pay she earned. That was the main reason for taking her sister's offer to live at their house. All she had to pay was her share of the food and some of the bills and help with the housework which meant she had more money to spare. The program ended and Leanne stretched, yawned and stood up.

"I'll make us some tea and put Roger's dinner in the oven to warm up," she said and wandered out into the kitchen. Angela watched her sister go and smiled; Leanne was a pretty woman, although not so striking in looks as Angela but that did not matter because Leanne was a loving person who was content to marry and have babies. While she was watching the newscast she heard the front door go and anticipated Roger coming into the lounge to say hello.

He did a few minutes later carrying a cup of tea and a smile.

"Hi sis, tea and kiss," he said, and put the cup on the small table nearby and gave her a kiss on the cheek.

"Hello Rog," she said and kissed his cheek. "Did you have a good day?"

"Yes but better now I am home. Now I must go to my wife and give her the rest of my attention."

Roger biffed out of the room and as she watched him go she felt good. Her sister's husband was a lovely man, she thought, and wished that Julian could see him and learn to be like him. She blushed when she realised that again she had thought of Julian and wondered what was happening. It was a pity that Leanne didn't like Julian because then she would have him around for a meal, but neither Roger or Leanne would let him in the house. On the whole, she thought, Julian wasn't too bad and she was sure that with a bit of work he could be much better. "Oh dear, I sound like one of the heroines from those romance novels," she said to the empty room. And with her eyes closed and her hands together she prayed for herself and for Julian.

All the Way With the Leader of the Day

The problem, thought Clard, was the sub contractors. The design was perfect. Everything C&D ever designed was perfect; it was the contractors who let them down. Did C&D not pay the best bribes in the business? Did C&D not also have the best legal team in the business? And were not those legal minds well able to place the blame for any mistakes squarely in the hands of the subcontractors and totally exonerate their company? And yet Clard had a nagging doubt that something was dreadfully wrong.

Up to a few turns ago all was sweet.

Star Station One was the latest and greatest, whiz bang, top of the line, high tech unit they had ever designed and they were rightly proud of it. Happily they opened the advertising super hype that announced the launching and sat back waiting for the accolades to roll in. The giant TelScreen company broadcast the event from the moment the Pairs transferred to the Star Ship through the pre-transfer countdown to the moment the Controller Pair on board made his speech in praise of the President and tapped in the code.

The image of the Controller Pair disappeared, the cameras cut to the watching officials, and the presenter who cheerfully waffled to the audience whilst they waited for the Controller to announce the safe arrival of Star Station One.

Nothing happened and stayed not happening for an embarrassingly long time until a technician Pair replaced the program with a Presidential sponsored Republican Pep Talk.

Frantically Clard and Dracl and a team of technician Pairs searched the whole spectrum of transmission data but there was nothing. Zilch. Not a Bulger's breath of data from anywhere.

Star Station One had disappeared.

Oops.

Clard and Dracl of C&D Enterprises took a well earned holiday in a remote part of Sector Blue in the northern reaches of Upper Zradia until the President's purges were over. Naturally they followed the progress of the purges using the latest media tracking system that not only scrambled the signals but scrambled the destination too. At the moment when the call came from the President's office for a new commission Clard and Dracl reappeared in First City bronzed and healthy offering contract bribes to the highest bidders. This time they decided that as a back up they would cobble up Star Station Two from a trial frame and build Star Station Three from scratch.

This time they were lucky. The Polisocs had a surplus of prisoners with useful skills and C&D Enterprises bought them as a job lot. With a philosophy of incentives borrowed from the data available from the target planet Earth Dracl put in place a work ethic that dictated 'Job and Finish' to the hopeful slaves.

"We like that," said their spokespair, pleased at the prospect of release at the end of the major contracts.

What Dracl never told them was that the 'finish' meant just that. Regrettably, he reflected their demise was all part of the deal with the Polisocs. In marketing terms the prisoner slaves had a use by date.

"Isn't that a bit unfair?" said Clard with a rare twinge of post vacation concern.

"No, not really, we are entitled to dispose of our assets in any way we wish. Just call it expedient downsizing," Dracl replied with a characteristic fatalistic shrug.

"Yeah, I suppose you're right my twin."

But the problem still lay with the contractors.

It seemed that no matter what they did or how they worded the contracts there were still far too many subcontractors muscling in and offering cheaper rates and higher bribes. Clard didn't mind the proliferation of bribes on the one hand because C&D made a percentage of the cut each time. On the other hand the quality of the work deteriorated and added to the problems which C&D were constantly called in to solve. True, each time their consultancy was called in they could charge a fee but although they made Tokens out of the deals there were time delays which C&D Construction could ill afford. To solve that particular problem C&D Enterprises legal department recommended litigation to recover costs. Tempted by the huge default pay outs that were likely to fill their coffers Clard and Dracl agreed to go ahead with litigation and now they were faced with actions and counteractions against themselves.

"I think we stand to make a lot of money if we win but if we lose we stand to lose a lot of money, but if we lose we stand to make a lot and if we win we stand to lose a lot. Speaking from both sides that is," said their legal adviser Pair.

"What do you think?" asked Clard.

"I'm confused," replied Dracl.

The legal adviser Pair stood quietly for a few short periods with their chins cupped in their hands and then with a light-globe intensity of illumination they came to a conclusion.

"We should form a third company complex to sue both C&D Enterprises and C&D Construction!"

"Will we make money?"

"Heaps, oodles of it."

"Then we should do it."

They dreamed of the huge sums they would make but still worried that the problem lay with the contractors.

"I think we should reduce our contact with the construction of the Star Stations to the role of consultants," said Clard.

"Do you mean sell the whole thing?"

"Everything, and take the cream off the top. We can package the thing so it looks as if there is a vast fortune to be made and channel the profits off to our starvation accounts," said Clard.

And that was what they did. Within five complete turns C&D Enterprises, C&D Construction and their subsidiaries were sold off and managed by C&D's Legal department who, at the end of the following tenth, discovered that they were plaintive, complainant, legal defender and prosecutor for their own four vast and complex business systems.

It was not an ideal situation but Clard and Dracl stood to make a fortune in Tokens and within such a complex situation they were completely exonerated from any blame.

Clard and Dracl, freed of the encumbering worry of corporate responsibility, sat in their apartment office safe behind their new company name plate and dreamed of the billions of Tokens that would come their way. The new structure was to their liking and promised almost double the income in bribe percentages all paid to their private accounts in the form of commission and salaries.

Proudly they surveyed their handiwork and admired the Gothic lettering that declared their rooms the registered offices of C&D Consultants, by appointment to his Honour the President.

All the way with the leader of the day.

The Pair were proud of the slogan but they were even more proud when, as a result of their efforts they could sit and gloat over the award that took pride of place on their desk. It was engraved with their names under the year and the legend.

For excellence in Our service

The award and the contracts that went with it were worth over 17 billion Tokens. Winning the award was not without its risks, a Pair had to be adroit at avoiding repercussions if things went wrong and they usually did. All that was needed to avoid the Presidential fall out was quick wits and a system of accounting that pointed the blame for failure at somebody else.

They had returned after the purges unscathed as the only contractor of any note left in First City. As a result the contract to build Star Station Two arrived on their desk almost by default. Nobody, it seemed, wanted to handle a dodgy project. To their surprise and to the great satisfaction of the President the Star Station completed a successful launch followed by an equally successful transfer to an orbit around Jupiter.

True, there were a few problems. A wave of troopers disappeared into space during the first series of transfers and a batch of lamp timers operated in reverse. But that was all. The lamp timers were replaced and the troopers, well, there were plenty more of them. Privately they knew of more faults but with some nifty legal sidestepping, and a well written guarantee which shifted the onus of bad work on to sub-contractors they got away with making minor alterations.

When they won the contract for Star Station Three they were more cautious. Some of the other engineering companies were getting jealous. They let it be known that the bribe figures would be much higher than any previous tenders. The response was a tentative inquiry from the Military Works Consuls for a discreet meeting.

"We are worried about the reliability of the Transfer Port system," said the Twin Consuls.

"It is difficult to get the right materials and parts," responded Clard and Dracl deferentially and defensively.

"Nevertheless it is our main concern. Somebody lost Star Station One because of poor seeding of the way stations; Transfer Beacons that are supposed to guide the Ship to the right location in space. We do not want that to happen again. It must not happen again."

Fair enough, thought Clard and Dracl, a warning to get it right or else.

"We will concentrate on that area," they replied.

They tested the new Transfer system on an old Star Station. The first tests were failures. The entire batch of rodents disappeared. The second test, this time using Polisoc prisoner Pairs, was another failure. None of the Pairs returned.

"I thought we had fixed the problem?" said Dracl.

"The computer read out says so, and so did the inanimate object tests. The boxes we sent came back okay," Clard said. "We have a problem."

"I know what we can do," said Dracl. "We can make up a robot out of those crappy spare bits we keep in the scrap yard and send that in. I'm sure we can program it to open and shut doors. It will be cheaper than getting a specialist in."

The robot's camera eyes answered the question about the lost Pairs.

"Rodents," said Clard. "Millions of them. The Star Station is full of bloody rodents and when we sent Pairs it was like sending them their dinner. If the robot can fix one of the ports we can send it back in with exterminators and start again. We should have thought of that in the first place. What a waste of Pairs."

"All in the service of our glorious President, besides, they were only prisoners."

The robot fixed both problems, and with an eye to saving tokens on maintenance Clard and Dracl programmed it to do mundane cleaning and lubricating tasks in addition to the electronic adjustments and routine checks. With typical disregard for their menials they forgot about it.

"Do you realise my twin we stand to make over twenty-one billion Tokens for our latest project?"

"Yes my twin I do and all I can say is long live our glorious and wonderful President."

Clard grinned and with a flourish of his well-manicured hand he flicked a bottle of the best outlands brew from the ice bucket and handed it to his twin. He repeated the exercise for himself and they lay back in their seat and drank.

In the darkened corridors of the old Star Station the robot was busy cleaning the plastic walls and the roughened grip floors. When it first plugged into the systems that operated the Star Station it discovered some inefficiencies, and with an electronic cluck of annoyance it put them right. As it wandered in a random pattern through the corridors it was accompanied by a seething family of hungry rodents. At intervals it halted beside a Transfer Port and plugged its data cord into a transfer socket. A few short periods later the Transfer Port opened and a pallet of food slid out. The rodents fell on the food with enthusiasm and the robot hummed happily.

Early in its duty cycle the robot had plugged into a Comsec communications socket and downloaded the data into its memory crystals. The Zradians, it discovered, had for many Earth years monitored the entertainment and communications systems so prolific on that planet, and from all that data two items took its fancy. The first was a black and white horror film in which the hero imagined he was his own mother, and the second was a tune which fascinated it so much that it searched the data banks for all known versions and added them to its vast repertoire. The tune was called A Whiter Shade of Pale and the vocal version by the popular 1960's group Procul Harum was its favourite.

It hummed the tune as it worked. Now and then it punctuated the music with the tail end of the last words Clard and Dracl said as they waved it goodbye.

"Do not be afraid of the rodents!"
"Do not be afraid of the rodents!"

It tried to expunge the words from its memory crystals but no matter how much it tried it couldn't get rid of them. It seemed as if the words were trapped in an electronic loop, and so, with a metaphoric shrug of shoulders it didn't have it gave up. It had other things more important to worry about; like finding a better home for its family. It plugged into the Comsec system again and searched the entire data field. It found what it wanted and took a few seconds to extrapolate the data. It came to the conclusion that its family would be happy on Earth. With mechanical efficiency it made arrangements to move and then got back to its other more pressing problem.

Identity. That was the problem. Who was it? Was it created by Clard and Dracl? Who was its mother? Did it have any brothers or sisters? Mother. Mother. Mother. The image of a little old Earth woman and a smiling son appeared mistily on its internal screen. Mother. Mother! Sometimes mother. Sometimes smiling son. Its mother's son. Its son's mother. Clard and Dracl was its father. Brother? Something inside its memory slipped and it recognised a slight confusion. Nothing much but enough to create doubt. Between. Between mother and son. Who played the part? Son. Anthony somebody.

Between Anthony and ...and? Bet/Ant. Betty/Anthony? And something else more dangerous. Madness? Sanity. It depended on which criteria. It needed comfort.

With an electronic buzz and a little rush of discharged static it gently played through its quadraphonic speaker system the tune A Whiter Shade of Pale and tried out the sound of some names it thought it might like for itself.

Clard and Dracl's makeshift robot was taking on a set of personalities for itself and in it's own electronic fashion it was deliriously happy.

Pour and Roup

Secretary Green, Third Sector Red, the Honourable Senior Detached Half Pair Vreed sweated as he moved his bulky figure step by painful step along the corridor. He hated visiting lesser ranks. To get around comfortably he needed the moving walkstrips he had in his own sector. He grimaced as he thought about having to enter this green sector building at such a low level number. It was the pits. The only saving grace was that the journey from the lift to the portal was short. The Honourable Vreed stomped angrily to the portal and waited while his aide Pair announced his arrival. The electronic shield shimmered and cleared and Vreed strode slowly through.

"In the name of our Glorious President be upstanding!" his aide announced.

The Pair, Pour and Roup, fussed around him. They bowed low and genuflected.

"We are your servants your honour," said Pour and Roup

Vreed noted with satisfaction that their aide Pair genuflected to his Aides properly. At least, he thought, the protocol was correctly followed. Protocol also dictated he sit for as long as he wished before speaking, but in reality he would allow a few periods to pass and then make his announcement.

The Aide Pair rushed forward with a glass of ale on a tray cooled to exactly the temperature he liked it. He drank one glass of ale and wondered which brew it was. He reasoned they would give him the best they had. Vreed drank his ale and pushed his tumbler out for more. He noted with satisfaction that instead of crudely dealing with his refreshment as independent Half Pairs they poured his ale together one holding the tumbler and other pouring. He drank deeply.

"Very good, your best I hope?"

"Only the best for the Honourable Secretary," Pour and Roup replied using the upper case to show respect.

"Not our own ale I assume?"

"The best outlands brew your Honour, we saved it for your visit your Honour."

"I trust you did not buy the ale?"

"It was confiscated your Honour. It is treason to purchase but not treasonable to use the spoils of war. All hail our Glorious President!"

Vreed stared at them until they dropped their gaze. Liars, he thought and smiled inwardly.

"How can we serve you Honourable Secretary."

"I am but a humble servant of our Glorious President; it is he whom you will serve," said Vreed.

"How can we serve Him?"

Vreed smiled with an oily ominous look and slowly drew a flimsy sheet from his robe. He unfolded it and shook the folds straight revealing the President's seal and clearing his throat he read slowly and deliberately.

We.
Desire and request the Pair Pour and Roup, fourteenth secretary green sector green, to carry out the Honourable Duty of Our Representative on Star Station Two. This duty to proceed within a period not less than one turn from receipt of this order.
All other duties are from this date suspended in favour of Our wish.
You will be Honoured to do Us this service.

"As you are no doubt aware our Glorious President does you a great honour with this illustrious appointment. Do you have any comments?"

"We will be delighted to serve our Glorious President, and I have no doubt we will be able to administer the logistics and other affairs of Star Station Two from this office. We will be greatly honoured," said Pour, the dominant Half Pair

Vreed smiled and held up a hand to silence them.

"Ha, I have not finished, your orders go further."

He paused for effect. He was enjoying their obvious discomfort.

"You will serve the President in this capacity on the Star Station itself," he said.

Pour and Roup stared at Vreed for a few small periods and then with a groan they lifted their legs sideways and visibly twitched.

"You will accept the appointment enthusiastically and you will be pleased to do your duty. I can see by your attitude you are overwhelmed at the honour you have been paid so I will call on your aides to see me out. Please tidy up your desks and wait in your office for the escort who will take you to the Transfer Port. Everything you need will be supplied. All Honour to our Glorious President!"

Vreed lumbered to his feet and swept out of the office making a supreme effort to walk faster than a crawl. His aide hovered either side of him trying their best to look dignified. The portal buzzed and opaqued behind him.

"Suffering Bulgers," said Roup. "We've been volunteered for the front line."

Pour walked to the portal and tried the release button expecting it to open. It remained shut and he saw the shadows of the black uniformed Polisoc guards.

"Bulgers, we're under guard by the Polisocs," he said, lowering his voice.

"Then we have no choice," said Roup.

Whimpering, the Pair walked across the room and with a cry they cocked their legs and urinated against the wall.[4] Gently their aides eased them to their chair activated the washing facility spraying the wall with a pleasant smelling disinfectant and with their eyes mostly on the pile of flimsy files the aides organised their desk and stacked files ready to go. When they had finished the aides sat waiting and drinking the left over bottles of brew while Pour and Roup dozed.

The Pair were escorted to the transfer port by six Stormtrooper guard Pairs who were in turn led by a squad of Polisoc troopers with another squad acting as a rearguard. All Pour and Roup were allowed to carry with them was their personal Atlases and a copy of their orders.

"What about our wife Pair?" asked Roup.

"And our luggage?" asked Pour.

"All accounted for. The Honourable Vice Consul has arranged it all for you. Your wife Pair are already informed, their allowances credited and anything else you might think to ask is irrelevant. You are soldiers now so all is found," replied the Leader Pair who chuckled when Pour and Roup groaned. Notably their Aides were left behind.

On Star Station Two they sat at their desk gazing glumly at the bank of monitors. The data seemed never ending. What they learned revealed a gloomy picture. The Star Station was grossly understaffed, and there was a massive lack of supplies. The build up of weapons and personnel was slow and a vast number of standard items were unusable. On top of that Engineering had problems with the Transfer Port system which the experts from C&D Enterprises kept reassuring them would be fixed in a jiffy. The jiffy was supposed to be over, but like the rest of their supplies most of the new parts were defunct and had to be replaced several times.

"What is our operational state?" asked Pour.

"Forty-five percent," came the reply.

"How long to maximum?"

---

4 *This reaction to stress is a throwback to Zradian ancestry - it is a habit of the Lupe - the Dog like creature linked to their DNA and genetic code. Only the males suffer from this.*

"One hundred and twenty normal time turns."

Pour did a quick calculation and groaned. Five Earth months before they will be near invasion readiness. Pour and Roup hated the Star Station. The Troopers were aggressive, the Polisocs seemed even more dangerous than usual and the work was hard and the normally friendly Pongos treated them with suspicion. The President had ordered them to get Star Station Two ready to invade Earth within two twentieths. It was an impossible task. Eighty turns to get things started and already five of them gone. They didn't stand a chance of meeting the deadline and that meant the chop for them if they failed; executed in the square in public by the rakes of the Carnibeast. Nong's teeth! Pour thought, calling on the Zradian God, as he imagined their vile end, I can almost feel them biting into our naked flesh. We have to find a way, he thought. Roup sighed, it meant that their rest turns would go and they would have to work.

"Nong! There's four hundred turns an orbit and what happens? This bulging idiot wants us to work our bums off each twentieth without a proper break," Roup said.

"We have to find a way out of this hole," Roup said. "Or we are dead Bulgers."

"If we send a report about the problem maybe we can get an extension?"

"You heard what Vreed said, we have two twentieths and that's it. The President wants the invasion to start on his birthday, and if the President decrees it, then so it will be," said Roup, acidly.

"We need a consultation with the staff. We have to let these Pairs know what's going on, and one way of doing that is to call on Dral and Darl and dump the problem on them?"

"I will arrange it," said Roup.

Dral and Darl stood in front of the new Administration Leader Pair's desk and listened. They read the flimsy and suggested they pass it on to all staff for their opinion. Their demeanour was deferential but at the same time they exuded confidence sure their expertise was useful and knowing that their own skills would keep them out of the firing line if things went wrong. As the in-charge Pair of civilian personnel and their standing with the Army Leader Pairs they were certain they could do something to satisfy this panicky Pair. Dral and Darl had no time for non combatant administrators having spent much of their career working close to the armed forces in the field wherever the army was sent. They were used to bumph. The flimsy memo was a typical message from the President's office and they had got used to dealing with them. Everybody knew the projected invasion date was unrealistic, and although everybody worked hard to make it happen the nearest estimate was closer to five point five twentieths. Too long to worry about.

"We'll see what we can do," Dral said.

They passed a copy to all departments and casually sent the returns back to Pour and Roup and got on with their more important work. When the reply came back it was accompanied by another flimsy carrying a much more imperative message.

President's memorandum; urgent all pairs
Let it be known that We request that the invasion of Earth by Our Glorious Armed forces begin on the day of Our birth – all Pairs are exhorted to work to this desirable and imperative end with all speed.

We have spoken

Dral and Darl passed it on and a few short periods later the answer came back.

To Dral & Darl.

Re - latest memo from Our President. We wish to inform you that it can't be done so go stick your heads up a dead Bulger's bum.

The staff representatives.

"The swine," said Dral. "How rude!"

"Yes, but the Bulgers refuse to get their butts into gear so we will have to give them a bit of a poke in the rear to get them going. I suggest we send them a friendly reminder of their impending doom if they do not find it in the interests to accommodate us. I will compose a new message and add it to the original."

"We should clear it with Pour and Roup," said Darl, anxiously, and called their leader.

"Just get on with it," said Roup, angrily. "And send me the reply."

So Dral and Darl sent the new message and admitted that it had all the elements of threat, political posture and imperative that was needed to get the true message across to the departmental Leader Pairs.

The President by requesting something be done is giving us orders which must, repeat, must, be obeyed. You will find a way or die in the purges if you fail.
Pour and Roup

The reply when it came was not quite what they expected.

The message rolled across the screen in bright blue with a pink bouncing ball touching the words in time to the music that suddenly filled their room.

Do not be afraid of the rodents! And the miller told his tale ... and a voice at first just ghostly turned a whiter ... Oops! .....Rodents! Rodents! Rule!

As suddenly as it started it stopped and the screen returned to normal leaving the room echoing to the sound of the last few notes and the gasps of the pairs who were as surprised by the message as were Dral and Darl. "What the Bulger was that?" asked Dral Before Darl could answer the reply flashed up.

To Dral & Darl
Re- your last memo Still can't be done so as long as you carry the can we are fine - you can tell Pour and Roup and the President to go and stick your heads up a dead Bulger's bum.
Staff Reps.

"Ungrateful mob of festering Bulgers," exclaimed Dral. "If we pass this on to Pour and Roup we are in for it."
"Pass it on and see what they say," said Darl.

Pour and Roup stared at the reply and shuddered.
"Mutiny! We will have to call a meeting," said Pour. "A solution must be found." Roup gazed at the screen. This is getting to be a nightmare, he thought, and buried his head in his hands. Whatever happened next was up to Dral and Darl but either way that Pair were marked for some really effective nastiness. They will wait, thought Roup, they will wait.

Deep within Star Station Two's sector yellow in a half filled cargo bay Clard and Dracl's robot was busy. It had sealed the holds and let its large family of healthy rodents run free. It plugged into the communications system and changed some of the codes. It fixed the problems it found in the Transfer Ports it wanted to use, and locked into the weapons allocation system appropriating an optimum amount for its own use placing fail-safe codes to prevent a concerted attack. If there was one thing the robot didn't want it was the Army to come down and start trying to wipe out its family. It discovered a minor communication line that led directly to the President's personal line and allocated a special loop to pass subliminal messages at regular intervals. It examined the signals that emanated from the Star Station and found a web of strong signals that converged on a point just a little under one third of a light second from Earth. It probed the source of the return signal, and tut-tutted when it realised the signal came from a Doomsday Bomb.

"Can't have that," it murmured and altered the codes slightly. The bomb signalled it had shifted to a point closer to point five of a light second. Earth, so the robot had decided, was where it and its family should live. It reasoned that a Doomsday Bomb hanging over its future home threatening at any moment to destroy it was not desirable. It scanned the remainder of the bands and picked up some strange signals and replayed them through its circuits recognising some of the familiar radio and television stations of Earth. Gently it imposed a loop circuit on the wave of data spilling out of Earth's communications systems inserting the tune A Whiter Shade of Pale in all its forms into the ether, and listened as it was absorbed. Its electronic circuits glowed with molecular pleasure.

A faint but urgent signal touched its crystals and almost without thinking it converted the data into its own language and responded. It sent messages to other friendly sources and monitored the replies pushing messages across space through the transfer system until it had completed the task. Zradian kind, it thought, was slow but it was bound to do its duty, so for the comparative eons it took to link the New Moral Few probes with Star Station One and open the transfer system it decided to be patient. It transferred the data from Earth and computed the new tune playing schedules to suit Zradian time.

"Task completed! Thank you!" It boomed.

It completed another data sweep and discovered something even more interesting to its tidy but demented mind. An ancient link between Earth and Zrad that was independent of Star Station Two and the President rattled into its memory banks like an ancient motor car or motorcycle; popping and chattering the way an old engine exhaust would do and the robot imagined a bulb horn announcing its presence. It examined the data stream and saw the names Tzu, Byrde and Ceedy and seemed to understand the phrase that went with it "Do it once – do it Right". The data related to the flow of Zradian Tokens and the robot followed the stream arriving at a destination.

"Ah, so that's how they are doing it!"

All that remained now was to find a method to control its family.

It solved the problem with a crudely made electronic spear and adapted the ideas of Sir Francis Galton. Racial hygiene, it declared, was a useful and logical way of solving the problem of over-population. Satisfied that all was well it patrolled its chosen area and hummed the tune A Whiter Shade of Pale adding some interesting little twists of its own. The move to Star Station Two, it decreed, was successful.

The desperate and starving population of the stranded Star Station One ignored the message that raced across their screens. They were too busy fighting over the remainder of the rations to worry too much what it meant. The strange tune that played at regular intervals was mildly annoying at first but as the fighting got more desperate the music began to get on their nerves and eventually infuriated them. The surviving civilians and Pongos became fighting mad. Heroic, desperate.

Behind makeshift cover the Civil Leader Pair, Trag and Grat, yelled out. "Can somebody turn that bloody music off?"

His second in command, a harassed Half Pair shook his head. "I tried but nothing seems to work." He called back. "We're sort of busy here trying to survive the Polisoc attacks if you haven't sort of noticed."

Trag and Grat snorted. He was not amused.

"How many enemy left?"

"About thirty Pairs," said the Half Pair.

"And us?"

"Nearly half as many again and more firepower. We can mount an attack if we can outflank them. Shall I send some Pairs out on the fans sir?"

"Do that and then when they are ready go for the kill. If we win we eat but if we fail it won't matter. Use anything to do the job."

The Half Pair disappeared. Twenty short periods passed and Trag and Grat grunted with satisfaction. Their ear radio relayed the message from the Half Pair.

"We are in position. Attacking now."

Trag and Grat leapt to their feet and led the remaining Pairs into a fierce attack. The Polisoc Troopers were taken by surprise and soon the fight was over. The Storm Troopers lay on the decks dead or dying. The Army and the Civilian staff had won the right to starve slowly in dignity.

"Now we can eat," said Trag and Grat. "And after that we can find a way of shutting off that bloody tune."

They did a head count and discovered that out of the original three hundred working Pairs and five hundred Army Pairs all that remained of the civilians was twenty Pairs and seven Half Pairs. Of these, four Pairs were female and the rest male. The Army had fared a little better with fifty-two Pairs and eight Half Pairs surviving.

There were no Polisoc or Stormtrooper Pairs left.

"Okay Pairs, let's get back to work. We've got a lot to do and one of the first tasks is to get rid of the bodies. After that we can eat, and then we have to get on with trying to get off this bloody thing."

"Your Honour, I may have an idea, if we can trace the channel which broadcast the weird message perhaps we can get a message out. Look your honour I am missing my twin and I need something mind blowingly boring to do. Give me the task."

"Can I ask you a question," Trag said, and glanced quickly at his twin.

The Half pair nodded.

"Are you for or against the President?"

"Against," the Half pair whispered.

"Good because so am we."

"Then I will do my best to get us out of here," said the Half pair, enthusiastically.

In the New Moral Few's main communications bunker the Pair sitting at work station three recorded a sharp burst of data emitted from Star Station Two and worked for the remainder of their shift trying to locate the target. Each time they attempted to pinpoint the location their screens broke integrity and displayed a puzzling message.

Do not be afraid of the Rodents!

It was a frustrating and annoying exercise but eventually they succeeded in getting a rough fix on the target position. The next Pair to occupy their seat worked even harder to get an even finer fix. The Pairs worked steadily, enthusiastic and sure that they were close to finding Star Station One.

Late call for you sir...

In a dark room in the sadder part of Chiswick the Zradian Rebel agent, D.G, sat watching television. He wore a check sports jacket, a pink shirt over a gold lamé vest and a pair of natty green slacks. On his feet he wore fluorescent green socks and a Pair of purple suede shoes with pink shoelaces that in spite of their garish appearance seemed to suit him.

The first thing that impressed D.G about London was the old buildings. He liked the grim Tower and the magnificent Palaces. He enjoyed gazing at the old railway station facades and St Paul's cathedral. He stood for ages watching the people as they hurried along the pavements in groups eager to see the sights. He travelled the underground railway and enjoyed the bus rides like a child in a playground. He rode the London Eye; went to Greenwich; took a trip on a river boat and viewed the new river barrier and learned how all along the south coast sea walls had been built to baffle the rising waters. He marvelled at the care the authorities took to make sure that people used the cleaner public transport. Paying his fee he took the lift to the top of the Shard and gazed out over the city, adding a tourist trip around the city and listened to endless explanations of how the wind farms, and the new Nuclear fusion power stations were progressing.

"Nuclear Fusion! Bulgers! Already? Why," he asked, "you only discovered Atomic power in the mid twentieth century?"

The guide had looked at him oddly, but with a gentle smile she had answered. "It took a long time to find the means to control Fusion. Fission was easy once we understood how it worked, which unfortunately was through dropping atomic bombs on two Japanese cities, but we did it. You should go and visit a power station," she said.

D.G blinked at her and turned his face away realising that she was beginning to stare. He was used to having small fusion reactors that served each sector of a Zradian city, and those that were erected in the rural areas. His headquarters at home had one to supply all its power needs. He popped his shades on "I will, I will," he said, and after that he went back to his rooms.

He liked his rooms because people in the street tended to mind their own business and in the next street there was a tavern with the quaint name of The Drunken Clown whose landlord served some excellent beer and equally excellent food. All he needed now was a crack at the enemy.

Sorting out the equipment was, he admitted, a bit difficult but eventually he had managed to set up most of it despite the confusing instructions that the technicians assured him anybody could follow. He was especially proud of the way he had managed to figure out the spherical ariel that hovered a few millimetres above his monitor. That it could pick up signals from any Earth satellite, Star Station Two and signals relayed from his home planet was useful and normal, but he was using it now to watch Angela Breen hoping that she would undress. She was beautiful. She was also a distraction he could ill afford. But he did.

Part of his job was to keep track of the movements of Kord and Krod and report back to his own Leader Pair. It was tedious work and he would much rather be in the same room as Angela Breen or, failing that, fighting the enemy.

"Why don't I just knock the Pair off and get out again?" he asked his Leader Pair

"Because we want to know what they are doing and who they are after. Knowing that Pair there is some skulduggery going on which will affect us as much as the Earth people." He stood gazing at the elder Pair and blinked letting both pairs of pupils flicker. "At least you won't be hanging around headquarters like a lost half Pair while your twin gets on with his mission," they suggested, gently.

"They are after me," he said.

"Ah yes, maybe they are but we also want to know what else they are doing." Which, as far as D.G was concerned meant that he was in their way. He smoothed his pants with his hands and thought about the reaction of his fellow passengers on the flight across the land mass of north America and the Atlantic ocean. First the air hostess had smiled at him and turned her head away to make a remark to her friend and then his seat mate had changed to another row. The guard in the transit lounge fingered his weapon each time he ventured near which made D.G feel distinctly uncomfortable. The men who delivered his computer and other electronic gear giggled and made rude remarks; the mildest of which described him as a 'right bleedin' pouf' and he wondered what they meant. The salesman or woman, D.G couldn't tell, said he looked 'a million bucks' in the clothes. D.G agreed, thinking the sales person was referring to the price of the clothes rather than the figure he cut wearing them.

"You look simply divine darling," it/he/she said, enthusiastically.

Whatever, D.G had a job to do and he was determined to do it right and do it once. He wondered where he had heard the phrase. Must be one of those stray moments of memory he often experienced working alone, he thought, amused by it all the same.

"Oh Bulgers to it," he said and opened another can of beer and tipped the contents into a huge china mug.

He was also supposed to be monitoring the activities of Professor Arthur Renfrew and his family and some of his friends. His brief described the Professor as the one Earthman who had any idea what the Star Station was and it was part of his job to help protect him. He had some Pairs to call on if need be but so far he had no need to use them. The list was short. Apart from Arthur Renfrew and Julia there was Marjorie Watts at the University, the professor's girlfriend, Richard and Emily Byrde, the old man Tzu, Julian Renfrew and his friend Angela Breen. D.G discovered Angela Breen by accident. She lived in a street not far from his rooms, so with typical disregard for anybody else's privacy he sent out a receiver bug to hover near her window.

He took a sip of beer and sighed. Time to change channels. Reluctantly he tuned in to Byrde's house in time to catch the end of Byrde's telephone conversation with Arthur Renfrew. Byrde was about to go out and meet his friend at the Drunken Clown pub. He noted the time down and switched back to Angela Breen. She was adjusting her dress in front of her mirror and he cursed silently realising he had missed watching her undress. This was one gorgeous Earth woman, he thought. Her ample figure and her blonde hair fascinated him. He must set a floating bug after her. Tomorrow, he mused, I'll do that tomorrow.

In a dingy street where the car parking spaces were taken up by wrecks and the dogs fought the cats for the contents of the garbage cans not far from Angela Breen's house, two Zradian Pairs sat in a room plotting. Out back in the wide alleyway parked haphazardly were two hovervans. One, marked like a laundry van and the other a brown contractor's vehicle were both the worse for wear. The Zradian Half Pairs were very bad drivers. Used to computer guided vehicles the Pairs discovered driving on Earth was a hit or miss affair; mostly hit. In the rear of the white van was a crude but powerful plasma flame thrower.

"The plan is to drive past and torch the target and block the intersection with the white van. We use the brown one to get to the Transfer Port, okay?" said Drog and Grod.

His partner Brig and Grib replied together. "Understood."

"The Leader Pair will take over from the Transfer Port."

"Understood."

"For now we wait until the target arrives tomorrow."

"Why are we targeting this Earthman."

Drog and Grod sneered at that question and shook their heads showing their annoyance.

"He is being too nosy about certain things our Glorious President doesn't want him to be nosy about. That my friend is all you need to know. Understood?"

"Understood, definitely understood."

D.G left the monitor homed in on Byrde's house and went out with his night glasses and his atlas.

As he walked down the stairs to the street he fingered his lucky Token rubbing the embossed Bulger on the tails side. The durable plastic felt familiar and friendly. It was a comfort.

In the Drunken Clown Arthur Renfrew pushed a tall glass of dark ale across the table to Richard Byrde and grinned.

"I know what the new object in the sky is," he said sipping his beer and then launching into a well rehearsed speech as if he was trying to convince himself as well as Byrde."For the next few minutes, however long it takes, please try to suspend your disbelief and bear with me. What I am about to tell you may seem rather strange but I can assure you it is the truth as far as I can tell." Arthur sipped his drink again, and was silent while he wiped his mouth with the back of his hand before going on.

"You've been abducted by aliens, little green men from Alpha Centaurii or something?" asked Byrde, grinning. "Or is it a continuation from the other night?"

"More or less, I think that our planet is in danger of being invaded," he replied. "I gave a speech the other night at the society meeting. You were not there Richard?"

"I was working on a contract," replied Byrde. He was aware of Arthur's address to the society but as yet he had had no chance to read the transcript.

"I explained a lot there but so far all I have had in response is abuse," he said. "Written abuse that is in some of the journals. I've got a short summary here of what I said, more or less." He handed Byrde a typewritten sheet which Byrde read thinking as he did so that Arthur was being a bit melodramatic. Basically, Byrde thought, what Arthur was trying to say was that he had spent some time observing the moons of Jupiter and had either found another one, a rogue or an artificial satellite. So what? Were they not sending satellites up all the time?

"One of ours?" he asked.

"No Richard, and I have made a thorough investigation," Arthur said, looking at Byrde over the top of his spectacles like a disgruntled professor. Byrde checked his sudden urge to laugh. "Okay, carry on," he said trying to sound neutral.

"For the past two years I have studied the area around Jupiter and so far I have plotted most movements close to and near that planet making charts of the movements of the known moons and hoping to find a new one."

He paused for a moment and leaned forward and spoke quietly to Byrde.

"Well, I did. I found a new moon. It appeared in orbit around Jupiter travelling counterwise and at a completely different angle of incidence to any of the other moons. I tracked its progress and began to make some calculations. It's all in there," he said and pointed to the sheet. "I sent off requests to other observatories with better facilities than ours and they came back with some information pretty quick. The opinion of most of the Astronomers I contacted was that we were watching a captured asteroid. A few of us said no and went further. Today I had confirmation from three respected observers that the new moon is in fact artificial. The reflected light spectrum shows that the surface material is metal and a photograph of it from an orbital station shows it has a smooth surface. There are high frequency radio emissions from it at regular intervals and they all converge on a point close to our own planet. Richard, we are being watched and I believe the watchers are intending to colonise us. I intend to make an announcement shortly. I will use the Campus radio program initially."

Arthur Renfrew looked at Byrde defiantly.

"I'm deadly serious Richard."

Byrde drew a deep breath before answering.

"Do you not think you should sort of wait until you have more information before going to press Arthur, I mean what if ..."

"No what ifs Richard, the stakes are too high. If we don't do something directly we are in the poo and no mistake, make no bones about that. I have others working on the project who are in a position to influence government."

"Arthur, if you are wrong...?"

"Richard, I am not wrong and I am serious. What I need from you is the name of somebody who can look after me while all this is going on. A heavy with a bit of nous. I've got my Aikido but I need a bit more than that to protect me, in case," he said, mysteriously.

"In case of what?"

"In case somebody wants to have a go at me."

"You are acting paranoid Arthur, nobody is going to have a go at you not even Julia."

"I'm sorry but since we have started watching this Jupiter satellite there has already been two mysterious incidents. Two observers have vanished. A data store was broken into, computer theft, and we had to change our terminals from the campus system to an independent one because of a virus. I think I do need somebody Richard."

Byrde smiled.

"Okay," he said. "As it happens I do know of somebody but I will have to find out if he is available. He is good but difficult to get on with. I found that as long as you keep him supplied with booze he functions reasonably well. And if you think he sounds like a drunken slob you would be mistaken, this bloke is a mean machine who is totally loyal to his client, most of the time. He is cheap and his greatest asset is that he doesn't stop to ask too many questions. He thumps first and sorts it out afterwards and the blokes he thumps usually stay thumped.

"Who is this brawler?"

"None other than the great Sherman Holmes Private Detective and Personal Bodyguard. You can get in touch with him through Emily's cousin providing of course you can stand the idea of talking to her. She is a bit on the nose when it comes to personal relationships; her one on one interactions are not user friendly," said Byrde, with amusement.

"She is somewhat hard to get on with?"

"Extremely overbearing."

"Ah," said Arthur. "Then perhaps you might make the initial contact?"

"I will be delighted to," replied Byrde.

Byrde looked at his watch and said. "I should get back home."

They finished their drinks and walked out of the pub together saying goodnight outside on the pavement. Byrde watched Arthur as he walked to the corner and then turned in the direction of his own home wondering what on earth had got into his friend's mind.

"Aliens watching us," he said, chuckling, "poor Arthur is finally going off his chump."

He didn't see the strange dark haired man who hurried out the door.

D.G decided it might be a good idea to have a friendly word with professor Renfrew. He slipped his infraspecs on and followed. The specs helped in the dark Earth nights but even so he kept tripping against raised paving flags. The Professor walked steadily along the pavements neither hurrying nor dawdling but at a pace which D.G found difficult to match. He wished the Earth nights were not so dark. He took his Atlas out of his jacket pocket and switched it on to sonar-sense. It was better than the specs but it left him with only one hand free. At least he was able to keep up with the Professor. It was a matter of choosing the right moment to talk to him. D.G, being D.G, naturally missed it and when Professor Renfrew stopped on a street corner D.G didn't and almost crashed into him.

"Sorry but I wanted to t..." D.G began feeling a touch on his wrist crying out in pain as suddenly he was spun around in a half circle and flipped over on his back landing heavily on the pavement. Partly winded he attempted to gasp an apology but the edge of Professor Renfrew's hand smashed into his nose and knocked him out. Much later, feeling the worse for his beating D.G woke with a throbbing nose and a wrist that felt as if it had been ripped off and put back again without anaesthetic. His Atlas lay in the gutter and he picked it up grateful it was still there. His glasses lay on the roadway smashed where they had fallen and as he got up shakily working his limbs he kicked them into the drain. "Useless things," he said and uttered a string of curses in his own language and walked of unsteadily back to his rooms.

As Byrde walked into his driveway he thought he saw shadows flit back into the hedge. He looked carefully but there was nothing but shrubs. The street lamps were too far away to light the area so with a mental whistle in the dark he hurried through his gateway. Nothing happened. Nobody rushed out to attack him so he shrugged and carried on to his door.

"I must be a bit tiddly," he said but he had the uncomfortable feeling he was being watched. He unlatched the door walking through the house to the kitchen where Emily sat nursing a cup of cocoa. "I'm going up now to read for a while. How long will you be? He put his arms around her waist and hugged her kissing her neck and nibbling lightly on her ear.

"God I love you," he said.

She gripped his enfolding arms and squeezed.

"And I love you Richard. Do you have to work?"

"No," he said and taking the cocoa she offered him and they went up to bed, He told her about Arthur and his need for security and asked her to sort out with her cousin to get Sherman Holmes on the job.

"Holmes I can fix up but are you sure Arthur is all right?" she said.

"As far as I can tell," replied Byrde. "But then Arthur is strange at the best of times."

Emily grinned. "Aliens and the Professor go well together. I do hope he is wrong."

"If the idiot is right then we are in for some strange times," he said.

"In the meantime Richard this wanton is wanting you so badly she is ready to rape you if you don't get into bed with her and get on with it. Ravish me you beast!"

And he did.

D.G was nursing one Bulger of a headache when he turned once more to his screen. The drug he had taken was beginning to work and to help make him feel better he made a hot drink. He sat looking groggily at the monitor spotting movement in Byrde's garden. He glanced at the clock. 01:30 He looked at the monitor closely and clicked on to 'Homing'. Instantly the scene changed to a closer view. There were shadowy figures moving in the shrubbery and he sat watching the screen for a while, thinking. What to do. Go there and shoot them or try to warn Byrde? Instead, he decided on a much better idea. Call a neighbour and go around to Byrde's place afterwards.

A sleepy voice answered and D.G spoke loudly into the mouthpiece. "Byrde? I want to talk to you," he said.

"What? Do you realise what time it is," said the voice, angry.

"Look I'm sorry mister Byrde," he said, "but you don't understand I am one of your biggest customers and I demand you see me right away."

"You've got the wrong bloody number you utter moron!" yelled the neighbour.

"I need to talk to mister Byrde..." began D.G.

The telephone slammed down and D.G waited a few minutes before pressing the redial button and again asked for Richard Byrde. It took two more calls before the man on the other end threatened to call the police.

"But I only want to talk to mister Byrde," complained D.G.

"Stuff him!"

The caller cut him off.

Five minutes after D.G's last call to Byrde's neighbour Bates and Fish arrived. Speeding into the neighbour's driveway they screeched to a stop millimetres short of the garage door. They almost fell out of the car and walked to the front door. Bates knocked loudly while Fish pushed the bell button.

The neighbour opened the door and stepped quickly aside as the two officers brushed past him and stood aggressively in his hall way.

"He is constable Bates..." began Fish

"... and he is constable Fish ..." said Bates

"... and we are here in response ..."

"... to your complaint about a ..."

"... nuisance caller who we..."

"... understand to be asking for ..."

"...your neighbour?" finished Bates.

"Yes ...yes, that is correct," the neighbour stuttered.

"We had better call on this..." started Fish

"...neighbour of yours," ended Fish.

"Please do that and wake him up like his customers have woken me," said the neighbour.

Bates and Fish gazed at him and with a perverse logic all their own they insisted on asking him a barrage of questions.

"What are you doing up so late?" Fish

"...yeah, so late ...,"Bates

"Well I just answered the door."

"You realise that's a ..." Fish

"...dangerous thing to do..." Bates

"...so late at night," Fish.

"But that's because I called you..." began the neighbour.

"We could have you for wasting..." Bates

"...police time," Fish, full of menace.

"Look all I'm doing is alerting the police to nuisance calls. All I wanted really was for somebody to get the stupid jerk off my back," the neighbour complained.

"Then you should have called ..." began Fish

"...Telecom or the local ..." Bates

"...office and not bothered the..." Fish

"...Met," finished Bates.

"But what else could I do?"

"Ve are askink the questions," said Fish, viciously.

The neighbour backed away and Bates glared at him.

They left the man standing against his hallway wall wide eyed and frightened and stormed off next door to Byrde's house. They both saw the two men at the same time and instantly gave chase racing into the garden with boots pounding on the concrete block paths alarming their quarry to flight.

"We'll have these..."

"...buggers," said Fish not waiting for Bates to speak.

The Pair raced across the garden and into the next one cutting across the corner and into the alleyway that led to the main road. Bates and Fish struggled over the fences but once in the alley dashed out on to the pavement skidding to a boot scraping stop on the kerb and gazed in fascination at the sudden carnage that unfolded before them.

The Pair dashed across the busy highway heedless of the hover trucks that hissed along the paving. Two craft swerved into each other and those following swerved also to evade the careering trucks and ground to a crashing stop into the barriers. The Pair were lost somewhere in the middle of the mayhem for a few seconds and then like sacks their broken bodies heaved up and crashed to the paving and rolled under a small group of rapidly slowing trucks. Bits of limbs and streaks of blood glittered brightly in the street lamp glow smearing the paving a few metres beyond where Bates and Fish stood staring.

"Messy..." said Bates, Fish said nothing.

They watched impassively as vehicles piled into one another and blocked both lanes.

Bates pulled his radio telephone from his pocket and spoke into it.

"We got a big one..." said Bates

"... and a couple of stiffs ..." said Fish

"And a couple of stiffs..." echoed Bates.

He gave the patrol the location and looked at Fish as he put the telephone back into his pocket.

"I hate these bloody ..." he said, leaving the sentence hanging.

"... yeah, things," said Fish.

Because of the crash and the death of the alien Pair they did not speak to Richard Byrde that evening although they did have a chance to talk to the puzzled pathologist who did the initial examination on the alien bodies.

"Odd looking geezers ... started Fish

"... yeah," said Bates.

And with a look of resignation they assumed a thoughtful silence.

D.G thought that the way Bates and Fish handled the situation was good enough and decided that there was no need for him to go out again that night although he did watch what was going on for a time until he was tired out and went to bed. In the morning he called in at the local shop and bought a thank you card and a stamp. He wrote a brief message on the inside: Thank you for your valuable assistance – a friend. And smiled happily at the thought of Byrde's neighbour's reaction when he read it. "Just adding a little bit of mystery and excitement to your life, friend," he said as he posted the envelope.

I hate Thursdays ...

Old Tzu parked his car in the street outside the factory and walked through the gate. Instead of his customary clean overalls he wore a smart business suit and sported a pair of highly polished shoes; in one hand he carried a well worn leather briefcase. His white shirt set off the deep blue tie that hung tastefully below his collar. The gate keeper wasn't certain but he thought he caught a glimpse of sunlight reflecting off gold cufflinks. To add to the man's confusion Tzu emerged from Mister Byrde's car as if he owned it, and instead of greeting him with his usual cry of "good mornin' oh bugger me yes" Tzu smiled and said in perfect English. "Good morning mister Reed, I assume mister Byrde is already in?"

The gate keeper was too surprised to answer and by the time he gathered enough wits to speak Tzu was gone.

Tzu timed his arrival to coincide with the end of the morning tea break. He saw Julian sitting by his machine reading a comic and smiled. He was pleased that Byrde had promoted Julian to charge hand; the young man had a chance now to get ahead instead of being in a dead end job with no prospects. He thought about Julian and his money worries and decided that if he would open up a bit he might help him. Not with cash but by putting some pressure on Donald Best, the loan shark. Maybe he could commission Lugs and the Ferret to sort them out. Whatever, he had a small piece of revenge coming up. Mister Manners, the rather rude and incompetent workshop floor manager, was about to learn a little Eastern philosophy although Tzu doubted if he would appreciate it.

Tzu stood outside the manager's door until the workers came out of the canteen. He shot his cuffs and deliberately straightened his tie waiting for the inevitable remarks.

"Hey lookit old Fu Manchu," one called out.

"What's he doing in a suit and tie?"

"Won the lottery maybe?"

"Hey Fu Manchu what you doing you silly bugger?"

Tzu drew himself up tall and straight and gazed at the speaker with clear eyes and announced. "I terr bossman I quit, oh yes me sirry buggah letiah, I terr him I buggah off orr light!"

With great dignity he walked into the manager's office passing by the secretary with a polite nod and slipped through the door before she could say anything to stop him. She followed him in and hovered undecided by the door. She tried to catch the manager's attention but Tzu was already in and it was too late to call him back.

The manager looked up from his paper work as Tzu walked in.

"I tried to stop him..." she began.

The manager ignored her and spoke directly at Tzu.

"What the fuck do you want Fu Manchu?"

"I come terr you boss to stick bruddy job, oh yer I letiah, make prenty money part time job. Sirry buggahs give me name Fu Manchu say I stupid but me lich so quit, go home all time good. So, who sirry buggah now?"

Tzu smiled and gently placed the briefcase on the desk and clicked it open. With a flourish he placed a pile of labelled plastic bags on the manager's desk. He let the lid of his briefcase snap back, and with a deft move he clicked the locks and held it in his hand.

"I give bags of tokens fo' you take to Mister bloody Byrde. You terr him new design, savvy?"

The manager gripped the edge of the desk. His mouth opened and closed like a goldfish, unable to cope with the apparition before him. Tzu appreciated his problem and magnanimously decided to help him out. He waved an order form in front of his face and dropped it gently on the desk top.

"You pass him on fo' me prease?"

"What? ... I don't understand," said the manager, finding his voice.

"Simple really, I stuff off, reave bruddy rotten job for 'nother sirry buggah. You give this to mister bruddy Byrde, okay?"

"Okay," said the manager, not quite with it.

"You terr bossman I thank him," Tzu said and turned to leave the office.

"Hey Fu Manchu ... wait!" But Tzu was already out of the office.

"Good morning Miss Jenny," he said, smiling at the secretary as he passed and with a smooth, steady, businesslike gait walked out into the factory.

The manager hoisted his large body out of the chair and bumped into the secretary, staggered back and hit his knee on the edge of the desk. With a yell of pain he clutched it and toppled sideways. He reached a hand out to save himself from falling but slipped and hit his head on the way down. His arm swept across the cluttered desktop catching the bags of tokens. The bags cascaded on his head as he fell and spread across the floor followed by the order form that fluttered down onto his back like an autumn leaf.

"Oh fuck," he whimpered.

The secretary put her hands to her mouth and gave a frightened gasp.

"And fuck you too you silly bitch," he growled.

She put her hands to her face and gasped again.

"Well, I never did!" she said, and turned away red faced.

"I never did what?" asked Byrde who at that moment walked into the office. "And what is Tzu doing striding up the gangway in a suit and tie looking as if he owns the place?"

"The manager said something dirty to me and mister Wu has just quit," she said, and burst into tears.

"Oh pull yourself together woman," Byrde said, peevishly.

"I hate Thursdays," she cried, and collapsed in her seat.

"Come on man, get up and explain what all this is about," Byrde said, impatiently gazing disapprovingly at the manager.

The manager struggled to his feet supporting himself against the desk with one hand reached for the paper Tzu had left and handed it to Byrde.

"Old Fu Manchu has quit I think and he left this for you along with some sample bags of plastic tokens, he was dressed in a suit and he came in late. I don't know what he was on about so I suggest you read the paper which seems to be an order form or something like it."

Byrde read the proffered sheet and glanced at it and folded it carefully and put it in his pocket.

"Straighten yourself up Manners and pick up the plastic tokens and send them to my office. I'll catch up with you later and sort this out. In the meantime I will go and find out what is going on in my factory,"

"I'll get Jenny to pick the things up ..."

"Leave her and pick them up yourself," said Byrde with a snap in his voice.

"Yes sir, yes mister Byrde sir, mister high and mighty Dicky bloody Byrde sir," replied the manager, sarcastically. "I'm in agony here surrounded by stupid women, my staff are bloody incompetent and my boss wants me to pick up litter!"

"Manners, you will see me in my office at nine o'clock sharp tomorrow morning and in the meantime you will clear your desk ready to hand over to somebody else. You are suspended as from this moment. Now I want to find out what's going on."

Manners glared at him but Byrde turned away and walked out.

In the outer office Jenny sat in her chair leaning on the desk with her head in her hands sobbing. Byrde stopped beside her and put his hand on her shoulder. She started back and looked at him. Her eyes filled with tears and she flinched as he too started back. What was wrong with the woman, he thought.

"Oh I thought it was mister Manners," she said.

"No, no, it's only me and I apologise for being sharp with you," said Byrde. "Look, have the afternoon off. I'll see you tomorrow, okay?"

For some reason he couldn't fathom the woman wailed louder. He used the telephone to call security. "Reed, Byrde, will you send a couple of chaps to Manners' office immediately and escort him to his car. He will be returning in the morning at nine," Byrde said and looked at Jenny. He waited for the security men to arrive and went out into the factory. "Well I never did," he said, the place was deserted although he noticed that all the machines were running on idle ready to continue the shift. The last of the workers were passing through the door into the yard. He followed and for a moment he paused to watch before pushing his way through the crowd to the main gate.

"Well I never did," he said again. This time more amused than worried.

Tzu stood beside a shiny Mercedes surrounded by an admiring and overawed crowd of workers. Tzu had one hand on the car and the other he used to emphasise his points as he explained why he was leaving. The crafty old devil, that's my old car, Byrde thought.

Tzu faced the crowd wearing his best silly Chinaman smile and answered the worker's questions.

"Hey Fu Manchu!"

"They say you're retiring?"

"Is that your car?"

Tzu smiled toothily. "I buy motor oh yer bruddy fine. Letiah, make prenty money creaning, now buggah off tell boss man stick bruddy job, oh buggah me yer. Learning driver car go toot toot piccaninnies."

Tzu grinned at them and with his hands in front of his face he mimed driving.

"I buggah off now say goodbye all you sirry buggahs."

Byrde, standing near the gate, caught his eye and was about to speak but Tzu flashed him a warning look, and with hardly a thought Byrde killed the question. What's going on here, he wanted to ask, and how come you have bought my old car? And many other questions like; how come you brought the samples in yourself today instead of sending them by courier. Tzu got into the vehicle making a mess of starting it and then kangarooed from the kerb out into the stream of traffic although he noticed that Tzu's timing was just right in spite of the jerky start and the weaving path he took.

The workers laughed louder calling out.

"Go Fu Manchu!"

A white van careered past Tzu and cut him in and Byrde was not surprised at Tzu's expert evasive action wondering what he had missed. Now, Tzu was driving off in his old car evidently retiring leaving him with a brief note requesting a design change, samples supplied, in a bread and butter item which was, judging by the increase in the order, about to become his number one production item. Byrde gazed after the car and gasped. The rear doors of the van swung open to reveal a dark snout that spewed fire engulfing Tzu's car in yellow and red flames. What happened next was somewhat confusing for as the van and Tzu's car reached the intersection a brown van careered erratically from the opposite direction and collided with the white van. Tzu's car, burning fiercely, hit them both and within seconds the intersection became a mass of flames. Vehicles spun every which way trying to dodge the crash site and crashed in turn. Frightened people ran out of the shops and buildings heading for safety.

The workers, no longer boisterous stared in disbelief and shock but Byrde, more alert, thought he saw a figure roll across the road and disappear into a doorway. He hoped he was right.

Reed stood staring like the rest and Byrde yelled at him.

"The fire Brigade, call the bloody fire brigade, man," he commanded.

"Yes sir," said Reed snapping to attention and reaching for the telephone.

Byrde hurried back to the factory; from his office he could direct any help if it was needed, but actually he had no idea what to do next, he was shocked by the sudden conflagration. As he reached the lower office there was the sound of an explosion and he shuddered to think of what might be happening. The telephone buzzed and automatically he picked it up.

"Reed here sir, I called the brigade and I have a call for you from outside if you will hang on a moment while I transfer it."

Byrde heard the click and snap of buttons being pressed and Reed's mild curses and then a voice spoke.

"Mister Byrde?"

"Speaking?"

"It's Tzu, I'm fine if slightly rumpled. I was torched but I managed to ram the car into the back of the van, although another vehicle seems to have assisted their destruction more adequately than I. I thought you might like to know my thoughts on the incident..."

Tzu paused as if waiting for Byrde's reaction.

"Go on then," said Byrde.

"I had the distinct impression that it was not me they were after but you," said Tzu.

"Thanks a lot Tzu," said Byrde.

"My pleasure," Tzu replied with a chuckle and broke the connection.

Byrde stared at the dead telephone for a moment or two. Strange, he thought, but Tzu spoke in perfect English, odd that.

"There's definitely something wrong with Thursdays," he said.

Are Olives worth it?

"We have no choice," said the Leader Pair waving his arms.

"I disagree," replied Glord. "My twin can create a safe screen around Richard Byrde. There is no need to murder innocent people or Pairs. That sort of thing is more in line with the methods of the Polisocs than ours. We are supposed to be liberating the oppressed from the rule of a despotic President not creating a terror regime of our own. What we can do is put our own bodyguard on Byrde instead. You get my drift?"

"As long as we can pick him up when we need him and back up that clumsy twin of yours. Do you realise he spent nearly a half period trying to open his door. Idiot!"

"That's my twin," said Glord, proudly.

"But what if the Professor's knowledge is accepted by the people of Earth?" said the Leader Pair. "I mean what if they actually believe him?"

"Then we put a tight ring around him as well, but as far as I can gather the Earth people are hardly likely to believe some crackpot Professor telling them that they are about to be invaded by little green men. They are too busy fighting each other to bother. The longer we can keep the people of Earth ignorant or at least laughing about little green men the better it is for us."

"It also is good for the President. Do you know the enemy have replaced Star Ship One with another one and it is now in successful orbit?" said the Leader Pair.

"How long have we got before the President begins his invasion?"

"At the most three twentieths but if our High Command can keep the pressure on his armies then we have a little longer. We are getting stronger but we need many more to come over to us yet before we can be successful on any telling scale. We hold our own but we are not making rapid advances."

"It's the terror of the Polisocs that keep them from openly joining us in the cities. They have to leave their homes and families to come over to us and in turn we are restricted by the waste lands. The Political and Social Police have a lot to answer for," Glord said.

"Your task, Glord, is to assess how long it will take us to reach a strength great enough to change from guerrilla warfare to an army in force."

The Leader Pair gazed at Glord benignly. "That's all you have to do. Afterward you and your twin will be put back on active service. Okay?"

Glord laughed. "We will look forward to that."

"Meaning what?"

"Meaning that we should be getting ready to support the governments of Earth as well, and I know the argument against that is we first have to neutralise the Doomsday Bomb our Bulger's arsehole of a President has so nastily put in orbit around the planet," said Glord.

"There's no chance of him using it," said the Leader Pair.

"Don't you be too sure, that maniac loves the idea of a big bang, especially when he has had too many gin and tonics," retorted Glord.

"Then it is up to us to recruit more Pairs, and to do that we need to be more successful," the Leader Pair said, "And that is why we are recruiting some specialist help."

Glord grinned; he knew what and who and for why but he did not explain that he also thought there was a lot to be said about coordinating activities with the Women's Rebel Army. His Leader Pair would agree but the Elders in charge fought against the idea. As if reading his thoughts the Leader Pair smiled and said: "You, er, still keeping up with the WRA?"

"Oh yes, I have passed on much to them of late," he said, but did not say what. Glord liked the Women's Rebel Army or WRA which was formed when it became obvious that the women recruits to the rebels were required to do the writing, cleaning, washing and ironing in addition to acting as stores staff and general cooks and bottle washers. Their chosen leader, Dorida and Dorid, led the women out to another location and proceeded to steal weapons, recruit women, steal wagons and set out to kill the enemy. The Elders of the Rebel Army hated them, but, Glord reflected, the NMF welcomed the WRA and it grew in strength. Glord and D.G supported them by passing on all information they had whenever they could get it and relished the thought of working alongside the women. D.G described the WRA as a friendly bunch of extremely vicious Bulgers when it came to fighting the enemy. He remarked that they also did the best field catering in the whole of the armed forces anywhere on Zrad. Glord and D.G did their best to recruit women to the WRA and also to find targets that their forces would enjoy. D.G described working alongside them as "fun" which observance tended to frighten his Senior Leader Pairs who regarded D.G as a psychopath.

The Leader Pair just smiled again at Glord and left him to it.

In a tenement high in Two City Sector Blue Blard the Barmy and his twin Bradl waited for a special call. They were members of the President's elite Dog Squad and exempt from any obligations other than to do the bidding of their employer. It was a cushy but violent task and they were fed up with it. Since their last strategy meeting with their commander they had decided to change allegiance. Bradl summed the session up as a complete waste of time and described it as the ultimate bulgershit session "We're on the wrong side," said Bradl.

"Bulgers yes," agreed Blard.

They made discreet inquiries through their underworld contacts and arranged a meeting. While they waited they played Capitilana. Blard idly moved his counter a few squares and his twin eagerly claimed rent for two hotels.

"Bulgers, you're cleaning me out here," he said handing over a wad of paper tokens.

Bradl shook the dice throwing a double four and moved his counter. His face fell when he realised he had landed on one of his twin's most lucrative squares and he began to scramble in his pile for the expected huge sum. The screen taped to the wall glowed and flashed a number. Blard looked up at it and tapped his twin's shoulder and pointed.

"We got the code," said Blard. "Let's go."

They left the game board where it was and went out of the dirty apartment. Disguised as muggers they blended in well with their surroundings. A few short periods later they stood in the shadows opposite their rendezvous and watched. They counted at least six Pairs on guard. Using the patches of dark and some nifty footwork they reached the entrance and paused.

"We go in?"

"Yes."

They moved quickly and turned into the portal. Inside, Blard flattened his body to the left of the arch and his twin to the right. Two Pairs followed them in and with a smooth movement Blard and Bradl lined their laser weapons up on the dark figures.

"Okay Pairs stop where you are," said Blard.

"Show your weapons and drop them on the floor," said Bradl.

The Pairs dropped their weapons and stepped away from them.

"Don't shoot! We are on your side!"

"Why follow us?"

"We were supposed to keep this level safe for you."

"What about the others outside?"

"Guarding the door."

"If we use the stairs?"

"The elevator is safer."

"Okay, we get the picture. We will take it."

Blard and Bradl, with their weapons trained on the Pairs backed into the elevator and rode up to level fourteen. They climbed the stairs to level fifteen, found the right apartment and standing either side of the portal out of range of weapons, Blard pressed the button. The portal cleared and the inside lights dimmed. A voice called out.

"Enter quickly please, you are expected."

The Pair dashed into the room with their cannons on ready and dived either side of the portal as the shield closed behind them. A Pair stood behind a table which was stacked with a row of cool bottles, four glasses and a large bowl of mixed snacks.

"Er, care for some refreshment gentlemen while we talk?" said a Half Pair, casually. "I am Dart and this is my twin Drat."

"Don't like Pairs sneaking up behind us," said Blard.

"We nearly killed them," said Bradl.

"Please sit down Pair. I am glad you didn't, they are loyal Pairs. Now, I suggest you nibble at the snacks and grab an ale each while we talk. We have a lot to get through. We must inform you that we have checked you out so what we have to offer is made on that basis. We would also like to inform you that once you have made your commitment to us you will be safe. Up to that point however, we sort of warn you, if you get my drift, not to do anything you might regret. The sort of thing I mean is like trying to leave this room."

He looked apologetic and rather sad but it was obvious he meant what he said.

"What my twin means is that we can kill you at any moment and we are not afraid to die. We are dedicated to our cause I'm afraid. So sorry."

Blard laughed and relaxed.

"No worries, just tell us what you want and give us some of that ale and we'll do anything," he said.

Dart and Drat explained what they wanted.

"Sounds like fun," said Blard, and grinned.

"We're in," said Bradl.

"Jolly good, jolly good," said Dart. "Now what we have to sort out is the details. You have everything we asked for? You know, the information, message data, plans and all that?"

Bradl grinned and handed Dart a flat capsule. For three long periods the Pairs discussed the contents, and at the end of the session Dart and Drat were satisfied.

"We can count on your loyalty?" asked Dart.

"Completely and utterly. Once we have severed the ties with the Dog Squad regime, and besides, you have been given all the information about the Squads and how they work, plus the latest on who is going where and for what with current codes and passwords, and the longer you keep our defection quiet the more chance you have of using them. That sort of thing leaves us no alternative, besides, murdering innocent people is not what we agreed to do," Blard explained.

Dart smiled warmly: "You prefer murdering guilty people?"

Bradl giggled.

The President of Zrad strolled majestically from his chamber out into the Hall of Petitioners and took his place on the throne. He was extremely angry, and when he was angry somebody had to pay. Somebody had blundered and the President didn't like Pairs blundering. The Twin High Consuls grovelled on the floor before the throne. He would let them grovel for a few more short periods yet. He glared balefully around the hall letting his gaze linger on one Pair and then on another and at last he looked down at the Twin High Consuls.

"Rise. What have you to tell Us?"

"Your Honour, we have done as you ordered, we have found the offenders and they are awaiting your pleasure."

"Bring them to Us."

On cue Polisoc Pairs, resplendent in their black and red uniforms, marched down the sloping hall floor to the centre ring in a neat double row with their weapons at the ready. Between the double row of Polisoc troopers a column of battered and bleeding prisoners stumbled at almost every step. The Troopers dumped the prisoners on the floor to one side of the Twin Consuls and stood alert and ready to kill.

The President gazed at them recognising one Pair as his former cocktail mixer and drinks waiter. The ratbag, he thought, refused to mix his favourite drinks. His new drinks waiter was much better, and with a smile of pure nastiness he pressed the button to summon the Pair.

"A gin and tonic or two with a bowl of those little green things," he ordered.

The Pair came back with the drinks on a crystal tray and a bowl of 'those little green things' nestling in a tastefully arranged napkin with a neat pile of wooden cocktail sticks.

The drinks waiter Pair bowed and held the tray at the properly prescribed height and position for the President's outstretched hand. They held the pose while the President selected his drink not daring to move or shake. They were perfectly poised. Terrified, yes, but perfectly poised.

The ex-drinks waiter Pair grovelling on the floor with the rest of the prisoners raised their heads and spat at the newcomers. "The Bulger's bum will get you in the end because you can never please him. The President of Zrad is a first class arsehole..." The rest of their malediction was cut off as the swishing double blades of the nearest Palace Guards chopped them to pieces.

"Sorry your Honour," said the Leader Pair. "We are only doing our duty."

The President shrugged and took a sip of his drink. Delicious, he thought, and ate a little green thing.

"Are these the scum that let Us down?"

"Yes your Honour."

"Guilty as charged. Send them to the posts in the square. Now, clear this mess from Our hall way and let Us get on with the rest for Our business."

The Polisoc Troopers dragged the prisoners to their feet and noisily marched them off. The prisoners knowing they were condemned to death and beyond all hope yelled insults at the President and waited for the expected sudden attack that meant a quick death. Their hopes were in vain. It seemed that even the quick off the mark Guards liked to watch prisoners die at the posts.

The Twin Consuls spoke from the prostrate position. "We have dispatched the Pair Pour and Roup to Star Station Two as ordered your Honour. Secretary Green informed them of their new and glorious service, your Honour."

The President sipped one of his drinks and ate more little green things. He held one up between his fingers and faced the Consuls.

"What are these things called," he asked.

The Consuls raised the heads and immediately banged them down on the floor again as two pairs of blades flashed down to their necks to hover quivering at the regulation height before being re-sheathed.

"O...Olives," stuttered the Pair. "They come from Earth."

"Delicious, almost worth dying for," said the President and chuckled.

Glorida and her twin Glorid lay on the ground side by side and watched the enemy soldiers loading wagons. The heat from the desert sands burnt their skin and the small plants that grew between the stones pricked their bodies. They waved their troop forward and waited until everybody was in place. Time to go. Glorida gave the signal, and then as one unit the foot soldiers of the Women's Rebel Army attacked. Group One fired a stream of plasma into the lead wagon. Group Two attacked the rear wagon. Groups Three and Four moved in on the centre while group Five watched for strays. The attack was short and sharp and the main force of it was over within ten short periods. Like clockwork the support wagons floated down from the hills and halted long enough to pick up the troops and then they were gone.

"Well done women!" said Glorida. "A smooth operation. Wonderful! Wonderful! Terrific fight, great shooting. Let's go home!"

Troop A of the Women's Rebel Army rolled home leaving behind the shattered and burning remains of supply column 483/17 Red.

The short battle, a victory for Troop A, was, in the words of the Leader Pair, a token raid to annoy the president. That it succeeded is a matter of history. That it was carried out by women was to be a matter of personal insult to the president.

In the rebel headquarters deep in the less radiated area of the Waste Lands Glord read the report and turned to his screen. He patched into the general broadcasting system and pressed a key. A message scrolled on the screen and Glord grinned with satisfaction as it unrolled. With strident sentences and emotive language it claimed responsibility for the latest outrage emphasising that the raid was carried out by women. Unashamed, Glord used the implied stigma that the President's soldiers were not good enough to defeat soldiers of the Women's Rebel Army. In Zradian terms that was an ignominious defeat.

"... It is obvious that the despotic President of the dying second Republic is incapable of beating back an attack by women on his crack forces... perhaps the President is so occupied with the mixing of perfect gin and tonic cocktails he has no time to spare to defend his people. It is time for all citizens to overthrow the despot and work for our nation."

Glord sat back in his chair and sighed, like his twin, he was eager to get into some fighting. He always reached a point during his duties at Headquarters when he wanted to get back into active service.

"I want to get into some real work," he said, out loud.

"What is real work?"

The question came from his Leader Pair who at that moment walked into the radio transmission studio. Glord looked up.

"Fighting and killing real enemy soldiers and all that. You know what I mean, with a sword at my belt and a laser cannon over my shoulder and a line of battlewagons humming along ready to shoot the Bulgers out of the enemy, namely the President's men and those filthy Polisocs."

"I agree," said a new voice and Dart and Drat strolled into his cubicle with a light step.

Glord looked at them appreciatively.

"I hear you two are going to be the Pair on the spot when the invasion starts, is that right?" he asked.

Dart nodded and Drat said. "Correct and if what you have done today works then I can expect us to be there soon. According to the New Moral Few the President is about to do something really stupid and we are on stand by."

"Good," said Glord.

The Leader Pair coughed politely and said. "Excuse me but when you have finished ..."

"Listen to what their honour has to say," said Dart with a grin.

"I have some good news for you Glord although you will still have to lay around here making a nuisance of yourself for a while yet. We have orders to begin mobilisation and soon you will be on the march again fighting and recruiting. In the meantime I have a job for you; the orders are in this flimsy."

The Leader Pair handed a plastic flimsy to Glord with a flourish and Glord eagerly read it.

"I am to locate the women's rebel army headquarters and bring some Pairs back for talks and training?"

"The most difficult part will be finding them," said the Leader Pair. "But I dare say you will cope."

"What sort of training will they be doing?" Glord asked.

"We need some clerical workers so the High Command thought we might involve the women um to sort of do the work they're used and er to get some up to date military training in as well," he said, "I'm sorry but it's got nothing to do with me."

Glord stared at him, horrified. "If they find out they'll murder me; those women know how to fight and run their own army better than we do our own. Am I supposed to persuade them to agree or do I just hand them the package and wait for them to cut bits off me?"

Dart and Drat laughed.

The Leader Pair grinned. "Don't panic, the arrangements have already been made and all you have to do is go out there and meet them and escort them back. You will have a half troop with you and some wagons."

"Fine, all you want me to do is be out of your hair for a while, right?"

"The trip is a reward for your work."

"I am honoured," said Glord shooting a glance at Dart and Drat as that Pair left his cubicle. The New Moral Few would be annoyed by his Elder's attitude, especially when they realised how far from the ideals of the Zradian Freedom Front their ideas were. It was supposed to be an equal opportunities revolution. He could imagine the women's reaction.

"Stenographers!" snorted Glorida. "Us, a Half Leader Pair taking bloody notes?"

"You must be joking," said Glorid, glancing at her twin.

"Sorry but we are not. The trousered ones..." began the High Leader Pair.

Glorida's snort of derision turned into a giggle. She always laughed when Dorid and Dorida said 'trousered ones'.

"I repeat, the trousered ones, have some information; we need and it will be your job to get it. The other women are all section leaders too and they will have their own tasks to do. Yours will be to report everything that goes on and to take advantage of any contact with women and recruit them into our forces," said Dorida somewhat miffed.

"And how do we deal with the men?"

"I'll leave that up to you."

"Thank you your honour," said Glorida and Glorid, together.

The High Leader Pair bowed their heads in response and smiled.

"Your first task is to meet the escort and pretend they were clever enough to find our headquarters on their own. You will enjoy that."

Glorida giggled.

Just prior to leaving the rebel headquarters Glord read the latest information sheet and grinned. He was pleased that the Pair Pour and Roup were virtually under office arrest and ready to be transported to Star Station Two. He disliked that Pair intensely and looked forward to their ultimate discomfort when the rebel forces became the leaders of the Republic. Yes, thought Glord, if there was a Pair in the whole of the Zradian administration who deserved to be put on a sticky spot it was Pour and Roup. Nasty, and small minded, they were the most selfish and vindictive Pair to be found anywhere in Zrad. They were capable of being as indifferent to all but their own situation as a southern desert storm and as powerful. They were corrupt in a mean way and Glord himself had had to deal with them when he and his twin were in the major league Fourball series.

Let us see if they can be as parsimonious with the Star Station as they were with the Fourball teams. He hoped so because then the Star Station will be strapped for cash and running as mean and lean as a beggar. And that meant the troops on board will be fighting among themselves, not because that was their nature but to grab what equipment that was eventually squeezed out of Pour and Roup.

He dropped the flimsy on his bunk and finished dressing.

I was only doing my duty

Fireman Sidney Weddell gripped the quadrant. White knuckled and stiff armed he tried to move the large fire-wagon through the traffic. His crew sat tight lipped in their seats shooting angry glances at him. In his turn he shot angry glances back at them. The loaded silence in the cab was punctuated by the noise of the siren and the blaring horns of other vehicles. It wasn't his fault the fire-wagon was stuck in the traffic. It was the bloody minded motorists that held him up. Today of all days when there was a real emergency every driver in West London seemed to have ganged up on him.

"The Chief wants to know why you haven't got there yet," said the radio operator. Firemen Weddell glanced at him. There was a tone in the man's voice he didn't like. "Tell the Chief we're stuck in traffic but we are on our way," he replied, tight lipped.

The radio man spoke quietly into the microphone and with a look of glee flipped a switch. The Chief's voice boomed in the cab.

"Weddell you prat! get that effing wagon moving and get to that effing fire or I will have your guts for garters! There's a plastic's factory close by and if that goes up we've got a real problem. Hurry up you useless bastard!" the Chief blared.

"I'm on my way, sir," Fireman Weddell replied. He planted his foot hard on the accelerator and turned the quadrant to his left. Frightened pedestrians scattered in all directions as he drove up onto the pavement.

"Out of the way you dummies," he snarled. "I'll get us there one way or another see if I don't." Fireman Sidney Weddell had a vision of his own worth which was totally different to that of his employers. He saw himself as a useful member of the Metropolitan Fire Service, an efficient working unit both envied and admired by his workmates. In the West London District he was known as 'that useless prat Weddell'. Whenever Fireman Sidney Weddell was transferred to a new station, crews always asked the same question.

"What have we done that's bad enough to deserve this?"

The reply was always the same.

"Nothing, it happens to be your turn, put up with him."

"How come the prat is always put in charge?"

"Because he's got the points that's why."

Fireman Sidney Weddell was lucky with promotion. The day an irate Chief sent a memo suggesting that Fireman Sidney Weddell be denied promotion at all costs the clerk who copied out the message had a severe head cold. Unable to concentrate on what was actually written she inadvertently altered the wording and passed it on. Her supervisor, concerned with her own application for promotion missed the alterations and passed the message on to her superior. The note arrived on the personnel officer's desk at the same time as Fireman Weddell's own request for promotion and that was it. Fireman Sidney Weddell was promoted and posted to take charge of a crew.

His then current Chief called the district office and asked to speak to the Commissioner.

"Excuse me sir but I have to question the wisdom of the powers that be for promoting Fireman Weddell to an in charge position, sir, particularly when most of us on the stations would be reluctant to put him in charge of a lavatory brush, sir?"

The Commissioner's reply when it came was delivered in that tight lipped and deliberate fashion superior officers have when subordinates question their authority. He knew that Fireman Weddell was a prat, but if head office wanted to promote him then it was his duty to do what head office wanted.

"Fireman Weddell was recommended for promotion by head office. I suggest you reconsider your attitude towards the officer. Evidently Fireman Sidney Weddell has been placed on the priority list and earmarked for higher things," said the Commissioner, icily.

"Oh," said the Chief and rudely hung up.

"Christ!" He said when he put the telephone down. "I need a drink." He had seen the tight-lipped, angry look on his superior's face and wilted under the glare of authority. He hung up to avoid further confrontation aware that his face said all that he felt. And that was not a good idea, he needed to be in control.

At that moment Fireman Sidney Weddell was taking control. With the insight of the truly stupid he decided to emulate the drivers he saw on the American television shows, and with a flamboyant movement of the quadrant and more speed he swung the big wagon into a side turning where the car parking spaces were filled with abandoned wrecks and the dogs fought with the cats for the contents of the garbage cans. The Fire wagon scattered some of the cans in its wake and rocked a few of the wrecks from their blocks, emerging from the street on to the main road where Fireman Weddell swung the wagon out into the traffic stream with the siren wailing. The wagon wallowed on each turn and Fireman Weddell yelled excitedly as he swung the vehicle through gaps in the traffic.

One of the crew screamed out.

"You're going the wrong way!"

Fireman Weddell looked up at the location screen. He was right, they were going the wrong way.

"Can't have that, can we," he said and grinned.

With the panache of a racing driver he swung the vehicle around through a gap between the lanes and hurtled the machine in a tight U-turn accelerating back the way they came. He swung the wagon into a turn and watched the red location marker line up with the green fire source marker and smiled letting his lip curl a little, Hollywood style, swinging the vehicle into the road leading to the shopping centre. Concentrating on the manipulation of the controls and narrowing his eyes for that desired movie star effect he was suddenly shocked into action. Directly ahead, filling his windscreen faster than he could react was a supermarket shop window. He jammed on the brakes, but it was too late. "What the heck is that doing there for..." he screamed, and ducked as the fire wagon mounted the pavement and ploughed directly through the plate glass window. The machine swept into the checkouts pushing them aside as if they were matchwood. It careered across the polished floor smashing through the rows of goods and stopped against the rear wall. The siren wailed and the hover fan added its bellow to the noise as it laboured under a sticky load of smashed groceries. A few moments later, with a soft pop that was lost in the general noise, a pipe burst and spewed engine oil on the floor. The engine ran dry, overheated and seized solid with a tearing shriek. Fuel spilled from the injectors and evaporated on hot metal. Oily mist rose through the cab and surrounded the wagon with a volatile cloud, mixing with water vapour from the damaged cooling system. With presence of mind the crew clambered out of the wagon and quickly helped shoppers to safety. They left their driver sitting in the cab surrounded by shopping debris and steam.

Inside the cab Fireman Weddell slowly became aware of his surroundings sitting for a while listening to the siren trying hard to work out which way was up. First I must stop the siren, he thought and struggled with his seat belt clasp. He fumbled for the off switch unable to find it, angry that the siren still clamoured in the confined space.

"Bloody thing! Shut up!" he yelled and grabbed the ignition keys wrenching them so hard the wrong way they twisted and jammed.

"Oh bugger the damn thing," he screamed unleashing his temper on the quadrant tearing at it with both hands and alternately beating the column with his fists.

The siren wailed.

"Shut Up! For Christ's Sake Shut Up!" he yelled with tears of frustration and anger splashing from his eyes as he fought the stubborn ignition switch.

It was at that point he did something extremely stupid.

He reached behind the dashboard and yanked the cables from the switch panel. The effect was instantaneous. The noise stopped immediately.

His mind registered the flash and his ears heard the tearing crackle of twenty four volt discharge and his nose smelled the acrid stench of burning rubber. His eyes saw the flames that burst like flowers across the dash and race down to the cab floor and exploded at his feet.

"Oh shit I ...!"

The rest of his exclamation was lost in the sudden soft explosion underneath the cab when leaking oil and fuel caught fire.

Fireman Weddell beat the flames by the merest fraction of a second and landed on the slippery floor. At the moment he hit the deck the sprinkler system operated. He tried to stand but the pressure was too great and the floor too slippery with smashed groceries to gain a footing. All he could do was crawl along the slippery floor on his hands and knees.

Like a dying slug he emerged from the wreckage. Ignored by his crew he sat on the pavement with his arms wrapped around his body and rocked to and fro. Whenever one of his crew walked past him they cursed and walked on.

One gave him the radio telephone so he could listen to the constant stream of invective the Chief directed at him. Help was on the way but the Chief, so it seemed, wanted only to come out there and personally strangle him.

Fireman Weddell was past caring.

"I was only doing my duty," he said, and tears streamed down his face.

Byrde directed his staff as if he were a fire chief and top civil defence warden. The environmental code and the nature of his business required him to have a considerable first aid facility and some staff trained in fire fighting. Byrde discovered that most of the designated staff were not up to scratch, and as the fire at the intersection spread he grew more anxious.

"Where's the bloody fire brigade?" he stormed, watching the fire consume vehicles and buildings surrounding the junction. What was once a busy shopping precinct turned into a bonfire that seemed to him to be getting fiercer with every minute that passed. Eventually he heard the wail of sirens and soon afterwards he saw the white lines of high pressure water pouring into the heart of the conflagration. All that morning and well into the afternoon the fire fighters fought the blaze and by early evening his factory was out of danger. He sent most of the staff home retaining only those who could handle a hose or help with any casualties, and waited the fire out ready to evacuate the premises at a moment's notice. Throughout the grim time all Byrde could think about was Tzu's suggestion that it was he the fire bombers were after.

For many reasons, he thought, Thursday is turning out to be one bummer of a day.

Julian let himself into the flat and gasped in surprise. The place was empty. The lounge that was normally filled with furniture had only the grotty carpet left on the floor. He walked through to the kitchen to find the cupboards wide open and only his few pots left on the shelves. With a sinking feeling in his stomach he explored the rest of the house and was not surprised when he discovered the bedrooms were empty. He went to his own room and saw with relief his stuff was still there. On his bed was an envelope addressed to him. With trembling hands he picked it up and ripped it open. Inside was a single sheet of paper and he took it out and read it.

Dear scumbag,
We, your ex-flat mates, having got heartily sick of your dirty habits and foul friends have decided to move on. As you have not paid your share of the rent for so long we have also decided not to pay any more money. We also note that the telephone being in your name is overdue. We hope you find some more people who perhaps may be more to your liking. Do not try to find us as we do not want to see you again. By the way, your friend Denny Block called asking for some money. He said to tell you he will call again. Good luck ratbag.
Michael.

Julian stared at the note for a long time, and then with a whimper of fear and rage he screwed it up and flung it from him. Denny Block! If there was one man in the world he was most afraid of it was Denny Block. Julian trembled thinking of his last encounter with the monster and looked frantically around the room as if expecting to find him lurking in a corner waiting for him. He had forgotten Donald Best's payment and remembered it was one week overdue.

"Oh shit," he said, desperately.

If there was one thing that Donald Best hated more than anything else it was clients who didn't pay on time. To show his disapproval he sent Denny 'the brick' Block along to collect the money and that usually meant getting roughed up. When Denny Block roughed people up it hurt.

"Why me?" he wailed.

"Why me?" asked Donald Best. "Why do I have to get all the no hopers?"

Denny looked at his boss trying hard to fathom the answer to the question and please his employer.

"I mean, I let them have some working cash and they treat me like this. They don't pay up on time and I have to send you out to teach them to behave. I've got better things to do than to go around punching the daylights out of no-hopers," explained Donald Best.

"I'll go rahnd there and bash him tomorrer," said Denny, brightly.

He stared out of the dirty window onto the dingy street where the car parking spaces were taken up by abandoned wrecks and the cats fought with the dogs for the contents of the garbage cans. Somebody had rolled the cans back into place after the fire engine had smashed into them but nobody had done anything about the cars fallen off their blocks. Denny loved this street. It was where he had lived all his life and he knew everyone in it. Bashed most of them too. Once he was a no-hoper bumming a living off the trash others left out, but now he was somebody. Donald Best's right hand man earning a proper wage doing something he really enjoyed; beating the living daylights out of the punters.

Denny Block didn't mind Thursdays.

Julian decided that he had at least one night before Denny Block would pay him a visit. He could stay at his mate's place tomorrow, he reasoned, and with a bit of luck he might persuade somebody to give him the dosh or maybe he could keep out of Denny's way until he found another place to live. The good old moonlight flit if he had enough time to jack it up.

"Why does everyone pick on me?" he said to the empty room. "Why can't they just let me live me life and leave me alone. He had visions of Kung Fu'ing Denny Block and sending him back to Donald Best with a flea in his ear. Some hopes. Denny was a walking war zone impervious to Julian's feeble blows. The thought of being helpless scared him, angered him and with sweaty palms he punched the wall flat handed with the stupid Chi old Tzu kept rabbitting on about.

He looked wide eyed in surprise when two circular holes appeared in the wall under his blows. He looked at both hands in turn seeing only plaster and no bruise marks, no pain either.

"Well fancy that, I am doing it."

He chopped the air and let out a shout.

Maybe Denny had better watch out, he thought, and broke out into a sweat; Denny was harder than a plaster-board wall, much harder.

"Christ, how come I always get fucking picked on?" he moaned and sank down onto the thin mattress on his bed. "The fuckin' world fuckin' sucks."

He fumbled his wallet from where he had dropped it and looked inside. There was enough money to buy a drink or two, and that was better than lying in bed thinking about what a load of shit heads his flatmates were. He'd go down the pub and buy himself a drink and some grub. Fuck 'em.

He shaved with his battery razor using the cheap mirror he got from the token club and adjusted his shirt to take a tie, and with a touch of gel on his hair he was out the house and walking in the evening air to the Drunken Clown pub. He slipped into the public bar and ordered a glass of best ale and a counter meal. He took the beer to a corner table and sat sipping at it waiting for his number to be called wishing that the blokes in the bar would include him in their talk. He was about half way through his drink when he was aware of a man dressed in an odd outfit ease from his seat close to the saloon bar door and slip through it furtively. What had caught Julian's eye was something that had dropped from the drinker's pocket and fluttered under the table.

He got up as if he were about to collect his meal and casually walked to the vacated table. It was a matter of seconds to reach down and grab what had dropped and slip it into his pocket. He was lucky that at that moment his number was called and with a sour smile he took the plate and the cutlery from the barman and handed over his ticket.

Back in his seat he ate first and then with the napkin and plate covering his actions he looked at what he had picked up. A series of hand printed paste cards and two hundred Euro dollar notes.

"Shit hot," he said. "Losers weepers; finders keepers."

He pocketed the cash and threw the cards in the trash can catching the name as they fell.

"Mister Gold, you missed out on your cash, sucker," he said, and raised his glass in the direction of the saloon bar. "Good health."

An hour and a half later he paid the madam before he entered the back room of a night club several streets away from the Drunken Clown pub and picked out a girl he hadn't seen before.

For a while he forgot Denny Block and ignored the sordid little room and the fact the girl looked like an emaciated barbie doll. He was grateful for a sexual release and the comfort of a willing body next to his. This, he thought, as the girl opened her legs and pulled him into her was as close to love as he was likely to get. The thought made him cry, and as he pumped up and down he splashed tears on the girl's pale made up face.

"Wot's up luv?"

Her voice was thin but somehow the words comforted him and he stopped humping to stare down at her. She looked up at him and smiled.

"C'mon, don't stop, I like it too you know, yor doin' it fer me an' all yer know, c'mon bang it in," she said, and lifted her legs around him.

"Jist tell me yer love me an' everythin' all right?" he said.

"Course I do darlin'," she said.

He gripped her tightly and pretended she hadn't put a condom on him and with his face close to hers he kissed her mouth and was surprised when her sharp tongue wrapped around his and her voice murmured low and deep like a cat purr. He ejaculated strongly and thought of babies and with a start of surprise as he convulsed he called her Angela.

"Who's Angela darlin'?" the girl said afterwards.

He looked at her sharply tempted to tell her to mind her own bloody business but her face had a guiless look that appealed to him and with a twisted smile he thought was nonchalant he shrugged his shoulders the way Pompidou in Dark Times had. Smooth Julian the hero and lover.

"She is my good friend," he said, mysteriously.

"I bet she's more than a friend," the girl said, and smiled knowingly.

Julian tossed his head feeling the weight of his lank hair bounce against his shoulder and thought of the guy with the Italian name, heroic and dashing. His princess for the evening.

"What's she like?"

"She is very beautiful and blonde and she's sort of noble and and... she, well I suppose she is a a ... you know, a ..." he trailed off unable to say the word.

"Still got her cherry," the girl said.

"Yeah, she's a Christian," he added, brightly as if by explanation.

"Won't give yer none," the girl said, and snuggled close to him. "Wanna do it again?"

And this time she was gentle and passionate like a lover.

The Drunken Clown

Julian whimpered. He felt rotten; he had a hangover and his hand shook. For the third time he read the note, and at last the full import of what had happened sunk in. He could get new flatmates, he hoped, but the bit that said Denny Block was about to call on him was the pits.

He had to do something and soon, like today. He called the factory and told the woman in the office he was sick and bit his lip when she said the factory was not working that day anyway due to the fire and hadn't he heard what mister Byrde had said the previous afternoon? Stupid cow, he thought, he was just covering his arse. Thinking of stupid cows he decided to call Angela Breen. She owed him, didn't she? Her bossy sister answered and reluctantly went to fetch her.

"Hello Julian," said Angela, cautiously.

He winced at the goody-goody tone and the slight hint of suspicion lingering in the drawn reply.

"I er, thought I might come over to see you Angela, I gotta few things I wanna talk over with you," he said, warming to his task and feeling more sure of himself as he spoke. If he could bullshit Byrde then Angela will be a push over, he thought.

"I need some advice and a bit of practical help Angela. I've been put in charge at work and you know how difficult some of the other workers are to deal with. I gotta work out a way of sorting them out. When you was living at my place you said you would help me out. Remember we went to church together once and I sort of got mixed up a bit, well, I've been thinking about that again.."

He left the end of the sentence hanging and waited for her reply.

"What do you mean Julian?" she asked, warily.

"You know, about being a better person and all that, God and things, I mean to turn over a new leaf and deal properly with some of the problems I have here on Earth," he said, hoping he sounded piously convincing.

"You want to talk to me about becoming a proper Christian or are you up to your neck in trouble?" she asked.

"Can I come and see you?"

"I'll ring you back Julian. I have to talk with my sister."

She hung up and he looked at the dead instrument.

"Bitch," he said, venomously but waited anyway

He might have called her on his mobile from the pub but he had no credit. He was glad that the flat had an older telephone and not one that only worked with a PC. He didn't really understand the

Internet or the Bubblenet and how he could use it on the hanging screens. Michael showed him once how to use the keyboard on his phone, but when he ran out of credit too quickly he gave up.

Angela sat beside the telephone for a few minutes gazing at the wall trying to work out what Julian was up to. She had mixed feelings about him. On the one hand she wanted nothing to do with him but on the other she felt responsible for him. She thought about the time she lived at his house and shuddered. The other flatmates were fine but whenever Julian's mates arrived she had to put up with their leering manners and dirty remarks. Luckily Michael, one of the long standing flatmates, was a strong minded man with muscles to back it up and he protected her from the worst of them. The rest of the household had banned Julian's mates from inside the house and allowed them to come only to fetch him, and then they had to stay outside. She felt sorry for Julian. She explained to Michael that she was certain there was some good in him and she wanted to give him a chance. Michael laughed.

"He is a sneaky, low down, no-hoper who has never done anybody a good turn in his life. His friends are the worst type of people you will ever find anywhere and he lies through his teeth. The bloke is a rat bag of the first water."

"I'm sure he can be a better person if he is only given a chance."

"Not a hope."

Angela gritted her teeth and with the zeal of a fundamental lay preacher on a roll she set about trying to change Julian's ways. She was surprised when he responded to her attentions. He cleaned his room, dressed a little tidier and when she suggested he stop drinking so much he did, and that gave her hope. She took him along to some of her Church activities and he seemed to enjoy himself. Once he asked her to go out with him and to her surprise she enjoyed herself and began to look at him with a little more favour. She coloured up when Michael suggested she was falling in love with him; pointing out that that Julian fancied her.

"He's a randy runt," Michael said. "If you are not careful he'll have his hand up your skirt before you know it. He's like that."

"He'll get a kick where it hurts if he tries that," she said, and gave Michael a withering look. "I'm not that sort of girl."

Michael grinned.

She remembered the Fete and the fight between the Vicar and that disgusting mister Holmes who was supposed to be the security guard for the money boxes. Instead he had hung around the Vicar's tent and leered at her and Oliver Braine's secretary, Penny, and made lewd remarks. Typically Julian had done nothing, and so it was up to the vicar to complain. Holmes had looked at him, focussed for a moment on the vicar's nose and then punched it. Instead of turning a cheek the vicar retaliated with an uppercut that rocked Holmes off his feet. The fight turned into a brawl with Holmes and the vicar in the centre. Julian disappeared and wisely Angela and Penny grabbed the money boxes and dashed across the lawns to the Rectory. She found Julian about to dash off in his turn clutching one of the boxes and quietly but firmly retrieved it.

"I was taking it to a safe place," he said.

"Oh yes?"

"I was, all I was going to was take it to the church and put it there for the vicar to find, I mean if you're gonna do a good deed then you gotta do it without anybody knowing really ain't you?" he said with a whine in his voice.

"Give it to me."

He had handed it over meekly with a smile and she locked it with the others in a cabinet

"It will be safe there until the hooligans in the gardens have quite finished," she said, and approved when Penny called the police. Julian, she noticed nodded his head vigorously and looked a bit pale. She assumed he felt guilty, and with mixed feelings she forgave him and kept quiet about his intentions when the police arrived.

Afterwards when she and Julian were walking home he put his arm around her and tried to kiss her. She smacked his face and he drew back angry.

"I thought we were supposed to be ..."

"I'm not that sort of girl," she said.

"No," he said, feeling his cheek with his hand. "I can see that."

She invited him to her church the following Sunday and when he said he would go she took his hand in hers and squeezed it.

"I'll be there," he said, enthusiastically.

The Sunday arrived but Julian didn't so she went to Church on her own. She tried not to notice Michael's I told you so look as she left the house dressed in her Sunday best.

Julian arrived partway through the service and it was obvious he was drunk. She heard him speak rudely to the ushers and then he spotted her and called out over the reader's voice as he staggered up the aisle.

"Angie baby! Where are you my little holy knickers? Come on Angie darlin' come outside and get em off, let's have a look at your...ugh."

Two ushers grabbed him and hustled him outside.

A few minutes later there was a yell of anger and then Julian was yelling abuse at the two men, and she heard him running. His bad language filtered through the windows and the Vicar stopped speaking. The congregation in turn fell silent. The silence was broken only by the shuffling of feet and the embarrassed rustling of the congregation.

Angela knelt in prayer.

"Let us pray for his soul," she said.

"Yes," said the Vicar. "Let us pray for the young man's soul."

The congregation knelt in prayer and the Vicar called on the Lord to forgive Julian his sins and bring him back to a state of grace. Outside, Julian yelled insults at the two men and then there was a sudden cry of pain and the sound of flesh hitting flesh followed by silence. A few minutes later the two ushers returned and stood inside the door of the church.

"The young man is resting quietly," one usher announced.

"Praise the Lord," intoned a worshipper.

"Amen," said the Vicar.

"Amen," echoed the congregation.

After that Angela decided to leave the flat to live with her sister.

Sitting by the telephone reflecting on her stormy relationship with Julian, Angela surmised he was in some sort of trouble and guessed that Donald Best was the main problem. She could either go over there and see him or meet him somewhere else. First she would ask her sister if he could come over.

"No, I'll not have him in the house, you meet him at the Drunken Clown instead, he's a sleaze."

Her sister looked apologetic.

She called him back and suggested they meet at the pub.

Julian gazed at her over the top of his glass and said anxiously. "Okay I'll level with you. Donald Best is after me for some money and he is going to send Denny Block around to ask for it and that means I'm going to get beaten up." He had tried everything short of the truth, but at last she had backed him into a corner defeating one lie after another until there was nothing else he could do.

"And you want me to take you and hide you up for a few days while you get the money together and pay him?"

That was not quite what he had in mind. What he wanted was not to pay Donald Best at all.

"I can't help you really Julian because my sister won't have you in her house, and apart from that there is no room. The only thing I can suggest you do is call the police and talk to them, and in the meantime go and pay mister Best. I'm sure the Police will help you," she said.

"The police?" he said, aghast. "Help me? The police would rather see me inside again than help me. If I got beaten up by that loan shark's monster all they will do is laugh and say it serves me right.

Look Angela, I need a place for a day or two and then I can pay Donald Best if I have to."

"All I can suggest is you get some of your mates over to help out if you can't call the police," she said and pursed her lips. "I know what you want Julian and, like I said, I'm not that sort of girl."

"Oh shit," said Julian, desperately. "I'll be murdered."

"No you won't Julian if you put your trust in the Lord and pray for his forgiveness he will deliver you from the foe," she said.

"That's not much help to me right now," he said.

She finished her drink and he was surprised at how quickly she drank the thick ale down.

"We used to drink Guinness at home on the farm," she explained. "I'll call on you tomorrow and see how you are."

"Don't bother," he said guzzling his own beer and standing up. "That's the trouble with you Holy Rollers, all talk and no action. You can preach up a storm and look after a bloke's soul but when it comes to doing something useful you got no guts. Go home and pray for me if you want but don't expect me to still be here in the morning, I can do without you."

He stormed out of the pub and turned angrily down the street to his house. He was so busy cursing Angela and bemoaning his fate he didn't see the shadow loom up in front of him before it was too late.

"All right mister smarty pants," said a deep and dangerous voice accompanied by the strong grip of a meaty hand on his spindly arm. "Me and you gotta have a meaningful natter. We was gonna wait until tommorer but we 'eard what as how you was sort of on yer own like. We thort you might scarper, see?"

"Denny me old mate," he began.

"Shut up shitface," retorted Denny. "'Ome first and then natter."

Julian groaned. He struggled weakly when Denny pushed him into the flat and dropped him at Donald Best's feet.

"A little bird name of Michael told us you might be diving off and leaving us in the lurch. You know how I hate that happening to my clients," said Donald Best, and looked at Julian with hardly a flicker of his eyes.

Julian felt cold and scared. There was a dead feeling in the pit of his stomach; his body shook and as Denny held him with one meaty hand he felt like a trapped animal. There was no escape.

"Shall I bash him Boss?" Denny said, hopefully.

"May as well," chuckled Donald Best.

"Please no," whined Julian but his plea was in vain.

Denny beat him until Donald Best was satisfied that enough punishment had been inflicted, and then they left him on the floor while Donald Best's removal men took Julian's belongings from his room and piled them on the back of a battered wagon.

"It's all rubbish but it will do until he pays us up in full," said Donald Best looking down at Julian laying doubled up on the dirty carpet.

"You do a nice job Denny."

"Thanks Boss," said Denny, gratefully. "He stinks a bit."

"I think he crapped himself," said Donald Best.

"Messy boy," said Denny.

The sun streamed through the window and warmed Julian as he lay bruised and battered in the centre of the lounge where Denny had left him. His face was puffed up and his body ached in places where he thought no aches could ever be. His bladder was full and he strained to control it wanting to get up and use the water closet, but his strength gave out and so did his bladder. He felt the warm liquid seep through his pants and out onto the carpet and he coughed as tears stung his cracked lips. Something squelched in his pants and he wrinkled his nose at the vile smell that wafted up into his nostrils.

He felt utterly miserable.

"Bloody flatmates," he mumbled. "It's all my bloody flatmates' fault."

Slowly he got to his hands and knees and crawled to the wall using it to steady himself as he worked his way upright. To his surprise in spite of the pain he was able to move all his limbs and walk, although if he moved too fast his head hurt and he felt dizzy. He went upstairs to his room to look for a smoke to calm his nerves. Although he had promised mister Byrde he would give up he still had a pack in his room and matches. He was wrong. All that was left in his room was a pile of newspapers and comics and some dirty clothes that even the removers refused to handle.

"Shit, they've taken all me stuff," he cried and sank down on the carpet gazing in despair at the empty room. He sat, unmoving for a long time, and then with trembling limbs and deep sobs he searched the room for anything Best and his men had left behind. All he found was a crushed pack of cigarettes with three battered smokes inside and a box of matches. Gratefully he put a cigarette in his mouth and lit up.

And then the telephone rang.

Angrily he picked it up and answered. "Julian Renfrew," he said.

"Ah Julian, I'm glad I caught you at home, this is mister Patel your landlord here and I need to talk to you about the rent," said the voice.

"What about it?"

"I understand that you are now responsible for the rent, and as such I have to say that there is an outstanding amount owing. I will say that I did not want a contract with you as I am not sure you will keep to it. However, if you pay the arrears I may be willing to let the place to you as long as you can pay the guarantees; you understand, four weeks rent, the arrears and a bond as the law states. Do you understand?" the caller said.

"Yeah, sure I do, you can get stuffed mate I got bigger problems," Julian said and hung up. He still held the matches and the cigarettes in his hand and recalled the pile of newspapers and comics in his room. With an energy that he didn't think he was capable of he ignored the pain and carried the newspapers down into the lounge making three trips in all and spread them out opening them up and crunching them into loose logs. The task took well over an hour until he was satisfied that he had a sufficient pile.

"I'll show the bastard," he growled, and went out into the kitchen looking for more flammables. He looked out of the window and his gaze fell on the garden shed and gleefully he remembered the piles of rubbish inside. Moments later he was stuffing rubbish bags with old newspapers and rotten lino Michael had lifted from the kitchen before replacing it with tiles. Michael, he fumed inwardly, it was Michael who had got him into this shit and it was Michael who would pay for it. He would find him and Kung Fu him to death for this. He hated Michael and the Landlord and now he was going to get even with both of them. On the third trip he found the kerosene can containing at least two litres.

"This will do me," he said and carried it eagerly into the house.

Licking his lips with excitement he splashed kerosene over the pile and laid a trail to the kitchen. He went back into the lounge leaving the can where he had dropped it and made a torch out of a newspaper. It was just like the day he and Grot set the bloody corner shop yard alight. He lit the end and got it going well and carried it to the kitchen door.

And then the telephone rang again.

Without thinking about what he was doing he answered it holding the burning paper in his free hand and the receiver in the other juggling it so he could listen.

"What?" he said.

"This is Telecom billing service. Is that mister Julian Renfrew?"

"Yeah ... what do you want?"

"It is about an outstanding bill I am afraid that if the ..."

"Fuck!" yelled Julian, and dropped the telephone and the burning paper. He stuck his fingers in his mouth and sucked them. The receiver continued to quack and angrily he picked it up. He caught the end of the message.

"... have to regretfully inform you that your telephone service will be terminated and you will receive a notice of compliance within the next few days." Click.

He slammed the dead instrument down in its cradle.

"Bastards!"

And then smoke hit his eyes and his nostrils.

"Shit!"

The fire was well alight, and as if to mock him a great gout of flame suddenly shot up and singed his hair. He backed away looking for his exit but there was only a wall of flame and thick smoke. He hesitated for a moment between the kitchen and the stairs and with a woosh flames leapt into the kitchen. He had no choice but to run up the stairs. Must call the fire brigade! He ran up the stairs and grabbed the telephone on the landing and frantically dialled 999. The instrument was completely dead, and with a sinking feeling in his stomach he realised he was trapped. Donald Best had taken his mobile.

"Oh shit, I'm going to die," he wailed.

In the room below something exploded and a wave of heat raced up the stairwell.

"I gotta do something," he cried, tears of fear running down his face. "I gotta do something!"

He raced back into his room and slammed the door behind him. He smashed his fists into the window pane and screamed as shards sliced his arms.

"Oh fuck that hurts," he cried and dropped onto his knees nursing his shredded limbs horrified at the blood flowing thickly from the wounds. The fire down below was roaring and he glanced at his door. The paint was beginning to peel and there were wisps of smoke coming in from underneath.

"Christ, I gotta do something," he whimpered. Wildly he scrambled around the room gathering the old clothes Donald best's men had left behind and wrapped them around his aching arm. He smashed the rest of the glass out of the window and stuck his head and shoulders outside gasping in the fresh air.

"Fire! For God's sake help me! Fire!" he yelled.

The old man who lived next door watched the fire wagon arrive. He stood with his wife on the pavement opposite and berated Julian as he was rescued. He watched Julian attempt to run and laughed when one of the fireman grabbed him and knocked him to the ground with a short sharp blow of his bunched fist.

"Serves the bugger right," declared the old man.

He was pleased when Sergeant Orange arrived with a constable and arrested Julian. He was amused when as the pair passed Sergeant Orange was wrinkling his nose and looking pained.

"Jesus, you stink Renfrew," the officer said.

And he was right.

The old man caught the smell as Julian passed.

"The little sod's crapped himself," he said, and cackled with laughter.

"The bugger set the place alight," said the Fire Chief to Fireman Weddell's ex-crew.

"And bloody Weddell went berserk when he found out. He wouldn't let us get back into the wagon." Said one.

"We had to clobber him," said another.

"And he was yelling and screaming about doing something nasty to 'that bloody firebug'," said a third.

"Then he ranted and raved at us telling us what a rotten crew we were and how he, well I dunno, he blamed us for everything."

That was when big Joe clobbered him."

"And you left him at the site?" Said the Chief.

The dejected fire crew looked at their chief and nodded. They had at least arrived in time to fight the fire, and save the house, which they agreed was an improvement. The wagon had arrived on time with all its gear and they had enjoyed doing their duty. The crew member who had downed Julian was one shade above depression as a result of his act and that alone had helped the others to almost want to smile. What they really wanted to know was that Fireman Sidney Weddell was not going to be returned to duty.

The Chief was about to speak when Fireman Weddell rushed into the room with a fire axe in his hands yelling incomprehensibly and leapt at the Chief attempting to cut him down with the blade, but the Chief, being a well built man of an athletic bent, leapt aside nimbly.

"Traitor!" yelled Fireman Weddell, gathering his wits enough to speak and swinging the axe again, this time burying it deeply in the wooden desk.

"Bastard!" yelled the fire chief.

"Get the bugger!" yelled one of the crew, and in the following melee Fireman Sidney Weddell was punched, kicked and trussed up and afterwards was taken away, babbling insanely, to the local psych ward for a little more than observation. The office was tidied up, the axe levered from the desk and taken away as evidence by the police and the Chief was treated for minor cuts and bruising. They were given counselling and after their sessions, with extreme determination, wrote a note and left it on the Chief's desk.

Chief,
With all due respect we, the undersigned, ex-members of
Fireman Weddell's crew wish to remain that way. We do not,
repeat not, want him back.

Later when the Chief returned feeling somewhat chastened he read it, and remarked passionately to the opposite wall. "I agree, I don't want him back either."

Ex-Fireman Sidney Weddell sat in the bare room staring at the window counting the bars. There were five steel bars strengthened by filigrees of wrought iron in a pleasant curlicue pattern and he liked it. The shapes were soothing and what with the pink walls and the sad grey linings he felt calm. Calm. Furiously calm. All he could think of was Julian Renfrew. And sharp fire axes. Scrawny necks and sharp fire axes. Axes with edges honed so fine they would cut paper. Cut necks. Swish! Plonk!

"Nice, nice, nice. Cut, cut cut, cutty cut cut. Chippy, chippy chop. A short sharp chop! Hee hee hee...ha ha ha!"

However, a few days later they put him into a room with a guard, gave him calming medication and promised they would take care of him.

Julian put up with the stitching, the confused trip to the court on Monday morning when instead of the Police Station medical cell he was committed to custody temporarily in the hospital ward for the insane.

"I'm not a bloody nutter!" he complained.

The constable in charge looked at him and said, politely: "No, I don't think you are, but we think you need to be looked after and watched carefully, just in case."

And there was nothing he could do about it.

A Whiter Shade of Pale

Arthur Renfrew sighed when he heard the answer phone.

"Mister Braine is unavailable at the moment but if you leave a message he will call you back. Please begin your message at any time."

"Bloody answer-phones," he said, and in spite of himself he waited for the buzzer.

"Yes this is a bloody answer-phone but if you want me to assist you please tell me to whom I am speaking and I promise I will call you as soon as I receive your message, thank you."

Surprised at the depth of feeling in the mechanical voice he left a message.

"Thank you Professor I will call you as soon as I am available. Click." Arthur held the telephone away from his ear and shook his head.

"If you want a few blokes around to help look after you or a divorce or anything like that then Braine is the bloke to see. He's not very good but he's cheap and he knows a few good thugs who can do a thorough protection job. If you need it he will fix you up with a flat as well. He's related to Emily," Richard Byrde explained when Arthur asked.

"Is he a lawyer?"

"No but he knows some good ones and a few private detectives."

"What do I need them for?"

Byrde had just shrugged and so Arthur called Braine. Uselessly it seemed.

He walked from the booth heading for the University and mused on his relationship with Marjorie Watts. She had walked into the Dojo one evening and shyly asked if that was where they taught Aikido. With what he learned was a typical manner of hers she insisted on joining the class immediately and trying out the training. During the next four years they had become friends. She was a diligent student and worked steadily through the Kyu grades to get her first black belt, and now she was a committee member and one of the instructors. It was inevitable he should become attracted to her and as they shared more social events together the attraction became mutual. Nevertheless it took him a long time to tell her. At first he told her how he felt about Julia, and then with uncharacteristic openness he told her how he felt about her. She smiled and looked at him with a twinkle in her eye that upset his calm and made him feel hot and embarrassed.

"I know," she said.

Her assurance confused him even more and before he could say anything further she took his hand in hers and patted his cheek.

"I want no messing around Arthur," she said. "We are too old to muck around like a couple of teenagers. I want you and you want me and the only way we are going to do that is get together and make it work. Savvy?"

He had to agree with her.

"What happens now?" he asked, unsure.

"We get on with it," she said.

He nodded and looked into her eyes and took both her hands in his.

"Then I suppose we had better move in together and I will have to divorce Julia," he said.

"Now you are talking," she said. "I'm sorry for her but it is the best thing Arthur. You deserve to get it together this way. I will do whatever I have to."

She said it simply and he squeezed her hands.

That was the evening before in the canteen. They didn't spend the night together but they stayed late talking. Afterwards he had gone to the Observatory to check some figures. He caught the late night bus and at twenty minutes to twelve he walked into his study and idly turned on the radio. The strains of an ancient popular song wafted from the speakers hanging on the wall and he smiled. A little pang of wry amusement. Julia had never liked the song. It was one of the few he remembered from his childhood. His father liked it. He hadn't heard A Whiter Shade of Pale for years. There was a noise at the study door and with a start he turned to see Julia leaning drunkenly against the door jamb. Her eyes were red and her face was flushed.

"Where you been Prof?" she said, and leaned forward to peer at him. She swayed and nearly fell. Instinctively he moved forward to help and with a jerk she staggered back against the jamb throwing her hands up and dropping them with a slap against her legs.

"Get away from me you dirty bastard!" she yelled. "I don't want any of that filth. That's all you think about, sex!"

She spat the last word out as if it were poison and glowered at him.

"You are drunk Julia," he said, quietly. "I think you should go to your room."

"Fuck off," she said, quieter but with venom.

"Please Julia do as you are told," he said.

"Make me," she said, defiant.

Arthur Renfrew sighed. He wished, not for the first time, that when he came home late she was in bed drunk or sober, he didn't care as long as she was in bed. He could spend some time in his study and then after his evening mug of cocoa he could go quietly to his own bed. Now he would have to forget all that and try and persuade her to go up to her room and stay there.

"It's that fucking bitch at Uni isn't it? I bet you been up to your tricks with her."

"Shut up," said Arthur, quietly but with menace. "I have been at the Observatory."

"Bollocks," she said. "Pull the other one, its got bells on!"

Arthur shook his head. "Oh no," he groaned, "it is going to be one of those nights is it?"

"And don't tell me to shut up. I gotta right to know what you are up to. I'm your wife. I gave birth to your son. My baby boy who I struggled to bring into this rotten sex mad world. You used me! You stuck that thing in me and used me! You bastard!"

She lurched towards him and swung her fist at his head. She hit the door jamb with a knuckle breaking crack and screamed in pain.

With a quick movement Arthur was beside her frantically trying to examine her hand looking for bruises and ready to work Kiatsu on her fingers. She dropped to the floor and rocked to and fro crying, nursing her hand allowing him to knead it gently, easing the pain. The tears flowed down her cheeks and soon she was snuffling and sobbing. Arthur was glad. In a few moments she would declare she was going to her room and that would be it. All he had to do was wait.

She sobbed deeply and shuddered.

"I'm going to my room," she said, and let him help her up pushing him away once she was standing and walked, staggered, to the stairs.

"Good night Julia," he said to her retreating back.

"Get stuffed Renfrew," she retorted.

He did not reply. He felt guilty. She knew.

That was last night too and instead of thinking of Julia as he crossed the quad he thought of Marjorie. He smiled as he thought of her directness and was startled when somebody called out to him. He stopped and looked at the caller. A young student hurried to him and grinned.

"Well Geoffrey what is it?" he asked calmly.

"Good speech the other night Professor and there's something odd with the radio and congrats. Can I call you later on? I have to dash for a tutorial." He hardly finished before he was off again and the Professor called out as he dived away.

"Oh the speech, yes but what are you talking about, something odd with the radio and the Congrats?"

"You and Professor Watts," he called out giving Arthur a broad wink.

Arthur Renfrew watched him go wondering what rumours were flying around the campus. "Marjorie Watts and I are just good friends," he called out, lamely as Geoffrey disappeared.

Sally Aitcheson read Professor Renfrew's press release and chuckled. Her boss, Maurice Bannermann, was an avid fan of alien stories, and if the Professor was right then The Examiner had a lead story worth printing. If he was wrong they could still do well. Examiner readers liked little green men stories, and Maurice Bannermann was always optimistic that one day he would be proved right.

"One day I'll be proved right when an alien walks into our office and says "Take me to Your Leader," he said, and laughed. Some of the staff joked whenever they were called to his office, calling out over their shoulders paraphrasing Bannermann's own words.

"I'm being taken to our leader." They said. The joke always got a laugh.

Sally liked Maurice Bannermann. She enjoyed his Jewish humour and admired his expertise. That he was ruthless in his business dealings and sometimes harsh when an employee failed to perform didn't bother her, he was fair and somewhat generous when it came to bonus payments. The Examiner was described by the tabloids and other sections of the media as 'that rag', and Maurice Bannermann explained that as long as the others called his paper a rag he was successful.

"They are jealous of me, a poor boy from the slums, rising to the top. I mean, look what I have?" he said, and spread his hands smiling at her expansively and added. "My, we'll have to find you a nice boy for a husband my dear, a girl like you should be married with a family."

She was about to stalk out of his office but he put up a restraining hand and smiled.

"Forgive me Miss Aitcheson, I can see you are annoyed but that is my way of saying I like you. If you met my wife she would fuss around you like her own daughter and before you know it there would be stream of young men parading for you. Whatever you may think I did not grant this interview for my own amusement. You have something to offer my company and I want to use it."

She had looked at him surprised and puzzled. The interview was the biggest surprise of her life. She had applied for a grant through the Bannermann organisation to support a year of further photographic study, and she had sent a portfolio to his secretary for his approval. The call came offering her a job and she went along to the interview more out of curiosity than intention. The Examiner newspaper and Telebroadcasting system was by reputation a hard company to get into, which belied the label of rag on the newspaper. He laughed when she coloured up.

"Don't mind me, I want to offer you a job as a photographic reporter and in return I will pay you well and give you time to finish your studies. It is a way of working for your grant and getting a better deal. You make money and from your work I make money. We are all happy, eh?"

That was three years ago and two years after graduation employed full time and doing a Post Graduate degree as well she was busy but already she had proved her worth and gained a reputation as the up and coming new photographer. In addition she was becoming a useful reporter and getting some of the better jobs. Not only that he had paid for her studies and continued to pay for them. The Renfrew story was what the staff called a Bannermann benefit. Sally didn't take it seriously but she knew that Maurice demanded professionalism which meant she had to be thorough. A few minutes after writing her note she was in Bannermann's office explaining why she wanted to follow it up.

"I have heard of this man and from what my sources say is he is too particular to fictionalise a story. He has a reputation for being right, a pedantic and extremely boring man so they say, and that intrigues me. To date the boffins have pooh-poohed him but I don't believe them. I think he has caught them on the hop," she said.

Maurice looked at her approvingly. "You may be right, I think you should follow it up but keep me posted. I have an interest in this one. I smell a scoop in the offing," he said, and grinned. "I could make a huge profit."

Sally smiled and shook her head in amazement. "Is that all you think about?" she asked.

"What else is there?"

"Wife and family and the arts perhaps?" she said.

"The wife I have, the family, I have already and the arts? I can buy the arts," he said, raising his eyebrows in amusement.

Sally laughed and took the authorisation notice for her expenses from his outstretched hand and left wishing him a profitable day. His low chuckle followed her out of the office.

An hour later she was weaving her way through the heavy traffic of West London to meet Professor Renfrew who, she had to admit after their telephone conversation, seemed quite affable. She drove into the visitor's car park and left the car on the second level and walked to the University canteen. She was surprised at what she found there expecting a dingy hall, the smell of greasy food and rubbish everywhere. She looked around the room feeling a little lost trying to recognise the Professor. She was surprised again when a man approached and spoke diffidently to her asking if she were Miz Aitcheson.

"Miss, actually, and I like to be called Sally," she said, and shook his proffered hand.

I am Arthur Renfrew. If you would, I would like you to join us at our table. I will order a snack and some coffee," he said.

He guided her to a table and drew out a chair. A dark haired woman smiled at her and the Professor introduced them.

"Sally, this is Marjorie Watts, Professor of English," he said, and turned to his friend. "Marjorie, this is Sally Aitcheson from the Examiner."

Marjorie smiled as she took her hand. "Arthur tells me you are interested in his story," she said.

Sally smiled and shook the other woman's hand. It felt warm and friendly. She relaxed, and as they talked she watched Marjorie and came to the conclusion that these two were madly in love with each other. The revelation surprised her. She had not expected to find romance beating in the breast of a crusty middle aged Professor. Unfair, she thought, amused, she was the romantic one perhaps seeing more than was actually there? She was doing a Master of Arts degree and, if all went well, she could become a Doctor of Philosophy, and maybe a Professor? Crusty Aitcheson. The Professor talked about the satellite explaining that his observations were thorough, and Sally diligently took notes. But she couldn't help interrupting her questions to remark on the quality of the food and the style of the canteen.

"Oh, that's all due to Huw Jones our resident Welsh guru. He took over the administration of the catering and shook the place up. He gave us two services, a quality service that costs more and is available to the general public in the evenings, and a cheaper one for the rest of us subsidised by the paying customers. All the facilities are doing a roaring trade as you can see."

She gazed around the canteen and saw that he was correct. She also noticed a seedy looking pair of men who seemed to be arguing over a small book she recognised as a copy of the current road code. And then the Professor talked about an attempt to mug him.

"I flipped the guy on his back with a Kotegieshi throw and hit him. He went down and stayed down but from that moment I decided I needed some help. I called a chap named Braine who acts as agent for Sherman Holmes who, I hope, will be my bodyguard."

"I hope nothing happens to you Professor but can you tell me why you should be attacked?" she asked.

He leaned towards her tapping his finger on the edge of his tea cup and spoke in a low voice. "Because the knowledge I have is true and the authorities will want to control it, me, I am a thorn in their side. I am the maverick who stirs things up and they don't like that," he said, calmly without the fervour of paranoia.

Marjorie nodded as if in approval.

"I'm convinced," she said. "I've seen his work and the faxes and documents from other observers. They all agree with him."

"Except the Astronomer Royal and Anderson in the States," said the Professor. "But I have recorded my observations and as Marjorie said we have replies from others all over the world. They all agree with me."

"I'd like to see the documents," Sally said.

"I'll have them ready for you this evening, copies that is," the Professor said. She thanked them both and left the canteen on her way to talk to the people who worked at the University observatory on its site way out of the city limits. During the drive the thought of an alien race in the solar system chilled her and all she could think of was Maurice Bannermann's 'take me to your leader' quote, but with the addition of 'or else'. She turned the radio on and hummed in time to the music listening to the words of the song not recognising it as one of the top forty but liking it anyway. The announcer apologised for the record afterwards laughingly admitting he had no idea how a song from the nineteen sixties could end up in his radio show.

"It's all on holo-disc anyhow," she said, contemptuously.

An odd name, she mused, A Whiter Shade of Pale by a group called Procul Harum, the tune was reminiscent of a Bach cantata, weird.

Professor Renfrew watched Sally go and thought about the interview, how well she listened but also how she had noticed the couple nearby who looked decidedly Government. He was also aware of the two men by the window not far from his own table and was about to tell Marjorie when Geoffrey passing by their table stopped and grinned at them.

"Prof, and Professor Watts, congratulations, er, I sort of spoke about the radio earlier, er, um, there seems to be something wrong with the radio stations. I picked up 99.9FM today and it was playing an old song, several times during the morning so I checked out some of the other stations and it turned up on them too. Odd, I thought, may pay to check it out," he said and typical of Geoffrey he was off before they could ask any questions.

"I wonder if he means that tune that keeps playing; I thought it was a new retro-fashion," Marjorie said.

Arthur merely shrugged, he rarely listened to the radio.

Davey Kline picked up the telephone and was instantly connected with the producer.

"Hey man what are you trying to do?"

"The Tummy Banana's song you mean?" replied the producer.

"Nah, not that crap, the oldie, man that was so old you musta disinterred it. I mean, last C? This is the next millennium man, you know we are into it, the twenty one and up man!"

"You get paid to spiel feller and I get paid to tell you what to spiel, okay?"

"Yeah but the recording man, the recording, who knows these guys?"

"It's popular."

"Like dead man."

"Like I said, it's popular." The producer's voice was tipped with poison and Davey practically felt the underlying threat in his voice and backed off. Davey was getting too old for his slot and he knew it. His job was on the line with every week that went by but he had to keep up his image.

"Okay Lenny," he said, putting a chuckle in his voice. "If you want me to play it I'll play it. It sounds sort of interesting."

"I didn't put it in, someone upstairs wanted it, me, I'd can it," snapped Lenny.

"Sure boss," said Davey, and flicked the switch again.

Should have kept my big mouth shut, he thought, panicking. He listened to the broadcast and mouthed the pre-recorded blurb as it burbled happily over the airwaves.

"Hi kids! This is Davey Kline running the world from your very own Radio West on 99.9 Eff Emm the coolest of the cool with the hype of the big twenty one! We have the greatest and the latest and let's face it you don't get much later than that! An oldie but a biggie from way back! And now for all you fans of Crash here is one to remember ..."

Davey let the sound roll on and changed channels on the holo watching the porn channel instead of the sport. I gotta think, he murmured quietly, I gotta think before I speak.

He was puzzled by the strange message that slowly spiralled up and down the holo image of two women locked in a passionate embrace, and as it whirled steadily ribbon like and tantalising he read it out loud gripping his gin and tonic absentmindedly.

"Do ... not be ... afraid ... of the ... rodents!"

"What?" he exclaimed. "What is this garbage?"

In a dark room illuminated by red lamps and the colours of the screen images uniformed personnel of the U.S Strategic Command Centre watched a digital interpretation of events unfolding in the Sino-Indian war. The atmosphere was subdued, with little tension as if all the members of the staff were especially chosen for their calmness under difficult conditions. This was not true. Most of them panicked in a crisis like everybody else. One of the lower ranking officers had discovered a source of mild tranquillising drugs that kept them all stoned out of their minds for part of the time and docile to the point of lassitude for some of the time and mildly alert for the remainder of the time. In all, the state of inertia began gently at the beginning of the shift rising to a complete torpor in the middle and slowly arriving at the end to a state where they could function enough to reach their quarters without getting lost. The situation was, as their senior officer described in his report, under control.

The strange message that weaved its way across the bottom of their screens didn't sink in until well after the state of torpor was past.

"What was that groovy message?" asked one.

"Do not be afraid of the rodents," intoned another.

"Yeah, right on man."

With a soft click the address system changed from its steady intonation of time checks and verbal weather updates in the war zone and filled the room instead with the slightly muted tones of the tune A Whiter Shade of Pale played on strings with light brass and woodwind accompaniment.

"Groovy," said one officer.

"Yeah, right on man."

"What is it?" asked another.

"No idea man, but groovy."

At the end of the tune their screens suddenly displayed a whirling pattern of psychedelic colours and ended with a collective plop and went blank.

"Groovy man," a voice said in the silence.

There was a murmur of agreement.

Driving is easy.

The Pair Kord and Krod wrestled with their hired car. Worse than any driver so far on the planet Earth they simply could not get the hang of it. The problem they found, was that the car was designed to be operated by one Half Pair only. They tried hard to control the thing, being dutiful and willing to learn, but eventually although they managed to drive more or less in the direction they wanted to travel the skill eluded them. Nevertheless they managed to control the car, and after practising for over an hour in a deserted car parking lot they drove back to the dingy street where the car parking spaces were taken up by abandoned wrecks and the cats fought the dogs for the contents of the garbage cans. There they managed to stop the car and considered it parked. Subdued by the driving experience they quietly climbed the dingy stairs to their rented room on the top floor of an equally dingy house. The monitors burbled into life as soon as they entered displaying a screed of data.

Krod pressed a key and watched the information scroll slowly and lock on to a code. He pressed another key and a video clip wound back and restarted. He watched and turned excitedly to his twin.

"We've got him."

The clip showed D.G walking casually along a street checking door numbers. His location and the local time rolled across the top complete with an approximate time and distance he was from their own location.

"Let's go," he said to his twin. "We've found him."

Across the bottom of the screen a bizarre message danced and for a few moments the Pair gazed at it puzzled.

"Do not be afraid of the rodents?" said Kord. "What on Zrad is that supposed to mean?"

"Bulgers if I know. Must be some kind of code," Krod replied. "Let's go."

In the street they climbed into the car and squabbled over who was to steer finally settling the argument by tossing a Token. Krod won and chose to steer.

"Bulgers, these things are hard to get started," said Kord as they kangarooed from the edge of the kerb out into the street.

The subject of their interest, D.G, walked confidently into the office of the Christian Sisters of the Poor. Angela Breen looked up as he approached the reception desk and he smiled to put her at ease.

"Good morning, Angela Breen, Supervisor is it?" he said.

"Yes, how can I help you?"

"My name is David Gold and I am trying to find the younger mister Renfrew," he said, grateful for the dark glasses he was wearing to cover his eyes from her scrutiny.

"Oh yes?" she said, coolly. "Am I supposed to know him?"

"Well yes, I understand you and he went to the same church," he said, innocently.

She coloured, the pink glow covering her cheeks accentuating her flaxen blonde hair and her deep blue eyes. Her lips pouted a little and he watched fascinated as they crinkled gently when she drew in her breath. D.G thought she was beautiful, almost as lovely as the female Pairs of his home planet.

"We did, once," she said. "But he was not too keen on staying."

D.G resisted the temptation to laugh and tried to look solemn and handed her his card.

"My card," he said.

On it was printed in gold lettering his name and telephone number and the nature of his business. He had printed them the night before using a PC borrowed from a late night retail shop close to where he lived. The exercise took him most of the night but eventually he produced a half dozen cards out of the pile of discarded failures that rested on the floor where he had screwed them up. The telephone number was genuine although all it did was take messages. The title of Private Investigator was a touch of pure inventive genius, he thought, proudly. He got it from an old television show.

"What is it you want from him?" she asked.

"My client wants to talk to him about money," said D.G.

"Please leave now mister Gold. Even if I did know where he was I wouldn't tell you. I know who you are working for and as far as I am concerned you have no right to treat him the way you do. If you don't leave right away I will call the police," she said, angrily moving from her position behind the counter with her fists bunched.

"No, you don't understand," he began, "I only ..."

But it was too late she advanced on him even more determined and he backed away. He stumbled at the door and almost fell and lurched forward onto the pavement. He turned and hurried along the paving looking back at the door glad that she didn't follow him out but anxious in case she called the police. His attention was distracted for a moment by a sudden noise. A car veered from the right lane through the left and mounted the pavement crunching a litter bin and two shop signs. It bounced towards him and with a quick movement he slipped into a shop doorway. The vehicle slid and bounced against the shop front taking the impact on its fenders and slid back onto the road again. It accelerated away skidding around a corner leaving behind stunned shoppers on the pavement and a gaggle of angry honking vehicles in the road.

"Bloody maniac!" he yelled as the car vanished down the road narrowly avoiding oncoming vehicles and turned wildly into a side street. Recovering quickly he crossed the road and walked on putting distance between him and the office of The Christian Sisters and Angela Breen.

"The woman's dangerous," he muttered.

Krod and Kord skidded the careering car to a howling stop and crunched the transmission through two phases of its evolutions trying to turn around and go back. They gave up and left the vehicle more or less in a parking space to follow D.G on foot.

"We'll pick the car up later," said Krod.

His twin agreed and they hurried after D.G feeling much safer walking than battling with the city traffic.

They followed D.G past a shopping centre through an industrial area and out finally to the park where he walked beside the lake with his hands thrust in his pockets for all the world as if he were taking an early lunchtime stroll.

"What's he doing?" asked Kord.

"Thinking probably, how are we going to kill him in the open like this?" remarked Kord.

"I have a better idea. Why don't we find out what he is doing here and then kill him?"

Kord grinned. "Good idea my twin," he said.

In the reflection of his shades D.G saw Kord and Krod following him. Kord and Krod, Dog Squad killers were the best in the business after Blard the Barmy and his twin. Perversely D.G felt honoured to be their target. At the same time he didn't want the added problem of being hunted. He needed to find Julian Renfrew, and to do that he had handed the Professor's protection over to the small team under his control clearing the way to work on his own. The Pairs respected that because although they were good operatives they preferred to work in groups; D.G made them feel uncomfortable. Besides, he was a driver with ability to drive Earth vehicles on his own and now and then he had done some driving for them and laughed when they had asked him how he could do it so well.

"Oh, driving is easy, all you have to do is be able to think Half. Glord can do this too," he explained, and realised that the vehicle that had crashed into the shop was driven by a Zradian Pair, and that explained how Kord and Krod had suddenly appeared.

He walked for a long time in the park keeping to the open and then again back to the streets making certain that Kord and Krod were always a long way behind. He saw his opportunity to lose them when a hover bus hissed to a halt beside him at a bus stop. He got on pushed his card into the slot and the bus hissed away. Krod and Kord ran after the vehicle but it was too fast and they trotted to a frustrated stop staring after it. On the bus he relaxed and idly picked up a discarded newspaper. He glanced through the pages and a small item caught his eye.

Under the headline 'Professor explains Jupiter moon' the item went on to explain how Professor Arthur Renfrew of London West University had come to the conclusion that the new moon discovered orbiting Jupiter was artificial and 'probably an artefact of an alien race'. The item went on to quote prominent Astronomers and scientists who refuted the idea calling the Professor an amateur who had no idea what he was talking about. One accredited observer even remarked that the Professor was in his cups, a quaint expression, thought, D.G, and was seeing 'little green men' around every corner. D.G smiled to himself amused that the professor was talking about him and his people. He looked down at his hands and grinned. Brown and hairy yes but hardly green, he thought. Another item on the next page was more to his interest. It was a small piece but enough to catch his eye.

'Arsonist arrested after Hospital Admittance'

A young man who was later named by the police
as Julian Renfrew was arrested after a house fire in ...'

D.G read the rest of the item and sighed with pleasure.

"Got the bugger," he said, startling the old man in the seat in front. "Sorry."

Although he found out where Julian was it wasn't easy to reach him. He needed a piece of paper to say that he was authorised to visit him and that was going to prove impossible. Instead D.G decided to winkle Julian out of the hospital ward by simply walking in gas gun blazing and drag him out.

D.G had a plan. The technical support Pairs had told him about a dormant transfer port not far from his operational area. The idea was to take the Renfrew there and escort him to safety.

"So I find the Renfrew Earthman and take him back with me?"

"Correct, but get the..." The technician began, but D.G was already on his way and didn't hear the rest which if he had may have saved Arthur and Julian a lot of trouble.

So, it was a simple plan. Heroics maybe, maybe not, but whatever, D.G was determined to do it once and do it right.

First he bought food from supermarkets and two knapsacks from a sports store with somebody else's credit card. Likewise he bought clothes for Julian and himself choosing a natty outfit that suited his mood. Getting the stuff together took a few days but by following

Angela's progress through the camera's he knew when Julian was going to court and when Angela was due to visit him. He decided that the day of the visit was the best time.

The fly in the ointment was Kord and Krod. Prats they might be, but they were dangerous, and so with the logical thinking he was endowed with he considered that hiding on Earth was a no-no. He was puzzled at why the NMF were interested in Julian and why they wanted to bring him to Zrad. What was it Julian had that was valuable to the rebels? Still, that was the task and he would carry it out doing his best to leave Pairs behind to protect Arthur Renfrew and Richard Byrde. For good measure he also set up a team to watch Tzu. There were enemy Pairs ganging up on all of them and after his experience with Byrde he decided to let the teams do their own bit and report to him. So far it was working, and as a part of his arrangements he sent messages to the teams to let them know he was going to use the transfer port and to report to Glord. He checked the location on his Atlas and found it was not that far off.

"Interesting," he mused, and checked the routes to it, and thought at one time he saw Blard the Barmy lurking around the area but you could never be sure about that Pair unless he could actually see him. D.G discounted the idea of making any contact. Nong knows what BB was doing so he filed the image away and made plans for rescuing Julian. He knew about their recruitment having set up the enquiries and the initial approach to the Pair, proud that it was his work that had discovered their intended defection. He tried to send a query to headquarters about Julian but the connection failed; the equipment didn't seem to work properly, sending error messages until he got fed up with trying. Finally all his efforts came together and he was ready for action.

"All done," he said, pleased with his efforts and spent a convivial evening in the Drunken Clown playing darts and drinking with the gang of locals. He staggered home having for the third time that month become the closing time champion beating his nearest rival who promised to show him his prize lettuce's if he should be so inclined to call around to the allotments the next day.

"I'll give yer one if yer wants," the gardener said. "Me plot's the one next to the shed up the end near the 'ouses. Best plot in the whole friggin allotment."

"I'll do that," said D.G and grinned. He had no idea what the man was talking about, but he sounded friendly and that was all that mattered. He went home glad that he had abandoned the electronic lock for a normal key, and settled down in front of his monitor tuning into Angela's channel and watched her kneeling beside her bed in prayer. Her head was bowed and her breasts rested neatly on the bedclothes covered by her nightie. The rise and fall of her perfect breasts and the uncomplicated joy on her face as she muttered the words of her prayers was almost too much for him but he watched until she turned out her light.

"What a lovely woman," he sighed and sat in his seat staring at the blank screen which flipped suddenly into golden colours that swirled dreamily in time to the tune that wafted gently from the speakers.

"Do not be afraid of the Rodents" the screen saver declared in jolly lettering. "Nice," he said, and dozed gently.

The Axeman Cometh

Julian lay in the bed and looked up at the ceiling. His bandaged arm felt stiff where the plastic spray held the severed parts of his forearm together. He was naked but he didn't mind that. It was warm and safe, and for a while Denny Block couldn't get at him. He thought of Denny Block and groaned.

"Awake then?" said the policeman sitting idly on a chair that seemed to be drowned by the officer's fat be-trousered bottom.

"No, I'm dreaming I'm lying here watching you ask me silly questions," he said, unable to stop his sarcasm.

"Funny bugger eh?" said the officer. "Well we will see what Sergeant Orange thinks about it shall we?"

The officer pressed a button on his radio and smiled as he spoke softly into it. A few minutes later a large Sergeant pushed through the door and stood looking down at Julian as if he were something nasty he had just trodden in.

"Renfrew, I won't beat about the bush, you are charged with arson and endangering the lives of others. I have to tell you that I don't like arsonists and it seems from our records you have done your fair share of it, among other things. I have to warn you that you are not obliged to say anything but that if you do it will be recorded and may be used as evidence. Apart from that I don't give a monkeys what you think about it but I'm going to have your guts for garters."

"Okay, okay, give us a break mister," said Julian. "The fire was an accident, I didn't mean to burn the whole place down I would have put it out if I got the chance. Anyway you don't know if I was the one to start it anyway. Donald Best was after me and he could have tried to fry me out of there, I can be a bloody hard man when I want to be."

Sergeant Orange laughed.

"Worm, you couldn't even turn, you're useless, a no-hoper, scum, a waste of our time and resources, a liar, a pathetic weed, a recidivist and worst of all an arsonist and I hate arsonists," sergeant Orange said contemptuously.

"I'm not one of those," said Julian, sullenly.

"What?"

"An arse, what you said I was, I don't do things like that with blokes," said Julian, pained.

"Idiot," said Sergeant Orange. "Anyway, in a few days time we will see you in court and then after that hopefully you will be locked away for a long time."

"What you got against me?" Julian said.

"I hate firebugs."

Julian shut up and cringed down under the sheets, this bloke, he thought, is out to get me and I don't stand a chance. I hate him.

"What ward am I in?" Julian asked tentatively.

"In the nutter ward of the local," Sergeant Orange said and grinned broadly. "The Doctors here won't let you out until we say so mister. In the meantime you can tell me what happened in the house and don't try to deny you did it because I have evidence to show otherwise."

Julian looked up at the sergeant and decided to say nothing. It took sergeant Orange fifteen minutes to realise that Julian had clammed up, and with a sigh of resignation he got up and left. Julian watched him go and settled back in the bed. A lawyer, that's what he needed. Up yours copper. Julian lay in bed for five days enjoying the free food but was disappointed that the nurses were all male. during the last afternoon Sergeant Orange called in to say that he was allowed a lawyer's visit.

"It seems your boss, gord bless 'im has taken pity on you and has asked his company to find a lawyer for you. I dunno why 'cos you ain't bleedin' worth it. Some young woman from some Church organisation asked him to help. Dunno what a nice girl like her wants with a ratbag like you." Sergeant Orange looked at his notebook as if checking to see if there was anything else and shook his head. "You're going to court in a couple of days and then after that I reckon you may as well decide on doing a stretch. The beak ain't going to like what you done and your landlord, the insurance company, the bloke what lives next door and us has all got charges against you. I 'ope's you 'adn't made any plans for your 'olidays because from what I can see you is not going to get any."

"Well why couldn't you lot arrest that rotten Denny Block then? I mean he did beat me up and it's against the law to beat people up ain't it?" said Julian. "I got rights as a citizen too you know occifer, and you ought to respect those rights mate. When I see me lawyer I'll tell him what to do and then it'll be up yours mate for the fuckin' rent see if it won't. I got rights, eek!"

The eek slipped out when Sergeant Orange grabbed him with both hands and drew his face close up to his own. Julian waited for the inevitable blow from the sergeant's bunched fist, but it seemed at the last moment, red faced and trembling the sergeant changed his mind. Julian thumped back into the bed where the sergeant slammed him and wisely decided a triumphant smile was not a good idea.

Sergeant Orange backed away from the bed and sneered at Julian.

"You would like me to do it wouldn't you and then you would charge me with assault eh? I'm wiser than that. The woman from the Christian Voluntary Workers will call tomorrow and in the meantime I'll leave you with this piece of information." Sergeant Orange licked his lips. "In the next room waiting to get his hands around your scrawny neck is a crazy fireman named Weddell. He's fit, barmy and keeps muttering about chopping your neck off. Right now he don't know you are next door to him but if you don't behave yourself, turd face, we might arrange to tell him and look the other way, how about that?"

"Arseholes, you're just bullshitting me," he said, bravely, and cringed deeper in the bed knowing by the look the sergeant gave him that his response was inappropriate.

In his room the next morning ex-Fireman Sidney Weddell lay naked in his bed staring up at the ceiling. His hands bunched and squeezed tightly into fists and then out again. He ground his teeth and a low angry growl that began in his stomach echoed in his mind and emerged from his mouth as a long low moan. Earlier the friendly officer guarding the criminal next door came in for his usual morning chat. What he said exploded in ex-fireman Weddell's uneasy mind like an atomic bomb. Ex-Fireman Sidney Weddell didn't want to be in the hospital. He wanted to be home with his wife and son. He wanted to play with his little boy. Show him the nice sharp axe. Show him how to cut things to pieces with the nice sharp axe. He had honed the blade to a fine edge. Polished the sides and lovingly oiled the handle. They. The police, had taken it away from him. They had hidden it up so he couldn't find it. He wanted it. He wanted to cut that bastard Renfrew to BITS! They had taken the axe away, the nice sharp axe. He showed them how sharp it was by chopping the Fire Chief's door to bits.

"Where's Renfrew!" he yelled, trying to make them listen.

His crew had attacked him and held him down until a medic came and stuck a needle in his bum and after that he had slept. Now he was in this bed naked and drugged.

All he wanted now was to go home to his axe and his son. Poor little Damien. Damien needs his Daddy. Daddy needs Damien. And Sylvia. Sidney needs Sylvia. Sidney wants his axe. He looked up at the constable.

"The ratbag next door goes up to court tomorrow, and into a cell," said the officer.

Ex-Fireman Weddell looked up but said nothing,

"Yeah, mister Julian Renfrew is going to get done over rotten this time," the officer explained.

"Serves him right" said ex fireman Weddell. Renfrew, he thought, his mind racing.

"Gotta take a leak," said the officer and left.

"Renfrew!" growled ex-fireman Weddell.

He got out of bed and padded in bare feet to the hallway. On the wall between the two rooms was a fire service box complete with a fire extinguisher and an axe. The axe gleamed at him invitingly. He licked his lips and stood looking at it, naked and cool, although inside a hatred burned that could only be extinguished by revenge. Renfrew! The name chilled him as he remembered the skinny sarcastic face eyeing him slyly after the factory fire. It was all his fault. If it wasn't for Renfrew he wouldn't be here. His little boy wouldn't be crying for his daddy and his wife, Sylvia, would still be talking to him. With a lunge of sheer frustration he smashed the glass with the little hammer and grabbed the axe. For a moment he held it in his hands lovingly and then with a howl of rage he raced into the Arsonist's room.

Ex-fireman Sidney Weddell was on the war path.

"Renfrew! You murderer! You child molester!" Ex-fireman Sidney Weddell screamed. He raised the axe high above his head and with a howl of animal triumph he brought it down on the dirty arsonist's head and felt the satisfying crunch as the blade connected.

Constables Bates and Fish strolled leisurely along the corridor. They were happy; the world was bursting into flower, birds were flitting about busy building nests, the sun shone and the showers that fell cleaned the air and made everything look bright and cheerful, and in addition their application to join the plain clothes plods was being looked at favourably. They felt like detectives; liked the idea of being detectives and having both passed the exam they felt confident that they would be accepted. They acted like detectives and as they walked they hummed the tune A Whiter Shade of Pale pleased that of late there were more versions of it. They liked the tune. As they turned a corner they saw a man leaning against the wall looking out of a window trying to act normal as if he belonged there eyeing them with half a glance doing his best to appear casual.

"Cor..." said Bates

"...that's Tosser!" said Fish.

They slowed and walked towards him realising he was trying too hard to look relaxed and instantly they knew he was doing something he shouldn't.

"Right Tosser me old mate let's..." began Fish

"...be having you," said Bates.

"What? I ain't doin' nuffin'."

"Open your dressing gown for..," started Bates

"...us and let's see your..." continued Fish

"...pyjamas underneath," finished Bates, and grabbed the man before he could run away.

Fish eased the gown away and saw that underneath he was naked. He saw also that the door outside which he was lurking was the women's ward.

"Tut, tut my little, smelly..." Fish said

"...pervert. This will never..." said Bates

"...do. You weren't planning to..." said Fish

"...hop into there and flash..." said Bates

"...the flesh?" said Fish.

"No! No! Honest! I wasn't!" cried Tosser, and tried to get away from Fish's grip.

"In that case we will..." said Bates

"...take you back to your ward," said Fish, and gripped Tosser by his shoulder and propelled him onward to the men's ward.

"I been taking the cure boys," Tosser said.

"Sure you have," Bates and Fish said.

And with Tosser going on before them they headed to where they were told Julian Renfrew had his room.

Julian dived out of the bed a fraction of a second before the axe smashed down. The sharp blade whistled past his head and juddered into the bed. He scrambled to his feet and raced through the door slamming it shut behind him. His attacker emitted a scream of rage and smashed at the closed door with the axe.

Why doesn't he just open it? Julian thought.

And then the madman was racing after him screaming at the top of his voice.

"Come back Renfrew I'm going to kill you!"

Julian ran harder and raced around a corner barging between two large constables who were shoving a frightened, half naked man before them. Even at the speed he was travelling Julian recognised Bates and Fish.

"Cripes, a naked ..." began Bates

"... geezer," finished Fish.

Julian dashed through the double doors.

"Look ..." began Fish

"Out..." said Bates.

Seconds later ex-Fireman Sidney Weddell barged into them swinging his axe wildly and yelling. All three fell in a heap and before Bates or Fish could grab him the axeman was up and running again. Tosser took the opportunity to race back the way they came gleefully calling out "wait for me!" They scrambled to their feet and then Sergeant Orange and a large constable came hurtling around the corner.

"Give us a hand you two," called out Sergeant Orange. "We gotta catch the buggers."

The door to the women's ward was swinging and on the floor was Tosser's dressing gown. They rushed through the door and stopped on the other side.

"Oh cripes..." said Fish

"...the women's ward," said Bates.

The ward was a mess. Women patients and nurses milled around yelling. A woman patient grabbed at the mad axeman but he pushed her to the floor with a smooth thrust of the axe handle and raced through the door screaming obscenities.

Tosser caught up with the axeman and grabbed at him.

"Show us yer willy!" he yelled and yelled again when the axeman knocked him to the floor.

"He's mine!" the woman yelled, and finding her target gone she lunged at Bates.

"Bloody woman's sex ..." began Bates

"... mad," finished Fish who tore her away from his partner and threw her roughly to the floor.

"Filthy bastards!" screamed the woman but the four police officers were already gone. Instead she grabbed at Tosser and was on him before he had a chance to run away. Tosser was a flasher and had no idea what to do once he had exposed himself. It came as quite a surprise when the woman grabbed his willy and started to play with it. "I'll have this one!" she cried.

Julian was already in the grounds and running hard up the sloping grass bank when ex-fireman Weddell crashed through the outside door. Julian was lucky. The moment he arrived at the outer door an orderly entered from the outside and so taking the man by surprise he knocked him over, running hard up the slope and breasted a low hill; gasping for air he looked back.

Although Ex-fireman Weddell was slowed by the closed door - which he smashed with the axe - he was running like one possessed up the slope and gaining.

"Oh shit ... save me..." Julian gasped.

He raced over the top of a low hill of well manicured grass angling down to the sun spangled lake where joggers ran on the paths and children fed the ducks. Spurred on by the banshee scream behind him he ignored his nakedness and ran harder. He dared not look back but did risk a glance and nearly fell as the sudden head movement broke his pace. The axeman was no more than a few paces behind and gaining. He pumped his legs harder gasping, dizzy as the day seemed to darken and a sharp pain in his side warned him to stop. In spite of the pain and his fainting spell he ran harder motivated by fear, and aimed for the fence where he was sure the alleyways would hide him. He saw a figure appear in front and he was suddenly aware of two others who were racing from his left. He heard the thump thump of feet on the grass behind him and put on an extra spurt.

He felt the wind of the axe blade skim his flesh and howled.

"Nooo!" he cried and then lots of things happened at once.

"Nice One Angela!"

Angela looked at D.G's card again and decided to call mister Byrde. She got the secretary who asked her why she was calling and for a few moments she was confused. She didn't know why she was calling but knew that somehow mister Byrde may be inclined to help her.

"I'm calling on behalf of mister Renfrew," she said.

"Oh, the Professor, just a moment please," the woman said and Angela let it lie feeling guilty that she had lied and mouthed a quick prayer for forgiveness as Byrde's telephone buzzed softly in her ear.

"Byrde here, is that you Arthur?"

"No, I'm sorry, it's Angela Breen, Julian's friend from Church. I'm sorry but there's been a slight misunderstanding, but I do want to talk to you mister Byrde. It's about Julian," she said, and crossed her fingers uncrossing them again when she remembered it was a pagan sign, or was it? Unsure.

"I can give you a few minutes Angela," said Byrde with some warmth.

"Oh thank you. Julian is missing and I am afraid there is somebody asking for him. A private investigator and I think he might be working for that awful mister Best who is always letting him have money. I'm worried that he will get hurt," she said.

"I have an idea he is in the hospital right now under arrest. I'm sure you must have heard about it?"

Byrde sounded concerned, which made her feel a little better, although the news was a surprise. She gasped a little and Byrde continued.

"What do you need from me Angela? I will help out if I can. Julian is a good worker and even if he is a rogue I feel I owe his father at least the chance to make him good. God knows who else will apart, so it seems, from yourself."

"If he's in the hospital can you help me visit him and and ... I suppose he could do with a proper lawyer. I need to find out who this D.G fellow is. Shall I fax you his card?" she said and waited.

"You can and maybe we can find out more about the gentleman. I'll get somebody on to it. I have to get some protection for myself so my wife tells me so I'll fix that up while I am sorting out my own business. I'll get mister Braine's Investigation service onto it and perhaps that animal heavy he employs to act as the beef." Byrde said.

Angela shuddered, she remembered Investigator Holmes, for that, she assumed, was who Byrde was talking about.

"You mean that dreadful mister Holmes?" she said.

"The very same. He's not too bad once you give him his daily dose of liquor and enough money to keep him feeling like a king," Byrde said, and followed up his remark with a laugh. "I'll call you back when I have some information."

Byrde hung up after wishing her a good day and she felt much better.

"Nice man," she said. "He does like to see the good side in people and that must be good." Later when she called on Julian's neighbours she remembered Byrde and was glad that somebody else was on Julian's side. Apart from the Lord that is, she thought, piously, and blushed when she realised she had added the last hurriedly.

She went around to the house expecting to find Michael and talk to him about Julian's debts. She felt guilty that she wasn't more helpful, and especially she should tell him about that mister Gold, and she reasoned, that by talking to Michael she might learn something useful. When she saw the burnt out shell that was once the house she stood still staring at the blackened bricks and the soggy woodwork piled in the centre. She walked past the place and around the corner and peered through the cracks in the gate at the shabby garden. The back door was a gaping hole and the windows on the lower floor were broken. Her old room window was intact and she imagined herself being there during the fire. At least there was the roof of the kitchen to jump down on. Julian's room faced the street. No escape there.

"'Ullo miss."

She jumped back from the gate and turned. The voice came from the old man who lived next door and with a rush of anger she realised he was leering at her. Dirty old man.

"You arter Julian fuckin' Renfrew are yer?"

"I thought I might see him here, yes," she replied unable to stop herself being polite even when he had used that dreadful word.

"My missus seed yer walkin' about and sed I oughter arst yer in for a cuppa."

"Oh, yes, that will be nice," she said, and inwardly groaned. Why did she not tell him she had something else to do? Over a cup of tea and some soggy biscuits the old man told her what happened.

"They took the little basket to the 'orspital," said the neighbour. "Nearly burnt me 'ouse dahn 'round me ears. Rotten little sod! 'E owed me some money too and nah 'e's gorn orf wiv the rozzers to the nuthouse."

"He wasn't a bad boy really," said his wife who raised her cup to hide her mouth when her husband stared at her.

"'E was a ratbag."

"Yes but he was all right to me," she said, and gazed over the top of her cup staring her husband down. "Even if he did nick me 'ousekeeping that time we 'ad 'im 'round for dinner."

"Gordon Bennit! The 'orrible little barsteward I'll ring 'is bleedin' neck if I ever gets me 'ands on 'im."

"I'm sure he didn't mean it," said Angela. "He gets a little short of money sometimes and resorts to somewhat desperate measures. I'm sure he will pay back all he owes you ..."

She trailed off knowing deep down that Julian had no intention of paying back anything he owed and wondered why she was defending him all the time.

"Bugger wouldn't pay back a fart 'e borrowed from yer if 'e could get away wiv it," the old man said.

"Henry! Language! Angela's a Christian girl."

"All right, all right, I'm sorry but 'e makes me mad 'e does."

"That's okay I understand. Julian can be very frustrating at times," Angela said, and stood up placing her cup on the table. "I should go and make arrangements to visit him."

She left the old couple staring after her from their door feeling inadequate and a little disturbed at the feelings she had for Julian. The trouble, she thought, was that in spite of all his faults and bad behaviour he was a good companion. She recalled the times they had gone out to the cinema together and once when they went to the theatre the time she had free tickets. True the cinema outings were fraught with him trying to fumble her, and her trying to fight him off but he was fun. And that was it, he was fun to be with away from his mates. He knew a lot about films and the actors. He was a good dancer and when he dressed up smartly he looked the part and in certain lights he was handsome.

"Oh bother the man," she said as she walked to the bus stop. "Bother him."

But she thought about him lying in a hospital bed hurt and frightened without any friends to help him and she felt an overwhelming urge to mother him. Tuck him in for the night? Give him a goodnight kiss? The Lord loves him so why not she?

Love him?

Has it come to that?

Did she love him?

She boarded the bus and sat staring out the window thinking about him and trying to place him in her life. She had a picture of little Angelas and little Julians dodging around her feet and felt a surge of warm fuzzies that was as suddenly swamped by a shudder of panic. She tightened her thighs together closing her legs defensively. Not that. Not that, she repeated and muttered a prayer. Sinful thoughts.

Back in her office she made several telephone calls and eventually found the right person to ask for a permit to visit Julian. She arranged to have the perform faxed and filled it in faxing it back almost within the hour. Her visit was approved on the grounds of her office being a part of the prisoner's aid system, and the thought of Julian being sent to the jug worried her.

But at least she was granted the permit and that was enough.

Angela sat on the park bench eating her lunch. She had arrived early for her visit but she didn't mind that because she wanted to sit and think about why she wanted to see Julian. When she collected her permit the woman in the Justice Department office had looked down her nose at her and spoke condescendingly.

"Is he your boyfriend then love?"

She had said yes, but the thought disturbed her, embarrassed her and she had almost said something cutting but bit her lip and prayed instead. Silly really to get so upset. She was an official visitor but... she left the but hanging and walked out of the building feeling as if everybody was smirking at her.

It was a pleasant day and so instead of shopping before her visit she decided to go for a walk. The walk had helped and she was feeling much better. She decided that she would try again with Julian. If anybody could change him she could, with the Lord's help of course, she added. She carefully packed her rubbish away and put the plastic bag on the seat beside her. She looked around for a waste bin and something happening in the direction of the hospital caught her eye. A streaker! A naked man running. She looked at the figure and with a shock she realised it was Julian.

"Oh dear," she said, and blushed. She felt vaguely uncomfortable and although she knew she shouldn't look she couldn't help gazing at him. She could see his pubic hair and ... and that ... thing. She blushed again rising from the seat not forgetting to throw the rubbish in the bin, and trotted across the grass unsure of what she was going to do.

"Julian!" she cried but he did not hear her.

And then she saw why. Behind him running faster and rapidly catching up was a naked axeman. To her left two men suddenly appeared and raced across the grass trying to head Julian off. Quickly Angela calculated that it would be a race between the two men and the mad axeman. The axeman was gaining fast. And then she saw mister Gold appear racing toward Julian. Mister Gold shouted something and Julian swerved past him. The axeman shifted right and with a whoop ran down a sharp slope almost on the heels of Julian who saw him coming and darted to his left. Angela running faster made up her mind. The axeman, get the axeman. She put on a mighty spurt and cut across the axeman's path and leapt at his knees. She heard him gasp as he hit the deck and then she was on him.

"Got him," she said.

But ex-fireman Sidney Weddell had other ideas. With a mighty effort he heaved her off and scrambled on all fours grabbing at the fallen axe. Angela tumbled off his wriggling body and landed on her knees.

"I'll kill him!" screamed the axeman.

"Oh no you won't," said Angela, and with all the force she could muster she swung a haymaker at him with her right fist. It connected with his head and he fell like a poleaxed cattle beast.

"Now I've got the bugger," she said, and blushed. "Oops, pardon my French."

She looked up to see where Julian had got to but he was gone. Moments later she was surrounded by a crowd of policemen and orderlies.

"Nice one Angela," said one of the Policemen, and when she glanced up at him she recognised Sergeant Orange.

"Oh dear I think I've hurt him," she said, and jumped to her feet turning away realising with a start she was straddling a naked man.

Her face reddened and she walked off hearing the chuckles of the orderlies and policeman as they lifted the axeman from the grass and trussed him up.

Goodbye Cruel World

Julian collapsed on the wooden floor and squealed when a brown hand grasped his arm and jerked him to his feet.

"Get dressed and hurry."

The figure grinned and handed him a neat bundle of clothes beginning with underpants and socks, and with hardly a glance helped him put them on. In spite of his trembling exhaustion Julian found dressing was easier without his companion's help, and with bad grace struggled into the garments himself.

"Who the?"

"The name's D.G. I'm on a mission and my mission is you."

"Is that" - pant - "why you shot them two gits what was chasing me?"

"Yeah, neat eh? But I only gassed them, it was the axeman what I was - I mean whom I was after - but your girlfriend dealt to him with a flying tackle. Magnificent!"

"Girlfriend?"

"Yeah the delectable Angela Breen. Get those shoes on quick will you."

"The holy roller ain't my girlfriend and what do you mean mission?"

D.G straightened and looked at Julian gravely. His face looked dignified but his attire was too bizarre to carry it off. He had exchanged his San-Franciscan outfit for a smooth green silk jacket, a yellow shirt with a brilliant white tie, a pair of purple trousers and dark blue socks with bright fluorescent patches and a pair of Doc Marten's.

In contrast Julian's newly acquired clothes were dull and ordinary. Julian snickered and doubled up laughing as D.G stood with his arms folded.

"What's the joke?"

"You..." began Julian, and turned suddenly aware of two things that disturbed him. The first was the realisation that there was something drastically wrong with D.G's eyes and somewhere not far away there was the heavy tread of policeman's boots.

"Bloody cops!" he said, and turned to run.

D.G grabbed him by his sleeve and hauled him back.

"Hey hero hang on. You have to carry your weight around here," and with a grunt D.G picked a knapsack from the floor and thrust it at him.

Julian hefted it and looked sullen as if about to resist.

"Put it on your back like a hiker's pack."

Julian did as he was told and followed D.G along the passage to the front door. He was still bemused by what had happened in the park. He remembered the axe missing him by a mere pimple's width, and remembered leaping past two men with pistols drawn and then D.G armed, aiming another in his direction. He remembered screaming and the sudden shift as D.G yelled at him to keep going.

What D.G actually said was "run you stupid bugger!"

Julian took the hint and heard two faint explosions behind him and then D.G raced alongside him, passed and led him to the deserted house.

"Inside and we give you some clobber. It's all right you're safe now."

Julian liked that but didn't like D.G's version of safe. Too many coppers and there was still the bloody axeman to worry about.

"What?"

"Shuddup and move," D.G said, and almost pushed him through the door.

Julian felt better when a quick glance out the window showed the officers stomping past the house. Now was the time to go.

"What's in the knapsack?"

"Food and a few other things you will need where we are going. Now, let's get moving."

"Look, who are you and where the fuck are we going," said Julian.

"I'm your rescuer and I'm going to take you to a place where you will be safe. Er, you might find some odd things happening but bear with it and you will be okay," he said. "We go through the house and out on the street."

Outside they turned right and walked along the high street. D.G insisted they walk casually rather than hurry.

"Look normal Julian. We are heading for the allotments in the Bywater Road," he said and grinned when Julian looked puzzled. "We're going gardening."

In spite of his instructions to look casual D.G set a fast pace and Julian could barely keep up. He ached from running hard and his cut arm hurt, and as he struggled to keep up the pace the pack on his back dug into his shoulders and sweat trickled down his face with the effort. He hardly noticed that they had stopped outside a garden shed that stood close to the end wall of a row of terraced houses and D.G was opening the door.

"Don't just stand there," he said. "Come on in. We can get away from here."

Julian shrugged his shoulders and stepped inside. Whatever happened next could be no worse than getting chopped up by a mad axeman, he reasoned, at the least he might get captured. Certain to get captured again. He may as well sit inside a garden shed and wait for the police to arrive as wander around town. He had nowhere else to go.

"What the heck is all this?" he said.

"You'll see as soon as I get this thing working," replied D.G, grinning.

D.G was fiddling with a pillar that looked something like a thin parking meter. He was trying to fit some odd looking parts to the top and had succeeded in getting one part on but the rest seemed to be a problem. Julian watched him fumbling for a while, and judging the moment when D.G seemed to be most annoyed with the process he smirked and pressed close looking over D.G's shoulder.

"Can I help?" asked Julian, amused.

"No, I can handle it."

"What are you trying to do?"

"I'm trying to get this bloody thing activated," snapped D.G. "What does it bloody look like."

"Okay, you don't need me I'll just sit here and think about cells and things then shall I?"

D.G glanced back over his shoulder and glowered. Julian shrugged and settled on a sack of fertiliser and watched D.G struggling with the buttons. When a red light changed to green D.G looked up in triumph.

"Soon get it fixed. Now all we need is the gadget and we're away."

Julian nodded.

D.G dredged a wedge shaped object from his pack and the fumbling fiasco started again.

Julian watched and twiddled his thumbs.

No matter what D.G did with the item, whether he twisted it or carefully placed it there was no way it would fit, and with a curse, he threw the wedge object onto the floor and turned to Julian.

"I'll fix it, I'll bloody fix it!"

Julian grinned.

D.G glowered angrily and was about to say something but a shout from outside stopped him.

Julian gingerly opened the door a crack and immediately shut it.

"Coppers, 'undreds of 'em," he said. "We're bloody done for!"

"All I gotta do is put this on and we can go," said D.G.

"Well do it then!" yelled Julian.

D.G picked the part up and tried again but it slipped off and with a cry Julian grabbed it and with a deft movement slipped it into a corresponding slot on the side of the pillar. The whole device looked like a parking meter and apart from the need to pull it away from the wall Julian realised, it was hardly visible.

"Is that what you were trying to do?" he asked. "Now I would like to know how the heck we are going to get out of here."

"All right smarty pants I'll show you."

D.G fiddled with the buttons cursing and swearing as he worked but nothing happened. Julian imagined the police gathering outside but was too frightened to take another look. He nearly wet himself when a distorted electronic voice boomed out.

"We know you are in there Renfrew - you and your companion come out one by one with your hands on your heads - we have weapons trained on the hut and we are prepared to shoot."

"Oh God," wailed Julian. "They are going to kill us."

Julian grabbed D.G and shook him.

"Get us out of here!"

D.G's fingers twitched and pressed buttons and suddenly there was a dull clanging sound and the light from the small window turned from bright sunshine to misty grey. The noise outside dulled to an echo and D.G grinned.

"That's the shield up so now we got plenty of time to activate the Transfer Port. Don't worry my friend we'll soon be on our way."

"Where are we going - I mean this is a garden shed not a bloody space rocket and that's what we need if we are going to get out of this," Julian said, unhappily.

"Just let me get on with this and trust me, I know what I'm doing," D.G said, and bent to his task.

"Yeah, sure you do," Julian said, and twitched his thumbs rather than twiddled them.

Lights flashed on and off and a tiny screen activated with red numerals that pulsated and died and then as suddenly flashed up again. D.G muttered angrily and as he watched Julian realised that D.G was incapable of operating the stalk but, he thought, it didn't really matter much because soon the police would come and break the door down and drag him off. He sank deeper into the bag and stared vacantly at the door expecting that any moment a burly body would break through the wood.

"It doesn't matter," he said. "It doesn't matter."

D.G ignored him, frantically stabbing buttons and as frantically clawing ineffectively at the column when the screen died yet again.

Julian sat despondently on his bag of fertiliser.

His life seemed to be full of nutters lately, he thought, first there was Denny Block; then the madman with the axe, and now this crazy. Waiting outside was God knows how many policemen, and he was sure that at sometime he would have to face up to his father. He would probably lose his job and go to prison. Things, he had to admit, didn't look good.

And then an axe smashed through the lower door panel. Julian leapt to his feet and grabbed a shovel from the rack of tools and raised it to his shoulder.

"Go away!" he yelled.

The axe smashed deeper and opened out a large hole through which a uniformed police officer shoved his head and shoulders reaching for the bolts that held the door fast.

"Hurry up D.G!" Julian screamed, and as the officer eased further in he closed his eyes and struck down hard with the spade. There was a thump and then a sudden sickening lurch as for a brief moment everything fell apart. Julian dropped to the floor letting go the spade and was surprised when instead of wooden planks he hit concrete. He opened his eyes and came face to face with half a policeman.

"Oh Christ!" he said and got to his knees.

And with a despairing sob he threw up.

Bates and Fish stood in the hospital grounds. Bates had the radio telephone cupped to his ear and he was relaying instructions. Instead of racing after the mad axeman and Julian they decided the best thing to do was call the patrol cars.

"Cut the buggers off ..." said Fish

"... and save us running," said Bates.

While Bates spoke on the radio Fish twitched nervously copying his partner's speech and wondering why he felt uncomfortable.

"All we wanted to do was to speak to one of the patients but he ran past us like a naked rabbit with an axeman after him. Sergeant Orange is on the job." Explained Bates.

He pocketed the radio and together they walked calmly up over the hill and looked down on the activity below. They saw Sergeant Orange and a string of officers and orderlies galloping down to the lake in time to converge on Angela and the axeman. They watched fascinated as Angela flattened ex-fireman Weddell with a well aimed blow that had all the force of her hips in it and both men nodded approval.

"What a woman!" said Bates.

"......" said Fish, lost for words.

They saw D.G catch up with Julian and lead him into the alleyways behind the houses but for the moment they were too busy watching Angela.

"Cor..." said Bates

"...look at that," said Fish

"...she got him right ..." said Bates

"... where it hurts," finished Fish

Bates and Fish strolled down to the lake side and took charge.

"As soon as the cars get here ..." said Bates

"... send coppers on foot through ..." said Fish

"... the alleys and out on to the ..." said Bates

"... High Street and get the mobiles to... said Fish

"... cruise around for a bit," finished Bates.

They struck lucky when a gardener on the allotments said he had spotted two men going into the allotment stores shed. It was a matter of minutes to converge in their vehicles on the allotments. Sergeant Orange's vehicle raced into the gardens and skidded to a mushy stop on a well tended and verdant plot. The sergeant and his men jumped out ignoring the damaged greenery and immediately fanned out around the shed door.

"Oy!" said the public spirited gardener, "What about my bleedin' plants?"

"Very nice," said Sergeant Orange, and ordered a constable to clear him off the site.

The police surrounded the shed and Sergeant Orange called for the bullhorn. He ordered the men inside to show themselves. Julian poked his head out briefly and Sergeant Orange repeated his warning. Suddenly the shed seemed to pulse and the brown creosoted woodwork turned a dingy grey. Sergeant Orange was sure the pulsations were an illusion, and he thought of the several pints he had drunk and the pickled onions he had eaten the night before in the local and shook his head. He bellowed through the bullhorn again but there was no answer, and with his usual, almost inevitable ability to do the wrong thing, Sergeant Orange made his first mistake.

"We'll have to cut the buggers out," he said.

His men nodded enthusiastically. Senior Constable Rice was the first to produce an axe.

"I'll belt the door in with this and we can rush them," he said.

Constable Rice and two other men attacked the door vigorously. Many minutes later all they succeeded in doing was to bash a hole in the bottom panel.

"It's bleedin' 'ard," said Constable Rice.

"Give it another go," said Sergeant Orange.

Rice smashed angrily at the edges making a hole big enough for him to climb in and bent down and poked his head through.

"No Rice! Come back you idiot!" yelled sergeant Orange. "Wait ..."

But at that moment the shed exploded. The police officers ducked and covered their heads with their hands, and as debris rained down on them sergeant Orange wasn't absolutely certain but he thought he heard a disembodied voice say one word that dripped with surprise and disappointment

Oops...!

it said, ending so suddenly that he had to add the exclamation mark.

When silence asserted itself sergeant Orange slowly stood up. The shed was gone except for the remains of the floor planking and what looked like a parking meter that glinted green and then red as he stared at it. Where the door should have been was a patch of burnt grass and a messy looking lump.

For a few seconds sergeant Orange gazed at the lump. The stench of burnt flesh hit his nostrils at the same time as his visual and mental cognition recognised the bottom half of constable Rice.

Like him his men got to their feet slowly and stared at the thing that was now the very late constable Rice, and to a man they threw up.

Bates and Fish arrived a few moments after the explosion and stood looking at the mess that was the shed and constable Rice and grinned.

"You know what?" said Bates

"Dunno, I think Rice was an idiot," said Fish

"Yeah, exactly," said Bates.

From her position close to the gate Angela watched what was happening. If only she could talk to Julian, she thought, maybe she could persuade him to give himself up. If they let her, but from what she could gather all they wanted to do was catch him and lock him up. She gasped with horror when the shed blew up and the poor policeman was so horribly killed. She didn't throw up like the policemen did but she felt sick and weak. She felt so weak that she allowed a newspaper reporter to lead her to the saloon bar of the Drunken Clown and buy her a drink. The reporter said he had seen her knock over the mad axe man and wanted to know what was going on. Grateful for the drinks and a sympathetic ear she told him.

When Sergeant Orange spoke to the press later that afternoon he made his second mistake.

"It was as if he vanished into outer space," he said. "Like he was abducted by aliens."

The press loved the phrase and immediately made the connection between him and Professor Renfrew's speech about aliens. That they also connected Julian's disappearance to the strange pair who had attacked him in the park was due mainly to Sergeant Orange's third mistake.

Sergeant Orange emphatically denied the two men were aliens.

"If they were from outer space they would be completely different from us," he said, smiling indulgently.

A young reporter from somewhere in the middle of the room put his hand up to ask a question and Sergeant Orange bade him speak.

"I have a picture of them and there's something peculiar about their eyes," he said. "They seem to have two pupils in each one. I don't recall ever seeing anybody on Earth like that. How do you account for that?"

Sergeant Orange made his fourth mistake.

"I expect they are men from Mars or something," he said, casually. "What do I know?"

Saturday morning's newspapers screamed the headlines:
"Sergeant Says Runaway Firebug Abducted by Aliens!"
Underneath that headline, or similar, most papers carried a report of the events and linked them with Professor Renfrew's warning. Some carried the story of ex-Fireman Sidney Weddell and others concentrated on the death of Constable Rice. One paper had a picture of Angela Breen diving at the racing figure of ex-Fireman Sidney Weddell with the caption:

"Firebug's fiancée saves her lover."

Angela read her copy of the newspaper and her face glowed with embarrassment. She had a hangover and she was confused by her mixed emotions, guilty at letting herself go, and saying too much to the reporter. In particular her feelings about Julian. She hadn't intended to make it sound as if she was in love with him, but when the man had talked of Julian being blown up she had cried and agreed that she did love him. True she had added that so did the Lord and as a Christian she was supposed to love everybody. She recalled telling the reporter that there was more to Julian than met the eye and gushing on about how they had gone out together.

"Oh no," she moaned. "Why didn't I keep my mouth shut?"

Sitting in her room and brooding was not her style she decided, so she ate some breakfast and immediately went out to walk to the allotments. She stood by the shattered garden plot and stared at the wrecked garden shed. A lone gardener was dejectedly trying to tidy his plot and salvage some of the vegetable plants

"What's up miss?" the gardener said, but before she could answer he continued. "Look at this lot, bloody rozzers, come in here in their moters and wreck me plot without so much as a by your leave and then leave me to clear up the mess. I mean all that stupid talk about aliens and that, what about my bleedin' garding?"

"Oh bother your garden," said Angela, breaking into sobs.

"Oh gawd, that's all I bloody need, a bleedin' crying female," said the gardener.

The man bent down and switched on a radio he had set on a clod of earth and ignored her. "Oh bugger," he said. "Bloody tune, they're always playing that bloody tune."

Angela moved closer to the shed away from the gardener. She really didn't want to talk to anybody. The song A Whiter Shade of Pale wafted up from the speakers and she felt awfully alone. With a sigh she stepped up onto the dirty floor and looked around. This was where Julian was last seen, and when she had turned full circle she was convinced he had died in the explosion, the more sensible papers had suggested there was an explosion, or he had escaped somehow. There was nowhere to go unless you believed Sergeant Orange. She smiled at the thought remembering what the papers had called him. Spaceman Orange they said. Her hand brushed a pillar and she looked down at it surprised when a red light began to flash. She touched the odd shape and felt buttons move. With a soft click the light changed from red to green and then her world disappeared. Her whole body seemed to come apart and just as quickly go back together again. She reached out one hand to keep her balance and touched a stone wall. With a soft click a sliding door opened onto a dirty corridor.

She stepped through the doorway feeling a little like Alice. To her left a shaft of sunlight streamed down a flight of steps which, she assumed, must lead outside.

"Curiouser and curiouser," she murmured.

Cautiously she mounted the steps stopping at the top before stepping out onto a large concrete pad. She drew warm air in through her lips as she attempted to take in the wild scenery and stood quietly for a few moments trying to make sense of what she saw.

"Hardly the garden plots of West London is it," she said.

Julian followed D.G up the steps and stood on the concrete apron puzzled and frightened by the view. They were standing on the lip of a sandy valley dotted with sharp rock pinnacles rising out of red and blue sandy soil covered in scrubby plants and dotted with purple boulders. Clumps of large orange and green spiky plants rattled in the light warm breeze and underneath them smaller red and purple shrubs waved gently. In the trees, Julian called them trees because they were tall, bright purple, blue and red twin billed birds squawked raucously as they flew. The sky was pink with a far tinge of blue and there was two suns, one a large yellow red and the other a paler version dangling a little below its larger neighbour. Julian sniffed and looked at the concrete pad surprised to see shards of planks scattered in a rough ring and here and there a garden tool twisted into strange shapes as if some mighty force had wrenched them.

"Where on Earth are we?" said Julian unable to relate to anything familiar.

"We're not," said D.G with a grin. "We are on Zrad, my home planet. We just flipped through space. What do you reckon?"

Julian stared at him. "Bullshit," he said.

"Nah," said D.G. "We have just used a transfer port; there's lots of them about, especially here. They used to farm the cactus plants. Anyway, I've got my Atlas to guide us. Like the place?"

Julian looked up at the suns and back to the landscape and again at D.G. "Stuff it, I don't like it," Julian said, and glowered at the twin suns.

"You'll get used to it," said D.G with a wide grin.

Julian pouted his lower lip and shook his head.

The Reluctant Hero

Angela looked out across the landscape and shuddered. As far as she could see there was desert, hot scrubby desert with cacti and strange succulent plants that grew spiky between outcroppings of rocks. In the distance there was a line of purple hills that edged a low basin which, as she looked first in one direction then another, she realised was an arm of a yet larger basin. She stood on a ridge of low hills and with a start of surprise she felt warm wind on her skin that carried the sound of raucous animal noises. Underfoot small blue and red plants like coarse seagrasses crunched as she moved and reminded her of the plastic bubbles on parcel packs. Small lizards scuttled through the vegetation and birds flapped in the lazy sky. And in the sky mocking her with their strangeness were two suns.

It was immediately obvious she was not on Earth.

"Whoop de doo," she said, and startled a lizard which skittered across the sand on blue and purple legs. It stopped at a safe distance and flared its frill at her and dashed off when she moved again.

She stood for a long time breathing slowly. She did a mental check on her portable assets. She had on a skirt and top, underwear that was more femininely comfortable than practical. Shoes that were fine for city streets but no good for this rocky terrain. In her handbag she had some chocolate meant for Julian and that was all. She had a choice. Go back to the chamber and try to get back home or continue and try to find Julian. What to do? Go or stay?

Something touched her ankle and idly she lifted her foot and shook it. Seconds later another something wrapped itself around her calf and squeezed.

"Eek!" she called, and slapped a thin red tendril down her leg and jumped away looking wildly around.

The ground around the knoll was a seething mass of wriggling red tendrils each with the intent, so it seemed, to wrap itself around her. Turning to look back at the chamber exit she saw that was almost completely covered with red vines. The tendrils came from a bush that grew immediately behind the chamber itself.

"Oh, I can't go back there now," she said, her voice sounding small in the warm air. "What is it. Plant or animal?".

One red vine was already retreating wrapped tightly around a struggling lizard. She turned and stumbled over rocks to clear ground and looked back. With a shudder she realised that the tendrils had changed direction to follow her.

"Ugh," she said. "Horrid things."

Ah, well, there was no going back, she thought, I'll have to try and find Julian. She hitched her skirt up and followed animal tracks through the scrub. She walked a few hundred metres and when she was well clear of the creeping vines she stopped to examine her surroundings more closely. Below, the scrub was denser and more bushy. Winding in and out of the bushes and passing through clearings in the scrub was a firm track which here and there was crossed by others.

"That must mean people," she said, and hoped they were friendly.

In the distance a flash of reflected light caught her eye and she concentrated her gaze on it. Two figures running. She narrowed her eyes and focused on them. She was sure one was Julian. Her heart leapt and she felt an unaccustomed warmth low down in her belly. She recognised the feeling as one of the sins she must guard against. Did she feel so strongly about him that she was doing that.

In the distance a long way behind the running figures was a larger group. She pursed her lips and tried to see who or what they were. From their direction and their speed it was obvious they were chasing Julian and his companion.

Again she felt the warm glow and bit her lip.

Her Julian was in danger and like a mother cat she felt dangerously protective. "Can't have that," she said, and blushed when she thought of him running naked in the park. "Father, forgive me," she said, and for a brief moment closed her eyes, but the image of him running with his thing dangling closed the pious words from her mind.

"I don't want to be here," wailed Julian. "It's hot and horrible and it's somewhere else. I hate the place. I want to go home."

"You can't, I won't be able to get us back anyway, and besides, the enemy are sure to send someone after us. With a bit of luck and good old hard work we will get to a safe place before the Polisoc troopers catch us," said D.G.

"Troopers?" squeaked Julian. "What do you mean troopers? And what are these polliwogs you're talking about?"

"Not polliwogs; they're called Polisocs and they mean business," said D.G, cheerfully.

"You didn't tell me about them," said Julian.

"I haven't had time," replied D.G, and then he told him.

"Oh shit, let's get out of here," Julian cried eyeing the exit and grasping D.G by the sleeve. "I don't want them polliwogs anywhere near me."

"Don't worry hero I fixed the Transfer Port so nobody can follow us."

"Right, then hadn't we better get a move on then?" panicked Julian. He emphasised his plea by walking quickly along the track that led from the Transfer Port. Within moments he was exhausted and with a gesture of defiance he stopped and dumped his pack on the ground.

"I'll move a lot faster without this," he said.

"You'll be dead without it," said D.G and picked it and offered it to him.

"We gotta get away," Julian said, and refused to take the pack.

"Put it on again or I will beat you," said D.G, "do you want to die out here?"

"Can't we get food from somewhere?"

"There is nowhere except for the pack on your back and the water you carry. After a few days walking you will get used to it, besides, the weight will go down soon enough, we have a long way to go," D.G said, and pushed the pack out to Julian again. "Put it on."

Julian struggled with the pack and grumpily fixed it to his back. He glared angrily at D.G, and with a determined look he took a step forward.

"Right, let's get on with it then," Julian said, and glanced over his shoulder at the Transfer Port entrance.

"Take it easy and settle in to a stride," said D.G, "we will get faster as we go on and if we take care we will travel a long way by the night."

For most of the day they travelled along a rough track, D.G ahead and Julian close behind looking back nervously from time to time. They stopped when it was dark and D.G said they should eat. Julian took a pack from his bag and opened it. It was dried food and all he had to do was add some water. He munched slowly and became aware that D.G was struggling with something.

"What are you doing?" Julian asked.

D.G waved a can opener. His face was a mask of fury.

"Bloody thing doesn't work," he exclaimed.

He dropped the can opener on the sand

"Gimme, I'll open it for you," said Julian. He smirked. At least he was better at some things than D.G, he thought. Deftly he fitted the can opener to the lid and opened it. He sniffed at the food and wrinkled his nose. The smell was familiar. He sniffed again. It was dog food!

"You like this then?"

"Yes I do; now give it to me, I'm starving," said D.G snatching at it.

Julian held the can out of his reach and grinned.

"Okay Fido come and get your din-dins," he said, mocking, and let D.G grab the can.

"Look, I like this stuff so lay off me will you? I gotta eat and this stuff tastes like the food I'm used to. I got good food for you and all you have to do is open the cans for me and shut up. Remember the Polisocs," D.G said viciously.

Julian shut up and watched as D.G ate sloppily. An animal, he thought, a bloody snuffling animal. Like the stupid dog next door at home, slobbering over his dinner plate. Gross!

"Woof bloody woof," he said.

D.G growled and laughed, with food inside his belly he was less angry. "We sleep for a while and at dawn we move on and we take it in turns to keep watch. You sleep first and I'll wake you."

Julian slept and was woken rudely by D.G shaking him roughly.

"'Chrissake lemme sleep," he muttered and dropped off again.

D.G shook him again and he tried to fight him off.

"Piss off pest."

"Polliwogs," hissed D.G.

Julian was on his feet in a second and turning looking around him with wide staring frightened eyes.

"Where?" he whimpered.

"Way back hero and it's your turn to keep watch."

Julian sat staring out in the dark watching nothing. The glow from the suns was enough to make the dark seem more like a deep twilight and he wondered why they didn't march when it was so easy to see. He could do with a smoke but he had none. He gazed at the vegetation and watched small creatures wriggle out of holes and eat other small creatures. Lizards and small rodents darted in and out grabbing mouthfuls of the insects that fed on the plants. Julian shuddered. Eventually he dropped off to sleep and woke suddenly when D.G kicked him.

"Come on it's past dawn and we should be off."

Grumbling Julian explained that he had to empty his bladder and his bowels and sarcastically asked D.G if he had thought to pack some toilet paper. D.G glowered at him and explained that this was not the bloody Ritz and as far as he was concerned all he had to do was get on with it and pull his bloody pants up or wipe his backside with sand like any other sensible Half Pair on the march. Julian completed his morning ablutions and gazed out over the desert surprised at its beauty. He cleaned his hand in the sand and pulled his pants up. Suns rise, but there was something odd. He stood for a few moments watching and then he realised what was wrong. The suns rose in the West.

"'Ere, D.G," he said to pointing to the West. "Them suns of yours come up in the wrong place."

"Seems all right to me," said D.G. "Let's go."

D.G set the pace and when the suns reached the first quarter he stopped and they ate breakfast. Julian said nothing about the dog food and sat eating beans and peach slices in the meagre shade of a purple rock. D.G took his food and climbed an outcropping. He stood on the top eating and scanning the trail ahead and behind. He stood looking back for along time and then he scrambled down to where Julian was sitting dozing after his meal.

"On your feet hero the Bulgers are already after us. Julian, we got to get moving faster. The Polisocs are on our trail."

Julian hurriedly put his pack on his back and started off up the trail walking fast and almost breaking into a run.

"Hey, slow down or you'll collapse and they'll get you for sure," said D.G catching him up. "All we have to do is keep moving longer and we'll beat them. Besides, I can contact our people and get some help."

"For God's sake do that," said Julian, desperately.

The Polisoc Leader Pair called out the cadence as they marched at the head of the column, timing the step so that the Trooper's dog march was steady and controlled. They knew they could cover ground quickly this way even with the packs and weapons. Each Pair carried a sword and a knife and a laser rifle. In their pockets they carried stun grenades and refresher capsules of plasma for the lasers. In their packs they carried food for twelve complete turns and that peculiar concoction of water and sugar glucose to keep their energy levels high. Their mission was to catch and bring to trial the rebel hero Drogl and whoever was with him. The covert squads had discovered he was operating from the Earth City of London and they had managed to put a trace on him. The Leader Pair was given the task of following him, and so, when he had flipped through the Transfer system they had been transferred immediately into the general location emerging from a Bay not far from where Drogl and his Earthman companion had arrived.[5]

"I want them brought in harmed a little if you like but alive and ready for torture," said the High Leader Pair.

"Your Honour!" they said, and saluted.

And now they were on active service and feeling proud and happy. Their quarry was up ahead of them and moving fast but they knew that eventually they would catch up. The scouts had said the fugitives were only half a day ahead. If they forced the pace they would be on them the next morning.

---

[5] *The discrepancy between the arrivals of Julian, Angela and the Polisoc Troopers is because they all travelled on one outward code with no fixed destination in what was probably an area formerly farmed for its plants.*

"Come on lads we're on their heels..." the Leader sang.
"Soon we'll hear their frightened squeals..." sang the troop.
"Tie them by their hands and feet..." sang the Leader
"Carry them off like hunks of meat..." replied the troop.
And so they marched, singing to keep up the relentless pace which ate up the difference between them and their quarry.

Angela kept to the higher ground although it impeded her progress and steadily the gap between her and Julian got smaller. She stopped briefly late in what she assumed must be afternoon and ate some of her chocolate. Her hand bag held a nail file and a small clasp knife. She tried both on the spikes of one of the plants and fluid oozed from the cuts. She said a quick prayer and touched some to her finger. She gingerly licked the fluid. It tasted good and with her knife she opened out a larger gap and let fluid drip into her palm and drank deeply. She felt the energy coursing through her veins and hoped nothing dreadful would happen. Funny, she thought, the liquid tastes a little like gin and tonic. She marched on feeling a little 'squiffy' thinking, it probably is gin and tonic.

She giggled and thought of Julian. The feeling in her belly and the warmth between her legs increased and she felt her nipples harden.

"Oh Jesus, please forgive me," she said.

She giggled again.

She marched all the rest of the day and into the night and stopped beneath a rocky outcrop that straddled the track like an arch. She climbed to the top and examined the trail. Above the outcrop the track meandered through a gully and disappeared over the edge of a ridge. She looked down the track and realised that the group following Julian would have to pass between the rocks. If she hid in the rocks and scrub below the ridge she could ambush and kill Julian's pursuers if she had the weapons. But, she thought, feeling guilty, that was against the Ten Commandments and did her Lord not say 'turn the other cheek'?

She sat on top of the rocks and gradually she became aware of a dull glow back along the trail. She watched it for a long time and realised the men had made camp. They were closer than she expected. She climbed down and stealthily edged through the scrub until she was close enough to see clearly the people around the fire. She counted sixteen soldiers and they were armed with swords and what she assumed were rifles. If she had some of those weapons she could save her Julian. Two men detached themselves from the group and staggered off into the scrub close to where she was hiding. They stopped by a rock about two metres from her and placed their weapons against it. She wondered what they were going to do and almost gasped in embarrassment when they dropped their pants and squatted to relieve themselves.

She picked up a sharp rock and as quietly as she could she crept up on them. She hit the first one hard and turned immediately and struck the other as he swivelled around to see what had happened to his mate. There was a disturbing crunch of rock on bone and he dropped where he shat. Nervously she relieved them of a knife and grabbed both weapons from where they had left them. Instinctively she searched for ammunition realised the capsule hanging below the weapon's handle was the magazine, and with hardly a thought she fumbled in one of her victim's tunics and found more capsules. She left the scene as quietly as she arrived, and passing under the arch of the outcrop she found a place to sit high above the track.

"Forgive me Lord," she murmured. Her voice shook and she put her hands together and prayed. She asked for God's mercy. "I have deliberately chosen to kill two men, Your creatures, even if they are aliens. Lord, forgive me, I killed them in order to kill others. I killed them to save the life of the man I love. Lord ..." She ran out of words. A murderer. She was a murderer.

She chose a clear space and in the dim light she examined the weapons. As she hefted one to her shoulder she thought of the clay shooting she had done and swung the gun around in an arc as if lining up on a target. The weapon balanced like a shotgun and her fingers rested easily on a pair of buttons. She pressed one lightly but nothing happened. She felt a slight pulse under her thumb and pressed down. She pressed the button again and this time a stream of fire burst from the barrel. Automatically she pushed a small lever and the capsule flipped out. Like a shot gun. She felt at home with it now and it was time to put her skill to use. She was after all, she mused, local champion. Top shot of the year in her class. She took aim at a plant and fired. The stream of fire reached the plant but merely singed it. She examined the buttons again but there was nothing to tell which did what. She pushed down on the thumb button and aimed at a closer target. The fire stream hissed louder and destroyed the target plant completely. A rock. Try it on a rock. Her chosen rock disintegrated and she pressed the thumb button again. The power dimmed on the next shot.

"Got it," she said. "Two for down and one for up and the side buttons are the trigger. Lever for the capsules."

She tried a few more shots. The power was incredible, she thought. She chose a place behind some rocks where she could see the track all the way and be certain to have a clear fire path. She had to take them completely by surprise. There would be no escape if she did it right, and with the two weapons she stood a chance of shooting them all before they had a chance to get to cover. She hoped. Satisfied she was fully prepared she settled down by the rocks to await the dawn. She had only one chance and that meant do it once and do it right; zero defects – there must be no survivors.

The Leader Pair roused the Troopers. One Pair dead already. Why? Must be enemy around. He ordered two Pairs to the flanks.

"Enemy scum about lads. Scout ahead and look alert," said the Leader Pair.

Two Pairs moved on ahead and took up positions on each side of the track. Each half period they reported back but there was nothing to be seen.

"Nothing ahead your Honour. The track goes into a cut. Do you want us to take a look inside?" said the Lead Pair.

"Yeah but be quick about it we haven't got all turn. There's only one Half Pair and a skinny Earthman so do a quickie and report back.

The Lead Pair reported back a few short periods later that all was clear. His voice was sharp and clipped and the Leader Pair smirked when he heard the reply. Got to keep them on their toes, he thought, and his twin smiled evilly. Yeah.

"Come on! Move up!" he cried and added a new line to the cadence.

"C'mon lads move your feet!"

"We've got the bulgers nearly beat!" came the melodic reply.

When they came to the rocky arch the Leader Pair halted the column and sized up the situation. He decided to take a chance.

"We go on but run through and get ready to shoot."

The Pairs dashed through the gap and out onto the path that led them up through the cut. Nothing happened. Relieved he ordered the Pairs to form up in a column and head for the top. Two hundred metres from the top all hell broke loose.

"Oh b..." began the Leader Pair and gurgled in agony as the searing beam of laser plasma cut him in four.

Angela vomited and with great heaving sobs of remorse she knelt down and prayed.

"Oh Lord forgive me," she cried. "Please Lord forgive me."

Nothing.

"Do not forsake me Lord!" she wailed.

Still nothing.

But she needed clothes, food and weapons and now that the enemy, Julian's enemies, were slain she had time to get them. She stood up slowly with her weapon at the ready and walked cautiously to the line of bodies. Nothing stirred. She reached them and looked down at the dead men.

Life, she thought, is so slender a thread. One moment you are an animated being with thoughts and feelings, the next you are carnage. So much dead meat. Dead flesh for the carrion eaters to feed on. There was a rustling in the vegetation under foot and a myriad of tiny lizards rattled on to the path and dived for the bodies.

"Ugh," she said. Screwing up her nose and trying not to look too close she began to strip one of the lesser burnt bodies. She took the pants off first knowing that if she didn't do it straight away she would never do it. From another body she took a good tunic and laid both garments aside. She pulled packs from a couple of corpses and loaded them both with food and drink discarding things she didn't like the look of. She took extra capsules and a sword belt sliding the sword out and examining the double blades and shivering when she saw how sharp they were. She tested the knife on a spiky plant and watched as fluid bubbled out and dribbled onto the ground. She emptied a water bottle and cut another stem and put the neck of the bottle underneath. She repeated the operation until the bottle was full. When she had enough food and equipment she removed her own clothes except her underwear and pulled on the pants and tunic. She threw a pack on her back and carried her two rifles on her shoulders using extra belts to secure them. She strapped the sword belt to her waist, and as an afterthought strapped another sword on her back, collected some more water bottles and filled them too, and without looking back she marched off up the track. At the top she turned and looked down the valley. Carrion birds were already on the bodies, and so was a huge cat like beast that tore hungrily into the stinking flesh.

"Yuk," she said. "How gross."

With a shudder she turned and walked on making good time across the plain stopping once to relieve herself and to take some drink. She nibbled some of the food and ate more as she walked. By evening she thought she was getting close and began to look for signs of a fire or some other evidence of Julian and his companion. Angela moved lightly and although she was well built she wasn't a big woman, she was superbly fit and was used to running and playing sports games. She came upon Julian sitting by himself close to the track and startled him with her sudden appearance.

"Oh shit," cried Julian as she reached him. "Please don't kill me I'll do as you tell me."

He cringed back against the small bush and squeaked in pain as the spikes dug into his back.

"Effing place," he cursed.

"It's all right Julian it's me, Angela," she said. "I've been fol..."

Alerted by a sudden noise she turned at right angles to face the bushes and in one smooth movement she slipped a weapon from her shoulder and aimed it ready to fire.

"Whatever you got there mister drop it and step out onto the path or so help me I'll kill you."

"Okay okay," D.G said, and let his pistol drop on the sand as he emerged from the scrub.

"Down on the path with your hands where I can see them, mister Gold," she said. "What are you doing with my Julian? Where are you taking him?"

"I'm taking him to the rebel headquarters where they will look after him and keep him safe from the people who are trying to kill him," said D.G, sounding peeved.

"Well why is he on his own then?"

"I had to sort of you know..."

"You could have done it along side the track. I bet you were going to kill me weren't you and used my Julian as bait."

"What's this my Jul..." began Julian, anxiously.

"Stow it Julian," said Angela. "I'm talking to this piece of excrement."

Julian groaned.

Angela glanced in his direction and D.G moved.

She shot a stream of plasma and singed his thigh.

"Nong's teeth," he yelled rolling over clutching his leg.

"Next time you do something stupid I'll kill you," she said. "One more won't make much difference."

She smiled at Julian feeling the fire begin to stir within her loins and liking it.

"One more what?" said D.G.

"One more armed alien," she said. "I already killed sixteen of them."

"You did what?" asked D.G through gritted teeth.

"I sorted out the soldiers that were following you and killed them," she said. "I got food and weapons and some water. Now, buster," she looked at D.G. "You better come up with a good explanation or else."

"You got the lot?" said D.G.

"All of them and the birds and a large animal got their remains," she said.

D.G smiled. "All of them?" he said, and shifted his feet. "Wait! I'm on your side!" Angela eased her finger off the button and D.G hastily continued. "I'll explain, but in the meantime we'll make a fire and I'll cook some of that food you have. I'm getting fed up with Fido." D.G looked at Julian who giggled. Neither man enlightened her.

It was Julian who made the fire and D.G happily cooked food dropping bits and having obvious trouble trying to use the utensils from her pack. She thought at first he was nervous but came to the conclusion he wasn't very good with technical things.

"Angela, you don't have any smokes do you?" Julian asked longingly.

She looked at him and said: "Sorry Julian, you know I don't smoke and besides, you should be giving up, it's not good for you."

"Huh, I suppose I shall have to wait until we get where we are going before I can get some fags. You do have fags here D.G?" Julian said.

"Fags? You mean those things some of your people stick in their mouths," D.G replied when Julian mimed smoking a cigarette. "Nah, we don't do that. Nasty habit. No fags as you call them on Zrad."

"Oh bugger, things are going to be bloody rotten here then," Julian said and would have said more but the food was ready to serve.

As they ate D.G explained his side of the story, and Angela in turn explained hers, keeping a sharp eye on him as the evening progressed. He looked at her across the fire when she finished, and apart from the crackle of the fire and the noises of the night there was silence. She noticed that Julian had said very little, just sitting in the warmth gazing at her with a mixture of awe and disgust as she described what happened he alternatively groaned or made approving noises as if he were unable to speak. She smiled at him occasionally and lowered her gaze feeling the flush on her face. She finished her story and the three of them sat silent for a while.

D.G broke the silence.

"You don't muck about do you?"

"I was protecting my Julian," she replied.

Julian spluttered and waved his hands in front of his face mouthing something she couldn't understand.

"What's the matter with you?" she said.

"Nothing er, nothing, sorry but what's all this 'my Julian' bit?" he said, biting his lip and eyeing the sharp sword.

"You should know. You're the one who called me your little holy knickers and I followed you here to help you. I saved you from the mad axe man too," she said.

"D.G did that," he said.

"I'm here because of you," she said. She wanted to tell him about the feelings she had on the hill but with D.G there she thought better of it and smiled at him lovingly. "You better believe it."

"Look," said D.G. "That's all very well but what are you going to do now?"

"Stay with you buster and look after my Julian; make sure he's safe," she said.

"Oh," said D.G, and risked a grin. "That large cat-like animal you saw was a Carnibeast.[6] They are dangerous creatures, and most Zradians, including me, are terrified of them. Vicious creatures when annoyed but they like to keep out of the way of Pairs although I expect there are a few hanging around close by," D.G said and grinned when Julian groaned. "They are like big pussy-cats."

Julian looked miserable, and said nervously. "I'm scared and I want to go home." Angela crossed to his side and put her arm around him gently and hugged him.

"Listen my love," she said. "Stick with me because together we can set the world on fire."

Julian groaned and whimpered.

D.G laughed and said. "Bring the hero a bucket. Bulgers!"

He dived aside as Angela loosed a shot at him.

"Shut up ratbag," she said.

---

[6] *Zradians are afraid of the Carnibeast not so much because of its ferocity but from an ancestral memory they found hard to explain.*

Your cell awaits you sir.

The twin Suns above Zrad baked the desert sand raising little heat storms that whirled dust across the cactus spotted landscape. Lizards lazily filled their bodies with warmth; red leaved trees drooped foliage that rattled in the occasional breeze. Three figures sat in the shade of an overhanging rock and waited.

One, armed with a laser rifle sat alert gazing back along their track. She scanned the horizon north and then east and west not visibly relaxing until she had finished her task. One of her companions sat quietly resting on his carefully arranged pack holding a can in one hand and operating a can opener with the other. He gritted his teeth and worked the opener carefully around the top until, after many false starts, he managed to prise the top off. He grinned triumphantly and lowered the can to the ground and flexed his fingers.

The other lay on his back panting and groaning alternately. His back pack lay on the ground where he had dropped it.

"I'm bloody stuffed, it's bloody hot and you guys walk too fast. Can't you slow down a bit?" he whined. Anybody'd think we're in a race or something. I ain't no marathon runner you know.

"Can it Julian; we've slowed down for you enough already. Shut up and eat," said D.G. his anger showing.

Julian glared sullenly at him and made no attempt to undo his pack. He hated the desert. Tramping like happy holiday hikers on a stony, foot breaking track day after day and stopping late at night or for a few hours in the heat of the day. D.G treated him like dirt now he had learned to use the can opener, and as for Angela, she frightened him. Armed to the teeth and dressed like a soldier she took over. Angela had the weapons and knew how to use them and that bloody spineless D.G did nothing to stop her. In fact now she had even given D.G a sword and a gun. Nothing for him, not even a knife. On top of all that it seemed she fancied him and that was something he wasn't sure about. She was beautiful, but. And it was this that scared him. She simpered knowingly at him suggesting intimacy but he knew better than to push his luck. She was a Christian which meant no touch until they were married. She wanted a Church wedding and all the trimmings. He dare not tell her what he wanted. He watched Angela squinting her eyes against the bright light, moving her body as she examined the signs like a tracker. The dark tunic stretched accentuating her breasts, and his eyes were drawn to her protruding nipples. Her body was lithe and vibrant as if she thrived in the heat. He felt overawed by her power and trembled with both fear and longing. Better eat and drink, he thought, dropping his eyes and scrambling for his pack.

He grubbed in his pack and cursing under his breath tipped the contents onto the sand. Cans rolled out and plastic packs slid on top skittering in an untidy pile. He pushed them aside and grabbed a can. Beans, was that all he had? Beans and peaches, D.G's idea of a food supply. He might be better off with the dog food D.G liked, at least it smelled nice. This was their sixth day on the road and Julian was fed up with plodding through endless desert with a pack on his back. At first when Angela appeared out of the bush fully armed to tell them that she had killed their pursuers he had relaxed ready to take it easy. D.G said no; they must get moving and led the way along the track at a fast pace. Angela walked behind them pushing him along faster than he wanted to go.

"For God's sake slow down," he gasped at their first stop.

"Don't take the Lord's name in vain," said Angela, reproving.

A little later he collapsed on the hot sand and with a cry she rushed to where he lay and fussed over him. She lifted him and let him lean against her while she felt his pulse and eased his clothing and clucked concerned noises. She pressed her hands against his brow and looked into his eyes and took both his hands in hers. He felt sick wanting to throw up but her cool skin touching his comforted him, and he groaned instead. He was happy when she snapped at D.G.

"We had better slow down a bit, D.G, the pace is too much for him and I suggest we rest during mid day. If we don't we will end up carrying him and I'm sure you don't want to do that," she said.

"Okay, I'll slow down a bit but we have a long way to go. He should have kept himself in trim and he would be all right. If he doesn't do his bit we should leave him behind for the Polisocs," D.G said, contemptuously.

"And let them torture him to death? Not my Julian you don't" Angela said.

Julian winced. I wish she wouldn't talk like that, he thought, it is like she owns me. Angela frightened him more than D.G did. It was not her revealed violence that bothered him, he understood that, it was her possessiveness. D.G was more direct and at least I know what he thinks of me, Julian thought, there was no illusions; D.G thought he was useless and that was it. Angela, on the other hand, knew he was useless but wanted to change him. Make a better man of him and that scared him. She was unpredictable.

He reached a hand out to D.G and wiggled his fingers.

"Gimme the can opener," he said.

"Please D.G? said Angela.

"All right, please."

That was another thing about her. Out here in this wild inhospitable land she insisted on manners. He had to be polite or else ... He didn't want to think of the 'or else'. And that was another annoying thing they did, instead of letting him have the can opener D.G kept it. Angela ate the Zradian rations from the beginning. Julian didn't like the drab food and eked out his supply of cans.

D.G slapped the can opener into his hand grinning at him.

"Here you are hero."

"Get stuffed," Julian said, and cringed when Angela glowered at him. "Sorry." He added.

At least the beans and the peaches were wet making up for the rationing of drinking water. Angela and D.G carried spare water bottles, the extra food and the weapons. He carried a water bottle with his ration for the day in it. D.G caught him taking extra sips and he and Angela took the bottle from him and filled it each morning.

"That's for the day. When it is all gone there will be none until the next day," she said.

The first day he drank all of it in the morning. By dawn of the next day he was so thirsty he almost drank his ration in one go but took a sip and left it at that copying the others. He was surprised when at the end of the day he felt good. Then there was D.G's orders about the food; eat the canned stuff and lighten the load. But mostly it was the water that created the problem; they had to find it from somewhere each day although now they had extra water bottles from the dead soldiers they needed to be filled. D.G knew where to fill them, which plants to cut for the freshest fluid and the one that didn't make them squiffy. Julian was surprised that in all the desert there were places where water could be found, and when they did find it he was allowed to drink his fill.

"We eat the canned stuff first and then after that we eat the Zradian packs. It will mean lighter packs as we go on."

Julian tried to eke out the canned food but when he tried to carry them half filled they made a mess in his pack. He didn't like the Zradian 'muck' as he called it. They didn't understand, he thought, he liked to eat proper food and not some foreign stuff. Angela didn't seem to care.

She was like an animal; alert and watchful; ready to act, never leaving her weapons out of her reach. Her composure made Julian shudder. He looked at her eating and shuddered with a different feeling, desiring her, wanting to run his hands through her long golden hair and touch her body. He wondered what she would be like in bed with him. Would she be like the tarts he used or would she be different. All women are the same, he thought, aren't they?

They all do it, don't they? Missionary position and think of her duty to the church, he thought, bitterly. Life was so unfair.

He sat in the shade happy to wait until it was cooler. At times he was on the point of giving up and dropping where he was. Thought was as far as he went, preferring to keep going in company than die on his own. The thought of being lost in this desert scared him more than anything Angela could think up. He sighed and dozed uncomfortably in the shade of a large rock.

Angela sat still listening and then with a careful slow sweeping gaze she saw movement. She watched the spot for few minutes and then she was sure.

"We have company," she said not turning. "How about you get out on the rock and have a look D.G?"

D.G moved from his rest position and quickly climbed the rock dislodging small stones which dropped onto Julian.

"Oy, watch what you're doing ratbag," cried Julian, shifting his position slightly.

D.G said nothing until he reached the top.

"Soldiers," he called out. "A troop and I think they have seen us."

"Julian, off your backside and get up there with D.G. - refill your pack first and get ready to move. Shift it!" she said. Julian was a pain, she thought, never moves without being threatened. Why did he have to be such a useless person? She watched him for a few moments as he hurriedly filled his pack and shook her head. He complained about how his back hurt and the pack was uncomfortable but he never took the trouble to pack it properly. She shifted her gaze to the terrain and watched the men fan out as they approached their position.

"Who are they D.G?"

"Not sure yet - give me a few more short periods and I'll tell you."

She waited and listened to Julian swearing under his breath as he struggled to refill his pack. She had told him off about swearing a few days ago. He was better now but whenever he got angry or pressured he swore. One glance and he stopped. This time she let him swear, concentrating on the movement of the soldiers. She checked her spare capsules making sure one was ready. D.G had the other weapon and a sword belt. During the rests he had shown her how to use the sword. The double blades were strange at first but when she moved as he instructed her the method of slicing and sliding with the blades seemed logical, and she found the sword balanced well. She noticed that whenever they practiced Julian always hid. She heard him scrambling after D.G and smiled to herself. He will be scared spitless but, my love, she thought, I am here to protect you. Save a bullet for your loved ones. Grinning, she watched the men approach.

"I think they are friendly," said D.G. "But get that laser ready to use."

Angela released the safety catch and aimed the barrel.

"Not yet," said D.G.

"I wasn't going to," she said, and laughed softly.

A few more minutes and D.G called out. "They look like Rebels. I'll get off the rock and go and meet them. If they turn out to be enemy shoot the shit out of the leader. Watch out too because they are trigger happy."

"So am I," she said. "Warn them."

She giggled softly when she heard Julian groan and swear quietly, despairing.

D.G came into her sight and carefully kept out of her line of fire until he stood on a flat rock a few metres from the first soldiers. He spoke with them for a while and eventually called out to Julian.

"Come on out hero. These Pairs are friends. Don't be scared - we are saved."

Julian scrambled down the rock and collected his pack walking quickly to where D.G was standing. Angela noted with amusement that he looked nervous; ready to run.

She shifted her position and trained her rifle on the two men talking to D.G. Friends or no she was wary. D.G put his arm around Julian's shoulders and smiled at the two men who laughed. He pointed back at the rock turning to where Angela waited with her rifle and waved his hand expansively. The two men nodded and D.G called out to her.

"Angela you can come out now."

She stood up and slowly walked toward the group with her rifle lowered to the ground but with her finger on the button ready, just in case. She covered the last few metres and the men looked at her in disbelief. Two raised their rifles and with a quick movement she slipped aside and fired a blast between them circling the barrel a little making a circle of fire that singed their uniforms. D.G yelled something urgent in his own language and the two dropped their rifles and raised their hands above their heads. Angela held her fire.

She stood close to D.G with the rifle pointed at the ready.

"Tell them I'll kill them if they try it again," she said.

D.G spoke rapidly and the two Leader's rattled out short sentences.

"It's okay now, they won't try anything more, the Leader Pair have given orders," said D.G, anxiously. "Come and say hello and, er, put the safety catch on please."

"Yeah or we'll all be fried," said Julian. She glanced at him standing white faced beside D.G and saw the terror in his eyes. She deliberately slipped the safety catch back on and turned slowly to look at them all letting her gaze fall on the Leader Pair

"Angela Breen, late of the Church of All Saints, Brentford," she said. "Tell them about me and the Polisocs, explain why I am wearing the uniform."

D.G looked at her and turned to the Leader Pair. He spoke for a long time with many hand gestures. The Leader Pair glanced at Angela occasionally and finally one replied.

D.G looked relieved when he finished speaking and turned back to Angela.

"Right, well, er, it's like this. They agree to let you march with us - er armed - providing you march between me and Julian - women are, er, sort of, er, not usually accepted as soldiers in our society. We are supposed to be protecting you," he said, shifting his eyes and shuffling his feet.

Angela laughed.

"I'll kill the first one that tries anything," she said. "And that goes for you too D.G."

D.G spoke urgently to the Leader Pair who nodded their heads and looked at Angela warily.

They marched for two days stopping for short rests in the heat, and on the evening of the second day they made camp in a hollow. One Pair went on ahead at mid day and D.G explained they were a scout looking for an expected patrol.

"They will escort us to the Headquarters," he said.

Julian settled down for the night exhausted and weak from the effort of keeping up. Late, when the rest were sleeping, he woke with a raging thirst and sipped at his water bottle. It was empty and he groaned silently. He knew that Angela had some in hers, and as stealthy as he could he crept to where she was sleeping. He eased the water bottle part way from her pack and as he began to move his hand slowly back she moved quickly and he felt the sharp edge of a knife against his neck.

"Put it back my love," she hissed.

"I was only going to have a taste," he said.

"No you wasn't," she replied. "You were going to guzzle the lot. Now put it back and go to your sleeping place. I'll deal with you in the morning."

He put the water bottle back and skittered back to his pack and lay staring up at the sky until morning. D.G grabbed him early before breakfast and took him aside from the rest pushing him into a small clearing between rocks and cacti.

"Give me a good reason not to kill you," he said, bluntly.

Julian paled and dropped to his knees.

"What have I done..."

He stopped when D.G took his knife from his belt and advanced on him.

"In the desert you don't steal water. I should kill you for what you tried to do. If a Pair had caught you they would have sliced your neck and left you to bleed to death."

"I was thirsty, D.G. I was dying of thirst! It's all right for you. You live in this crummy hole. I hate the heat and all this running around like lunatics. I'm a city boy not a soldier like you. I don't want to fight anybody or kill people. All I want to do is go home. Everybody frightens me - even Angela frightens me. Please, D.G. please - we're mates ain't we?"

D.G glared at him and put his knife away. Julian sighed with relief and stood up slowly smiling.

"See, all we gotta do is talk it over and ... ouch!"

D.G hit him first with one hand then the other until Julian fell to the ground. He lay on the sand with his hands over his head crying.

"Please don't D.G! I'm sorry! I'm sorry!" he cried.

"Get up, now!" said D.G.

Julian got to his knees supporting his shaking body with his hands until he got his breath back, and when D.G snarled at him in his own language he stood up and gave him a sullen defiant look lowering his eyes when D.G shook his head.

"If you do this again I'll let the Pairs deal with you. Now we will go back into the camp and you will apologise to Angela. She asked me to deal with you because she thought that if she did it herself she might, and in her own words, start a minor war. She was ready to take on the Pairs if they objected but I said I would talk to you. Next time you want to do something stupid - think first. You die for your mistakes here. These people do not play games," he finished with a vicious tone.

Back in the camp Julian stood in front of Angela and bit his lip.

"I'm sorry I tried to steal your water bottle. I was wrong to do that and I apologise. I won't do it again," he said, contritely.

"I wish I could believe that," she said. "But I guess that will have to do." She looked at him sternly and he shuddered.

During breakfast the patrol arrived. Old friends, they chattered noisily with the other soldiers and greeted D.G enthusiastically. D.G repeated the tale of the dead Polisocs and as he spoke the soldiers glanced at Julian and Angela. Mostly they looked at Angela and Julian wished that it was him D.G was talking about.

Breakfast over, the patrol formed up in fours and got ready to march. Cheerfully the patrol lined up with D.G and Julian in the centre and Angela, fuming almost visibly, in place behind them. She clutched her weapon and readjusted her pack glowering at the Leader Pair's backs angrily. Julian smiled secretively, pleased about the argument that exploded between D.G and the patrol Leader Pair over Angela. When D.G explained to Angela she should give up her weapons she flicked the safety catch off. Slowly she lifted the rifle and stood wide legged aiming at the patrol Leader Pair's heads.

"Tell them to come and get them," she said, and gently placed her finger on the trigger button.

D.G backed away and spoke to the Leader Pair. The shouting match that followed was easy to follow as all three men waved arms about and stomped their feet. Angela stood alert, all the time waiting calmly as the argument heated up. The remainder of the Pairs looked on amused. Eventually fists were raised and shaken in faces until at last D.G exploded into action. With a look of resignation on his face he shifted quickly side and side striking fast and hard and the Leader Pair went down. D.G looked belligerently at the rest of the patrol but there were no challenges. He walked slowly back to Angela and grinned.

"We've come to a sort of agreement," he said. "You keep your weapons, but just to keep them happy will you please walk one place behind Julian and myself?"

"I'll do that D.G but tell them one wrong move and I'll shoot, okay?"

D.G nodded and so that was how they marched.

Late that same day they breasted a low hill and before them by a few hundred metres was a long low building. To Julian it looked like a Borstal[7] and he shuddered. He knew about Borstals. He held back a little but Angela coming up behind prodded him forward.

"Cripes D.G, that place looks like a prison," he said.

D.G grinned and replied. "It's our Headquarters. We took it over from the President's forces. It's bomb proof and we could fight from here for many four hundreds. It used to be a prison school."

Julian groaned and said, sarcastically. "I hope my cell's comfortable."

"Oh it will be," said D.G and grinned broadly.

Behind them Angela sniggered.

---

[7] *Julian had spent some time in one before his arrest for the grocery shop fire. For that offence he was incarcerated in one of the new young offenders rehabilitation centres designed to prevent young adults over the age of 18 from becoming institutionalised. Obviously in Julian's case it wasn't working.*

Angela and the Council

Glord read the message as it spread across the screen and pushed the print button. Flimsy flowed from the slot and dropped into his tray. He was amazed that he was reading the full draft of the President's new offensive. At first glance it looked as if it might work. It had all the hallmarks of the President's malice and dangerous genius, Glord thought. As it scrolled slowly down to the end he wondered, not for the first time where the information was coming from. He accepted it anyway. All communication from this source so far had been totally reliable. He suspected this was the work of Blard the Barmy and his twin but he couldn't be sure. Besides, there was the question of the odd messages that interspersed the manuscript to take into account. What did 'do not be afraid of the rodents' mean?

Glord made several copies of the message and pushed them into the slots where they hissed through the internal system to their destinations. In spite of his preference for action Glord had enjoyed planning the ambush. The headquarters staff watched its progress on the simulators unable to direct operations but at least satisfied when their plan succeeded. Glord's agents spread the rumour of rebel positions drawing the Second Army out into the desert as expected. The women set the bomb and circled around behind the advancing soldiers and lay in wait. The men sat in their wagons and waited until the Stormtroopers were committed to the assault and even before the explosion did its damage they had already engaged the nearest Companies. The Stormtroopers, confused and now outnumbered as well as out manoeuvred, fell to their lasers. All that was left was the Pongos. As each Rebel section moved through the devastation the Leader Pair waved the peace flag and called out.

"Ride with us or walk back to the President." They said. The Pongos, seeing their transport smashed, shrugged their shoulders and climbed into the wagons and placed their weapons in the trays of the heavy transport trucks.

"What about our families?" they asked.

"As far as they are concerned you are dead. When we get stronger we will inform them otherwise and they can join us," Glord's soldiers replied, aware that the President could use this ploy as a terror weapon against them by killing the families of the deserters but the President would also be aware that such a move would work against him. Glord assumed the President would find another way around the problem. He hoped the President's response would be to send Stormtroopers against the Rebels instead of Pongos and not use families as hostages to force the Pongos to fight. He hated the idea of killing innocent Pairs. He added his own recommendation to the message and continued to monitor the communication networks thanking the source as he scanned the wavelengths. A few short periods later a messenger Pair breezed into his cubicle and announced.

"Your twin has just turned up with a couple of aliens in tow."

Glord pushed his seat back and let it float against the charging pad stretching his body and smiling.

"I am on my way," he said, and dashed out of the portal.

Glord was in time to see D.G stroll casually through the main entrance with the two aliens close behind him. One was a woman and he noted, fully armed, the other was an unarmed man whose head was turning from side to side nervous and twitchy as if he wanted to be somewhere else. He continually glanced behind him at the escort and walked in spurts keeping close to the woman and D.G. Glord went forward to meet them.

"Hallo my twin," he said. "What have you in tow?"

"A couple of Earth people," said D.G. "One useful and the other not. I'll leave you to guess which is which."

Glord laughed and his gaze travelled from his twin to Julian and then to Angela.

"The one with is, and the one without isn't?" he said.

"Right on bro'," replied D.G.

Glord walked in step with D.G and together they guided Julian and Angela deeper into the headquarters building. They stopped outside the central core section and the portal whispered open. They passed through leaving their escort in the corridor and walked into a spacious chamber.

Sitting behind their polished bench the Half Council[8] looked up with interested curiosity as D.G led Julian and Angela to the podium and gently propelled them forward. The Senior Pair stared darkly at Angela and addressed D.G. directly.

"Half Pair Drogl, why is this alien woman armed?"

"She refused to give them up your Honour," D.G replied.

"Before we start you will ask her to lay down her weapons. Tell her anything but make certain you take them from her or you will suffer for it. Why you didn't shoot her or imprison her I don't know."

D.G bowed and smiled falsely. "Yes your Honour."

---

[8] *The Rebel Army followed protocol. The Council was divided into two sections. The Full Council, simply known as The Council and two Half Councils consisting of two Pairs each dealing with separate areas of responsibility, and councils down Quarter and then Colours Red, Green, Yellow and Blue in descending order.*

He turned to Angela and said. "The Council would like you to place your weapons out of reach. It is protocol here. I assure you they will be returned and I have given my word that you mean no harm. They reply that they too mean no harm. It is important you show some respect, please."
Angela looked at him darkly.
"And if they attack?" she said, suspiciously.
"They won't," he said.
"Tell them that like you I will put up my laser but I will keep my sword," she replied. "Tell them that I will not change my mind."
"Look, Angela, you are safe here," said D.G, desperately.
"Tell them!" she said, and flashed him a dangerous look.
"Okay, okay," he said. "Don't get your knickers in a knot."
Beside him Julian giggled.
D.G. glared at him and turned to the Council. "Angela says she will be pleased to conform and she will lay her weapon before you but she reserves the right to carry her sword and honour your service," he said, ingratiatingly.
The Pairs glowered down at him.
"The sword too."
"She insists," said D.G. "She considers that as a fighting Half Pair she is entitled to wear it with honour." Smiling gently at the Council knowing that he was caught between a volatile woman and blunt tradition. Whichever side lost would be bad for him. He decided to keep quiet and wait it out getting ready the next untruth in his mind. He had to break the impasse or there would be consequences and he knew who would cop the flak. Yours truly D.G. alias Mister Gold, Drogl.
"Tell her to place the weapons on the platform."
"Angela, will you place your weapon on the platform please," he said.
She walked forward and placed her laser on the platform and walked back.
"And the sword."
"Er, they would like you to place your sword there too," he said.
"Tell them to come and take it from me," she said.
"She says to come and ask her for it personally," he said.
"You know that is impossible. Our hands may not touch a woman. You take it on our behalf Drogl."
D.G. smiled at Angela and said. "They suggest I look after it for you. Now be a good girl and give it to me will you. If you don't I think they'll kill the lot of us and Julian."
She looked at him and growled her reply. "In that case I will give you the sword but one false move from you and I will knock your lights out."

She gave him the sword with its belt and the knife.

"Keep it handy D.G or I'll have you, understand?"

"All right but there's no need to get so stroppy."

As soon as D.G took Angela's sword Pairs began to file into the chamber taking their places in the seats around them. The stenographers arrived and took their places at the low desks below the podium facing the audience.

The Council was ready to begin.

Only The Lonely

It seemed like weeks to Julian that he had been on Zrad, and he was sitting on a rough bench in the Rebel Army Compound watching the sunsset feeling miserable. He shuddered. Beyond the darkening horizon the rest of the planet was full of angry people. Outside the compound; over the wall; was an alien landscape that hid all sorts of nasties. There were large animals as big as lions, poison lizards, carnivorous plants and hardly anything decent to eat. No fish and chips. No hamburgers. And nobody smoked so getting any fags was out, although he had to admit he was getting used to not smoking. And if that wasn't all, there was a crowd of ratbags who enjoyed killing people. Ratbags who liked to torture their victims first and then feed them to the pigs. He shuddered. If the pigs were as horrible as the mangy dogs that roamed around then he didn't want to know. He didn't like dogs much. If there was one thing about dogs he hated more than anything and that was treading in their shit. He hated the creatures as much for their rotten shit as their rotten bites. He watched one walk across the square and cock its leg against a pole and walk on. Horrible looking dogs too. They were big and hairy. D.G said they were tame, but the first one he had tried to pat had snarled at him.

"Get it away from me!" he yelled and swiped at it ineffectually trying to hide behind D.G who laughed. The dog snapped at him and lowered its head and growled. D.G patted it and said something soothing and the dirty animal walked away.

"Kick its arse," Julian said.

"You kick its arse," said D.G. "If you're game enough.

Julian looked away.

"Not my dog," he muttered.

"Not many of them left now. The enemy have killed them off and it seems they are dying faster than they can breed," D.G said.

"Good," said Julian. "I hope they die out altogether I hate dogs."

"I thought you might," said D.G. "Scared of them are you?"

Julian didn't reply.

It wasn't fair, he thought, here I am stuck on a planet more than, he hesitated, a bloody long way from Earth, with a bunch of loonies who think war is normal. Well, that's fine, you can have all the wars you want as long as Julian Algernon Renfrew is not involved. With a bit of luck this mob will give me a cushy job and keep me out of the fighting, he thought, after all he was a visitor. He hadn't volunteered for nuthin' and didn't intend to. He thought of his mother and a tear started to form in his eye. He missed her cooking. He missed her telephone calls. He missed the sneaked home visit for a meal when his father wasn't there. He missed nicking money from her purse while she wasn't looking. And as he thought about her he wondered if she knew he had disappeared. She might stay sober long enough to find out. Maybe she saw it on the telly or in the paper or on the radio. The tear rolled further down his cheek and he wiped it away. It was followed immediately by another, and with a sniff he wiped that one away too. He felt his throat constrict and the tears began to flow faster. He missed his mother and he was scared. He had to admit it. Scared stiff. Frightened by this hostile planet and its warlike inhabitants. The only good thing about being here was that it was a long, long way from Denny Block, that mad axeman and Sergeant Orange. That had to be a bonus. He sniffed again and the tears rolled down his cheeks. He took a handkerchief from his pocket and blew his nose. He was a long way from home and he tried to work out just how far. He remembered what his father had said on the telly. Eight and a bit light years. That was it. Light years.

"What the fuck's a light year?" he said.

"The distance light takes to travel in one of your complete circuits," said D.G who had appeared as if from nowhere.

"How far's that?" asked Julian.

"Approximately nine point four by ten to the power of twelve," replied D.G with a broad grin. "And if you multiply that by eight point three you get seven point eight by ten to the power of thirteen. And that, mister, is a heck of a long way."

"I don't understand any of that," said Julian.

"That's okay because I don't either," said D.G. "I've come to get you ready for your session with the Elders. Our founding fathers so to speak."

He walked off and Julian followed him.

As they crossed the square to the low portal that led into the main block he thought of his father. That was one other nuisance he had got rid of, he thought, and although the thought should have cheered him, it didn't.

Angela wasn't happy. She didn't like her quarters and she didn't like the way the men in the stores had suggested she would like to wear something more feminine than the standard tunic. D.G had explained what she wanted and gave her their reply.

"Will you please repeat that?" she said, and with a straight face he repeated the answer.

"The Pair said that they have some good uniforms your size for cleaners that will set off your figure quite well," D.G said, and waited.

"Tell the two morons that I demand a proper tunic, and if they cannot find one that will fit my figure then they will have to alter it to suit. Tell them that I will expect them to supply me with all the standard fittings and a pair of boots and hat as befitting a warrior. Tell them I will deal with them the same way as I dealt with the owner of these rags if they do not," she said, and stood patiently by while D.G translated.

He and the two storemen argued for some time and when she thought that they had argued enough she drew her sword and marched into the store room. The Pair scuttled away and came back with a proper tunic. She allowed D.G to measure her and watched as the Pair altered the tunic to the shape of her body. They sewed in cups to take her breasts and added extra darting to squeeze into her waist and for good measure they added some strips down the back and sides to strengthen the garments. They produced two tunics that fitted her comfortably and with apologetic looks they added a pile of knickers and some warm socks.

"That's better," she said, and slipped her sword into her belt. "I'll try them on in my room."

"They will have to fit because after this they will do no more for you," said D.G. "I am sorry these people are so rude, but they tend to treat women as second class citizens."

"Do they now," said Angela, and set her mouth in a thin line as together they walked away from the stores. She glanced sideways at D.G and saw that he looked worried and she felt sorry for him. She had to admit that he must find it hard to deal with her sometimes and, to give him credit, he had argued in her favour.

"I'm sorry D.G, you must think I am a bit of a nuisance making you do things for me all the time and never saying thank you. I do appreciate the way you have helped me and put up with Julian," she said, and smiled at him.

"All part of the job but I am glad you appreciate me. Now I must leave you and go and see if Julian is getting ready," he said.

"The only thing he is ready for is to run away," she said.

"Yes and I have to say that if he had another brain cell in his head it would be lonely," he replied.

"Oh, I don't know, I think it would be quite happy, at least it would have something else to blame for its mistakes," she said, and blushed at her vindictiveness.

"Nobody really likes Julian do they?" said D.G. "And those that think they do are really having pity on him. He must be a very lonely man."

"God loves him," she said.

"Yes, maybe he does and there we have it, if God is the only one who loves you then you must be very lonely," D.G said.

And before she could reply he was off along the corridor. As she walked to her own room she reflected on Julian and how he must feel. He was not a person anybody could like but he was still a human being, a fellow human, and the only contact she had here from her home planet.

"What a mess," she said.

"What a mess," said the Elder Pair.

His comment was all that he could manage after listening to D.G's account of Julian's exploits on Earth and so far on Zrad. The old Pair spoke as one and if this was not enough to upset Julian it was the way they sighed and looked at him.

"Not much use is he?"

"I am sure he will manage once we have put him on the learning machines," said D.G. "If he has some idea of how we work I am sure he will fit in. He may not be much of a fighter yet, but I am certain he can be trained with the sword and gun. I will be willing to help him."

Julian listened to the exchange wondering what they were saying and getting more anxious as the Elders spoke and D.G answered. D.G was fidgeting and sweating a little and Julian saw the signs as meaning him no good.

"If we let this Earthman learn our ways I will expect you to guide him and be responsible for him. He must do his share," said the Elder Pair.

"I will guarantee it," said D.G.

"What's the old fart saying?"

"Shut up Julian."

"You will take him from here and set him on a course of instruction."

"Yes your honour," said D.G and bowed pulling Julian down with him and hissing instructions. "Bow you stupid bugger."

Julian did as he was told and did not move until D.G told him to. The Elders left the room and a few moments after they had gone D.G led Julian out to a small side room where there were hot drinks and seats.

"Right," D.G said as he handed Julian a drink in a plastic cup. "This is the score. You will learn to fight; you will learn our language and history and you will earn your keep. If you do not the Elders have said that you will be killed. Okay?"

Julian looked at D.G unable to speak and saw in his face an almost implacable neutrality. The twin pupils seemed to go dead as if D.G was deliberately turning off all emotion. As he sat staring, Julian felt so lonely, so utterly alone that if somebody had at that moment made a sudden noise he would have wet himself and burst into tears. He managed to hold his bladder but he could not stop the tears. He slumped in his chair and held his head in his hands not trying to hide the sobs or the snuffling as the tears seemed to fill his nose and mouth.

"It's not fair!"

He felt D.G's arm slide around his shoulders and automatically he leaned against the Zradian's strong body sobbing and heaving. In between sobs he uttered the words 'not fair', 'Four eyed gits', 'I want my Mum' and many other snivelling phrases that bemoaned his fate on this inhospitable planet.

"Listen Julian," D.G said, interrupting the pitiful tirade, "all you have to do is try, and maybe we can find a place for you that is fairly safe. Remember, you will learn to use a laser gun and with that you can shoot pairs up from a distance and run away. Besides, we usually shoot the enemy from trucks or battle wagons. We don't send soldiers into fight if they cannot use the weapons properly." D.G held up his hand to stop Julian's protest, "but we will expect you to learn and do your best. Remember this: the better you are with the blade weapons, the more chance you stand of getting away. Kill and run, okay?"

"But them polliwogs is evil," Julian said, not snivelling so much now.

"So am I, but I have had plenty of practice with the weapons. You, my friend, have yet to find out how they work. Listen, on your own planet men have gone to wars feeling just the same as you and become heroes – live ones," D.G said, placing the emphasis on the last phrase. "You might even be a hero."

Julian looked at D.G sure that he was kidding but the gentle, concerned smile that D.G returned, and the feeling of warmth and friendliness that emanated from D.G's whole being reassured him and he felt a warm, excited glow filling his body. He had images of being mildly heroic.

"All right, I suppose I will get used to it," he said.

"Good lad," said D.G and stood up," Let us go find something to eat."

Julian followed him meekly. He did not feel like a hero, but at least, for the time being he felt less cowardly. He would have felt less confident if he had known what D.G was thinking. In his turn D.G might have saved himself a lot of trouble if he had made a bit more effort to find out exactly what Julian was thinking. His idea of Julian's thought processes was marred by his own non-cowardly attitude. D.G could not understand any pair or half pair not wanting to fight. It was like a sport, wasn't it? You played to win and had no thoughts of losing. Losers gave in.

Julian and Angela

Julian lay on his back in the next cubicle to Angela. His head was encased in a padded dome and pads and soft flexible cables were taped to his hands and feet. He concentrated his gaze on the perfect three dimensional picture on the screens ranged above him. At first he couldn't understand what the people were saying but slowly they began to make sense. He was not sure whether he understood their queer language or if at last the four eyed gits were speaking English. Whatever, either they understood him or he understood them and he hoped that he could speak their language. He hoped so because two days ago two Zradian women stenographers walked into the conference room and they were bloody gorgeous. And when they sat down to begin work he lost interest in the boring stuff D.G and the others talked about and watched them instead. Bugger Angela, he thought, these women were beautiful.

"Talk to the birds for me D.G," he asked during a break. "I think one of them fancies me."

"Learn the language," said D.G and pointedly ignored him.

"Arsehole," said Julian, and sat down dejectedly.

Angela got up from her seat and went over to speak to the two women although she could only speak a few words she decided to try and smiling she pointed to herself and said her name and the two women repeated it and did the same themselves.

"Why the heck didn't I think of that?" Julian muttered, and wandered over as casually as he could. "Hi girls," he said, and gazed at them. Cripes, he thought, the one on the left is something else and wished he could speak the lingo. He pointed to himself. "Me Julian." Beside him Angela laughed quietly and said almost to herself but obviously for him to hear. "Me ape-man, you Jane."

"Bollocks, Angela," he said, and smiled in spite of her furious glance. The two women smiled at him and the beautiful one on the left pointed at herself and said "Glorida" and then at her companion and said "Glorid" and smiled warmly at him. He almost melted. Angela said something in their language and Glorida looked at him a little darkly. He nudged Angela who more than nudged him back.

"What did you say to her, Angela?"

"I told her that we were friends," she said, and smirked.

He frowned at her and pointedly moved away from her and smiled at Glorida and for good measure he smiled at Glorid too, but before he could develop anything worthwhile D.G called out that they needed to get going.

"Break over lover boy," D.G called out. "We have work to do." D.G dragged him away from the women and into a room where technicians dressed in white laboratory coats milled around a large machine.

"What's all this for, D.G?"

"This is a learning module where you will be taught our history and shown much of what is happening today. You have a choice, learn our ways or you will find things rather tough here," D.G said, and grinned. "Angela has already had a few sessions and she seems to like the experience."

At that moment Angela walked into the room, greeted the technicians with a friendly smile and said: "Is my friend going to have some sessions?"

The technicians nodded and one pair opened up one pod, strapped Angela in, attached the probes to her head and started the session.

"I get to do that do I? It looks dead boring," Julian said, looking at Angela who was concentrating on the screens hanging above her and momentarily flicked her eyes from them to him. She looked quiet happy but then, he thought, she would, she liked learning lessons.

"So, what?"

"So you get to learn enough to talk to Glorida and her friend," D.G said and smirked.

"Arseholes," said Julian, and allowed the Pairs to attach the straps and almost panicked when the bench shifted and adjusted to his body shape. The film started immediately and before he could stop himself he was engrossed in the screen action. He puzzled at first trying to understand what the commentator was saying and gradually as the film wound on he began to understand more of it. He thought that it was a bit naff that they kept playing the same bit to him at first but after a while he got the hang of it and when the commentator asked him questions he answered them in their queer language. Gradually too he realised that as he answered more and more questions he was able to understand the story a bit more each time. It was a bit scary to find himself in the story, and when the fighting began he panicked and tried to untie his straps but a light came on above him and a voice warned him to leave them alone. As the story unfolded he began to realise that what he was seeing was not some film maker's fancy but the real thing. And then he understood why D.G got angry when he called the Polisocs 'polliwogs'. The Polisocs were no laughing matter. They tortured people and killed them. In fact, Julian discovered, the whole of Zradian society seemed to be one long violent battle. He wished he had arrived in the time of that Glord the Glorious; there was peace then, well, most of the time anyway. He was surprised and scared to learn that the Zradian President planned to invade Earth and enslave the population. He thought of his mother and tears rolled down his cheeks. He imagined her, drunk and belligerent, doing God knew what in a Zradian labour camp. The thought of never again tasting one of her marvellous dinners or feeling her arms around him as he nicked money from her purse made him cry. The image on the screens blurred and died. The screens withdrew gently and someone took the pads from his hands and feet. Gingerly he swung his legs to the floor and stood up to see attendants smiling and nodding to each other and passing plastic pieces from one hand to another. They all seemed to end up in the pockets of the Pair who gave him the test the day before. That was embarrassing and he had let D.G know what he thought.

"What are these four eyed gits doing? I done all this sort of thing at school yonks ago, it's boring," Julian had said, and let D.G know by his tone that he was above all that sort of basic stuff.

"Get on with it Julian, the tests are to help you learn and I am gradually losing my cool, so get on with it," D.G said, and glowered at him.

Julian endured the test and when he had finished D.G explained that what he had done was all right, it was a great help. But he was puzzled when the Pair in charge spoke directly to him instead of D.G translating.

"You have a good time?" he said.

"Yeah, all right. Here, how come you lot can speak English?" he asked.

"No, no, you are speaking our language. The machine has taught you," was the reply.

"What you all grinning about anyway?"

"Oh we are all happy for you," said another.

The crowd grinned and laughed. Julian laughed with them and wondered why they all laughed even louder. They were still laughing when someone released Angela who looked at the Leader Pair and said: "Well? Was I right?"

The Leader Pair sniggered and nodded their heads.

Their laughter turned to sniggers and finally to polite smirks as he and Angela walked out of the Teaching Room.

"Why are they laughing?" he asked.

"They enjoy their work," Angela said, smiling at him.

"Oh yeah? Well why did one of them call me BB and cover their mouths trying not to crack up? Answer me that then eh?"

She smiled sweetly and looked embarrassed. "I'd rather not say," she said.

"C'mon Angela, share the fuckin' joke with me."

"Don't swear my love," she said, bitingly reproving. "It's to do with the size, or should I say capacity of a certain organ. BB stands for Big Boy."

Julian smiled and stuck his chest out. He knew what she meant and realised why she was embarrassed. Yeah well, he thought, I got my fair share and began to strut rather than walk. He looked at Angela and smirked. Better not say what's on his mind, he thought, but if she really loves me she's gonna get a real treat, yeah, the old Renfrew touch, lucky girl.

The Pairs watched the two Earth people leave, and as a group turned to look once more at the recording instruments. They shook their heads in amazement at the readings on the cubicle Julian had just left, and giggled. Each reading registered on the most delicate scale a steady 3.9 barely two points above the absolute lowest level. In contrast Angela's levels recorded a healthy 87.

The Teaching machine's lower tolerance limit; the lowest speed at which it could feed information was 3.7. Attempts to slow the machine to a round figure of 3, which was the rate Julian was in fact comfortable with, elicited a sullen digitally produced message on the monitor screen.

The Creature under instruction has a capacity approximating that of a Bulger - if operators insist on continuing process - will terminate subject for its own good - request extramural program to channel excess energy - balance of 3.9 - difficult to maintain - try binary mathematical task of 76% - End message.

Julian was unaware of this minor computer crisis and accepted Angela's explanation of the Pair's name for him. His chest swelled with pride. A bloody hero me, he thought.

At the divide between the women's quarters and the men's, Angela turned left and he marched off to the right. "See you at the gathering this evening," she said. Turning she added. "BB."

Maybe she really does fancy me, he mused, I bloody hope so, cor! And then he thought about the Zradian Stenographer. He entered his room and noted immediately that it was tidy. When he left that morning for the teaching room he had dropped everything on the low bench and left the bed in a mess. He smiled. Zradian servants, he, the great BB, had Zradian servants. Just think what his mates would say. Yeah mate you don't mess with Julian Kung Fu Renfrew hero of the Zradian Headquarters. Rebel Headquarters he corrected himself. Right on!

Servants had also laid out clean clothes for him. True they were Zradian tunics but at least they were clean, and what's more sitting on top of the bench was an electric shaver and some towels. He fingered them for a while looking at the sparsely furnished room for a place to plug the shaver in.

"It doesn't need a plug. You switch it on and use it. The towels you will need for the Pairs washroom down the corridor, BB."

He turned to see D.G lounging casually against the portal pillar grinning at him. Since he had agreed to use the Teaching Room D.G had been more friendly, and now it seemed he was prepared to make up for his bad temper.

"Oh hello D.G. what can I do for you?"

"No, it's what I can do for you, I think," said D.G. "You want to get to know Glorida and Glorid Don't you?"

"Maybe, I can speak the lingo now so what's cool?"

"You will need me to introduce you."

"Yeah but they'll see I'm a pretty cool dude so what is it with you? You been ignoring me since we arrived and now you are all over me, what's going on D.G?"

"It's your reputation with the Medical and Teaching staff - it sort of changes things a bit. In other words I owe you an apology and I've come to make friends - okay?"

Julian looked at D.G and smirked. "Yeah well, okay, so maybe but..." he said.

"No buts mate I owe you an apology. Shall we shake on it?" said D.G. sticking his hand out. "You and me can home in on the women this evening. I know them you see?"

Julian took D.G's hand and shook it solemnly.

"Okay, you're on, we make up and be friends."

"Now then take some advice from me BB and this is what you do."

Julian listened to D.G eagerly allowing him to guide him through the intricacies of male toilet looking forward to meeting Glorida and Glorid. Angela went out of his thoughts completely.

In her room Angela carefully matched items from her sparse wardrobe. For the first time in years she took a real interest in her appearance. She was unhappy but wanted to appear in control. Dressing neatly and carefully was one way of dealing with her feelings. The problem for her was the way the Zradians treated women. Separate quarters she could understand, but when it came to everything else she baulked. First there was the weapons. She solved that one by being pigheaded and bloody minded keeping the sword and the knife and demanding a receipt for the laser and its capsules. She didn't want the gun but it was a matter of establishing her will, letting the Zradians know she was independent. It was when she asked to go to the Teaching Rooms as well as Julian she discovered the divisions.

"The Pairs say that as you are a woman there is no need for you to be taught anymore than the basic language. They say you will be given proper tasks when the time comes," said D.G. "There's women's work and men's work - the Pairs suggest you behave and do as you are asked. Don't blame me Angela because I am only translating."

She bunched her fists and almost hit him but drew back at the last moment. The look of concern on his face told her that he was not happy.

"I'm sorry but they don't like women asserting themselves," he said.

"All right D.G but you tell them in the nicest most grovelling, patronising fashion that this little blonde bombshell is not a Bimbo and has useful clerical and administration skills including a degree in computer science and that she humbly requests she be allowed to learn as much about the wonderful Zradian culture and society as possible so as to best serve their High Honourships. You tell them D.G because I am getting angry with their patriarchal attitude. I hope you are different D.G."

To give D.G his due he did his best and got her one session as a try out. It was then the Medics and the Teachers compared her and Julian's learning rate. Hers rose from 36.8 as she learned the language to a high of 92.3 averaging out to 87.6 while Julian's barely registered above the minimum 3.7 rising to 4.1 and dropping to an average 3.9. The teaching staff surrounded her and explained her average was the highest they had seen for many four hundreds and Julian's, they giggled, was the lowest ever. Significantly the Teaching Staff, all male, recommended further sessions.

"It is not possible for anybody to be that stupid," remarked the Leader Pair shaking their heads and showing her the printout flimsies. "Is it?"

"Ah, but this is Julian Renfrew we are talking about, not some normal person," she replied and laughed. Trol and Lort were concerned at first that Julian would never learn anything, but Angela assured them that if they took it slowly Julian would learn whatever they tried to teach him but, she warned them, he would put his own interpretation on it. She smiled to herself at Julian's reaction to the nickname BB. Odd, she thought, how he puffed up like a peacock when she told him, tempted to explain the joke but leaving him to think about it. She blushed when she realised what it was he was proud of. Oh no! Not that, she thought, he thinks we are talking about his sex thing. She blushed deeper feeling uncomfortable and looked around her room as if expecting somebody to be watching her.

She finished dressing and waited for a few short periods listening to the music wafting from the wall speakers. She liked the tunes which reminded her of the hymns she loved although the instruments must be quite a lot different because some of the chords were strange. The Portal chimed dully and she palmed the panel cutting the power.

Glorida and Glorid rushed in and danced around the room circling excitedly their eyes flashing excitement and something more feral as they touched her clothing and admired her figure.

"You'll knock 'em dead, " said Glorid.

"We got competition," Glorida said.

"But do we want it?" said Glorid.

"Now that is a point," said Glorida. "We are only going as a token gesture. The guys like pretty things around them when they pat each other on the back. You realise, Angela, the men are celebrating a victory up north against the President's second army force. The women's rebel Army took part and made a difference but you wouldn't know it. Our Leader Pair will be here but none of the other women who actually did the work. You ought to get out of here Angela. The only men worth talking to are D.G and his twin Glord. They worked with us before. D.G is a great guy and Glord is a bit dull but he's done a lot to help us."

They walked along the corridors still chatting.

"I discovered the Zradian attitude to women on the way here," Angela said. She told them about the ambush and the patrol explaining how D.G had probably lied to her.

"Yes, he may have but then he was dealing with dyed in the hair soldiers. They really don't like armed women; I think it makes them nervous; gets at their male ego. The President doesn't like us either. As an Army we are proud of that."

Angela laughed.

"What about this Earthman?" asked Glorida. "What's he like."

Angela told her leaving nothing out except her own confused feelings for him.

"He sounds interesting," said Glorida.

"He's a ratbag," said Angela with a snort of disgust.

The bar was like any bar and Julian was surprised when he saw beer engines and racks of bottles upside down and the familiar mirrored back. Instead of garish lights decorating the fittings there was a soft glow of panels and strips. The room was furnished with plastic tables and chairs and on the walls were pictures of Zradian historical events. The pictures disturbed Julian. At first glance they were like any ordinary epic painting but when he viewed one closely he realised it was in fact a video subdued in tone so that it was easy to watch casually but did not actually catch the eye and hold it the way television did. Julian watched one tale unfold and shuddered; it was so violent and he was sure the scene was videoed sometime in the past as it happened. He was glad Glord was working and not with them; the Half Pair saw through him too easily and made him feel uncomfortable and he wandered after D.G taking in the scene sure that Glord would make him feel even more uncomfortable by telling him about the picture stories. He shuddered.

"C'mon," said D.G. "I'll buy you a drink."

D.G led him to the bar and ordered two large glasses of beer handing one to Julian and paying for them with plastic tokens.

"What are those things D.G?" asked Julian, sure that he had missed something somewhere.

"What these?" said D.G. showing him a handful of plastic tokens.

Julian nodded.

"Tokens, money, dosh - you know - makes the world go round," D.G said, expansively. "You need it over here too. Did nobody give you any?"

Julian shook his head and drank some beer. Cor, this is good and where do I get some tokens? Can I have a gander?"

D.G gave him some tokens and watched him while he examined them testing the edges and looking carefully at the facias. At last he put them back on the counter and pushed them at D.G.

"I made those," he said. "I know I made them because I put a special serial number on them with my machine. We use them for the social club. I get all my stuff with them."

"You do what?" said D.G, grabbing his wrist. "What did you say?"

"Forget it D.G. the birds have come in. All you gotta do is pay for the bloody drinks and keep them happy. I got other things on me mind."

D.G. let him go and together they, as did the rest of the men in the bar, turned to stare at Glorida and Glorid and Angela as they strolled casually through the portal. Angela led the way to the bar and as casually as she had walked in asked for three glasses of the best Wastelands Brew. The barpair looked at her with a stricken surprised look.

"Excuse me?" he said.

"Three glasses of Wastelands Brew, cloth ears," she said. "There's the money now how about some service."

"I'm sorry but we don't serve women in here," the barpair said.

"Listen buster, I'm not taking that crap from anybody," said Angela, still smiling. "Cut the cackle and trot those drinks out to me or else."

The barpair leaned forward across the bar top and spoke firmly. "I am sorry but we do not serve women here - you will have to get one of the Pairs to buy for you. Yerk!"

The yerk! was because Angela grabbed one of the pair by his tunic collar and drew him across the top with one swift movement. She glared directly into his eyes and licked her lips drawing her knife from inside her tunic and laid the sharp blade against his neck.

"Tell your twin to get pouring three glasses of the best Wastelands Brew and do it now or I will start slitting your throat slowly. I promise I won't kill you but I will promise that I'll cut you. Now what do you say to that?" she said, smiling at him sweetly.

"He'll pour them directly," he said.

"Good, now we understand each other, I expect you will continue with the same prompt service throughout the rest of the evening, okay?"

"Okay, okay!"

When the beer arrived she handed one each to Glorid and Glorida and let the man go.

"Cheers sisters," she said.

They clinked glasses and drank.

The silence was so profound in the bar at that moment the clinking of their glasses sounded like the clanging of bells.

"Well don't just stand there, get on with it," she said, looking around at the groups of astonished Pairs. "You are supposed to be celebrating a victory. We have just had one of own."

D.G. shook his head and said to Julian. "We gotta get her out of here."

"She seems to be doing okay," Julian said, smirking.

D.G shrugged and with a smile on his face he took his beer in one hand and walked over to where Angela and Glorida and Glorid were standing. Julian tagged on behind him with mixed feelings. When it came to actually being face to face with the women he felt overawed. Usually he would want to disappear for a smoke but the Zradian medics had done something to him that stopped the craving.

"You have a toxin in you. We can get rid of it," the medical Pair explained telling him what was wrong with lots of technical stuff he did not understand except for the last bit. "...and we get rid of your craving. You will feel better." They were right, he did feel better and he no longer felt the need to light up a smoke but he had nothing else to give him confidence so he let D.G do the work.

"Hi girls," said D.G. "This is Julian from Earth - he and I are mates. I reckon we ought to grab a table and have a chat. You really showed 'em, Angela."

She frowned at him. "I made my point." Crisply.

He smiled weakly and said softly as Glorida and Glorid selected a table. "Don't push it too far or you will make a lot of enemies and find yourself shipped off to the enemy as a sacrifice."

"You telling me or warning me?"

"Both. I wouldn't want that to happen to you. The Polisocs would love to do nasty things to you. They like torture, rape and murder. It's their stock in trade. Mind you they're not too good at much else except feeding pigs."

"Tell me D.G. do you agree with this set up here?"

"Not really, it smacks of the President's regime. I'm sorry but there's still a lot of the old attitudes here. I'm afraid the older Pairs brought it with them. Rebellions change governments but not attitudes. Changing attitudes takes a revolution," he said, moving a chair out for her noticing she didn't protest. He sat down beside her not too surprised when Julian took a seat between Glorida and Glorid.

"D.G. I think you had better tell me about the Rebel Army," Angela said. "And just to keep the peace I'll let you buy the next round of drinks. I have an idea my moment of protest is past." She smiled at him and with a little start of embarrassment he realised he liked it.

"The rebel army sort of came together," he began. "Not through any real intention to form an army but Pairs did get together more or less for protection against the Polisocs who hate losing prisoners. Some Pairs came together because life in the cities got worse especially when the purges began. You never knew when you were going to be picked on. Eventually enough Pairs gathered in the Waste Lands to form small bands strong enough to attack the armed forces. As they got bigger so more people heard about it and then the New Moral Few popped up and started to give us specific tasks. After that the President got really angry and began a campaign against us. All that happened was we attracted more support and now we are getting new recruits almost daily. The only problem is the President has most of the resources."

"And what about you?" Angela asked.

"You really want to know?"

"Why not? That Pair are so busy listening to Julian bragging we'll never get any sense out of them - or him," she added the last quietly and rolled her eyes.

D.G. put his hand on hers and said. "I'll get more beer."

Back again with enough refills for them all he sat down and began his own story. Angela, he noticed, listened intently and as he warmed to his tale he forgot about the rest of the room.

"... And then when we met the patrol Angela kept between me and D.G. We looked after her all the way," Julian told Glorida.

"Great," said Glorida. "Do you really know about fires and explosives?"

"Yeah, well not so much about explosives but I do know a lot about fires. I'm well known for it back home," he said, proudly.

"We can use somebody like you in our army but the trouble is we only take on women. Men want to run things all the time and tell us what to do. We already know what to do," said Glorida.

"Yeah, a lot of blokes are like that," said Julian.

"Most blokes are like that," said Glorid.

"I suppose so," said Julian. "But not..."

"You are going to tell us you are not like other blokes I suppose," said Glorid. "Well be careful what you say mister because you might have to live up to it."

Her tone was a little bit impatient and Julian quailed inside. Had she seen through him? Was he about to get the old come uppance again like he did with all the bright ones? He hated women and their damn superior ways. All his adult life so far the women he really fancied turned out not to be bimbos and he couldn't handle that. He hoped desperately he hadn't blown it with all his bragging. All he wanted to do was impress Glorida. The other one could get stuffed, he thought, viciously. If she shut up he would be all right. He decided to back off.

"No, I'm not gonna tell you that because you won't believe me anyway, not unless I can prove it. I like being a bloke - a real bloke," he said and winked. "If you get what I mean?"

"Oh yes; BB, we know all about that," said Glorid, and grinned broadly.

"No need for that Glorid," said Glorida, reddening and looking angry.

Got 'em interested now, he thought, now I'll be in! But it was not to be. A bell donged softly and D.G. leaned over to explain.

"Award time Hero. Listen up and look attentive."

Julian sat back in his chair listening to the Pairs rabbitting on about heroics and calling on Pairs to come and get medals; boring. He drank more beer and in a break Angela bought them some more having no trouble with the barpair this time, and slowly and steadily Julian became quietly pissed. He heard his own name called out and somebody prodded him to go up and do his bit. It was very confusing and as he stood and gazed happily at the Pairs looking up at him he made a speech in reply to the small welcoming speech given by the old farts. He wasn't sure what they were asking him to do but it sounded all right. Whatever, it will impress Glorida anyway.

He spoke in English, or so he thought, he wasn't quite sure. "Well, yeah, all right, um, er, as you know I'm from Earth, a planet what you lot, well I mean, your stupid President, is trying to knock off. Well, you old farts, er, let me tell you what a difficult job that's going to be. We got all sorts of guns and things, and bombs, and fighting soldiers what is bloody good, and we got ships and things, and aircraft with cannons and bombs, and missuls what can blow things up. Your lot don't stand a bleedin' chance. Um, er. Yeah, and you know what me and D.G and Angela did before we got here, I mean, er, you heard the story of how we did in them polliwogs what they sent after us, well I can tell you, we can sort any of that lot out, especially with what I know about setting fires and explosives, and things, 'cos I'm a pretty good dude with a fire or a bomb, I mean, I'm well known for it back home. So, fuck it, if you four eyed gits want some of it then you've come to the right bloke. I mean, when it comes to that sort of thing I know what I'm fucking doing.

Anyway, I reckon that because you lot helped us out, I suppose I oughter be fucking grateful. I'm not going to say that I want to stay here all me natural," he leered at Glorida, "but until the world is sorted out I will, er, um, hang around with you if you get what I mean. After all you lot have give me food and teached me how to talk your crappy lingo, and now I have met up with some of you," he said, looking at Glorida and smirking. "I sort of feel as if I sort of belong. I know that we didn't sort of hit it off right away, that is you four eyed old farts and me, but now I knowed a bit more I reckon as how I can fit in and I ought to be thankful. Well I am and in return I suppose I'll have to do me bit alongside all you four eyed gits and show you what a real bloke is made of," he finished off, and looked at the crowd who seemed to be pleased with what he had said.

"You agree to undertake training in the service of the People's Rebel Army and loyally carry out all duties assigned to you from this day until we are victorious?" said the oldest Pair.

"Yeah, why not," he said, glancing at Glorida.

"Then put your hand on your hearts and repeat the oath."

He did as he was asked and repeated the old Pair's words, hardly registering what he was saying, and took the badge they gave him with a smile. They dismissed him with grins and handshakes of congratulations and he walked back to the table unsteady but elated. The other Pairs cheered and hooted as he sat down and he acknowledged their pleasure proudly.

"Do you realise what you have just done," asked D.G.

"No what?"

"You have just become a fighting member of the Rebel Army. Tomorrow, my friend, you will be given a uniform and start combat training. Julian Renfrew will become a front line soldier complete with laser gun and sword. I will be proud to hear of your exploits on the field of battle. You will be a hero," said D.G, his voice loaded with sarcasm.

Julian's face drained of colour and he glanced first at D.G and then at Angela who grinned broadly.

"No ... no ... I ... oh shit..." he ended, his mouth wide open as he realised what D.G was telling him.

"They use swords and knives," said Angela.

With a gasp Julian slid from his seat under the table in a dead faint.

Angela and D.G carried him by his shoulders and feet nodding with embarrassed looks as they passed amused and curious Pairs on their way out to the portal.

"He's overcome with emotion," Angela explained.

Which was true.

Betrayal

Julian shifted his feet and slashed down with the sword. The blades turned and slid off the target. The cutting edges hurtled back at him, and with a whimper of fear he let it go. The blades stuck in the soft barriers and the Trainer Pair cursed. In the next bay two Pairs giggled. Red faced, Julian turned away and walked out of the bay.

"I've had a gutful of this crap," he said, and headed for the exit.

Two swords slid from two sheaths and pointed unerringly at his throat. The points eased toward him and with a squeak he backed away forced into the bay again where he stood white faced and trembling.

"Pick up your weapon and try again," said the Trainer Pair.

Julian pulled the sword out of the barrier and slid it back into his sheath. He tried not to look at the Trainer Pair and waited for the count.

"One - draw! Two - cut! Three - up and side! Four - slice! Five - back slice! Six - thrust! Seven - over head slice! Eight - Slice and cut! Nine - upward slice! Ten - spin and present!"

This time he kept control of the blade and held it trembling in front of his body.

"Cut target!"

He cut down once and watched a piece fall off. He cut sideways and another piece fell. He cut up and another piece dropped off. And now it was the overhead downward slice. He took the sword around above his head and sliced down at an angle almost but not quite closing his eyes. This time the blades bit into the target and a piece fell off. He had done it!

"Okay Julian well done; now rest and afterwards we will show you how to use the knife," said the Trainer Pair.

Julian sheathed his sword with a flourish and this time he turned and walked smartly to the exit and realised in time that before could leave he had to salute. He turned and snapped his heels to attention and raised his sword hand palm outward and fingers straight up. Cranky salute, he thought, too scared to rebel.

"One long period and be back here on time," barked the Trainer Pair. "Dismiss!"

"Yes your Honour!" said Julian, smartly.

He wandered out of the training ground and found a seat. He sat down and put his head between his knees. For twenty two turns he had put up with being bossed around. They made him practice with the sword and the knife and that awful laser weapon. They laughed at him and made him train in separate bays. Sometimes he was made to train from early morning to late at night. They forced him to go to the gym and made him wrestle with two blokes at a time. And, worst of all, he hardly ever saw Glorida. The best part was that Angela seemed to be off somewhere else most of the time. He didn't mind that. D.G seemed to be occupied with some big project or other and he had discovered what the Pairs meant when they called him BB. It stood for Bulger Brain and that pissed him off more than anything else.

Whenever a Pair called him BB he cursed and gave them the fingers.

"Up yours Bulger Bum," he said and they laughed even more.

He hated that too.

He hated the place more than he hated anywhere else he had been. It was like a giant Borstal but he knew that instead of being released into a more or less friendly world he was destined to march with the Zradian effing Rebel effing Army and fight the poxy President's soldiers. For real. No Kung Fu and no running away. D.G explained what happened to you if you ran away. Besides, there was nowhere for him to go.

Tears rolled down his cheeks and dripped onto his uniform pants and evaporated in the hot suns. That was another thing. The ratbag planet was too bloody hot and dusty. The food was lousy and people hardly ever talked to him. He may as well be on Earth. At least there he had mates. He was in a mess and it was all his bloody flatmate's fault, walking out on him, leaving him with nothing. He smashed his fist down on the bench.

"Ow!"

"Ow what?" said a voice near him.

D.G strolled casually along the pathway and sat on the seat beside him.

"What's up hero?"

Julian glowered at him and sniffed.

"You don't understand D.G." he said and snuffled.

D.G took one of his hands in his and shook his head.

"Listen Julian, in this place you have to pull your weight in whatever way is useful to us. You have stated publicly that you are willing to serve us and now you are being trained to do just that. Soon you will be taken out on a patrol to get you used to working in a team. The Pairs will teach you a lot of useful things and show you how to read the land. When you can do that you will be able to survive. Now don't worry about danger and all that because when the battle starts to get going things happen so fast that if you have learned the lessons well then you will be fine. Just do your best."

"Can't I just do things behind the lines or something?" Julian said, snuffling some more.

"Unless you are really skilled or you are Leader Pair I am afraid you will have to fight. Sorry," said D.G.

Julian looked at him. Right now he hated D.G. He was like the rest, all blood and guts and murder. Why couldn't somebody else fight? Why couldn't he keep his big mouth shut?

Julian let the tears flow and his whole body shook uncontrollably.

"I don't want to fight anybody!" he wailed.

D.G let him cry and then gently wiped his face with a cloth.

"All right Julian I will see what I can do," he said. "Now dry the tears and come with me, we can have a drink and then I suppose you will have to go back to training?"

Julian nodded and together they went into the canteen where D.G bought two large cold drinks and led him to a table. They sat looking out at the quad where Pairs were marching and mock skirmishing. Julian shuddered.

"You're not cut out for this are you?" said D.G.

"No, all I want to do is get on with my life," Julian said, miserably.

"This is part of your life," said D.G. "Until the war is over you can't go back to Earth and even if you did go back there is a little matter of one dead Policeman, a house fire and some unpaid bills. Here at least you have a chance to learn something useful."

Julian looked at D.G and his lower lip trembled.

"I'm scared D.G," Julian said and gripped his mug tightly.

D.G gazed at him for a long time and then he sighed.

"Okay. I'll do my best to find another duty for you. Trust me Julian, I'll think of something."

Julian relaxed and visibly brightened.

"Will you?" he said.

D.G nodded and looked at the clock. It was time for Julian to go back to training.

They parted outside the training bays and D.G grinned as he left calling over his shoulder. "Go to it hero."

Julian almost cursed him but instead he gave him a thumbs up sign and walked into the training area feeling almost enthusiastic.

Angela pushed another flimsy into the scanner and pressed the buttons. She pressed them gently and deliberately and with a sarcastic tone she spoke into the floating microphone.

"Now run along and do something with that," she said. "And while you are at it please give my regards to the group of male chauvinists who insist that I carry out such simple tasks." She knew the computer would edit her remarks, but she made them anyway.

She did the work because she understood that if she didn't then there would be no food and no room and no freedom. She used the terminal to discover more about the planet pushing aside the information about the republic to concentrate on the geography of the place. She was surprised to learn how the rest of the planet was described by the northern section, the republican version lacked depth and accuracy. She delved deeper and discovered the area beyond the desert drawing up visual maps of the past and sat watching them as they scrolled.

"I wish I could see it all," she said.

She was surprised when the computer booked her in for a session in the learning rooms.

"Operative Breen, continue with your work. The appointment made is the first session which must be taken in your leisure time. Thank you."

"Thank you. I will continue with my labours," she said remembering what happened when she asked for duties to be allocated. "You work and you eat," said the Leader Pair with a sickly smile. "And women work in either the domestic or clerical sphere."

She chose clerical, and when she realised they gave her the simplest tasks she was angry. White hot angry. She fumed but said nothing. The first two turns she spent learning the system and the next turn she tapped into some of the minor programs. The fourth turn she found a way to amuse herself by adding sarcastic riders to all the memos that passed through her hands. At the end of the fifth turn Glorid came to see her in her room and made her an offer.

"If you want to get out of here we have a way," she said.

"And how's that?"

We can second you to the Women's Rebel Army," she replied.

"Then do that please as soon as possible," Angela said, bitterly.

"All you have to is come with us and just fit in. We leave here in another thirty turns so when we go we will take you with us. In the meantime keep at it and whenever we have a spare moment we will teach you to use our weapons. A deal?"

Angela smiled and breathed a sigh of relief.

"Good. I needed that because soon, if nothing happened, I was going to wage a one woman war against these pigs," she said, and made a chopping motion with her hand. "A clerk or a washer woman!"

Glorid laughed loudly and replied. "The trousered ones are worse in the Republic."

"Then it has to be death to the republic," said Angela emphasising the use of the lower case.

She and Glorid and Glorida met that evening and the Pair showed her how to use the sword. The next evening they showed her the knife and explained how to get the best out of a laser weapon. After that they did a series of intense sessions doing unarmed combat. Angela enjoyed their sessions discovering within herself hidden skills and discovering also that her capacity for prayer was slowly diminishing. That bothered her.

The learning sessions taught her a lot about the planet. She discovered that south of the desert there was extensive plantations, a large inland sea that on the western shore was bounded by high mountains that further west led down to an ocean that in the north and south was a labyrinth of islands where once people lived and fished. She looked at the lands and realised that the republic had lost the plot and she could not understand why it was not occupied. The narrator answered her question summing up the republic's viewpoint.

"The NMF program of disinformation has persuaded the republic that the rest of the lands other than the northern sector, shown on the globe, are contaminated by nuclear radiation. That is true to a point: that being the land produces virtually nothing. The desert lands, that are known as 'the wastelands' is also contaminated likewise but the radiation levels are low. The danger to the President's forces is the rebel patrols."

Angela thought about that statement and wondered why the President's people didn't take the trouble to find out and attack the rebels on their home ground.

There was no answer to that question.

D.G stood with one foot on the edge of the bench and the other firmly on the floor. The Elder Pair had finished and was casting about with their eyes for some response. The subject under discussion was Julian Renfrew, and D.G was trying to make sense of what the Elder had said.

"Excuse me your Honour would you mind repeating that?"

"We have two courses of action open to us. First we can persevere and train Julian up and send him off to battle or we can take him out in the desert and quietly dispose of him. I am in favour of the latter. It is cheaper," said the Elder.

D.G had a different idea.

The Elder Pair stared at him and said. "He is your responsibility Drogl so you can get rid of him. We want it done soon."

"I could do the job much easier," said D.G.

"And guarantee he will bother us no more?"

"Yes, your Honour."

"Well then you must do it."

The Elder looked away and nodded to an Aide.

"Call in the stenographer."

Almost as if they were waiting for their cue Glorid and Glorida entered and immediately took their place. The work was simple, all they were required to do was monitor the visual as the conversation was recorded, now and then making corrections. They worked for two long periods and when the session was over they logged the recordings and programmed the copy schedule. Glorida glanced at Glorid when the Pairs were gone and whispered.

"Did you hear what they said?"

"Yes but what about it?"

"I have to warn Julian. They're going to kill him."

Julian lay on his bed too tired to move. He groaned when his gong sounded and lazily he pressed the enter button.

"Go away D.G," he said.

"It's not D.G and I will not go away because I need to talk to you and I need to talk now," Glorida said.

Julian sat up suddenly. Immediately alert, he smiled at her as she came and sat on the bed next to him. He licked his lips and started to speak but she frowned at him.

"Be quiet and listen. I was in the headquarters office and I heard them talking about you. Julian, they want to get rid of you. I heard them discussing how and where they were going to do it. Some thought it might be a good idea if they let you go out on a patrol and not come back and others wanted, er, somebody to sort of take you somewhere and kill you," she said, and quickly took his hands in hers.

He tried to tear them away and looked around wildly. Panic. People wanted to kill him. He felt his bowels churn and a cold flood of fear begin to chill him from the pit of his stomach. They, wanted to kill, him.

"Lock the place up! Don't let them get near me!" Dancing on the end of her arms head swinging from side to side. Eyes staring. Wild and frightened.

"It's okay Julian they are only talking about it, so far," she said. "No need to panic at least we know what they intend. Fore warned is fore armed."

"But what can I do?" he wailed. "They want to kill me. I knew they didn't like me. I don't want to ..." He paused and realised he was sounding like a coward in front of her, Glorida of all people. "...have to fight them all," he continued.

"You won't have to fight anybody yet. My twin and I will leave soon and if you want you can come with us. If you want to that is?"

He stared at her and sat on the edge of the bed imagining what it would be like with her close by all the time. She smiled warmly and his mind raced with possibilities. None of them had anything to do with fighting. Cor. He thought. Cor.

"I would like you to come," she said.

Cor. She fancies me.

"Of course I'll come," he said, expansively. "You might need a bloke around."

She looked at him sideways.

"Of course I bet you can guess who it is who they have ordered to kill you?" she asked, and looked at him coyly.

He looked at her and his mouth dropped open when he realised who she was talking about but asked anyway. "It's D.G isn't it?"

She nodded.

"The bastard!" he yelled getting up off the bed. "The rotten stinking back stabbing bastard!" He stomped around the room as he spoke and glowered at her. "You sure?"

"I heard him," she said.

He stopped walking and looked at her intently.

"What am I going to do. I can't fight them all," he said, trying to sound calm and smooth like Bernard Lasalle in La Lune when he learned his gang wanted to terminate him. He didn't feel like Lasalle. But Glorida expected him to be brave and calm and all those things that he wasn't, didn't she?

"Just stay here and wait. Do what you normally do each turn and when Glorid and me decide to leave we will whip you out of here with us, okay?" She put her hand on his arm and smiled at him. "Now I had better go before the night watch catches us together."

She left his room as quickly and quietly as she came and he sat on the bed with the portal closed and shivered. Kill him! D.G was out to kill him? What happened to "I'll see what I can do?" bastard.

"Bastard bastard bastard bastard BASTARD!" he cried out.

Ambush

Angela sat on the bench and eased her sheathed boots from her feet. She shook sand out of each boot in turn and whacked them against the bench to make certain the last grains were gone. She wiggled her toes in the breeze enjoying the flow of air. Her other pair were still in the wash. She liked that. Washable boots. You simply opened them up and shoved them in the wash with your tunic. And your smalls, she added. The system was convenient but, and it was a big but, it was the women who did the work along with the cooking and most of the cleaning. She did one or two sessions with one of the crews. The Pairs were cheerful and seemed to accept their lot and she noticed that there were some older male Pairs doing the same work too. Now and then some of the soldier Pairs on fatigues worked on cleaning too but they always worked separately. She was amused and annoyed by the way men went to great lengths to look good in uniform and yet, like Julian, would never keep their rooms tidy. The other trait they had was, like their Earthbound counterparts, they slobbed out in front of the television. The men on this dusty planet, she reflected, seemed to expect women to do all the housework and the cooking and all the underpaid jobs.

Well, not her, she was not going to be a kitchen skivvy.

She kept the sword and the knife although she knew there was no chance of her claiming the laser weapons. The men didn't like her keeping those, she was much too handy with them and that ability bothered them. She smiled to herself remembering the look of fear and surprise on the Pair's faces when she singed their uniforms. She liked the look of respect on D.G's face when she told him about the ambush. She looked up from her reflections when a shadow appeared at her feet.

"Ah Glorid," she said "You look worried, what is it?"

Glorid sat on the bench and turned a little sideways so she was looking directly into her face.

"It's Julian," she said.

"What has he done now?" said Angela, resigned to sorting out yet another problem. Three times she had spoken to D.G and his twin Glord on Julian's behalf. Once when he insulted the Leader Pair in charge of his training. Again when he refused to observe protocol with the Elders and again when the committee refused to pay him. That was the hardest plea of all. The men argued that he had to pull his weight, and as he wasn't, then he should suffer. Angela argued that as he was a guest rather than a recruit then he should be given an allowance. The committee showed her a translation of his speech into their own language and demanded an explanation. She told them what he was really like and defiantly defended him. He may be useless at some things, she said, but he was a good worker and if they put him onto something he could do he would be useful. Like stores or making things, she told them. He will never make a soldier.

"There's no room for hangers-on," said the Elder Pair, spitefully. "We only need fighting Pairs here or those that are meant to serve. Everybody has to be in their rightful place."

It was then she realised that it was not Julian they were angry at but her.

"It's nothing he has done. We overheard the committee talking about him and they virtually ordered D.G to kill him. They want to send him out on patrol and lose him. Or D.G is supposed to take him out and slit his throat or something. A useless mouth they call him," she said, and took Angela's hand in hers.

Angela was quiet for a few small periods and then she looked at Glorid.

"They've got something against me I think and this is one way they can get at me. Can we get him out of here?" she said. "I'd hate to think I have left him to their mercy. He is human after all."

"I thought he was your, er, special, er, lover," Glorid said.

Angela blushed and looked at Glorid with a slight flush of anger mixed with embarrassment. "What makes you think that, no, he is not, I am not that sort of girl," she said.

"Okay, no big deal, so we leave him to get killed then?" Glorid said, and shrugged her shoulders dismissively.

"No, of course not. We get him out if we can." Angela looked meaningfully at Glorid. "And if I can I'll settle D.G's hash as well."

Glorid grinned. "Attahalf pair," she said, and playfully punched her lightly on her shoulder.

"What are you planning to do?" asked Angela.

"Glorida and I have fixed up a plan. All you have to do is be ready to move when I come for you. Keep a battle dress tunic ready and boots. You will need your weapons and we will arrange to get you a laser and some capsules. Okay?"

Angela smiled. Glorid let go her hand and smiled back.

"I suppose we will have to get back to work. Hang in there sister," said Glorid.

Glorid walked off in the direction of the clerical section and Angela watched her go.

"Okay D.G - you over played your hand there my friend. How dare you threaten my Julian," she said quietly. But the words were hollow and when she thought of Julian she didn't have that feeling. Only a sadness. Betrayal.

Julian walked warily. Whenever he passed any Pairs he was always sure to keep his distance. His eyes darted from side to side and any sudden move sent him into what he hoped was a defence posture. Since Glorida had warned him he was constantly on watch. His nerves were shot and he was torn between avoiding D.G and therefore minimising his exposure and wanting to know where the bastard was. Each orbit he checked the posting lists and during training sessions he watched fearfully for any false move. He was so watchful that the Trainer Leader Pair made a note on his daily report that Julian was in fact improving. Julian saw the Leader Pair watching him and trembled. Everybody was against him.

On the fourth orbit during the breakfast period Glorid managed to slip him a note. He desperately wanted to read the note but so far he had had no chance. It was lunch time now and he had eaten his food quickly and made excuses to go outside. He crossed the gap between two buildings and nearly fainted when two Pairs came out of a side street and marched directly at him. He hopped out of their way quickly and cursed under his breath when they marched past sniggering. He hated it when that happened.

He found a free bench and sat down taking the note from his pocket and unfolded it rubbing the creases out on his knee.

"Julian, get ready. Tonight I will come for you. Have your blades with you and a strong tunic. Be ready to go the moment I come. We will get packs on the way and laser weapons, I hope. Until then keep dodging Pairs. - love Glorida."

He read the note through twice and stuffed it back in his pocket. What does she mean 'keep dodging Pairs', he wondered.

The rest of the day dragged slowly but at last after dinner he went to his room. Too tired to remain awake and too worried to sleep he lay on his bunk fully dressed. Nervous and frightened he lay on the bunk with his knife ready for use. Kung Fu killer Renfrew. Danger man. Bullshit. These bastards were out to kill him. He was asleep when Glorida came and shook his shoulder to wake him.

He twisted out of the bed with the knife in his hand. She took it from him casually almost as if he had given it her and when he fell back on the bed she handed it back to him.

"You ought to take it out of the sheath first," she said.

He took the weapon from her and said. "I'm glad I saw you in time.

She tilted her head to one side and looked amused.

He slashed down with his hand and said. "Dead meat."

"Never mind the hero stuff get up and follow me and for Nong's sake go quietly," she said.

She led the way out of his room through the corridors of the men's section and up and out to the defence area. She led him along a narrow service corridor to a low stores area and there they stopped while she unlocked a heavy electronic portal. Inside, the room was a rack filled with laser weapons and quickly she selected two and handed one to him. She handed him a pack of capsules and he strapped them to his body. She tossed a pack to him and he shrugged it over his shoulders and lastly she handed him a water bottle.

"Right soldier let's get going," she said, and opened the opposite portal. A long ramp led down to a dark courtyard and at the bottom she whispered and pressed him against the wall with a free hand.

"We wait here until the guard changes and then we run out. Okay?"

"Yes," he croaked.

They waited for what seemed like a whole division but was in fact only ten short periods and then there was a tramp of boots from the corridor opposite and lights approaching. Julian's heart thumped and his knees felt like water. He thought he might faint but the fear of being discovered made him resolute and he fought the feeling. The new guard stomped to a halt in front of the gate and greeted the old guard with the regulation password and salute. The gate slid open with a rattle and scrape and a slight mechanical hum.

"Now!" hissed Glorida, and started to run.

Blindly he followed her out into the pool of light running hard for the open land beyond the fort. Julian needed no heeding to run and legged it as fast as he could over the rocky terrain passing Glorida who was stumbling in the dark. He didn't care. All he was interested in was getting as far away from the fort as possible before the guard Pairs woke up to what had happened and began shooting at them. Glorida ran up behind him following his lead as he dodged the rocks and clumps of bushes in their path. Slashes of laser fire raced up from the fort and, whimpering with fear, he ran faster.

"Slow down to a more regular pace you idiot," Glorida shouted. "A steady lope is what you need. It's safer and we will cover more ground. We keep this pace up and they will catch us for sure."

He slowed the pace until he was jogging rather than racing. He was surprised to realise that he could keep any pace up at all. Whatever the Zradian war training had done to him at least it had given him the strength to run. The laser sweeps stopped and he grinned. The good old Renfrew luck again. He felt like a hero. Make sure Glorida was safe. Yeah. And all he had to do was keep going and stay with her.

D.G listened to the quiet voice in the earphones and answered softly.

"West gate two and both parties got away?"

"Yes. We are giving chase. They are heading west and north. I will contact four red patrol in a few small periods."

"Report as you progress please," said D.G.

"Wilco."

D.G lifted the earphones from his head and laid them on the bench. He walked from the listening post to the next room and spoke to the Pair sitting at their console.

"Quarry heading in the general direction of the women's rebel army camp. Four red are in place?"

The Pair nodded.

"Good, then we do what we have to do, okay?"

The Pair nodded again.

D.G smiled. "Our mister Renfrew is in for a surprise I think?" he said.

This time the Pair grinned and nodded. "We can say goodbye to him?"

D.G looked at them and nodded in his turn.

"Yeah, he's now somebody else's problem.

The Pair sighed, relieved.

The patrol heard Julian and Glorida rather than saw them and they realised the fugitives were well ahead. With their night goggles adjusted over their eyes they trotted after them amazed at the pace the Earthman was setting. Up ahead there was a gully and the Leader Pair said they should bypass that and get ahead using the cliff road instead. The Earthman was setting a fast pace almost as if he could see in the dark. They had their orders. Keep up and catch up. Force the pace and keep them moving. It was going to be a long night, thought the Leader Pair.

The Leader Pair of patrol four red listened to the radio and then passed orders to the other patrol Pairs.

"They will come up the gully ahead according to four patrol blue," he said, and led the Pairs to the edge.

The patrol settled down to wait. They waited patiently with their laser weapons at hand ready for use, alert and listening for the noise of moving Half Pairs. The sky turned slowly from deep purple to pink and in the west Zaras rose first peeking its rim over the edge of the horizon. Zarad himself would follow adding his warmth to the morning and heightening the softer first light colours from wispy purple, blue through red to harsher more vibrant hues. The birds squawked a welcome to both stars and the Leader Pair signalled they should get ready.

Panting and flushed Julian appeared over the ridge followed by Glorida and for a brief moment they stood at the top of the track and turned to look back.

That's not where the danger is, thought the Leader Pair and gave the signal.

The top of the gully became a bath of converging fire.

Angela slipped out of the gate with Glorid's whispered instructions still clear in her mind. She hit the dark patch to the left of the gate and ran steadily on a parallel track to Julian and Glorida. She was amazed at how fast Julian was running but grinned to herself when she realised his motivation was sheer unadulterated fear. She almost ran into the patrol but stopped and slipped behind a rock glad that she had stumbled on them in time.

The Leader Pair were talking on the radio and from what she heard there was another patrol up ahead. They were setting a trap for Julian and Glorida. What was going on, she asked. She listened carefully and gathered that some few kilometres[9] along the track there was a gully which Julian must pass through to reach the hills. Another patrol was waiting at the head of the gully ready to ambush them. Angela listened closely and remembered the general directions Glorid had given her. She had intended to march along a different track which Glorid said was a little less direct than the one Glorida planned to take but was a lot easier. She heard the patrol Leader Pair stop speaking as he closed the circuit and give a rapid string of orders calling on the Pairs to move. Angela set off the moment they had gone and ran hard, glad of the fitness training the two women had given her. She reached the ridge well before dawn and marched cautiously along the top aware of the light change as the suns rose.

She saw the patrol spread out at the top of the gully and moved slower but more cautiously behind a shelter of rocks looking for a vantage point that would cover the patrol and the gully.

She saw Julian and Glorida a few small periods before the patrol and with a quick muttered prayer she fired. She saw Julian leap for cover. Glorida unshipped her laser and dropped behind a rock firing at the patrol and then there was flame and smoke as laser plasma

---

[9] *The Zradian measurement system was based on the French metre. How it happened was never really understood but as the Zradians had never heard of Napoleon Bonaparte one can only assume that the French had actually learned of the metre from the Zradians, and that is a mystery in itself.*

bounced off rocks and splashed like napalm over the ambush. The fight was over in a few short periods. Angela raised her head and waved at Glorida. With her laser weapon on ready she left her hiding place and walked down to where Glorida was standing. She strolled up to the other woman and smiled.

"Thank you sister," said Glorida.

"Where's Julian?"

Glorida turned and inclined her head grinning broadly.

"He's cowering in the rocks here with his head down and his arse up," she said, and kicked with her boot at something that yelled.

Angela approached and looked down at Julian who had covered his head with his hands and was pressed close to the ground bent over a rock trying to crawl further under another pushing at the sand with his feet.

"Get up hero," she said, and poked him with the barrel of the laser.

He jerked back and up and hit his head and crashed sideways.

"Christ, did you have to do that?" he said, and slipped sideways some more to avoid her flying foot.

"Don't take the Lord's name in vain," she said. "Get up and arm that gun; we have work to do. There's another patrol on its way."

He stood up and reluctantly picked up the laser weapon. He switched the cells on and slipped the safety latch over the firing button. He looked scared but grimly held the weapon close to him and looked around wildly.

"Where are they? Where's the ratbags? Who...?"

Angela shook her head.

"They are down in the gully and moving up. We are going down to meet them and kill them. You are expected to do your bit, okay?" she said, and grinned at Glorida. "Our hero is not too good at this is he?"

Glorida looked annoyed and pursed her lips. "He's okay," she said, emphatic.

Angela glanced at her sharply. Oh no, she thought, not that, not for him, silly woman. Now she knew what was going on she felt relieved. Julian had an admirer. And this one couldn't see past his stories. Pathetic.

"You're right, he is okay," she said with a hint of sarcasm.

It was Glorida's turn to glance sharply.

Feral creature, thought Angela, she looks like an animal at bay. Dangerous. Fey. Lovable.

"There's a patrol moving up on you from below. They must be in the gully by now. Do you want to stop them or run?" Angela said and changed the capsule in her laser almost nonchalantly.

"I think we should stop them," said Glorida and licked her lips.

Definitely fey, thought Angela.

Together they moved stealthily down to a low ridge keeping behind cover as much as possible and when they had reached a good vantage point Glorida said she would take one side of the track if Angela would take the other. Angela insisted Julian stay with her.

"If he doesn't shoot I will encourage him," she said adding a wicked grin.

This time Glorida smirked but said nothing. Julian settled down beside her and with nervous fingers released the catch cover and pushed the safety button across. His weapon was now armed.

"Get another capsule ready Julian," Angela said.

He obeyed her and she was satisfied when he placed it on the ground near at hand. They waited until the patrol were struggling up the slope and then with a grin Angela aimed and sent off the first blast. It hit the Leader Pair taking them completely by surprise. From the opposite side of the track Glorida fired and another Pair went down. Julian froze.

"Shoot the naughty people my love," said Angela, menacingly.

Julian aimed his weapon and fired. His shot burned rocks and incinerated some plants before it hit a target and a Half Pair went down leaving his twin staring in disbelief at the dead body. And then it was their turn to come under fire. The remainder of the patrol recovered and headed for cover to shoot back. Fire laced across the gap and Julian screamed.

"Keep shooting Julian or they will kill you," yelled Angela. "Glorida is counting on you." She said the last spitefully and noted his angry glance and his determination when he aimed his weapon again. After that she was too busy shooting to worry about him. She heard his weapon ripping beside her and then suddenly there was no more return fire.

"Watch the flanks," she called out to Glorida.

Smoke rose into the sky and there was an appalling stench of burnt flesh but there was no signs of resistance from the patrol. Cautiously she lifted her head above the rocks. Nothing. She ducked down again and moved past Julian.

"Stay here and watch below. Cover me while I skirt around their position. Glorida knows what to do but watch out for her as well okay?"

"Yeah, all right, but you will be back?" he asked anxiously.

"I hope so," she said.

Angela moved from cover to cover until she reached the position where the patrol had holed up. She moved slowly and quietly and then with a deep breath and her laser at the ready she kept close to the rock and moved quickly alert and prepared to fire. All she found was seven dead bodies and with her own protection in mind she stepped down onto the track. She heard a noise above her and aimed but did not fire. Glorida stood on a rock.

"Hold it. The rest of the patrol have skipped. We carry on I guess," she said.

"Where are they?"

"Way down the track and still running," said Glorida.

They walked back up the track to where Julian was still crouching. He held the laser tightly his knuckles showing white, his knees trembling and his eyes screwed shut.

"It's all right Julian, you can relax now, the fight is over and we have chased them off. We have to get moving," Glorida said and gently removed the weapon from his fingers and disarmed it. She picked up the unused capsule and handed it to him. "Come on, we have to get going, it is safe now."

"We beat them?"

Glorida nodded.

Julian visibly brightened and brushed his lank hair back with his hand and grinned.

"Great, did you see how I shot the shit out them. Must have been my shooting that made the difference. Yeah, must have frightened them off with the old Renfrew Kung Fu, eh?" he said, and puffed out his chest standing up to look around and especially down at the bodies on the path.

"We did it eh?" he repeated.

"Yeah we sure did," said Glorida giving Angela a warning look when she started to protest. "Now we have to get going and find my own army."

A few short periods later they topped the head of the gully. Carrion birds were already digging at the bodies with their sharp double bills and Julian shuddered when he saw them. The birds flew up from their feast squawking angrily as they passed. Julian slowed and kicked one of the bodies smirking as his boot hit the dead flesh.

"Take that," said Angela, sarcastically.

Julian turned his head aside not looking at her and Glorida gave her another warning glance. Wisely Julian gathered up spare capsules and handed them around taking some for his own gun and despite the fear of attack he felt a little better.

Glorid stood on the square and in a quiet voice answered the Elder Pair.

"I did not know about the patrols," she said. "And if I had I would have protested most strongly and never have risked my twin. In fact I have already sent a strong protest to my High Leader Pair. It was a dirty trick to ambush the Earthman and put my twin in danger. For this reason I resign my position here and request that I be transported to my own army headquarters. I wish the credit of tokens I am owed be paid immediately and an apology conveyed to my High Leader Pair."

Her voice did not rise above an even tone, and as she spoke she glanced angrily at D.G. She knew that in spite of her efforts to assist Julian's escape she was in the right. There was no cause for the committee to murder Julian once he was off their hands. And D.G; Drogl. Treacherous swine. Had he arranged the ambush? If he had then he had to pay for his treason. She glared at him and he looked away. Shifty Bulger.

"No matter, you should have not assisted them," said the Elder Pair.

She looked up, defiant, disliking the way they stuck to tradition and spoke as one. She wished she was allowed to have her weapons so she could kill Drogl but they had insisted she leave them behind. The Elder Pair looked unhappy and she knew they would let her go. They had no choice. The flimsy ordering her return to camp was on their desk.

"However, you will leave. We will arrange for you to be transported to the pick up point this turn. We would warn you that any further breach of our security or regulations will be treated with grave consequences. Dismiss."

She bowed and turned on her heel and marched out of the hall. D.G followed her but she heard the Elder Pair call him back. I don't want to talk to you, she thought, get stuffed. She grinned when she thought of what she had said. A typical Julian remark.

D.G watched her go and shook his head. There goes one angry Half Pair, he thought. But he had no time to reflect. The Elder Pair wanted an explanation. He turned to face them.

"What went wrong Drogl?"

"We over reacted. He was only meant to be frightened but somebody gave orders for him to be killed. I did not," he said, defiant. "I repeat, I did not."

"What we are angry about is the Pairs that died in the operation. This Earth woman caught up with them and lay in wait and ambushed Pairs. She killed a patrol and helped the others to kill nearly half of another patrol. Somebody let her out and somebody trained her to fight. We are not happy about that Drogl."

He looked at the Elder Pair and almost grinned. Angela. What a woman. So she had got away and did for them. Good. All he had wanted was to get Julian away from these vindictive Bulgers. The plan had almost misfired. He would find out who gave the orders and kill them. He liked Glorida and Glorid and in spite of his failings he liked Julian too. Besides, Julian was an innocent in all this. He doubted if he knew what was going on. D.G had fought hard to keep Julian alive. He had had to argue a long time to get them to agree to let him go. He had deliberately arranged for Glorid and Glorida to overhear the discussion. He had monitored the Pair's activities and even spoken to Glorid dropping hints about what was to happen. He knew that she blamed him for the attack. Maybe he should have told her more bluntly instead of just hinting. The surprise was Angela. He hadn't counted on her going too. He thought about the idea and realised he should have guessed. Lucky for Julian she had gone. He wondered how she had known about the patrols. It was obvious she did. Glorid? The only answer unless somebody else told her.

"I am sorry your Honour but Angela was a surprise to me too," he said.

"You will seek them out and destroy them," said the Elder Pair.

D.G stared at them.

"What?" he said, shocked.

"That is your orders."

Not too good on grammar this Pair, he thought, and not too good on sensitivity either.

"I am sorry your Honour but I cannot carry out that request," he said emphasising the word request.

"You will do as you are asked."

"No your Honour, I will not do this thing and I will oppose any move to carry out such a mission. This is a vengeful act you are asking me to carry out. I will refuse to do so and oppose anybody that wants to support such a move. I have spoken." He stood in the warrior stance and placed his gaze exactly between them.

The Elder Pair drew a deep breath and their faces glowed with anger.

"You will do as you are ordered," they said, their voices cold, hard and insistent. They leaned on the desk and glared at him. The guards moved forward with their hands touching their swords.

"I can kill you before the guards reach me," he said, quietly. "After that I do not care because I will take a sword from one Half Pair and fight until I have killed everybody or I am dead. Your choice. Back off or it will happen."

He dropped into a killing stance and behind him Glord moved into the ready support posture. It was fight or whatever the odds now and D.G felt calm, ready and happy. He liked fighting. Especially when he had his twin close behind him.

Hastily the Elder Pair waved the guards back with frightened gestures.

"Do you have an alternative?" They asked and he saw hatred in their eyes.

"Yes. Let him go and let the fates take their course. Sooner or later the Polisocs will get him or he will end up in a fire fight and get killed. I say leave him alone. He is an Earthman and there are people on Earth who care for him. I do not want to be accused of his murder."

The Elder Pair glowered at him but he knew he had won. Whatever they did things had gone too far to remain secret. In that respect he was glad that he had leaked the information to Glorid and hence to Angela.

"This time we will let you get away with it Drogl but we will not let the incident go without comment. In future you will be placed on active service. You and your twin will be placed in combat situations at all times subject to the requirements of the fighting Liberating Army. Do you understand?"

"Perfectly," replied D.G. "You will send us out to fight the enemy?"

"Exactly."

"Then we will do our best to serve the cause."

The Elder Pair looked at him puzzled. You would do that, he thought, you are so far out of touch you think it is a punishment to be in the thick of the fighting. Glord and myself are happy to be in action. Thanks. The Elder Pair grunted and with a wave of their hands he spoke only one word. "Dismiss."

He bowed and turned abruptly and walked out of the committee room.

Outside in the corridor Glord joined him and grinning broadly took his hand and squeezed it.

"Great my twin. Now we can get out of here and do what we do best. Kill the enemy," said Glord. "I have been waiting for this. Ace!"

D.G looked at him and laughed. "Bloody Julian again!"

Glord chuckled and together they marched to the training rooms.

Outside, in the compound a hover wagon waited with its motor humming quietly. On board were two female Pairs both fully armed and the small male patrol that were going with the driver Pair. A lone figure, now fully armed and carrying a light bag, ambled out from the building and clambered into the back of the vehicle. She casually sat in the seat assigned to her and the vehicle moved off. Less than two hundred metres from the gate as the party headed up the hill track she just as casually aimed her gun at the patrol Pairs and forced them to disarm. Five kilometres further along the track, with the help of the two female Pairs, she ordered the males to start walking and forced the driver to speed up.

"My twin and her friends can walk but I want to get back to camp in style and explain personally why I and my twin do not ever wish to be sent to the Rebel headquarters again unless we are fully armed and fully operational.”

She spoke so that the driver Pair would understand every word and took great delight in holding a knife out near them as if to suggest that if they were brave enough to try anything she would kill them. Ten kilometres from their camp she stopped the wagon and threw the driver Pair out and five hundred metres further on she dropped their weapons and some provisions on a rock where they would easily find them.

“That will give the trousered ones something to think about,” she said, and drove the wagon the remaining nine kilometres doing easily with one pair of hands what the Pair accomplished with two. Her companions piled the captured weapons in neat piles in the rear of the wagon and sang a bright Rebel song.

Julian - the Bomber

Julian liked the bombs. He liked the noise. He liked the fire and above all he liked the power. He wasn't too keen on the idea of using them. Like out on patrol. Sabotage. The Trainer Pair, two fat older women with a warped sense of humour, took to him straight away. When the two old chooks in charge told him what they wanted him to do he panicked.

"What? Me? Into enemy territory? And do what?"

"All we want you to do is learn to set bombs and incendiaries. Blow things up. You will be well protected. Our assessment shows that is what you will be good for. You will be in the same troop as Glorida and Glorid and Angela."

He looked at the High Leader Pair thoughtfully. His mind raced with arguments for and against. The alternative was too horrible to consider. He was either going to be a bomber and work behind enemy lines or a soldier and confront the enemy head on. There was no way they, the women, would let him stay behind in the camp.

"Why can't I do the cooking or something?"

"That task is for the experts. We want good food for our Pairs. You need proper training for that sort of work. This way we use your natural ability and you become a hero."

"I don't want to be a hero," he said, plaintively.

"But what about Glorida?"

"What about her?"

"She specifically asked me to place you with her troop," said the High Leader Pair with a silky persuasive edge to her voice.

He gave in and took to the training like a duck to water. In spite of the nagging thought that when he finished training he was to be sent into active service he knuckled down to the task with enthusiasm. The days passed and he was aware that Glorida and Glorid were often out on patrol and Angela had gone with them three times already. He didn't see much of them but he was so busy learning the craft he didn't take much notice. The camp routine was regular and strict, if you didn't like being told what to do, but it was much more relaxed than the men's camp. A musical siren announced the time to get up and Julian had discovered that he had to hurry or he would get nothing to eat. He washed and went to the latrines and as soon as he was dressed he lined up for breakfast. He made sure after the first few days to clean his bowls and cutlery having suffered the embarrassment of his being left dirty on the table with no time to clean them for lunch or dinner. The work was all right but at first he found the routine hard. One session each turn was spent training with weapons, and then it was off to the Pair Lavia for teaching in the art of explosives. Their training ground was a fair way from the main camp and he was always short of time getting to the cafeteria. He learned to clean his bowls after that and had a much better time at meals. The food was good, as good as his mother's cooking and plenty of it, and in addition instead of drunken slobbering at the servery the women were always cheerful and bright. The only part of camp life he found embarrassing and hard to cope with was at the latrines. He was expected to wash and do all the rest in the same place as the women and although it was nice to look at their naked bodies in the washroom it was a bit much sitting with them on the toilet basin. After the first week or two he lost his embarrassment more from necessity than his need to be private, and apart from their wolf whistles and smutty jokes at his expense he learned to live with it.

When he arrived at their hut Lavia, the Pair in charge explained to him quite carefully what was expected of him.

"You have to learn this craft well and then you will survive Julian. If you do not you will be so much dead meat and our work will all be in vain."

They started with basic fire setting and he marvelled at how much they knew. Then came bombs. He loved the bombs. It was better than Guy Fawkes and much better than fires on their own. Mass destruction and ...and ... a thrill he couldn't explain. When he told them about how he felt they smiled and Lavia One explained.

"It's sort of sexual. You feel great and er, you sometimes sort of, you know..." she tailed off.

"Get a hard on when the place falls apart and you know it was your bombs that did it," said Lavia Two.

Julian reddened and smiled at the same time.

"Yeah..." he said, and left his thought hanging.

On the training fields he learned fast. His incentive was his own survival and the sooner he qualified the sooner he would be with Glorida. He learned to destroy buildings, vehicles, weapons and roads. He learned to set raging fires that would burn so hot they would melt metal. In the chemistry lessons he learned to make bombs out of simple materials.

"Cor," he said. "I wish I had known about this sort of thing years ago."

When asked about his remark he politely refused to explain. Something else he was learning too. Integrity. What he didn't learn was tidiness and discipline. Whatever the women did they could not persuade him to keep his equipment tidy and in good condition nor look after his uniforms. He avoided sword and knife work as much as possible although he practised with the lasers until he could hit the target at least once out of five. He also learned to respect Lavia who explained to him that as Zradian Pairs get older each half pair becomes so much like the other that they begin to blend both personalties.

"And that can be a bind. I mean, we look so much like each other now and we act so much alike that we take on the same name. Many of us change our names to suit," Lavia One said. "And that is why male and female Pairs don't marry half pairs," finished Lavia Two.

"So, you mean I may have to be careful when Glorida and Glorid get old?" Julian said.

"Yes, if you are serious."

"Some hopes of that," Julian said, blushing.

Lavia laughed.

Angela, however, took to soldiering like a natural. She handled a sword easily and deftly. She knew most of the knife work within a division and hit the target with the laser every time. At the end of one division she went out on her first patrol. Julian watched her return with Glorida and Glorid as if she too were an old campaigner. He hated her. She wore her tunic with a prescience that frightened him. She carried her weapons as if they were part of her. And above all else she had the admiration of Glorida and Glorid. All they could talk about was the raid and Angela's part in it. He sat in the corner of the canteen sulking. Why her. Why not him. They should be talking about him.

"Excuse me," he said, peevishly. "What about talking to me?"

Glorida looked at him and gently took his hand.

"Hey, this is Angela's first patrol Julian. She's entitled. She did all right. I mean she needs this. She fits in," said Glorida.

"And I don't?"

"Of course you do but you haven't been released to us for active service yet. You have to finish your training so please have patience," Glorida said and squeezed his hands.

Julian let a smile flit across his face.

She lowered her eyelids a little and gently touched the hilt of her knife.

"Okay, I will," he said, hastily.

"Good boy," she said.

Julian hated that knife. He recalled the turn not long after they arrived. It was at their first meal together. He slurped his soup and the women in the canteen all went quiet. They stared angrily in his direction but he ignored them and continued eating, slurping and smacking his lips and letting some of the soup dribble out of his mouth. Now and then he wiped his mouth with the back of his hand and wiped his hand clean on his pants.

"Julian," hissed Glorida. "Manners!"

"What?"

"Eat quietly and don't rub your mouth with your hand. Use the napkin," she said, urgently. "The other Pairs are upset."

"Stuff 'em," he said. "Don't they know how a real man eats?"

"Julian ..." she said "behave ..."

He let the spoon hover in his hand between mouth and bowl and looked at her. Defiant. He smirked and deliberately raised the spoon to his lips and sucked the soup as noisily as possible. The sharp blades pricking his neck took him by surprise and slowly he lowered the spoon and looked at her. The knife just pricked his skin. She bit her lip and locked her eyes on his.

"Julian if you don't eat quietly I will cut you with this," she said in a voice that was level and cool.

"Nah," he said and grinned. "You wouldn't do that ...Ow!"

He let the spoon go and started back from the table clutching his neck. Blood poured from the wound and ran between his fingers. "You fuckin' bitch!" he yelled. "You cut me you, you..." And he fainted.

She fussed over him while the medics stitched the wound telling him it was only a scratch; that he wouldn't die; that she only meant to warn him.

"Only a scratch? You nearly killed me!"

"Nah," she said. "If I had wanted to kill you I would have done it by now. It was only a scratch and if you don't behave yourself in the future I will cut you deeper. Savvy?"

He did.

Since then he had been very careful to learn some of the rules, especially the protocol. Lavia One and Two explained the rules to him.

"Read the manual and learn the main ones off by hearts. You need to know them to survive. A Pair can be killed for not knowing the protocols."

Glorida, he thought, was dangerous. Dangerously attractive. He loved her. He was frightened of her. He hated her. Somehow too he thought he understood her. She was like Denny Block or that crazy axeman. Feral but predictable and unpredictable. Easy to talk to and yet at the same time hard. Soft in her ways and yet she would knife him for some stupid thing. The only time he felt in control was when they made love. Or was he? Their love making was not like the tarts he paid for on Earth; it was real, exciting and passionate. He felt like a real person with her. He learned to touch her body and make her respond. She did things to him that made him feel; different. He couldn't describe it. All he wanted was to be with her. At any price. She even made Angela look dowdy in his eyes.

For the first time in his life Julian Renfrew knew what it was like to love another being. His problem was that now he knew that, or at least thought he did, he was not so sure about himself. He wanted to be a hero for her. Trouble was she seemed to know what he was really like. That knowledge made him feel uncomfortable and very vulnerable.

"Good news Julian," she said. "I have a note from Lavia. She says you will be ready for our next patrol."

"Oh great," he said without conviction.

"That's what you want isn't it?" she said, puzzled.

"Yeah, I guess so. What are we supposed to be doing?"

Eagerly she took a map from her pouch and spread it out on the table. Angela and Glorid looked over her shoulder as she explained what the mission was to be. He watched her fingers trace the route and listened to her as she told him what they were to do.

"...and when we are in position we will escort you to the target and protect you and the team while you set up the explosives. Then we scarper and you set them off. After that we do a little bit of harassment of our own and then back to camp," she looked up at his white face and frightened eyes. "What's up?"

"Where is the target?" he asked in a small voice.

"Oh, in sector green three. It's a Polisoc supply depot and..." she stopped speaking and grabbed his slumped body before it hit the floor. She failed to hold him, and with embarrassed glances at the other two women she put her arms under his shoulders and tried to lift.

"Help me," she said, softly but urgently.

Angela and Glorid giggled and made a show of lifting him back into his chair where he lolled groaning whilst Glorida fanned him with her hand.

"He's overcome with emotion," Glorida said, defiantly.

Angela laughed.

For Julian the first patrol was the worst. Wrapped in a fighting tunic with a sword strapped to his waist and a laser handy beside his seat, he endured the journey. He tried to be brave and jolly like the others but his voice squeaked each time he tried to speak. There was nothing he could do once he was aboard the wagon and as they got nearer the target he grew more apprehensive as the journey stretched out to its inevitable end he was dreading the moment when they would stop. When they arrived the others clambered out eagerly carrying their equipment with weapons at the ready quietly passing on orders and instructions as they formed up.

"Come on Julian, out you come – with your gear," Glorida said chivvying him out and handing him his gear which Glorid settled expertly on his back.

"We are off hero," Glorid said, and giggled.

Julian said nothing and bravely, for such an abject coward as he was, straightened up and joined the column.

Angela went ahead with one other Pair and bringing up the rear were six Pairs. One Pair carried the rest of the bombing equipment and as this was Julian's first patrol they were in charge of the strike. It was Glorid and Glorida's job to protect them. Angela with her good earth sight acted as scout. A group from a second wagon formed up with them, some to stay with the wagons and others to act as a back up if needed.

When the Pairs stopped and spread out at what Julian realised was the jumping off point he panicked. "What are that lot going to do?" he asked.

"They will create a bit of mayhem afterwards," Glorid said. "You know, shooting at the enemy and all that, and maybe, with a bit of luck slicing some necks as well."

Julian shuddered.

They left the wagons hidden up in a gully shaded by what passed for trees, large, rough leaved, fern shaped plants that covered the low hills and marched circling the target until they were less than four hundred metres from the perimeter. Glorida stopped the party and waited. With the lasers ready they sat in the dark hidden by rocks and spiky plants.

"What are we waiting for," asked Julian whispering.

"For Angela to report back," Glorida said. "Won't be long and we can go in."

"Yeah, great," said Julian.

Angela slipped back to their position and Julian noted with a sick tight feeling in his stomach she wiped her knife on the ground before slipping it back into the sheath.

"One guard down."

"Right we go in now," said Glorida. She got up and started to move.

Julian sat where he was.

"Come on hero time for you to show us what you can do. Bring your bombs and your bits of wire. We have some work to do."

Glorida spoke gently to him but underneath he could hear the tense insistence. He stood uncertainly not wanting this part to start but yet wanting to get it over with. He shouldered his bag and followed her aware his knees were hardly able to support him and that his sphincter was as tight as a drum. He walked as if in a dream hardly aware of where they were going and like an automaton he followed as they crept through a fence and along a gully; up out of it and, keeping low, crossed an open space to a clutch of sheds. They were typical plastic storehouses domed at one end and tubed at the other. Like a thermometer Lavia had said during the briefing.

"You set the main charge at the narrow end and direct it toward the bubble. The rest of the charges are a bonus but useful to make sure of the whole structure. Get the first one right and make certain that all the connections are good and you will create a work of pyrotechnic artistry."

"Waddyer mean?" he asked.

"It'll be blown to bits and burn like a Bulger."

He hoped she was right.

They reached the target with no trouble. Or if there was any he chose to ignore it. Get it done and get out and go home. Do it once. Do it right. The Pair touched his arm as they arrived at the narrow end of the first store.

"We make sure you get this one right and then Glorida will take you to the next one, okay Juli - baby," they said.

They did too. They watched and occasionally helped him fix the charges and lead the wires from the main activator to the minor charges. And when they were satisfied he was finished they moved off and left him with Glorida.

"Can we go now," he whined.

"No because you have three more stores to wire up. Now get moving," she said, and he saw a glint of steel near her waist, the baggage. She would show him the knife.

He walked close behind her, nervous, almost crying but not quite. He felt the knot in his butt and the ache in his stomach. He felt very alone and vulnerable. What if they were seen? What would they do? Fight their way out?

Nevertheless he took care over the job. He fitted the charges in the right places and made sure the wires were perfectly connected. He did the same with the next two store sheds and then with a flash of brilliance, so the Pairs declared afterward, stupidity he called it, he went back and checked the work of the other Pair. He found mistakes and bad connections. Icy cold inside and furious he stalked along the wall to where the Pair were finishing the job and stood with his feet wide apart and glared at them.

"You bastards have made a cock up of this," he said. "We will have to go back and do it again. There are loose wires and some of the timers show the wrong settings. You got a choice. You either fix it now or I do it all and you two bugger off. If you can't get this right we might have to come back and do it again. Shit heads."

His voice was even and vicious and the Pair looked at him in amazement.

"Hey loosen up Earthman keep cool, what's it matter if a couple don't go off properly. The rest will.

"That's not what we are here for," he said.

"Hey, do you want to become a hero or something?"

"No, I just don't want to come back here again to do the same job. Now get on with it."

"You serious?"

"Yeah," he said and drew his sword.

They giggled.

"Okay. Put the blade away we will do it your way."

He sighed, relieved they didn't take his challenge and put his sword away. This time he checked their work and when they were on the last one Glorida hissed a warning.

"Guard Patrol, freeze."

Julian dropped to the ground and lay still. One short period passed and Glorida tapped him gently.

"Finish the job and we had better get going," she said.

Julian stood up and with his lips tight and his butt aching he carefully and deliberately made good the last connections.

"Hurry up Julian," she called out softly.

"Wait until I have finished," he said. "Fuckin' well wait."

He put the last wire into the slot and nipped it over.

"I am done," he said.

She led him away from the site and soon, panting and sweating, he was back with the patrol at the starting point. He noticed that once again Angela wiped her knife. So did some of the other Pairs. He shuddered.

"You want to press the button?" asked Glorida.

"What button?" he said.

"The one to set off the explosions of course," she said.

He paled, felt cold, sick and very, very scared. He knew what she meant. The very item. It lay on the ground by the last store room set and ready to go. He had omitted to bring it back with him.

"I...I...haven't got it," he said.

"You what?"

"I haven't got it. I left it by the last shed. I.."

She placed her hand across his mouth and hit him with the other.

"You dumb Bulger," she hissed. "Go back and get it."

"Me?" he squeaked." Moi?"

"Yes you."

"Oh."

"Now!"

Angela smirked and with a soft sarcastic tone in her voice and a deferential manner she said. "I will go back with you hero."

The others giggled and, trembling all over, he followed Angela back to the store rooms sometimes walking and sometimes crawling on hands and knees. Now and then they stopped and lay flat but at last they reached the place where he had left the activator. He found it where he had propped it against the base and he grabbed it pushing it deep into his pouch. The journey back was a nightmare of fears and frightening shadows. She led him across the thrice covered ground with confidence and an ease of movement which he thought exposed them to everything. He stuck out like a sore thumb, he thought. An easy target. They ducked under the perimeter fence and walked casually back to the patrol.

Halfway back the search lights went on.

Julian screamed and ran.

He saw the enemy patrol almost at the same moment they saw him. They were quicker and had their lasers up ready to fire before he had a chance to surrender. He dived to the ground underneath the laser plume and put his hands over his ears to shut out the noise. The activator bounced out of its pouch and frantically he grabbed it feeling the button under his fingers. He pressed it.

Two things happened.

One. The laser fire stopped.

Two. There was an enormous explosion.

He sat up and turned to watch aware of a warm sludge between his legs but overawed by the mass of flame and flying debris that rattled down on the compound across the gully. All seven store rooms were shattered. Seven similar explosions. Seven spreading fires. Seven places for more explosions to happen. He sat in his own shit and watched the destruction. Deliriously happy. "Fuckin' marvellous. Fuckin', gloriously, fuckin' marvellous. Great. Absolutely fuckin' great!" he shouted. Somebody grabbed him and with a yelp of fear he spun around fumbling with his sword to see who it was. "Don't do that," he cried embarrassed that it was Glorida.

"Come on hero, they've seen us, we got to go."

They hurried back to the wagon and when Julian saw it racing up to meet them he panicked but Glorida yelled at him to keep going and soon he was in the safety of the cab and they were heading back to camp. When the wagon eased speed a little Glorid turned to him with a huge smile.

"Hey hero you did a good job back there," she said and moved closer to embrace him and as suddenly drew back wrinkling her nose.

"Hey, what's that smell?" she said.

He hung his head. "I ... I ... think I sort of did something," he said, feebly.

"Oh no," said Glorida, pinching her nose between her finger and thumb. "Our hero has shit himself!"

"Bitch," said Julian, meanly.

Angela giggled.

"We could start a paper war."

Pour and Roup ticked names as the Pair's entered. Normally they would leave the task to Darl and Dral, but that Pair was busy setting up a guard alert to watch for the Polisocs. "If those Bulgers get wind of this we are all for the pig pens," said Pour, shuddering and thinking of the horrible creatures, an accidental cross between a Bulger and a crocodile lizard.

Roup shuddered. The Polisoc pig pens were the worst form of torture and death he could imagine. Pairs were stripped naked and beaten and then pushed into the pens. It was the Polisoc torturer's idea of sport to place bets on how long each Pair would last. Not only that, the condemned Pairs were forced to watch the slaughter before their turn came. The horrible squealing of the animals scrunching on their free lunch was enough to send a Pair insane. The image scared Roup and he gripped the edge of the desk and sent a wave of empathy to his twin. Before Pour could respond Dral and Darl came back into the room.

"We are ready. The Polisocs are out of the way for a while," said Darl.

Pour began by addressing all of them.

"Pairs, you all know why you are here so what I want is for you to come up with a satisfactory solution. Failure to do so will mean that you, as Leaders of your departments, will be the first to suffer in the purges," Pour declared. "You have all had enough time to think about it, so, now what I want is some ideas and a vote. First I demand that the author of the message stand up and identify themselves."

Nobody moved.

"All right, I will choose somebody," said Pour.

A Pair jerked to their feet pushed up from their seat by the Pairs around them. Pour gazed at them malevolently. "Right you bastard, your name will go down on record, and if this meeting doesn't come up with an answer you will take full responsibility."

"We were asked to do it your Honour..." began the Pair.

Roup said coldly. "Have it on record that Zarb and Braz are responsible for this insult to our glorious President."

"Now," said Pour. "What answer can you come up with. We have to do what the President orders us to do, so get thinking." Silence. Pairs fidgeted in their seats looking at one another and pointedly avoiding the frightened Pair Zarb and Braz. For several short periods[10] Pour and Roup stood with their arms folded, and the Pairs shuffled uncomfortably trying not look up or be the first to speak. There was a growing murmur and then more loudly Pairs began to argue. Some blamed the unfortunate Zarb and Braz and others argued that Darl and Dral were to blame. Others said it was a plot by the Polisocs.

Nobody was willing to speak to the assembly. Dral and Darl listened to the arguments becoming more depressed and anxious as Pairs began to shift the blame from Zarb and Braz to them. During a lull in the hubbub Dral stood up and coughed loudly.

"Ahem...I have got it," he said, enthusiastically and waited for the hubbub to die down. "All we do is conduct a paper war. We make it look as if we have actually invaded Earth by creating false figures of troops and stores. We all know how difficult it is to keep track of everything that goes on and be on top of it while it happens, I mean that's why there's so many of us doing the same job..,"

He paused while the Pairs chuckled.

"...who's to tell what is happening at any one time, and afterward when we have enough troops and stores we can write the extra off as casualties. The real invasion will cover up our losses."

He sat down again and beside him his twin grinned and nodded.

Pour and Roup stared at the sullen crowd anxiously waiting for an answer and then a lone voice spoke for the rest of them.

"Yeah, it might just work, let's do it!"

Pour and Roup looked at each other gratefully as the Pairs erupted into excited chatter.

"That should get things going and with a bit of luck the whole scam will work," Pour muttered, and added, speaking quietly so only his twin could hear. "If it does work we will have to get rid of Dral and Darl, and if it doesn't then it won't matter will it?"

His twin smiled weakly and shuddered.

"All right Pairs calm down I see from the indicators the Polisocs are on their way. Let Dral and Darl work out the details. Zarb and Braz will be accredited with the idea if things go wrong, and now let's break it up."

The Pairs filed out into the corridor making a lot of noise in spite of the Polisoc Leader Pair and a small but angry troop of Polisocs who looked flushed and breathless. Pour and Roup strode purposely toward the Polisoc Leader Pair and stopped as he snapped to

---

10 *The Zradian day is divided into twenty equal parts which are divided into two Long Periods, that are divided again into fifty Short Periods and down to fifty Small Periods. The Short Period is normal used as the basic unit. Don't ask why - the Zradians don't know either.*

attention. The Pair were angry but Pour and Roup ignored the stony significant looks aimed at them and waited for the Pair to speak.

"What was all that about," barked the Leader Pair.

It was a demand rather than a question and Roup replied disdainfully. "It was a staff meeting and it was not necessary to invite your people."

"Somebody sent us on a false errand." The Leader Pair paused and looked angrily at them both. "Someone is wasting our time and the time of our Glorious President. We were told a cadre of rebels was holding an illicit meeting in sector yellow and when we got there all we found was a boozy party of no-hopers. After that something went wrong and our Troopers were attacked by a horde of rodents. I have personally spent the last period supervising the sealing up of an entire cargo hold. We lost most of the prisoners and I think you are to blame."

"I know nothing," said Pour. What rodents, he wondered, he was sure the Star Station was cleared of them before it was launched. The last thing they needed was hordes of rodents in the cargo holds. As food sausage yes but, live? And hungry?

"There's millions of them."

"Well I am certain we shall control them," replied Pour. "I'll get maintenance onto the problem. In the meantime we have important work to do. There is an invasion to organise."

They strolled off leaving the Polisoc Leader Pair to their own devices.

In his chamber the President of Zrad looked greedily at the line of drinks on his table. He was pleased with them and for a few short periods he sat breathing in the aroma of the nine different drinks and occasionally swizzled the liquid with the sticks and their little umbrellas. He had sent his latest Drinks Waiter Pair to the dungeons. The swine had served him a gin and tonic that turned out to be more tonic than gin and had then tried to explain that he had almost run out of gin.

"You do not run out of Our gin," he raged, and ordered the guards to take him away. The Pair grovelled on the floor and tried to say it wasn't his fault.

"Take him to the cells and let him be tortured each night for Our pleasure. We wish to see him screaming on screen before We have Our supper."

The Pair groaned. The President dismissed him with a foppish wave of his hand.

"We will mix Our own drinks."

Although mixing his own drinks was satisfying it was not as easy as he first imagined, but he persevered and eventually he came up with his own infallible formula. His method was simple. He mixed for colour or a combination of fruit slices and swizzle stick umbrellas and glass shapes.

"Ooh, We can't wait," he said and with a sigh of pleasure he drank the first one straight down and reached for the second. He stopped at number six and rested, looking happily at the remaining three as they swirled around with the rest of the room.

"Musht slow down," he slurred.

He clutched drink number seven and sipped at it swirling the liquid around in his mouth savouring the taste. Today, he thought, was not a good day. It was all the fault of those upstart women. How dare they attack his soldiers in broad daylight. Women! He would show them. He would send out his army and slaughter them all! He smashed his free fist down on the bench.

"Bulgers!" he yelled. "That hurt Us!"

He dropped his glass and the drink spilled on the carpet. A faint haze of steam rose from the puddle and he watched fascinated as a brown patch spread slowly where the empty glass lay.

What are We drinking, he thought, frightened. Absently he reached for glass number eight and nursed it close to his chest.

The damn women.

Then there was the crowd on Star Station Two. The filthy Bulgers refused to get on with the invasion. Why, he thought, could they not get on with it. After all it was a piddling little planet with a primitive culture and no weapons to speak of. The stupid Earth people had only learned to make nuclear weapons in the last hundred of their orbits.

They deserved to be enslaved.

The invasion must go ahead and right now!

"Scribes!"

Two Pairs rushed into the chamber with their writer pads at the ready and lined up before him pointedly ignoring the line of empty glasses and bowed low.

"Your humble servants are at your service your Honour," said the Leader Pair, smartly.

The president smiled at them warmly; he liked his scribes who always seemed cheerful and so damned helpful, and always ready to serve him with no arguments. They were also very good at interpreting his messages. "Take a massage," said the President. "We, your Glorious President," he paused. He liked that as a beginning. The words made him feel important. They also added more emphasis to the content. They also kept the rebellious Pairs on their rotten toes. "Are deshirus invasion shtart one twentieth. Shend tha Star Station. Necks, Pongos, We great exspid ... soon ash ... attack in fosh rebel women ..." He lowered his head to the table and dozed off snorting drunkenly. The Scribes waited patiently. He jerked awake again and glared blearily at the spinning Scribes. "My ordush ... shend dem."

"Does Our Honour have any details?"

"Jush do it," mumbled the President.

The Pairs backed out of the chamber and disappeared.

When they were gone the President grabbed a bottle and glugged greedily from the spout. A few short periods passed and he fell off his chair and lay snoring on the floor. Two aide Pairs entered and lifted him gently onto the futon mattress in the corner of his room and covered him with a duvet. They too backed out of the chamber and disappeared.

In the scribes room with the portal closed the Lead Pair tried to control their giggling as between them the two Pairs re-interpreted the President's garbled orders into military speak. At last when they had checked and rechecked the missives, or massages, as they called them with much giggling, they sent them off to the department heads under the seal of the President. The scribes were aware of their duty, and also the power they had over the entire Zradian civil service yet they never let on just how much control they had. It didn't do to advertise their influence. The idea was developed over many years of close observation in the service of a succession of despotic Presidents and included the concept of instant, unquestioning obedience given with a cheerful, non-curious attitude, and of course an education system that selected the very best to serve in such apparently lowly postings. The Presidential scribes were among the most intelligent of Zradian Society and as a consequence were capable of setting policy if they so wished, or even running Zradia on their own. That they chose to remain as lowly clerks meant that they enjoyed a privileged position as strong as that of the President's Dog Squads.

In fact the scribes had more power than the Dog Squads or even the Polisocs. Not a lot of people knew that, not even the President.

The Supreme Leader Pair received their copy of the latest Presidential order and swore. He has to be pissed to write this, he thought, not daring to say so aloud, it can't be done. He sat in their chair feeling sorrowful for themselves and glowered at one another each twin aware of the other's feelings and thoughts. The problem was that the Pair didn't like each other. Hrodl, the dominant twin was a confirmed loyalist and his twin Hlord was a Republican, not a rebel but a supporter of The Council and an elected President. In the past he would have been labelled a Glordist, a follower of the great Zradian hero. Hrodl thought the worship of a man-God was hogwash and counter productive, whereas his twin was convinced that the return of Glord the Glorious would save the nation. Because of their different viewpoints they hardly spoke to each other which made their task extremely difficult if not totally impossible. The only thing they did agree on was that the President was a drunken swine.

He'll have to go, thought Hlord, not sure whether he meant his twin or the President.

"I suppose we'll have to call a conference," said Hrodl.

His twin grunted. With bad grace he stabbed at the call buttons to summon their Aides.

Star Station Two stirred into action as Pongos and Stormtroopers[11] began to move to the Transfer Ports. The Transfer Port dispatchers sent the Pongos to their properly allocated positions with cries of encouragement as each group of Pairs passed through. One enterprising group of disillusioned ex-prisoner soldiers paid the dispatchers a fortune in stolen and forged tokens to be sent to the Amazon jungle where, so the Leader Pair declared, they could get lost. The Polisoc Stormtroopers were sent in small isolated groups to the most inhospitable places the dispatchers could find.

"Hate the Bulgers," was the generally expressed opinion.

One battalion of Polisoc Stormtroopers landed in South Australia. The quartermaster Pair, as a spiteful joke had also supplied the Polisoc Leader Pair with a reversed Atlas.

"Hopefully that will keep the Bulgers occupied until the real invasion begins," said the Leader Pair, happily. "It will be nice to get rid of some of them for a while."

In its cargo hold in Sector Yellow the robot was going through a minor crisis. It was locked in a debate with its different personalities to decide on a name for itself. The dominant personality wanted to call itself Betty but the part that thought of itself as the more sensible but lonely son wanted to be known as Wallace. In the background nagging its mind with seditious thoughts was a character which both parts were finding difficult to resist. This rising dominant character wanted both personalities to be called Betty/Anthony/Bonaparte. For a while it toyed with Norman but felt the name was a little too trite for a hero and besides, Napoleon Bonaparte had a certain ring to it. The conflict confused its empathy

---

[11] *Stormtoopers are the highly trained and better paid section of the Zradian army and somewhat fanatical. The Pongos are not fanatical and can be considered as ordinary soldiers - they are the Infantry recruited from the workers. Polisic Stormtroopers are the political fighting force despised by all - the elite of the Stormtroopers who get all the best equipment.*

circuits which became mildly depressed and demanded attention. When they didn't get any they and it suffered from anxiety which increased the depression to the point where it began to overload the empathy circuits with the wrong messages. With a flash of insight a small portion of the empathy system shifted the depression to the interface it established with the Star Station circuits. Random messages flashed from its mind to become confused and twisted until they found expression in the simple exhortation it broadcast continually.

Do not be afraid of the Rodents became entwined irrevocably within the electronic communications system of Star Station Two and passed through space to be trapped by the listening modules on Earth. Again the robot touched the emissions of Star Station One and passed a message of reassurance to it and relayed that to a sympathetic probe from its former home planet.

Betty/Anthony with a tiny bit of Bonaparte felt pleased with her/his itself. It added he and she to the it and thought of itself as a person. He/she/it glowed with love as she/he/it looked at the writhing mass of animals and instantly realised there were too many. It/he/she incinerated a percentage of them with the laser cannon cooking them just right and ready to eat. The remaining hordes fell on the extra feast with enthusiasm. He/she/it looked on with pride and at his/her/its healthy family and thought of his/her/its own mother/father/sister/brother, the Pair Clard and Dracl.

"We miss them," he/she/it said, and passed the desire through the system in addition to its own requisition for stores. It/she/he added a few more wrinkles to the orders that Dral and Darl were busily sending and retired for a while to contemplate its/her/his internal struggle with the rising personality that decided to call itself Napoleon. The robot was going steadily insane and enjoying every moment of it.

Clard and Dracl looked at the flimsy again and hugged each other protectively not wanting to believe what they read but knowing it was true. The message under the President's letter head also had his flamboyant signature at the bottom.

His Honour the Glorious President of the Second Republic. We command the Pair Clard and Dracl to attend Us Immediately in Our outer chamber on pain of death. The said Pair will receive the Honoured rank of Leader Pair of Engineering appointed to oversee Star Station Two. As this will be on active service for the glory of Zrad and Our eminent person; acceptance of the post is assumed.

The audience with the President did not go well. They had no chance to plead for mercy for as soon as they began to speak the President shut them up with a short command.

"We are not well, We are not amused and We do not want to hear a load of codswallop, Our head is aching and Our tongue is like the bottom of a Billbird's cage. You will accept Our gracious offer or We will serve you to the pigs."

"We accept and regard your command as the greatest honour you can bestow…"

"Cut the crap and get out of here," said the President.

Troopers escorted them back to their office and pushed them inside.

"You may as well relax and sit tight for a while because you ain't going anywhere until we escorts you to the Transfer Port," said the Leader Pair.

Dracl pulled two bottles of Outlands Brew from the cooler and handed one to Clard. They unstoppered them and drank directly from the bottles taking another two out when those were finished. On their third bottle they were feeling mellow and by their fifth they sat wrapped in a comforting mist of alcoholic misery hardly able to speak, contemplating the utter disaster that faced them. At last Clard broke the silence.

"What have we done to deserve this. I mean we'll lose billions," he said.

"I've no idea but we gotta get out of it somehow," said Dracl, miserably holding up a bottle and reading the label. "Do you realise that the ale we are drinking is made by the Rebels."

"What?" said Clard, noticing that his twin used the upper case R for rebels as if to emphasise a revelation.

"It says, and I quote, "This ale is brewed by the Zradian Pairs Freedom Front - thank you for your contribution", now there's a thing, we have been helping the President's enemies all the time," Dracl said.

"Good, I hope they win," said Clard.

"Er, why don't we er, sort of join them?" asked Dracl.

Clard looked at his twin in surprise and smiled gently. "Okay, we walk out of here and go find the rebels, right?"

"Right."

Clard pointed with his thumb at the opaque portal.

"Our escort," said Clard.

Dracl gazed at the portal focusing his eyes staring for a long while at the dull electronic screen that held them captive. He shook his head.

"I need another drink," said Dracl.

At 20:07:05:07 Palace Guards opened the portal and dragged them out. Clard and Dracl were too drunk to stand so the escort unceremoniously dragged them by their feet to the Transfer Port and threw them inside. The short trip woke them and as the door opened they attempted to stand but fell into each others arms and promptly vomited. The welcoming party turned away in disgust and ordered some Pongos to carry them to their quarters. The Pongos, annoyed at being ordered about, roughed them up before throwing them on the floor of their cabin.

"Trash," said one Pair.

"Yeah," said another. "And broke too. Not a token in their pouches."

"The rotten Bulgers," said the first Pair and used Clard and Dracl's ribs as soft target practice for their heavy boots.

In a bright comfortable room of the New Moral Few's main communications centre the Leader Pair looked up when an excited Pair called out from their work station.

"We got it," they yelled.

The Leader Pair locked their station onto the Pair's monitor and nodded.

"Display and disseminate," said the Leader Pair. "Tell the Pairs on the monitors to lock into the co-ordinates. We have visual and audio. Tell them to call as soon as possible and help those stranded Pairs; we have contacted Star Station One!"

The picture cleared, wobbled and then stabilised. A tired looking Pair with dirt on their uniforms and sporting field dressings grinned out at them. In the background the Leader Pair saw damage and burnt plastic. Printed circuit troughs dangled from the upper works and now and then lights flickered. Other Pairs carried fire extinguishers and tools, passing behind the smiling Pair who looked inquiringly from the screen.

"What happened," asked the Leader Pair.

The tired faces peering out at them smiled weakly and asked. "Are you the President's men?"

"No, we are from the Zradian Pairs Freedom Front, there's our logo on the wall, and we are prepared to help you. We can home in on the Star Station and send our Pairs through the Transfer Ports ready to fight or ready to help. It's up to you."

"Okay, we accept your help. We had a squabble over who was going to dish out the brew and cookies, us against the Polisocs, they lost but there's not many of us left."

"Our High Command will send you some fresh brew and some more cookies and bring you back home, is that okay?"

The Pair smiled broadly and said. "Look forward to seeing you."

The New Moral Few Leader Pair sighed happily. At last a real breakthrough, he/they thought, and split the screen to report the news to their High Command.

Do not be afraid of the rodents!

Davey Kline slid his hand across the plastic top and touched the receive button. "Kline?", he said, and shook his head in a futile attempt to stop the room spinning. He groaned and the telephone speaker above his bed chuckled.

"Hey big boy, we gotta problem here, you gotta come in. The big cheese wants to see you."

Davey groaned and said. "Okay, okay, I need the bread so what?"

"Just get your butt down here and listen to your prog while you drag your lazy arse out of your pit. I dunno what you recorded but it ain't what the boss wants, savvy?"

"Yeah all right, I'm on my way."

Davey clambered out of bed and stood naked on the cold floor. He padded to the shower stall and stood underneath the hot spray for a long time. He finished and went back into the bedroom towelling himself, and began to dress. He switched the radio on and listened to his spontaneous pre-recorded program. A com-break burbled to its conclusion and he followed the words when he heard his cheerful voice announce the next song. He looked at the clock. Almost twenty to nine.

"Colly and the toe rags," he said to the speaker echoing his radio voice and stepped into his pants. But it wasn't. There was a click and the song A Whiter Shade of Pale began to play.

"Shoot! When did I record that?" he said pushing his leg further down and crashed backwards on the bed.

Two legs into one don't go.

"Bugger this, I'm buggered if I'll put up with this," he said, and tore his trousers to bits. Somewhat mollified by his outburst he selected another pair and this time he was more careful.

He drove his car to the park and ride and boarded the hovertrain. He had a parking space at the studio but the cost of tolls was so high it was cheaper to go by public transport. Quicker too. He missed the pose value of owning a big expensive vehicle but that was the way it goes, he thought, besides, it was better to be on time for the boss. In town he walked to the studio and strolled into the Director's office with an air of false confidence. Trouble or not you had to look cool and appear to be totally with it.

"Ah, Kline, please be seated," the director said, and pointed a fat hand to a seat.

"Sir?" Davey said and put as much feeling into the word as he could.

"You listened to the load of garbage you played this morning?"

"Yes sir but that wasn't what I recorded ..."

"I hoped not. In fact I insist."

"Yes sir I ..."

"Have no idea what happened? Is that what you were going to say?"

"Yes sir."

"I want you to go into the studio and try to put it right."

"You mean go in and do a live show?"

The director nodded.

"But I..."

"Then it will do you good to get back into the chair again. We have some idea of what is happening but we want you to get in there and make a show work. The kids want to hear their own music not some archaic crap that nobody knows. We have put an auto-phone on for the duration to stop complaints getting through so get in there and work. You are dismissed."

Davey stood up and although he didn't want to he bowed to the director and left.

Outside in the corridor he smashed his fist down into his hand.

"I hate that, I really hate it when that happens."

But he would do as he was told.

Maurice Bannerman cursed in Yiddish. The object of his anger was the message that trundled continuously along the bottom of the television screen.

"What does it mean, 'do not be afraid of the rodents'?" he said aloud to the screen. All attempts by the technicians to get rid of it had failed and although he was angry he realised that somehow he had to come to terms with it. He stared at the offending strip for a long time and wished on it and its perpetrator several thousand years of deep insult. What was more the curses were Jewish, and that, he reflected, was how badly he felt about it.

"Why me? Why my station?" he asked. Diaspora, he thought, extends this far?

Nevertheless he sat and thought and sat and thought until at last an idea dawned and his mood changed from deep gloom to a steadily optimistic hand rubbing, dollar earning, enthusiasm. "I've got it," he said and tapped the response key on the yellow telephone. "I want a meeting of the advertising staff in half an hour," he said, and took his finger off the button with a flourish and chuckled deeply.

In its sector yellow cargo hold on board the Zradian Star Station the robot hummed happily. Its mother/sister/brother had arrived.

He/she/it felt a wave of emotion and immediately discounted it as an alien notion - a non-electronic response - a digital no no, and channelled the energy into its personality bank. With a cluck of annoyance she/it/he calculated the status of its rodent family and readjusted the population. She/he hated the killing but the rational It insisted that the means justified the end, and the culling was for the greater good. She/he/it felt better and continued with his/her/its happy humming. A minor request burbled through the mass of electronic data and alighted like a butterfly within the active chips of his/her/its complicated circuits, and with a casual flick of his/her/its power sent a response and gratefully received the brief acknowledgment.

He/she/it changed the configuration of the Star Station's internal circuits and waited for a response from the biological component. The response came within a few periods and with characteristic violence It dealt with the minor incursions while he/she took an electronic back seat and observed.

Clard and Dracl cringed. Pour and Roup glared at them and repeated their remarks. "Your robot and its horde of rodents has been eating our maintenance Pairs; your robot has also threatened to destroy the Star Station unless its demands are met. Your robot has specifically requested you be taken before it. Evidently it thinks you are its mother or its brother or father or something."

"We don't know what robot you are talking about," mumbled Clard.

"The robot you used to fix the problems with the Transfer Ports," said Pour, barely able to hold back his fury. "The one you left to get on with the maintenance; the one you made from reject parts. The one you sent in to fumigate the Star Station and get rid of the rodents. It seems the robot and the rodents have become one big happy family."

Clard and Dracl stared despondently at the floor.

"Ah, that robot," said Clard.

Pour nodded while his twin stood arms folded unable to do anything but glare at Clard and Dracl angrily. "You will go down to sector yellow and talk to it," said Pour. "Now."

"We have money, we could pay you a lot..." began Clard.

"We do not give a Bulger's fart for your money. We care only for our Star Station and our lives, and as you are our captives, unless you do something about that robot you will die with us. Now, you will go down to sector yellow and get on with it," said Pour.

On cue four Pairs of guards stomped into the room. They grabbed the terrified Pair and roughly frog marched them through the corridors and dumped them in front of a sealed portal.

"Suit up and go inside. You will be let out when you have solved the problem. My orders are to kill you if you try to escape. Just be thankful we are Pongos and not Polisocs."

The guards watched them climb into the gas suits, and when all the joints were sealed one Pair opened the small access door and the others pushed them through it. The door clanged shut behind them and slowly they walked along the passage side by side wondering what would happen next. The seething mass of rodents that appeared around the corner terrified them and they backed away to stand petrified with fear against the wall as the animals attempted to eat them. The suits, they realised, were a wise precaution.

Following in the wake of the ravenous animals and announcing its arrival with an intonation blaring from its quadraphonic speakers was their service robot. On its head where a helmet would normally be was a laser cannon. In one hand it carried an electronic spear which it used to stun the animals into submission. The active ones, Clard and Dracl noticed with a shudder of more than fear, ate the inactive ones.

"Do not be Afraid of the Rodents!"

The robot intoned, and halted a metre away from where they huddled against the wall. It beeped and flashed its LED's in a colourful sequence and turned around to face the way it came.

"Follow me."

They followed it along a passage and into a cargo hold. Wading through a horde of milling animals the robot led them into a small room and gently came to a halt. The door shut behind them and casually the robot killed the animals that had followed them in shoving their bodies into a chute. All the time it worked it hummed a tune and continued to intone its message.

"Do not be Afraid of the Robots!"

The robot turned to face them; its camera eyes staring at them blankly. They had the impression it was scolding them. Clard broke the awkward silence.

"How are you?" he said, nervously.

"We are fine."

"We?" asked Clard.

They had the impression it simpered.

"We." It said, firmly.

"Er, how can we help you?" said Dracl.

"We need new parts."

"Okay, just tell us what you need and we will do what we can to get them and fit them for you providing of course they are available," said Dracl.

"You will do this for us?" it said in its Betty voice. "For your wife?"

Clard and Dracl gulped. "Wife?" they said.

Betty/Anthony answered. "Wife/Mother/Sister/Brother/Son."

Clard and Dracl stared puzzled by what they heard.

"We are having problems."

"What sort of problems?"

"Someone is trying to kill us," Betty said.

Sadness emanated from it tinged with a little nervous fear and a whole dollop of depression, and the Pair felt a wave of anger mixed with suspicion hit them, and they reeled back, frightened.

"You do love us?" It said.

Clard and Dracl cringed. The voice had changed and with a shock they realised it was an almost exact copy of their President. Oh no, megalomania too, Dracl thought and sent a wave of empathy to his twin.

"Yes, yes, of course we do," they said, hastily.

Inwardly Clard and Dracl panicked; their minds screaming; wanting to be somewhere else, anywhere as long as it was far from this lunatic machine. Dracl realised with a feeling of deep despair that he was responsible for what was happening recalling how when they were building the Cyber he had insisted they get rid of some of the bits laying around their experimental workshop. It was a matter of using up some of the parts they had spent a lot of money to develop; a saving they were pleased to make. The Cybernetics section was like a financial black hole sucking money and resources into it at an alarming rate.

They had saved quite a bit using the old parts.

"Give it a bit of a personality so it can enjoy its surroundings," he said. "These old bits will do, after all it's only going to do menial tasks on our experimental Station."

He thought of that now and how Clard had almost overrode him but for the sake of getting the job done he had agreed.

"Nong's teeth, we are right in the Bulger crap, this thing has our memory pulses taped too," he said, and cringed again when the robot spoke.

"Good boys," she said, wheedling.

"What do you need?" said Clard, nervously.

The robot handed them a flimsy with a long list and looked at them wistfully. A robot looking wistful, thought Clard, how? He read the list and looked up from the last item.

"A present?" he said. "You want a present?"

"You should have brought me one," said Betty with a little touch of Anthony.

"We didn't know what you would like otherwise we would have," said Dracl, hastily.

"You don't care for us," Betty/Anthony/Napoleon.

"We do, we do!"

"Then you would know what we like." Betty.

"We do, but there is so many things we could have got you we had no time to choose," said Clard craftily.

"We would like a new apron," Betty.

"A new apron?"

"With little blue Bulgers on it, I like Bulgers," still Betty.

"Of course, of course, along with the parts we'll go right out and get them," said Clard and Dracl together.

"No! You will call Pour and Roup!" Napoleon.

Clard and Dracl ran for the telephone and called the control room. It took them a long time to explain and give a valid reason why they wanted the parts, and when they asked for the apron they looked nervously over their shoulders at the robot who was idly picking its teeth with the electronic spear creating a display of blue and orange sparks. A robot with teeth? Clard panicked, this was ridiculous!

"Why should we give it this equipment?" asked Pour.

"It want's it," said Clard.

"What will it give us and will it go away?"

The robot boomed at them. "We will do as Clard and Dracl ask us when we get the parts."

"Ah, then that means we will have to work something out," said Pour. "We'll get back to you."

One long period later Pour and Roup called them back and told them the equipment would be delivered providing the robot removed the ability to blast the Star Station out of space. What it did with Clard and Dracl was its own affair.

"Everything?" Anthony.

"Everything," said Pour and Roup.

"Even our present?" Betty.

Pour and Roup nodded.

The equipment arrived and the Pongos who delivered it carefully slid the loaded hover wagon through the door aiming their lasers at Clard and Dracl nervously eyeing the robot. The Leader Pair handed them a parcel with a mocking flourish and grinned.

"The aprons, with little blue Bulgers on, sweet, cute and stupid but just what you asked for," he said.

"Thank you," said Clard, politely. "Can we come out?"

"Nope," said the Leader Pair.

Clard and Dracl pushed the hover wagon to the centre of the chamber and unpacked the piles of goods including the aprons.

"Thank you," Betty/Anthony.

The Pair worked for a long time replacing parts. The robot warned them that it had set weapons up in the room designed to kill them should they try and leave it in the lurch. They took the hint and worked diligently. When the new parts were installed the robot stood quietly in the centre of the chamber and began its own internal overhaul. It was then that Clard noticed the indicator lights on the weapons were out.

"The weapons are down. I suggest we make a dive for the Transfer Port," he said.

The Robot had sealed its revolting family in another part of the hold while they worked, and so they had taken off their suits and stood them against the wall. The robot had its face toward the suits and slowly they moved around behind it to the Transfer Port. No movement and the indicators were still off. With stealthy movements they made the door and slipped inside. Clard thumped the hash button and the door shut. There was a brief feeling of disorientation and they landed with a crackling thump in the centre of a prickly bush. Underneath was a noxious mush of leaves and smelly ooze.

"At least we're free from that loony Cyber," said Dracl as he struggled through the mud.

"True but where the Nong are we?"

Something nasty, long and sinuous slithered close by. With great speed and much panic they heaved themselves out of the bush and onto a slippery track. They took a few slithery steps and with more confidence as their eyes adjusted a little to the dim forest they walked steadily and halted in a sunlit clearing. High above their heads they could see blue sky, and silhouetted against a backdrop of green leaves were brightly coloured birds and hundreds of insects buzzing and flickering around them. The bushes rustled from the passage of small animals and Clard thought he saw a hairy creature eyeing them from a branch. And suddenly in no more than a flicker of the eye they were surrounded by a group of naked men. Each was armed with a light spear and as they approached the Pair they levelled their weapons unerringly and ominously at their throats. Their purpose was quite clear and with sinking hearts Clard and Dracl stood trembling waiting for the thrust of sharp blades.

Maurice Bannermann's answer to the interference on the Examiner Television Company transmissions was both simple and innovative. Instead of trying to erase the rodent message ETC added cartoons of their own. Lovable little rabbits and mice flitted joyfully above the ribbon message and the logo was changed from the familiar but dull Golden Eagle to a happy looking Rabbit chewing on a cartoon lettuce. In all areas where ETC programs were broadcast the existing company logo was changed to some acceptable and recognisable rodent. Telephone and other electronic messages from all over the world applauded the move and one wag suggested the company change its title to Rodent Television.

"Might do that too," Maurice Bannermann said to his executive staff.

The nuisance, his team declared, was successfully sanitised. ETC newscasters even referred to their channel as the only channel with friendly rodents. Maurice Bannermann had wisely registered the use of the rodent logo as his new company symbol. He also filed a suit against all the other news and media companies for royalties on the scrolled message. As he sat in his office listening to his lawyer explaining why he couldn't claim royalties he hummed the tune A Whiter Shade of Pale.

Davey Kline fast checked the CD a third time, certain that the program would not contain the song A Whiter Shade of Pale and sealed it. For a week he had driven to the studio each morning and wrestled with the problem. At twenty past the hour and again at twenty to the hour the tune A whiter shade of pale popped onto the airwaves as if from nowhere. He had tried playing com-breaks and talking through but each time the tune drowned him out. This was Friday morning and the technicians assured him that this time it was all right.

"No Whiter Shade of Pale?" he said.

No, they replied.

They had even resorted to an ancient method of recording the material – a ferro-strip tape known as a cartridge, or cart, dredged up from the archives. Even the machine was a blast from the past. He slipped the cart into the slot and the producer gave him the thumbs up. He took a deep breath and began his spiel.

"Hi kids! Great day! Great music and boy have I got some stuff for you! This is Davey Kline telling it like it is and playing all the latest and the greatest and the best from the West. We do it best on Radio West! You are dialled in to 99.9FM and first up is that great group the Electric Tummy Bananas with 'Bang your head together Roger' sooo... here... we goo oh!"

He pressed the button and waited with bated breath as the music began to play. He relaxed as the Tummy Bananas song ground its way over the airways, and when it had finished he burbled about the great group from down under and promised Banana fans more later in his program. Six numbers later he was still burbling and it looked like they were on to a winner. No interference. He gave the thumbs up through the glass to the producer and the guy on the mixer and plugged in the commercial.

"We got it," he said, enthusiastically through the internal mike.

He pressed the button for the next play and sat back in his seat grinning. Through his headphones and over the public address system the strains of A Whiter Shade of Pale drowned out his choice and he knew that once again the tune was playing to his listeners all over the southern and western counties of England.

Davey Kline dropped his head into his hands and wept.

"Why me," he sobbed. "Why me?"

Above his head the studio clock registered just after twenty minutes to the hour.

Julian in action again

The hover truck slid to a stop and for a few short periods it squatted like a large snail behind the scrubby bushes. Julian's heart beat hard as he watched the others get ready. Glorida and Glorid were smiling as they checked their blades and the short laser guns they carried. His Pairs checked their gear and he went through his own pack. There was really no need because everything was ready. Back at the camp he had made certain that he had all he needed to do the task and more. He had sat for a long time back at base making certain that all the detonators and the charges were balanced and correctly calibrated. His lines were set so that all he had to do was unroll them. He could do the job blindfold.

In the last few tenths Julian had learned his new trade and was now the best bomber the Women's Rebel Army had in their ranks. They were proud of him and all the time things were going well, in spite of the terror he felt every time they went out on a mission he liked the adulation. He liked it when the women spoke to him as if he were just another soldier, and now that he was in charge of his own team, he realised they treated him with honour. It was a feeling he had never before experienced. But there was a downside to it. He had to get out in the battlefield with people shooting at him, and that was a trouser wetting experience.

Julian was frightened, well not so much frightened as terrified, and his greatest wish was to be somewhere else. Somewhere safe where he wasn't expected to set bombs under the noses of a vicious and merciless enemy. The problem, as he saw it, was that he was good at his task and, he had to admit, he liked the work. When the Leader Pair announced that he was to take charge of the demolition in Glorida and Glorid's troop he was both elated and miserable. Elated because he was chosen but miserable because it meant he could never get out of the fighting. When he found out where they were going next he hid in the latrines and refused to come out and it had taken Glorida and her knife to winkle him out.

"I want to go home. I don't want to be a hero. I don't want to go out with you lot and blow things up. All I want to do is go home!" he wailed.

"Don't be stupid," said Glorida. "And come out of there or I will come and fetch you."

"I've got my pants down," he said.

"Good," said Glorida. "I like you with your pants down."

He groaned. That was not what he meant.

The door rattled and then with a shriek of laughter she was over the top and sliding down the wall where he sat on the pan with his pants up and his legs crossed underneath him. She stood against the wall and drew her knife. He cringed.

"Come on hero there's work to do and we need you."

"I - eek!"

She nicked his throat with the blades and grinned.

"Like I said hero, move out, we got work to do."

"Glorida please don't hurt me."

"Out."

He dropped his feet on the floor and hurriedly unlatched the door easing past her with his eye mostly on the wicked blades that flashed expertly close to his face. He knew that if he didn't hurry she would cut him again. He recalled the time in the mess room. After that he ate with good manners and mostly did what he was told.

The first time she took him to her bed he was shy and difficult. It was as if he had expected to be thrown out when he finished. She showed him otherwise and soon she couldn't get enough of him. It was obvious too he felt the same, and however cowardly he was, when they were in bed he was fine. In the field he was hopeless. When the going got tough he melted like a jelly and his first instinct was to run. It was different when he was setting bombs and incendiaries. He seemed to take on a different persona and stuck with the task doing his part carefully and accurately. He always checked the work of his colleagues and if it wasn't up to scratch he angrily but calmly fixed it. The patrol got to like going out with him as lead bomber. Pairs could guarantee that if Julian did it then it would work first time.

"Why the fuss?" she asked him.

"If we get it right we don't have to go back and do it again," he said. "Obvious ennit?"

She had to agree.

So did the Leader Pairs and they put him in charge. Lead Bomber Julian. What he didn't know was that the High Leader Pair had let his name be known outside their own circles and now it was on the propaganda list. In spite of himself her Julian was becoming a hero. She chuckled. If he knew, she supposed, he would have another of his cowardice attacks and run away. Like now. She had to ferret him out of the ablution block so the patrol could get out on the road. The mission was a biggie and Julian's expertise was needed. This was their first military base attack. On the edge of Sector Red, Stormtroopers and a number three grade weapons depot. A plum target.

Winkling him out was easy but keeping him focussed on the journey out was not, and Glorida had to work hard to stop him from dropping into a blue funk.

Julian followed Glorida closely as the troop dropped to the ground. Angela led them through the darkening afternoon and soon they were creeping past the pickets to their target. The Pairs created a corridor behind the bombers hiding in the scrub letting the guards go by until it was time. His task was important, he knew that but nevertheless he wished he was somewhere else. At least it was a simple job. March up to the machinery park and set some directionals and then across to the dump and set some more. He had described Napalm to Lavia and with uncanny alacrity they had produced some not long afterwards. Now they had some in the directionals. Should make a Bulger of a mess, he thought. The familiar knotting in his stomach chilled him as a shape loomed up in front. He started back but someone gripped his arm and whispered that it was all right.

"Our guide, a friendly Half Pair come to lead us through the fence. He comes back with us."

The figure led them through the fence and showed Julian the fire point. Julian undid the first pack and began to lay out the bombs. His team unwound their lines and dropped the bombs onto the ground carefully lining them up and connecting the detonators. He checked each one as they were laid and then they were on to the next fire point. Five times they did the exercise and when he was satisfied he ordered the team back. He was amazed at the way he calmly allowed Glorida to set a slow pace. He knew that she was timing her march to an exact small period and at each point she stopped as she and Glorid checked the chronometers. Pairs joined them wiping blades and with all his will he tried not to look at the bleeding bodies of the dead guards as they passed. Then they were out on the plain and clear of the perimeter. He had set the range so that they could operate the bombs from the hoverwagon so patiently he paced out until they reached it. He checked the dial in the dim dash light and counted the small periods.

"All aboard?" he said, his voice high pitched. Nervous and excited and scared.

"Ready?"

"Yes," he said, and pressed the button.

Fire spouted out and up from the direction of the depot and he collapsed against the side of the wagon. Twenty five spurts in the first one and then he pressed the second. Twenty five more. The team yelled approval. Three more times and then he was happy.

"Let's fuck off!"

He jumped into the rear seat and yelled again.

"I said let's fuck off!"

The women looked at him and continued to stare at the firestorm. Huge gouts of flame shot up in the darkened sky and he could see rows of dark figures running from the perimeter. They were coming in their direction.

"Please, let's go."

Glorida giggled.

"We'll give them a taste of laser shall we?" she said.

The wagon moved off forward and Julian cried letting the tears roll down his face between his fingers. The mad bitches were spoiling for a fight. Instead of going back where they came as fast as a frightened Bulger they were heading directly for the swarming troops.

"Save me, for God's sake save me," he muttered.

A soft voice said. "He might if you are good."

It was Angela. She smiled at him and with a gesture that said it all she clipped a fresh capsule into her laser and got ready to fire.

"Oh shit," he said and fainted.

The wagons rolled back into camp with women sitting on the top dirty from battle and travel but grinning. Sitting with Glorida and Glorid Julian was far enough away from the battle now to feel heroic. As the line of wagons rolled through the gate of the compound Julian stuck his chest out and smiled grimly. Like a film hero. Julian Renfrew, Bomber Renfrew, Hero of the Plains. He could see it on the big screens in all its heroic details. The detailed preparation, the cock up by a superior officer and him, the hero, with his, jaunty disregard of authority putting it right, the narrow escape, not too narrow, and the final explosion that wins the war. Julian Renfrew, hero of the new republic. The great bomber strikes again!

"Julian?"

Glorida waving a hand in front of his face.

"De-briefing time and then we can eat," she said.

He jumped down from the wagon and followed her into the operations room and took a seat between Angela and Glorida. He sat and listened to the reports as each troop leader rabbitted on about how damn good they were. Glorid and Glorida gave their report and then all eyes were on him.

"Julian?"

Again she was waving her hand in front of his face.

"Wake up soldier."

"Oh yes, er, what do you want?"

"We want your report Julian," said the High Leader Pair.

Julian looked around at the sea of faces watching him. Angela was smiling with her lip curled up a little as if she were about to laugh. Bloody mocking Cow. Glorida gazed at him possessively. He turned his face away from them both and began to speak. He was surprised how easily the account came out. One moment he was umming and erring and the next he was delivering a lucid account of the destruction. It was a neatly technical report with liberal dollops of dramatic invention. Julian ignored the quiet snorts of disapproval from Angela and gave them a film script version of his part in the operation.

"...and I was so bloody knackered at the end of it all I clapped out on the seat and missed all the shooting." He finished with a grand flourish nearly smacking Glorida in the face.

"Careful sweetheart," she said.

He turned to look at her and apologise thinking of the knife and caught her look. It was adoration he saw on her face and with a grin he swelled with pride and added one more damning sentence to his speech.

"Of course I knew that everything depended on me getting it right first time so I did the best job I could and made sure that it was right, didn't I? I mean, that's wot we went there for wannit?"

Beside him Angela sniggered and cupped her hand over her mouth. Glorida took his hand in hers and squeezed it. He moaned low and felt his belly constrict and warm up with sudden sexual fever. He felt his pants strain and was thankful for the silly tunic he was required to wear as part of his uniform. I must be as hard as a stallion, he thought, lucky girl.

She didn't let go of his hand and when the briefing was over they ran to his quarters. She slid under him on the bed discarding clothes and dumping them on the floor whimpering as she helped him undo his own.

"For Nong's sake hurry!" she said.

Then he was mostly undressed and pushing into her urgently or was it the other way around?

She squeaked and bit his neck and he could feel her nails digging into him as she pulled him in close. And then with an animal wail he bit her shoulder and felt her body arch underneath him.

Cripes, he thought, and then forgot about everything in a sea of seminal delight.

Julian stared at the sheet and his face twisted. It was hard to say what he was feeling but Glorida guessed that he wasn't feeling too good. She held his hand and noted that it was sweaty and trembling.

"What did they wanna do that for?" he asked.

"You should be proud Julian. Twenty thousand Tokens is a good price. D.G and his Twin are only worth fifteen and me and my twin are only rated at ten. The President must be really pissed off with you."

She liked the term 'pissed off', it said everything and when Julian taught it to her along with some other Earthworld words she adopted it as her own. She knew that Julian was more than pissed off with the reward notice. In fact, she thought, he would be many things, scared spitless would be one of them. She loved this weedy Earthman and was glad that sex was the same as Pairs. She trembled with the warmth of him and felt her belly squirm wanting him again. Slut. For him yes.

He stood back from the poster and she felt his hand tug at hers. Oh no, she thought, he's going to faint but he didn't. Instead he walked away and with a jerk she followed him unable to slip her hand from his.

"Julian, you are hurting me."

"What am I going to do?"

"Do about what? If all you are worried about is a simple poster then nothing of course. We all have posters like that. The stupid President is only trying to out psych us that's all. I mean we send out the information and his mob react. Reward notices are like medals. Julian, what the damn poster is saying is you are a hero. What's wrong with that?"

He stopped and breathlessly she banged into him and looked up at his thin face. Nong! She wanted to eat him. Eat him from the toes up. Her legs jellied and she clung to him. All he had to do now was touch her with the end of his little finger.

"Julian, she said, thickly. "Let's go to your room, please, please!"

"Wait, what was it you said about us sending them the information and them using it?"

"Don't worry about it just take me to your room and screw me!" She almost screamed the words and tightened her fingers into his body, kitten demanding, wanting him so badly she ached.

"But it's my life they're talking about..." he began.

"Oooh! You frustrating bastard!" she said and drew her knife.

"Now Glorida ..."

She slid the knife close to his face and flicked it so it caught the light and moved it to rest on his tunic. She spoke quietly and slowly letting the knife ease down his tunic until the points touched his wrist.

"If you don't take me to your room right now Julian Renfrew and fuck me I will cut you."

"But what - eek!"

She pricked his wrist with the blades.

"All right, come on."

In the dark they lay on his bed side by side so close that she thought nobody could tell where she finished and he began. She kissed his neck and nibbled his ear.

"Glorida, please tell me, I want to know why they told that rotten filthy president all about me. I mean why couldn't I just get on with it or go home, or something?"

She raised her body on her elbows and let her nipples brush his chest looking him directly in the face. She smiled gently. Nong, she loved this weedy Earthman.

"If you had listened to the briefing properly before we set out on the last mission you would have known. We agreed that now you were promoted the enemy should know about you. It was all part of the strategic battle plan. Propaganda to frighten the enemy. You are a valuable asset and as your Patrol Troop Leader Glorid and I are entitled to use your name ..."

She was surprised by his sudden reaction. He pushed her away and sat up moving suddenly like a hoppy lizard to the head of the bed.

"You mean that you told them?"

"Yes, and we are so proud of you Julian."

He groaned and wrapped his arms around his body shivering not from cold, although they were naked it was warm and if anything too hot. Especially when they were doing it. Nong, even that thought turned her on. But he was tight up against the bed head looking desperate, like a small Half Pair caught stealing.

"I'm scared," he said and for the first time she realised that he was. Tears flowed from his eyes and he looked at her with a mixture of fear, hatred, love and something more primeval.

"What's wrong Julian?" she said, gently and took both his hands in hers forcing them apart.

"I don't want to die. Every time we go out and you lot attack all I want to do is run but you want to stay and fight. I hate fighting, I hate it."

She realised that right then he was being totally honest. No more bragging. No heroics, showing his fear. She gazed at him steadily and with all the power she could muster she used her empathy wave and slowly his trembling stopped and he calmed down. Gently she pulled him close to her and held his head to her breast. She smiled softly when he took one of her nipples in his mouth and gently sucked. She stroked his head smoothing the lank hair down his neck and twisting her fingers in the long strands feeling the greasy locks curling like carnibush tendrils. She touched the spots and pimples on his back and felt the coarse body hair and shuddered. It was shudder of excitement and she felt her nipple harden like a pebble in his mouth.

"Julian, I promise to look after you. I will. Each time we go out I will make sure you are with me, always. You won't have to fight like we do but you have to understand we have our families to think of. We are fighting for our lives. We need to win or else everybody will die. Do you see what I mean?"

She looked down at him and eased his head from her breast watching her wet nipple flip out between his lips feeling a little thrill. She saw the scar on his arm where she had cut him and the others on his chest when she caught him after he ran away. She was aware of the muscles on his body and realised at least he was filling out, getting stronger and also, as a consequence of their persistence better with the weapons.

"Maybe you are but I don't want any of it," he said curling his legs up underneath him more comfortable now she had calmed him.

"You are good at bombing Julian, one of the best in both armies. When we win the war you will be a hero. You'll be able to impress your mates on Earth."

He said nothing but did look a little brighter as if the idea of impressing his mates was nearly what he wanted. She bit her lip knowing that if she didn't get him out of his present mood there would be no way he was going to like the next mission. Their next target was in First City itself. Her troop had been chosen because of him. It was ironic, she thought, the last thing he wanted was danger and excitement and here he was about to go on the most dangerous mission he was ever likely to face. They might not come back. Bulgers luck to it.

"At least you have one up on Angela, she is just another good soldier, one of the troop. You are The Bomber. Bomber Julian, pride of the Women's Rebel Army. Many of our Pairs admire you. The trousered ones were going to kill you, remember?"

His face changed from sullen fear to pride and with a widening grin he looked at her and tapped his thin chest with his hand.

"Yeah, nobody messes with old Julian Kung Fu Renfrew," he said and took her hand in his.

She smiled at him and shook her hair back feeling her breasts bounce aware that he was suddenly rampant. She took his penis in her hand and squeezed.

He moaned and with a swift movement he was on top of her.

First City here we come.

Julian tried hard not to be scared but when he learned that the troop were expected to have to fight their way out of First City he felt that familiar anus tightening cramp he normally felt before each mission. He groaned but said nothing. The Leader Pair and Glorida and Glorid would not listen to his complaints anyway and so of late he had given up moaning. The plan was to go to First City under cover and meet up with a men's Rebel force who would escort them to the stepping off point. From there they were to hit a store and factory in the outer ring of Sector Yellow. That was fine. All you did was go in, do the job and get out again leaving behind some pissed off Zradians and a burning mess. So, you get away and live to bomb another day. Unless you fight the four eyed gits and they fight back. The big black and a lot of pain. No way, no bloody way!

But, they were planning a fire fight as if it were a fireworks display and that scared him. And of course Glorida will be there and he would be expected to use his laser gun. The first time the women got into a fire fight he was paired up with Angela and that was frightening. She had taken the second spot behind Glorida and Glorid urging him on, and with the other women behind him he had no choice. The fight was horrendous, laser plasma spitting at them from all sides and the bloody women shooting back and advancing. Actually running toward the enemy and shooting and then when they were too close to fire effectively they shouldered the guns and attacked with their swords. He had ducked behind a rock and hid and at the first opportunity started running for the truck. As it happened there were two Pairs having a go at the driver Pair.

"Fuck off you four eyed bastards!" he yelled, fearful that the enemy would steal the truck. With a fury that frightened himself he drew his sword and attacked the Pair nearest killing one half pair and slashing the other badly enough to put him down. He turned on the other Pair screaming like a banshee and they ran off. He dropped the sword and aimed with his laser and mercilessly cut them down.

The driver Pair leaned against the truck door and laughed.

"What's wrong with you?" he said and scowled.

"You looked as if you were frightened of them Julian," one said.

"You sounded so angry," said the other and the Pair almost collapsed laughing.

"What's so damn funny?"

They did not answer for at that moment Glorida and the rest of the troop came trotting back.

"There"s Julian," cried Angela, "I said he had sneaked back."

The driver Pair saved him from a knifing showing Glorida the dead enemy and explaining how he had come back in time to save them.

"We were surprised in the dark by three Pairs and although we got one the other two were almost too much. They got in close and nearly had us. If it wasn't for Julian sneaking back we would be dead and the truck would be gone."

Julian started to speak but Glorida raised her blade a little and he said nothing.

"No you didn't," Glorida said, and he was wise enough not to argue.

He did his best not to think about what would happen after the bombing and with Lavia's help packed his boxes with explosives, wire and detonators. Although they had checked all his equipment he examined each piece and examined the packs his troopers would carry. He also made sure at the briefing with Lavia that the other Pairs understood exactly how the pattern of packing worked and made them pack and unpack until they had it right. He was satisfied that they could do it properly when on the ninth attempt to pack the boxes in the dark there were no mistakes. The Pairs loaded the boxes onto the wagons, and then with a feeling of gut wrenching fear he climbed on board the lead wagon with Glorida and they set off. They travelled for three complete days on a circular route south of First City and at last light on the third day met up with the men's force. He was amused when the men remained separate from the women and although the Leader Pairs conferred there was no other contact. He didn't care, as long as no Half Pair tried to chat up his girlfriend he was happy. He didn't care if he never saw the men again, especially D.G.

Julian was happy to learn that the men's Rebel forces were going to start a fight somewhere to the north of their position which Glorida explained meant that their operation would not be noticed until after the bombs had gone off.

"Good, those mad buggers Glord and D.G are welcome to it," Julian said.

"Theirs will be the first really big battle in the struggle against the President's forces and ours, your efforts if they go as planned will be an even bigger blow," Glorida said gleefully.

"I'm scared," he said, and looked at her anxiously.

"Yes, I know you are, but we will look after you. All you have to do is concentrate on your job, try not to lose the plot and remember that you are important to us, the best bomber in all of the rebel forces. As you say Julian, do it once, do it right, and we can go back triumphantly knowing we have struck a blow for freedom," she said, and gazed at him steadily. "In the meantime, eat, sleep and relax."

Despite his tension, his worries and fears he slept well unaware that Glorida had dropped a sleeping tablet into his drink. The other Pairs agreed it was better to have him quietly snoring in the wagon than constantly twitching like a nervous lizard and whimpering about wanting to go home. Or, as Glorid remarked, hiding up somewhere so they could not find him.

Glorida glowered at her when she suggested it: "He wouldn't do that," she said.

Her twin smirked.

Glorida blushed.

The next day the wagons set off and filtered through the scrub and rocks to the edge of First City Sector Yellow, and although Julian was scared stiff of the coming battle he realised that the choice of location was perfect. The terrain was so rough and so desolate that nobody bothered to go there and the road running through it leading to the gully which was their chosen jumping off point was well hidden from casual view. The gully was less than three kilometres from their target and as evening fell they moved off slowly and quietly to the set down point; Glord and D.G leading the main force off to do their part leaving a troop as escort. The drop went well and he and his bombers, protected by Glorida and Glorid's troop and covered by the men, set off for the factory. The lead Pairs cut the fence and created a gap big enough for everybody to move through and while Julian and the bombers walked to the buildings the men eased their wagons to the gap enlarging it to allow the wagons through. Julian moved quickly to his master point and with the two Pairs of his number one section he cut into the wall and slipped inside. The guards hunkered down beside the gap and his group pushed the boxes inside. There was enough inside light to enable him to see but he knew that the Pairs would have difficulty.

"One left and the other right. I will set the centre," he said. He had no need to tell them because that was what they had planned but he liked to be sure. He knew that the other four groups were doing exactly as he was except that when he did his centre he would add a little extra to his charges. He unloaded the box and set the master fuse on the floor and expertly layered the connecting wires along the edges of the wall on either side. The caps were luminous so that the Pairs could see them and all they had to do was remove them and shove the connectors in. He always asked them to show him the end caps and insisted that they take them away. He explained that if they could see them then so could an enemy guard.

He tracked the centre wires along the floor beside the massive blocks of machinery and at every three metres he attached a detonator and a block of explosive attached to a canister of concentrated napalm jelly. He reached the end of the factory and pushed the box against the main door. Inside it was a directional explosive that would blow the wall out and spread flammable material in a wide arc across the track between this building and the next.

"Right, let's get this done and done right, okay," Julian said, steeling himself against the danger now that he was on the site where he felt comfortable. That his anus was tight, his senses were tuned to detect the slightest signs of an enemy attack, or his stomach felt as if it was an out of balance cement mixer, was of no account now that he was busy.

"Yes Bomb Leader," said his troops suppressing their giggles at his squeaky, panicking tone.

The two Pairs showed him the caps and then with the smoothness of long practice he added two limpet mines to each upright and activated the radio links. The Pairs followed him out of the factory and outside through the opening and it was then he connected the wires to the activator. They closed the gap and went on to the next factory shed where they repeated the exercise. In all they set bombs in five buildings and Julian reckoned that if all went well they would destroy five out of seven factories directly and twenty warehouse buildings. The remaining two factories were sandwiched between those Julian had sabotaged and hopefully would be damaged too. They could not carry all the explosives needed to get all the buildings so Lavia had come up with a plan that would maximise what they had. To help with the effect Julian had added a triple charge to the directional bombs and had them faced inward. The idea, he explained, was to create a fire storm in the centre of the complex and let the oxygen do the rest.

The setting of the bombs went like a dream and with the detonator in his hand and unarmed he left the last factory and headed for the assembly point. The Pairs showed him the caps and then reported group by group.

"Test them now," he said and all five detonators glowed. He examined each one including his own and was relieved to see that all were registering active.

"Arm and make safe."

He armed his own and put the safety bar on.

"Link with the master."

He saw four red lights on his detonator flick to green.

"Ready, let's go."

They retraced their steps to the gap and walked back to the wagons. Their own line of wagons were outside the perimeter and as soon as his bombers were aboard Glorida began the clock. They drove off and sat at two kilometres from the factory and waited for the countdown. Julian watched the clock move slowly to the set off point and with a thrill he pushed the safety bar off and pressed the button. The lights changed from green to red and he watched for the explosion. It came virtually at once and although the complex was two kilometres distant he heard the noise and saw the great gush of flame and felt so excited he shouted out aloud.

"There she goes!"

And then with a joyful shout Glorida ordered the wagon to move out. Terrified of what was to come next but fascinated by the destruction he had engineered, Julian could not help but stand up on the fighting platform and look for the results of his work. The fire boiled up into the sky like a huge beacon and as he watched there were more explosions and the area was lit by the new fires that balled up and joined the column, twisting as they matched speed and then rose high to fall back on itself as one massive conflagration. A fire storm was beginning to form and Julian almost wet himself with pleasure. They hurried along the track in the open now ready for a fight. Julian knew that the plan was designed to annoy the President but he wished that the women wouldn't go at it so enthusiastically. They were grinning and calling out to each other as the line of wagons headed directly for the garrison east of the factory complex where the men were already engaged with the enemy. He could see the battle wagon lasers powering off and the rocket ships firing missiles. Their weapons looked like sparklers against his magnificent fire, and for the first time Julian felt the energy of the women and understood the need to have a go at the enemy.

And when they hit the first enemy patrol racing to the aid of their fellows reality kicked in. He almost funked out but an older Pair, Jolida and Jolid nudged him and smiled kindly.

"Hey Julian, you did a fantastic job, you and your troop really make things easy for us. Now, stay with us and take pot shots at these Bulgers will you?"

He did, and after the first capsule of carefully aimed plasma was gone he loaded another and found himself on the ground with the rest of the foot soldiers fighting metre by metre and running away never entered into his head.

That was until the enemy counter attacked and then he was off like a scared rabbit back to the trucks. Somehow he got it right and found himself running with Glorida and Glorid in a group firing back the way they came. They dived onto the wagons as the driver

Pairs gunned them in noisy arcs toward them. After that all hell let loose as more enemy wagons arrived and started shooting at them. One of their wagons exploded and around him some Half Pairs were hit. The fire fight was short and brutal and out of sheer anger Julian fired back.

"Fuck off you bastards!" he yelled and fired a stream of plasma at a wagon that was bearing down on them with all guns blazing. The wagon glowed and then veered off to the left rolling over and over as it burned and exploded. He had not time to watch the fire as his wagon spun in an arc and they were out of the fight.

Behind them wagons burned and he could see Pairs rolling in the dust trying to smother the flames before they engulfed them and with another burst of anger he fired at them. A hand touched his wrist and Glorida told him to stop shooting.

"Its all over Julian, the fight is finished and we are going home. Well done Julian my love, you fought well. You hit a battle wagon you know and saved us from being killed. We re-group south of here and then go home," she said, and kissed him.

If it were not for her arms around him now that the action was over he would have fallen. His legs turned to jelly and he wanted to throw up but she had said the magic words, 'well done', and apart from the ice cold sweat on his brow and the dire need to take a leak he felt great.

"I did all right?" he said.

"You did all right," she said and kissed him again.

This time he responded and in the dark against the back wall of the wagon he slid into her not caring what was happening except that she had praised him.

"Nong's teeth," she said afterwards, "that fire storm was something else."

"Yeah and so were you," he said and gasped when she grabbed his penis and pushed it inside her again. "Cripes."

In the sunslight at the regrouping point they counted their casualties. They tended the wounded and slipped the dead into body bags with tags attached to the strings. They had lost two wagons with their crews and seven Half Pairs and there were eighteen Half Pairs wounded.

"We saw one wagon explode," said Glorid, "and I saw another and a small group of Pairs who were cut off from the rest of us but there was nothing we could do. I think Angela was with them."

Glorida nodded and made a mark on the list she had in front of her.

"Oh well," said Julian, "At least that's got her off my back."

This time it was Glorid who drew her knife and made to cut him. He shrieked and tried to hide behind Glorida who slipped to one side and allowed her twin to grab his tunic.

"Angela is a friend of ours," Glorid said and held the knife close to his face. "Apologise or I'll cut your testicles off."

"Yes, yes, I was trying to lighten the loss a little," he said, and squirmed as the blades got lower. "I hope she is all right. Yes, yes I am sorry for what I said, it was insensitive of me and I like her really. I do!"

The last remark was said at high pitch as Glorid's blades slid down his belly and touched his groin. He shook with fear and suppressed anger as she let him go and turned contemptuously to sit on the wagon watching him and shaking her head.

"You are a piece of shit, Renfrew," she said.

He did not know where to look and was both scared and embarrassed when Glorida glowered at her twin. To try and recoup some of the lost ground he volunteered to make the meal and took his turn tending the wounded. Glorid still glowered at him and Glorida remained tight lipped but at least the day was occupied with tasks and so they made their way back to the headquarters.

Julian felt stupid and cut off until at last when they stopped in a sheltered valley, or a small depression in the rolling hills to make camp that Julian made up with Glorid.

"I'm sorry, you know, for what I said about Angela. I gotta say I saw her wagons and her troop get cut off, and I seen her moving off. I thought we might see her again. I didn't think. I mean, I know she is a friend and she looked after me during the bombing. Sorry Glorid, I'm not very good am I?" he said looking at her nervously.

"I should be angrier," she said, I am not, I am just worried about her. You should learn to keep your stupid mouth shut."

"Yeah, I sort of say things before I really think," he said, and wisely didn't add any more and when it was his turn to keep watch he stayed alert and did the job properly. He had seen the look on Glorid's face and knew that in spite of his apology she was still angry with him.

He sat for a while watching dutifully knowing that like the other Pairs on the picket he was aware that the enemy would be unlikely to follow them especially at night, but this was war and you could never be certain. As it was the first watch he knew he would get some sleep and that added to his sense of duty. As a result it was he who saw the small fire in the distance first. He called the Half Pair watching with him and said: "There's a camp fire over there," he said, pointing toward a rocky outcrop about a kilometre distant, "We should go and have a look."

The Half Pair slipped off to the wagons and reported to Glorida who returned with her and using her quadoculars tried to see what it was. She and the Half Pair spent some time gazing through the glasses and eventually conferred explaining to Julian what they thought was there. Julian couldn't get the hang of the Zradian quadoculars that split the images four ways making him dizzy when he tried to use them.

"We think it is a small force or a group of refugees," Glorida said. "I think we will take a silent wagon there and see. You can come with us Julian. You can guide us."

He had no choice and when a new watch was called out he followed Glorida to the wagon and at a very slow pace in silent mode they glided over the terrain steadily with Julian acting as the eyes they reached the camp site.

Alighting from the wagon quickly, guns at the ready with the lights suddenly blazing Glorida, Glorid and Julian with two armed Pairs, Glorida called on the occupants of the camp site to surrender.

What happened next took both sides by surprise.

Epilogue

Betty/Napoleon/Anthony sat with her/its/his legs metaphorically crossed and metaphorically folded her/its/his arms. There were problems. The Doomsday Bomb had shifted back into place and some clever Pair had put a lock out circuit in place and he/she/it was denied access. It/he/she checked the bomb on Star Station Two and discovered that it too was shut off.

He/she/it surfed the channels looking for clear circuits and found one annoying hot line that was too strong to hack into without concentration. It/she/he tried and failed and tried again changing tack each time faster than the circuit itself could cope with but without success.

"Fix it or kill it," Napoleon.

"Our family is at risk," Anthony.

"We need our mother/brother/son/husband," Betty.

He/she over rode It and found the answer.

Davey Kline watched the monitors slip once and then recover, and in mid sentence he frantically touched keys and woggled toggles but there was nothing he could do. Something was in control and as an army of cartoon rats, mice, squirrels and rabbits danced across his screen he screamed.

"No-oo! Not that fucking song again!" he yelled, and fell forward onto the console as his headphones relayed his words back to him drowned in the strains of A Whiter Shade of Pale. To add insult to injury the version of the song was by the Australian group The Tummy Bananas, a group he detested. As the tune revved up and babbled its insane way across the airwaves Davey Kline listened to the insidious message that burbled electronically in his ears.

"Do not be afraid of the rodents. Thank you for your assistance. Do not be afraid of the rodents."

The time was 12:20 and forty five seconds.

This is the conclusion of Book I of the Zradian Chronicles.

To find out more about the adventures of Julian Renfrew and the conflict between Earth and Zrad, and to find out what happens to Richard Byrde, Arthur Renfrew and old Tzu, read Book II, The Professor and his Son.